PINELAND
SERENADE

— A MINNESOTA MYSTERY —

LARRY MILLETT

Book & Cover Design by:
Erik Christopher Ugly Dog Digital

Author photo by Matt Schmitt

Published by Millett & Ahern LLC.

Millett & Ahern LLC.
www.http://larrymillett.com/

ISBN 978-1-7357278-0-6

PRELUDE

On the first day of April, in the central square of Pineland, Minnesota, someone posted an anonymous message only hours after the town's wealthiest man vanished under suspicious circumstances. Typewritten on a plain sheet of white paper, the message appeared to implicate four local men in the disappearance. It also suggested an unknown woman might prove crucial to solving the case.

The curiously old-fashioned message came with a modern addendum in the form of an attached thumb drive. The drive's contents—a single audio file consisting of ten seconds of music performed by a not very proficient band—offered another mystery. The file was of poor quality, the music sounding tinny and distant, as though it had been recorded from far away. Technicians were able to enhance the recording, but no one recognized the melody.

Strange and violent events followed, along with more messages and more snippets of music. The snippets, adding up to sixteen bars in all, were eventually spliced together to form an unremarkable melody. It was only after we'd heard the last of the song, and unraveled the terrible story behind it, that we learned its name.

It was called "Pineland Serenade."

Our troubles, like those of the universe, began with a big bang. It happened on April Fool's Day and it was the high-decibel start to a month no one in Pineland will ever forget. Here's how the Associated Press reported the news:

PINELAND, MN—A massive explosion early this morning destroyed a hilltop mansion near this community 100 miles north of the Twin Cities, and its wealthy owner has gone missing.

The mansion, located about five miles west of Pineland, belonged to Peter Swindell, a prominent local businessman.

"At this point, we have reason to believe Mr. Swindell is in jeopardy, and we have begun an active search for him," Paradise County Sheriff Arne Sigurdson said, but would not go into further detail.

Sigurdson said it does not appear anyone was in the 12,000-square-foot home at the time of the blast. "We have not found human remains in the house," the sheriff said, noting that Swindell wasn't married and "as far as we know lived alone."

The explosion occurred just after 1 a.m. and could be heard as far as 20 miles away, the sheriff said. "I know it shook me and a lot of other people out of bed."

Fire crews from Pineland and three nearby communities responded to the scene. It took about three hours to bring the fire that followed the explosion under control.

A team from the state Fire Marshal's office will attempt to determine the cause of the blast, which tore through the roof of the sprawling brick mansion and left only a few walls standing.

Sigurdson said the house was heated with propane stored in a large tank on the property. "The fire investigators will be looking at that," he said. "They'll have to determine if it was an accident or a deliberate act of destruction. We just don't know at this point."

The sheriff said agents from the Minnesota Bureau of Criminal Apprehension (BCA) will be brought in to assist with the investigation.

"Obviously, this is a very disturbing situation," he said. "Mr. Swindell is a very well-respected man here who's made many contributions to our community."

Swindell, 70, built the Paradise Pines Resort Hotel, which opened in 2015. The hotel is next to the popular casino of the same name operated by the Grand Lac Band of Ojibwe.

"The hotel has been a big success and brought a lot of new jobs with it," said Martin Moreland, president of the Pineland Chamber of Commerce. "Peter is a tremendous force here and everyone is just stunned by the news."

According to Moreland, Swindell is a native of Paradise County who later became a highly successful real estate developer in Chicago. "He moved back here because he wanted to help the community where he grew up. He's a great guy and a true friend. I just hope he's all right."

Swindell's mansion "was by far the biggest house in the county," Moreland said. "He loved to throw parties and a lot of folks in town have had a chance to see the place. It was a real showpiece."

Swindell is "a millionaire many times over" and had been "welcomed with open arms" when he returned to Paradise County, Moreland added. "I can't imagine why anyone would want to harm him. He's done nothing but good things here."

Like any news story, the AP account requires some reading between the lines. Take Marty Moreland's fawning comments, for example. Truth is, Marty and Peter were not so much friends as co-conspirators. Marty helped Peter close some rather unsavory real estate deals and so was among the lucky few invited to those parties at the mansion, where caviar, champagne and hookers were usually on the menu.

Marty also lied about the Paradise Pines Resort Hotel, which hasn't been a tremendous success. Just the opposite, in fact. Word around town is that the hotel—as managed by Peter's deeply unlovable son, Dewey—lost piles of money from the start and may be headed for receivership.

And as far as Peter doing "nothing but good things," well, that qualifies as a howler. Yes, he spread around plenty of money, purchasing goodwill at the going price, as rich men always do. But he didn't return to Pineland out of deep love for his old hometown. Peter came back because he wanted to be king, a position unavailable to him in Chicago, where he was just another fast-talking real estate guy making deals for crappy suburban office parks.

Here, on the other hand, he became lord of all he surveyed, our very own royalty, Peter the Great. A man with wads of money in his pockets is always a local hero, and Peter received an adoring welcome when he returned to Pineland in 2010. There was no parade with confetti raining down on the streets, but our town's leaders were quick to embrace Peter and his marvelous plans for bringing a new age of prosperity to Paradise County.

If the resort hotel was Peter's signature project, the mansion was his ultimate personal statement, a shining testament to his regal aspirations. He named it Kingshill—subtlety was not Peter's strong suit—and he supposedly spent well north of four million on the place. It was a plump, steep-roofed brick-and-stone extravaganza in the faux French Provincial style favored by people with more money than taste. The mansion's carefully tended grounds included a formal garden, a greenhouse, and a pond stocked in summer by a small school of Koi carp said to be worth thirty grand. Presumably, when winter came, Peter ate them.

I visited the mansion only once, when Peter staged a grand opening and invited the local peasants to see what the king had wrought. It was quite the affair. Uniformed caterers roamed the mansion and grounds, offering up tasty morsels concocted by a chef allegedly trained at a three-star restaurant in Paris. Peter, resplendent in a white linen suit, mingled merrily with his humble subjects. The mansion itself offered many marvels. There was a "great room" roughly the size of Rhode Island, a baronial fireplace outfitted with andirons as big as spears, six bedrooms, seven bathrooms, and a kitchen heavy with Angolan granite and Italian marble. All that was lacking was a throne.

I suppose I should introduce myself. I'm Paul G. Zweifel, skeptic at large, occasional drunkard, failed husband, connoisseur of rue, and soon-to-be the former attorney for Paradise County, of which Pineland is the seat. As you'll discover, I was thrust into the middle of everything that happened here last year, and I barely escaped with my life. Even so, some conspiracy theorists in town continue to insist I was no innocent party. As they see it, the real story has yet to be told and terrible secrets still lie buried like rotting bodies in the dark woodlands of Paradise County.

But the "real story" is always elusive, if you think about it, and the best I can do now is tell the story as I lived it. Trust me when I say I'll offer the finest version of the truth available. You have my word on that. After all, I'm a lawyer.

One more thing: *Zweifel* means "doubt" in German, and a sublime sense of certainty has never been one of my defining characteristics. Maybe that's why some people around town think I'm just a smartass who likes to question revealed truths. To that charge, I plead guilty.

I may have been the only person in Paradise County who didn't hear the explosion that leveled Peter's mansion. Blame it on my friend Jack Daniel's. I'd spent much of the previous night in his company, watching ancient "Perry Mason" reruns and hoping the great litigator might elicit a confession from me. No such luck. And yes, I know what you're thinking and you're right. How pathetic. There's nothing sadder than a solitary drunk.

But I have my reasons. I drink on Friday nights because I want to forget the ones long ago when my beautiful Meredith and I would go out on "dates" and then come home and drink and smoke pot and make love. Those were the best nights of my life—probably the best I'll ever have. Meredith left me ten years ago, with good and just cause, and found happiness, along with substantial spending money, in the arms of a bald neurologist.

Now, in the dead hours of the night, I often marinate in regret. I used to call Meredith now and then, eager to hear her voice and remember what we had, but she was curt and uninterested, and now we don't talk anymore. As I like to say, the past is never free. I pay up with Jack.

Once I nodded off I entered the kind of deep, sloshed sleep that is much like death, only without the benefit of lasting forever. So when the big blast came, I was oblivious.

Camus, my existential border collie and faithful bedmate, was not. He began barking furiously and jumped on me just to be sure I'd wake up.

"For God's sake, Camus," I said, rolling over and glancing at my alarm clock. "Do you know what time it is?"

He didn't, clocks being of little consequence to dogs, but he wouldn't let me go back to sleep, much as I disliked the idea of being awake. My head felt like an overstuffed bean bag and my insides weren't any better. Eggs ala Alka-Seltzer would be on the breakfast menu, with a Bloody Mary to wash it down. The television screen on the far wall, which I'd neglected to turn off before falling asleep, blared with an infomercial promising me the most amazingly robust erection of my life. I would have settled for more sleep, but Camus was having none of it.

I stumbled out of bed and looked at my watch. One-ten a.m. I had no idea why Camus had started barking. After a while, I heard distant sirens. A fire somewhere? A big accident on the interstate? A mass shooting at the casino? I didn't really care. A bad hangover kills curiosity, among other things. All I wanted was more sleep. I went to the kitchen and gave Camus a bowl of food to shut him up. Then I went back to bed.

I should have stayed up and had the good sense to look at my phone.

My second awakening came just after seven, again courtesy of Camus. I peered out the bedroom window, toward my back yard, and saw nothing other than the usual vista of dim brown fields painted with gray piles of slush. Another glorious morning in Paradise County, which despite its name offers little in the way of sublime beauty. It looks especially dreary in April, Minnesota's month of false spring and dashed hopes.

My country manor, as I like to call it, is the only house on a cul-de-sac at the edge of town in a development known as Pine Ridge Estates, even though there's not a ridge or pine tree in sight. An ambitious young developer planned the subdivision back in 2007 and managed to build just one house—mine—before the Great Recession arrived to plunge him into bankruptcy. The solitude suits me just fine, neighbors usually being more trouble than they're worth.

Camus wasn't interested in the view. He raced to the front door, barking madly and circling, a sure sign someone was outside. I threw on sweatpants and a T-shirt and went into the living room to investigate. I looked out the sidelight and saw Sheriff Arne Sigurdson coming up the walk.

Short and barrel-chested, Arne has a butch haircut, a silvery beard he keeps closely trimmed, a twice-broken nose that invites speculation and gray eyes as piercing as a welder's torch. Although he's well into his fifties, he's still ox-strong and not a man to trifle with. A year earlier, he and five deputies raided one of the many small meth labs that do business in the woods of northern Paradise County. A wild shootout ensued. Two deputies were wounded and both meth makers—brothers with long criminal records—were shot dead. More than one hundred rounds were exchanged during the firefight. One of the brothers was hit three times, the other two. All five of the bullets came from Arne's Glock.

Arne wouldn't mind shooting me either, given the chance. We don't get along and never have. He'd been sheriff for twelve years by the time I came on board as county attorney and was used to doing things his own way. Like many sheriffs, he turned his office into a fiefdom, rewarding friends and even a cousin or two with jobs. But his vassals aren't always competent when it comes to criminal investigations, handling some cases so poorly I've refused to prosecute them. This makes Arne extremely unhappy, and our working relationship is coated in ice.

As soon as I let Arne in, Camus began to growl. He's never liked men in uniform.

"Go herd something," I ordered, sending him off with a tap to his behind.

"I tried calling you," Arne announced once we'd taken seats in my living room, which offers two shelves crammed with books and CDs, a collection of cheap IKEA furniture in varying shades of beige and walls bare of decoration except for an expensive, limited-edition print of *Gas*, my favorite Edward Hopper painting.

"Couldn't get an answer on either your land line or your cell," Arne complained. "I was wondering if you'd left town."

"In your dreams. I turn down the ring volume on my phones at night so people like you won't bother me. Clearly, that strategy has failed, since here you are. What's up? I'm guessing you didn't stop by for toast and jam."

Arne, whose sense of humor can best be described as deeply Scandinavian, stared at me and said, "So you didn't hear the explosion? That's funny, I'm pretty sure they heard it in Duluth. Maybe even in China. I'm thinking you should get checked for ear wax."

"Thanks for the hygiene tip. I'll hop right to it. Now, what's this explosion you're talking about?"

"Christ, it woke up most of the county. Do you sleep in a fucking vault?"

"No, Arne, I don't. But I do sleep soundly. Is that a crime?"

Arne shook his head, clearly disgusted by my talent for nocturnal oblivion, and said, "Peter's mansion blew up this morning and then it burned to the ground. It's basically a heap of ashes. We don't think the explosion was an accident. The fire guys believe somebody deliberately filled the house with propane. As for Peter, he seems to be gone with the wind. I'm thinking this all could be a big deal. How about you?"

"Jesus," I said. I don't usually invoke the Lord's name as a matter of surprise, but it was the best I could do at the moment. "How did it happen?"

Arne filled in the details, including a piece of information that hadn't been released to the media. "We found Peter's SUV not far from the house. The driver's side door was open and the engine was running. We think whoever blew up the house snatched Peter."

"So it's a kidnapping?"

Arne fired up a Marlboro, not bothering to ask my permission to smoke in the house. I passed a coffee cup his way to use as an ashtray. "Could be," he said, sucking in the poison, "but if it was a kidnapping, why would somebody go to all the trouble of blowing up the mansion?"

"Maybe the perp didn't like the architecture."

"What's that supposed to mean?"

"I'm joking, Arne. If I had to guess, I'd say the kidnapper destroyed the house because he didn't want to leave any evidence behind."

"Well, if that's the case, he did a good job of it. I don't think we're going to get much out of the place."

"What about the SUV? Anything in it?"

"Yeah, and it's strange. There was a photo on the front passenger seat. Maybe Peter left it there or maybe the perp did. We don't really know."

"What kind of photo?"

Arne fished out his cell phone. "Have a look for yourself. I took a shot of it."

The image showed a woman walking along a busy street. The woman—African-American, probably in her thirties, dressed in a gray business suit—looked to be a professional of some kind. It didn't appear to be a posed picture and might well have been snapped without her knowledge. Behind her, out of focus, skyscrapers loomed, suggesting the photo had been taken in a big city—New York, maybe, or Chicago.

"Any idea who the woman is?" I asked.

"Not a clue," Arne said, "but I doubt she's from around here." This was hardly a Sherlockian deduction on Arne's part. Most of the handful of Blacks in Paradise County work at the casino. The woman in the photo did not look like she dealt blackjack for a living.

"All right, anything else I need to know?"

"As a matter of fact, there is. When was the last time you had any contact with Peter?"

A peculiar question, I thought, so I posed one of my own, "Why do you ask?"

"Just answer the question, if you would."

"To tell you the truth, I'm really not sure the last time I talked to him. We're not friends, Arne, as you well know."

This was true. Peter didn't like me for any number of reasons. While I was still in private practice, I'd sued him in a case involving an historic family mansion in town he was trying to renovate. Later, when I became county attorney, there was a big dustup over his hotel project. He and his phalanx of clever lawyers had cooked up a scheme that would have saddled Paradise County with the full cost of new roads needed for the project. The county board, eager to please the king, was willing, but I challenged the plan's legality. I also leaked some of the more fragrant details to our local newspaper, the *Paradise Tattler*. An outcry followed, and the scheme quickly died.

Never one to take defeat lightly, Pater called me the next day and said, "You cost me a million and a half, you little shit, and I won't forget it." I told him, in a calm and measured voice, that I thought he was a crook as well as an asshole. More charming conversation followed. Later, we had other clashes in court, and Peter regarded me, not unjustly, as his biggest adversary in town.

Arne said, "So you're saying it's been quite a while since you had any contact with him, is that right?" Suspicion lurked in his voice. It didn't require any legal acumen to realize I was being interrogated.

"Okay, Arne, I can tell you're sitting on something. Why don't you share it with me and we'll go from there?"

"Well, here's the thing. We found Peter's phone. It was lying on the driveway next to his vehicle. Being the ace investigators we are, we looked at the recent calls and text messages. You'll never guess what popped up."

"A call from the Pope?"

"Oh, better than that, counselor. We found a message Peter sent to your cell number at midnight."

My first thought was, oh shit, which was also my second thought. I considered my situation and said, "Well, that's strange. I didn't even know Peter had my number, and I have no idea why he'd send me a message. What did it say?"

"You tell me."

"I haven't looked at my phone this morning, Arne, so I can't tell you what the message said, assuming there was one."

"Well then, I'll need to see your phone."

I didn't like Arne's tone, and my lawyerly instincts took over. Was the message in some way incriminating? If so, I wanted to see it for myself before I let Arne have my phone. It also occurred to me Arne might have an ulterior motive. Maybe he wanted to look at my phone for a reason unrelated to Peter's disappearance. Maybe I was being set up for something. Paranoia comes all too naturally when the law is on your tail.

"Well, if you've read the message," I said, "just tell me what it says. That seems fair enough."

"I'd rather look at your phone, to verify you received it."

"And I'd rather you not, until I have a better sense of what's going on here."

"You're beginning to sound like a man who has something to hide."

"No, you're the one who's hiding things. How about we quit playing silly games? What did the message say?"

"So you're not going to give me your phone?"

"Tell you what. You'll get it—later."

The blowtorch eyes were now cutting holes in my face. "Why are you being such a dickhead about this? Do I have to go out and get a fucking warrant?"

"No, you don't. I'll drop the phone off at your office later today and you can obsess over it all you want. How's that for a deal? Now, unless there's something else you want to tell me, I think we're done here. You can show yourself out."

Arne crushed out his Marlboro, stood up, and glared at me as though I was a naughty child. "You're not being very cooperative, counsellor. I really wonder why that is."

"Wonder all you want, Arne. It'll give you something to do in your spare time."

"Go ahead, be a wiseass. But guess what? You've got some real problems. Fact is, I'm pretty sure we're going to have to call in a prosecuting attorney from the state to handle this case. You're compromised, the way I see it."

Arne had finally done it, ticking me off to no end. "I'm compromised? Strange words coming from someone who's been in Peter's back pocket for years." This was true, more or less. Like every other public official in Paradise County, Arne had cozied up to Peter, attracted by his wealth and unapologetic hedonism. It was said Arne had been invited more than once to the bacchanalias at Peter's mansion, and there were courthouse whispers money had changed hands for favors rendered. I'd never been able to prove any wrongdoing, but Arne knew I didn't trust him.

"You haven't heard the last of this," he said. "You'd best watch yourself. You're in trouble and that smart mouth of yours won't help you."

"Again, thanks for the helpful advice," I said. "As always, it was lovely chatting with you."

After Arne left, Camus wandered in for a discussion. He gave me a long look, searching my eyes for secrets, then tilted his head a bit as if to say, "Now what have you done, you damn idiot?"

"Well, what do think?" I asked Camus. "Am I in serious trouble?"

Camus's light blue eyes gazed balefully at me before he delivered a sharp, quick bark, suggesting the answer was a definite "yes." As always, Camus proved prescient, and it became clear just how deep my troubles were once I looked at Peter Swindell's message on my phone.

3

I hate my smart phone and it hates me, and that's why I use it as little as possible. It's an outsized Moto—Verizon, wishing to have a laugh at my expense, gave me a deal on it—and I've come to think of it as a malicious elf living in my pocket. It finds many ways to torment me. Sometimes a screen appears out of nowhere. Sometimes the ring volume magically descends to zero and I miss calls. Sometimes the phone locks up without warning or drifts off into a mysterious setting known only to Google engineers and every twelve-year-old on the planet. Or maybe the phone is just a whole lot smarter than I am.

Now the damn thing seemed ready to implicate me in a crime. I went into the kitchen, where I charge the phone overnight, and started scrolling through the text messages. Arne, I found, hadn't been playing me. There was a message from Peter, at two minutes past midnight. To say the message was cryptic would be an understatement. It read: "I'm ready.

Come to Kingshill now & come alone. We can still settle this thing."

The message didn't make sense. Why would Peter have texted me at midnight and what was the mysterious "thing" we supposedly needed to settle? Was he still angry, three years later, about the road deal I'd scotched? That seemed unlikely. Or was something else sticking in his craw? The fact that Peter requested an immediate meeting at Kingshill was also puzzling. Why invite me to his mansion at such a strange hour when he could have talked with me any time he wanted?

Nothing about the message rang true, and I thought it very likely Peter's kidnapper, rather than Peter himself, had sent it. I could think of only one reason for doing so and it was chilling. The kidnapper wanted to cast suspicion on me. What I didn't know was why.

Second thoughts, like second marriages, aren't necessarily good things, but as I chewed over the message I had another idea, which was that Peter's supposed abduction might actually be a big show. Maybe he'd staged his own disappearance. Because of his complicated business dealings, Peter carried a lot of debt, and there were tales linking him to certain people in Chicago whose method of settling past-due accounts usually entailed the breaking of bones. Had Peter found himself staring at that unattractive possibility and arranged to vanish while implicating me just for the merry hell of it? It sounded far-fetched, but I couldn't rule it out. With Peter, anything was possible.

Whatever was going on, I had to be careful. I scoured my Moto looking for old messages or calls that might arouse suspicion. I found none, but that wasn't necessarily comforting. A smart phone is a harbor filled with hidden mines ready to detonate. Who knew what some clever forensic technician might discover? Even so, I knew I had to turn the phone over to Arne. It would look bad if I didn't and, besides, Arne could always obtain a search warrant if he had to.

Plenty of people in Pineland dislike me, despite my manifestly charming personality. One of them is Dewey Swindell, and I was surprised when he called my land line just before noon. Dewey is not a highly regarded figure in Pineland. Loud and relentlessly opinionated, he's the kind of man people walk across the street to avoid. He wears a MAGA hat like a crown—his right, I don't care—but he thinks it entitles him to share his profound political insights with everyone else, whether they want to hear them or not.

"Hello, Dewey," I said when I heard his grating voice. "Sorry to hear about your father and what happened out at the mansion. I hope he'll be all right."

Skipping the niceties of a preamble, Dewey said, "So what's this meeting you had with the old man this morning? What did he tell you?"

Dewey always refers to his father as "the old man" and it's not a term of endearment. The story around town is that father and son haven't gotten along since Dewey was tapped to manage the Paradise Pines Hotel, a plush assignment he took to the way a duck takes to sand. I'd heard rumors, not long before Peter disappeared, that he blamed Dewey for the hotel's problems and was about to fire him.

"I didn't have any meeting with your father," I said. "What makes you think that?"

"Don't bullshit me. It's all over town. He texted you and you were out at the mansion. Was he feeding you some crap about that Lorrimer bitch?"

Dewey clearly knew all about the message on my phone. I wasn't surprised. Criminal investigations in Pineland tend to be a community affair, powered by a wondrous gossip mill. Or maybe Dewey had simply been tipped off by Arne.

As for the "bitch" Dewey referred to her, her name was Jill Lorrimer and she'd once worked as a blackjack dealer at the Paradise Pines Casino. She was also reputed to be a pricey call girl who served clients at Dewey's hotel. Three months earlier, on New Year's Day, she'd been found dead in her car of an apparent drug overdose. Documents discovered in her apartment suggested Dewey had in effect been her pimp, taking a cut of her proceeds and possibly those of other prostitutes who worked out of the hotel. There were also tantalizing hints Dewey had bribed sheriff's deputies to overlook these indecent activities.

The allegations were juicy enough to prompt an investigation by the state Bureau of Criminal Apprehension. Because of my connections to the sheriff's office, a state prosecutor was called in to oversee the case, but so far no charges had been filed. Now Dewey seemed to be suggesting his father was also involved in the matter, possibly as a witness against his own son. This was news to me.

I told Dewey again that I hadn't talked to his father about Jill Lorrimer or anything else. "There was no meeting. It's that simple."

"You're a fucking liar, just like you've always been," Dewey said with his usual grace and good humor. "I know you're up to something. You haven't heard the last of this."

He disconnected before I could patiently explain to him that he was being a complete asshole.

Early that afternoon I decided to go into town. I wanted to drop off my Moto at the sheriff's department, thereby keeping Arne from going apoplectic. Then I planned to stop at my office to catch up on a little work. I'd also need to acquire a new phone, since Arne would undoubtedly take his time returning mine.

As I backed out of the garage, Camus riding shotgun, I saw a sheriff's cruiser parked in my lonely cul-de-sac. Apparently, I was under surveillance. I pulled up next to the cruiser. Robby Lindquist, a florid dumpling of a man in his early thirties and one of Arne's least brilliant deputies, was at the wheel. He rolled down his window so we could talk. Spotting a suspicious uniform, Camus went into his usual low growl but I quieted him with a disapproving stare.

"Hi, Robby," I said. "Anything I can do for you?"

"Just sitting here for a while. Catching up on some stuff."

"Kind of a strange place to do that, isn't it?"

He shrugged and said, "Good a place as any."

"Have you been assigned to follow me, Robby?"

"Can't say."

"Ah, I see. It must be a state secret. Well, do me a favor, will you?" I handed him my Moto. "Give this to Arne. He'll have fun with it. Now, just so you know, I'm heading to the courthouse. Feel free to follow."

Robby did just that, sticking to my tail all the way into town. Clearly, the surveillance wasn't going to be subtle. He was still behind me when I reached the Paradise County Courthouse.

Built in 1894, the courthouse is a towering pile of pinkish red sandstone that stands in Pineland's central square. A brochure in the lobby describes the building as an "outstanding example of the Richardsonian Romanesque style." That may be, but I've always thought of it as a giant ogre that wandered into town one day and decided to squat for perpetuity. The stone used for the courthouse came from a quarry north of town founded by my great grandfather—Paradise County's first Zweifel—and so I've always considered the building, ugly as it is, part of my heritage.

A big clock peers out from the massive central tower, and it was still keeping time with remarkable accuracy until vandals with no fear of heights somehow managed to break off the hands last fall. Maybe it was an omen of the disordered days to come, when time itself seemed out of balance. Or maybe it was just a coincidence. I'll let you decide. In either case, the county board—always a parsimonious lot—has shown no interest in budgeting the fifty thousand dollars needed to repair the clock. "Everybody knows what time it is anyway," a board member explained to me, "so why should we spend a fortune to fix the damn thing?"

I parked my blue Prius on one side of the square, then waited for Robby to pull in behind me. I didn't know if he'd get out of his cruiser or simply continue to watch me from his front seat. He stayed put, so I waved at him, put Camus on a leash, and walked toward the courthouse. It's closed to the public on Saturdays, but an after-hours entrance at the rear provides access for county employees. A line of white pines, planted as a nod to the county's history, screen the entry, and by the time I got there Robby and his cruiser were out of view.

A surprise awaited me. Taped to the courthouse door was a typewritten message on a plain sheet of white copy paper. At the bottom of the message, secured by another piece of gray duct tape, was a thumb drive. The message read:

Do you know what happened to Peter Swindell? Ask his son. Ask Sigurdson. Ask Zweifel. Ask Moreland. They all have secrets. They all tell lies. Await THE WOMAN. Let the truth shine forth.

The Serenader

I stared at the message, wondering if it was a joke. But the way it pointed to specific people suggested the author was dead serious. The "Serenader" was a complete mystery to me. I'd never heard of anyone using that name.

I also didn't know why I and the three others were being called out as suspects in Peter's disappearance. Raised a Catholic, I've always adhered to the cheerful view that pretty much everybody is guilty of everything. Even so, I couldn't think of any reason why I'd want to harm Peter. We'd had plenty of run-ins over the years in court but they weren't personal. True, I had no great love for the man, but if I started kidnapping people I disliked there'd be no end to it.

As for Dewey, Arne and Marty, who could say? But if one or all of them had good cause to spirit Peter away, I didn't know about it. Yet the Serenader was clearly implying a conspiracy of some kind surrounded Peter's disappearance. If so, how did he know? And who was he, or for that matter, she?

Trying to guess the Serenader's identity would soon become Pineland's favorite sport, but for the moment I was completely in the dark.

The uppercase "WOMAN" we were told to "await" was another question mark. Who was she and what wisdom might she have to share? Could it be the Black woman in the photo found in Peter's SUV? I assumed Arne was trying to track her down, but the photo wasn't much to go on. Then again, maybe she was someone Peter knew and her identity wouldn't be that hard to discover.

The thumb drive was equally intriguing. Presumably something was on it, but what? And why leave a digital file next to a message produced on an old-fashioned typewriter? I had my laptop with me and was tempted to plug in the drive and see what it revealed. I resisted temptation.

I knew I had to report what I'd found. Before I went back to retrieve Robby, I looked up at the security camera over the door and wondered if it would reveal who left the mysterious message. With Camus pushing ahead on the leash, I walked back to Robby's cruiser, where I found him working on a burrito.

"Don't want to spoil your gourmet lunch," I said, "but there's something you need to see. It's on the back door of the courthouse."

"What is it?"

"Just put down the damn burrito and follow me. "

I let Camus pee on the courthouse lawn, installed him in my car, and then went back to the door with Robby. He read the message with a suitably dumbfounded look and pondered the thumb drive as though in the presence of the Sphinx. "Weird," he opined.

"That pretty much sums it up," I agreed.

Robby got on his handset and contacted Arne to explain the situation. Fifteen minutes later Arne arrived with a couple of deputies and two rangy guys in their thirties I'd never seen before. They introduced themselves as Jason Braddock and Jason Grinnell. They were agents with the Minnesota Bureau of Criminal Apprehension, better known in law enforcement circles as the BCA, and they'd been sent to Pineland to assist in the investigation into Peter's disappearance.

Once everyone had a look at what was on the door, Arne radioed for a forensics team to process the scene. Then he turned his attention to me. I knew I'd be in for a grilling but there wasn't much I could say other than the obvious fact I'd stumbled across the message.

Before long, Pineland's Chief of Police, Jim Meyers, joined the crowd. He's an outsized ex-Minneapolis cop who found Pineland the perfect place for on-the-job retirement. Now he finally had something to do and the prospect seemed to perturb him, as did Arne's presence. The two titans of local law enforcement can't stand each other, and they squabbled over jurisdictional matters before determining both of them needed to talk to me. The two Jasons also had questions. I told my simple tale forward, backward and sideways over the next hour, sticking to the basic facts, which weren't especially enlightening.

"So what do you suppose earned you a mention in the message?" Arne asked.

"I guess I'm just a popular guy. How about you? Any thoughts on why you're also one of the anointed?"

"How the hell would I know? I didn't write the goddamn thing. Maybe some jerk is just fucking with us."

"Could be, but I'm not so sure. The writer had to go to a lot of trouble to post it here along with that thumb drive."

"Does make you wonder why he just didn't post a message somewhere online," Arne said. "Maybe the guy's not all that smart."

"Or maybe he's very smart," I said. "Anything digital leaves all kinds of tracks. But a typewritten message on a sheet of paper could actually be much harder to trace. I doubt the thumb drive will point us to the guy, either. I'm really curious what's on it."

"We'll handle that," said Jason Braddock, the taller and apparently senior member of the BCA team. "It'll have to be processed by our lab."

"Well then, I guess I'm done here," I said. "I've told you everything I know."

Jim Meyers seemed satisfied and left, but Arne and the Jasons wanted to squeeze me a little more.

"Mind if I have a quick look in your briefcase?" Arne asked.

"Be my guest. You won't find any duct tape. I didn't plant the message, if that's what you're thinking. By the way, why is Robby following me around?"

"Just a precaution," Arne said as he did his rummaging. "Wouldn't want anything to happen to you now that you're involved in this business."

"Thoughtful of you, but you can call Robby off. I can take care of myself."

"Whatever you say, counselor."

He handed the briefcase back to me and said, "Well, it was worth a try, wasn't it. And I still think that message on the door is pretty interesting. Almost seems like something you'd write, seeing as how you're so big on anonymous communications."

Arne was referring to my alleged habit of leaking news to the *Paradise Tattler*. He'd long suspected I was the courthouse's loose faucet, although I'd never owned up to it, my quaint philosophy being that a man is innocent of telling the truth until proven guilty.

"I have no idea what you're talking about," I told Arne. "I've always assumed you're the leaker-in-chief. Dewey would agree, I'm sure."

"What's that supposed to mean?"

I recounted my phone call from Dewey and said, "You must have talked to him, Arne. How else would he have found out about that message from Peter on my phone?"

"I have no goddamn idea," Arne said, leaning into me. "You're just looking for trouble, aren't you?"

Jason Braddock intervened. "This isn't getting us anywhere," he said in a level voice. "Speaking of your phone, Mr. Zweifel, do you plan to turn that over to us today?"

Robby, who'd been listening in on the conversation, chimed in: "Oh, I forgot. He gave it to me. I've got in my squad."

Arne stared at Robby and it was not the look of a happy man. "Why don't you go fetch it right now," he said, "before you lose the fucking thing."

Then Arne turned to me and said, "Your phone will go to the BCA lab, too. I hear the people there can work miracles. What do you suppose they'll find on it?"

"Less porn than on yours, I'm guessing," I said and went on my way.

The idea of doing office work had lost its appeal, so I returned to my Prius. I found Camus with his head out the window, basking in some welcome attention from his old pal Marty Moreland. Marty's surname nicely evokes his line of work as a real estate agent. He also heads the local chamber of commerce. Tall and balding, with a sandy fringe of blond hair and unthreatening blue eyes, Marty is in his mid-forties, well spoken and eager to please, and a salesman to the core. Everybody seems to like him, and he's our town's biggest booster, always upbeat and brimming with enthusiasm.

Like me, Marty owns a border collie, a rambunctious character named Rafferty, and now and then we join forces and take our beasts for a romp in a fenced dog park along the Paradise River. Marty's real estate office is across the street from the courthouse, and he'd been putting in some Saturday hours when he noticed the gathering of law enforcement outside his window.

"What's going on?" he asked. "Why all the cops?"

I wasn't sure how much I should tell him, but then I thought, why not? News of the message, every word of it, would blow like a jet of hot air through town. I gave Marty the lowdown.

"Geez," he said, "that's really strange."

Yes, Marty still says "geez," without a trace of embarrassment, and I guess that's why I like him, despite his shady dealings with Peter. He's hopelessly earnest, a Boy Scout lost in middle age, but it seems to come so naturally I've given him a pass.

"Can you think of any reason why you'd be mentioned in the message?" I asked.

Marty shook his head—earnestly. "No. I don't know anything about what happened to Peter. What about you?"

"It's all a mystery to me, too. How about the Serenader? Does that name ring any kind of bell?"

"No, not right now, but maybe something will come to mind."

"Well, let me know if it does," I said. "How's Rafferty, by the way?"

"Driving me crazy."

"Tell me about it," I said and got into my Prius, where Camus was looking anxious. Time to get him home.

The security camera footage proved to be of no help. When BCA technicians examined the camera, they found it had been disabled for thirty seconds at three-fifty a.m., only hours before Peter's disappearance. An ultra-bright LED flashlight shined directly into the lens had done the trick. The camera's positioning was also defective, so that someone sneaking up to the back door along the walls of the courthouse would be out of view.

As for the contents of the thumb drive, Arne and the BCA decided not to share that information with me. I knew why. They already viewed me as a possible suspect and suspects don't get to see the evidence piling up against them. Even so, I learned via back channels that there was a snippet of music on the drive. How it related to the typewritten message was anyone's guess.

In the meantime, my own problems began piling up as an old enemy saw a chance to gain a measure of revenge and force me to the sidelines.

5

After chatting with Marty, I drove to the Walmart Supercenter along the interstate to buy a new phone, and it was almost five by the time I got home. I was feeling tired and put out. I wanted a serious drink, badly, but I knew if I had one Jack another would quickly follow. I found a Summit Pale Ale in the refrigerator and I settled for that. A lot was going on and I had to keep a clear head.

Then more trouble came my way. My land line rang, identifying the caller as LaVerne Blankenberger, chairman of the Paradise County Board of Commissioners, the august body that sets and pays my salary. Vern is a devious customer and my spit travels much farther than my trust in him. Also, he views me as a giant pain in the ass. I'm not especially fond of him, either.

"Good afternoon, Vern," I said. "Whatever could you be calling about?"

There's a ritual here in Pineland—a kind of slow waltz that usually precedes getting to the point. To be fast and blunt is to be rude, especially if it's anybody you know. I've been at county board meetings where getting to the point is a journey along many winding byways, like swamping through the Everglades in an airboat, and if you aren't willing to go along for the ride, you might end up going nowhere at all. Vern, however, got right to the point.

"You know why I'm calling. We've got a situation here and we need to deal with it."

"Well, that certainly sounds alarming. If there's one thing that strikes fear into my heart, it's a 'situation.' Care to be more specific?"

"Sure. It's simple. You've got big problems. Arne told me about that text from Peter. Very interesting, if you ask me. And of course there's that thing on the courthouse door you discovered. Quite the coincidence, don't you think?"

"You're reaching, Vern. Just because the text came from Peter's phone doesn't mean he sent it. Or if he did, he was just trying to fuck with me because, as you well know, he hates me. As for that 'thing on the door,' I just happened to be the one to find it. It could just as easily have been you or the courthouse janitor who stumbled on it. And who knows what it means? Not me, and for sure not you."

"Doesn't matter. You're in the middle of all this crap now and we can't have our county attorney handling a case in which he's also a suspect."

"Since when am I a suspect?"

"Since Arne and the BCA said so. Here's the deal. We need to get someone from the Attorney General's office up here to take over. You're compromised."

Arne had used the same word, and I didn't think it was an accident.

"I'm not compromised," I said. "Far from it."

Actually, I was, and I knew it. The text from Peter had turned me into a legitimate suspect, and the message on the courthouse door hadn't helped matters. Recusing myself from further involvement in the case would have been the right thing to do. But something just didn't smell right. Vern wanted me on the sidelines, the sooner the better, and I wondered why.

Vern's voice turned hard and cold. "Listen to me, buddy boy, and listen carefully. People need to know there'll be a full, fair investigation into Peter's disappearance. That's the way I see it and that's the way the board sees it. We can't be screwing around with this. Right now, you're a problem. You need to go. Understand?"

"I'm not your 'buddy boy,' Vern, and never will be. Understand? But you sure seem eager to get me off the case. Why's that? Afraid something might come up and bite you?"

"What the hell are you talking about?"

"You tell me. You're a lot closer to Peter than I ever was."

"All right, enough of this shit. If you don't recuse yourself, we'll get a court order to force you out. Don't be an asshole."

And with that friendly piece of advice, Vern hung up.

My problems with Vern go back to 2014, when I ran for county attorney and then, to almost everyone's surprise, won by the resounding margin of fifty-six votes. My strategy was one of the oldest in the books. I ran a classic throw-out-the-rascals campaign, the rascals being two of Vern's fellow county board members I strongly suspected had accepted kickbacks in exchange for green-lighting Peter's resort hotel project. I thought Vern was dirty as well, but he was too smart leave much of a trail and I was never able to pin anything on him.

The resort was built on Clear Lake, a spring-fed body of water that used to live up to its name. I'd fished and swam there as a kid, at a cabin owned by my uncle. Now, runoff from the resort's perfectly manicured lawns chokes the lake with algae, and swimmers dip into the cruddy water at their own risk.

It shouldn't have happened. Two years before Peter unveiled his plans, the county acquired fifty wooded acres along the lake with the intent of developing a park there. But Peter saw the site as an ideal spot for his resort, and before long the county board decided to sell the park property to Peter at a most attractive price. The board approved the deal on a three-to-two vote, with Vern and his two corrupt pals in the majority. At the same time Peter began his maneuvering to stick the county with the bill for constructing a new road to the resort.

It was a naked sellout in the best American tradition, so blatant that local environmentalists filed suit to stop the resort project. I was their lawyer. We eventually lost the case—I knew from the start it would be a tough go—but along the way I managed to excavate plenty of smelly dirt about the county board and its dealings with Peter.

The whole thing pissed me off, plain and simple. Pineland is at bottom a pretty decent place, and I hated what Peter and his lackeys on the board had done. It didn't help that the county attorney at the time, a nice old fellow who'd held the post for years, seemed oblivious to the stench. So I decided I'd run against him. The fact the job paid over a hundred grand a year—far more than I'd ever earned since returning to Pineland—served as a marvelous catalyst for my newfound idealism.

After my unexpected victory, I wanted to go after Peter and his two county board pals, both of whom had been voted out of office, thanks in large part to the stink I'd raised. Arne, however, showed no interest in pursuing an investigation. I couldn't get the FBI or the state Attorney General's office to bite, either. Peter, meanwhile, donned the heaviest legal armor money could buy, and in the end I couldn't make a case. But I did make plenty of enemies in town, including Vern, and I knew he'd work tirelessly to screw me if he could.

Peter's disappearance touched off what would eventually become the biggest criminal investigation in the history of Paradise County. It did not begin well, however. Arne's deputies and a squad from the BCA spent days sifting through the ruins of Peter's mansion but found nothing of evidentiary value. Peter's SUV proved to be equally bereft of useful clues—no blood, no tissue, no fugitive fingerprints, no signs of a struggle.

Investigators did have Peter's phone, with me as the recipient of his last known text, and there was hope it would yield some promising leads. It didn't. The BCA went through his calls and messages going back for months and came up with nothing. It was all routine stuff. My confiscated Moto was another disappointment. Other than Peter's mysterious early morning text, it harbored no incriminating information, much to my relief. Unfortunately, it would be more than a month before I got the phone back.

As is usual in missing person cases, investigators monitored Peter's credit cards and bank accounts for any activity. There was none. Nor did anyone send a ransom note. A tip line was set up, and a number of callers claimed to have seen Peter here or there, but nothing panned out.

Agents were able to establish that Peter had last been seen by his secretary, Helen Forsberg, as he left his office near the hotel shortly after noon on Friday, the day before he vanished. Peter told her he was going home early to "conduct some personal business." Helen, a salt-of-the earth woman in her sixties who's worked for Peter ever since his return to town, explained to investigators that "personal business" was Peter's euphemism for spending some quality time with a hooker. Finding the prostitute in question became a top priority, but the search produced another dead end. If Peter did employ a local hired hand that night, none of the usual suspects would admit to it.

Investigators also talked to Peter's friends and co-workers as well as Dewey, but learned very little. No one knew of an enemy who would have gone so far as to kidnap and possibly murder him. The idea that Peter might have orchestrated his own vanishing act also fell flat. He had no financial worries—it turned out he had ten million dollars stashed in various accounts—and there was nothing to indicate he was upset or depressed. Nor, apparently, were criminal charges in the offing in the Jill Lorrimer matter or anything else. Peter simply had no good reason to go on the lam.

All of which left investigators with little to show for hundreds of hours of work. Peter was still gone, and no one knew whether he was being held captive in a shed somewhere or sunning himself on a Caribbean island or lying in a shallow grave out in the woods. But it wouldn't be long before investigators had other mysteries to occupy their attention.

6

Welcome to Paradise County! We're Minnesota's playground and there's lots to do! Boat and fish and swim in our crystal clear lakes. Take in the scenic wonders of the Paradise Dalles. Visit our quaint shops and stores. See Paul Bunyan's axe (yes, it's mighty big!). Oh, and don't forget to eat! Our fine restaurants are eager to serve you and you'll also find the best in clean, modern lodging at our resorts, hotels and motels. And wherever you go, you'll meet warm, friendly people. So come see us soon and enjoy your very own adventure in Paradise.

So states a tourist brochure from 1960, its anonymous author shamelessly playing on our county's name to convince visitors they were about to encounter heaven on Earth. For all I know, our little corner of the world may have been a sweet place back then, although I have my doubts. It's certainly not paradise now, but it's not some remote hellhole either. What's it really like? You'll get different answers from different people, but here's my personal guide to Paradise

County and Pineland, scoured of the usual chamber of commerce hyperbole:

The county is poor, rural and its year-round population is declining, although the casino and the resort hotel bring in thousands of annual visitors. It's not the whitest place in America but it must be close. Blacks, Hispanics and Indians make up only six percent of the population, and at last count there were no Hawaiians or other Pacific Islanders among the county's twenty thousand residents. I can't imagine why.

The climate is bitterly cold in winter, while the short summers seem largely designed to ensure that mosquitos do not go extinct. The landscape is mostly flat, consisting of hardscrabble farms and vast expanses of scrub trees that took root after the lumbermen cut down all the pines. Interstate 35 cuts through the county, providing easy access to the Twin Cities and Duluth. Like all interstates, it swerves around the small towns along the way, leaving them with dead main streets as small galaxies of gas stations, restaurants, and motels spun into existence out at the interchanges.

As for the county's lovely name, it would nice to think that an early settler, enchanted by the sylvan beauty of the surroundings, saw it as a veritable Garden of Eden. Not so. The county was actually named after Jonathan Paradise, a lumberman from Maine who arrived in the 1870s. His lumberjacks went after the prized white pines, felling one great grove after another and leaving behind a landscape of waste and ruin. In honor of this magnificent achievement, a grateful citizenry named the county after Paradise in 1878.

His work of deforestation produced thousands of acres of woody debris known as slash—a deadly fire hazard that ignited on a hot, bone-dry September day in 1892. What followed was the worst catastrophe in the county's history, known today as the Great Pineland Forest Fire, which claimed more than four hundred lives. The fire destroyed Pineland and a half-dozen nearby towns, torching hundreds of square miles all the way to the Wisconsin border. Pineland was completely rebuilt after the disaster, with new wooden buildings as flimsy as the ones that had burned down. Some people still wonder why anyone bothered.

As for the city of Pineland, here are a few essential facts:

Population: 2,847, according to the 2010 census. That's ten more people than the town had in 2000. Talk about a growth boom.

Elevation: 1,021 feet. Rising seas should not be a problem.

Year incorporated: 1882.

Original name: Chengwatana. This was an Anglicized version of the Ojibwe word *Zhingwaadena*, roughly meaning "white pine town." But when the time came to incorporate the village the old Indian name was ditched, maybe because people thought it was too hard to pronounce or because they didn't much care for Indians. Too bad. Chengwatana has a nice, lilting ring to it; Pineland, not so much.

Streets: Pineland is a standard Midwestern grid town, laid out like so many others around the rail tracks that gave it life, except for one peculiarity. All of our streets, instead of being numerical or celebrating the usual trees, bear biblical names. This happened because one of the town's founders was a deeply religious man named Josiah Preston, who despite his close relationship with God perished in the Great

Fire. Before going to his eternal reward, he surveyed the town's initial plat. In a display of faith he gave the streets names from *Genesis*, including Adam, Eve, Eden, Noah, and Abel. Cain didn't get a street, however, presumably because of his criminal record. Our main drag, Paradise Avenue, is actually named after the lumberman, who does not seem to have been a godly figure.

Tourist attractions: Not many. A weird mortuary designed in the 1950s by Frank Lloyd Wright pulls in a few visitors every year. Then there's Paul Bunyan's axe, a twenty-foot-high fiberglass artifact located in a small park at the entrance to town. I once suggested Paul Bunyan's penis might be a more spectacular and photogenic attraction, but the Pineland Chamber of Commerce disagreed. There also used to be a small amusement park called Bunyan World just south of town on old Highway 61. It offered a giant lumberjack smoking a corncob pipe, among other wonders, but the place went broke after the interstate hijacked all the traffic. The Pineland Fire Museum, located in the old Northern Pacific Depot, also roped in a few visitors until it burned down ten years ago—I believe this is what is meant by irony—and was never rebuilt.

Politics: Trump is king. He took seventy percent of the vote in 2016. Some people in town love him, but mostly he got the vote because people couldn't connect to Hillary Clinton, an alien in green pantsuits from some elite coastal world. Still, there's no denying Pineland is deeply conservative and hosts its share of birthers, conspiracy theorists, white supremacists, anti-vaxxers, militiamen, and even a handful of holdouts still fighting fluoride. But most people aren't at the fringes. They're just regular folks who adhere to beliefs—in

God, family, country, and duty—they fear are being lost elsewhere in America. It's also worth noting that in 2016 the people of Pineland, while voting heavily for Trump, elected an openly gay and avowedly liberal woman named Mary Jane Bakken as mayor. Go figure.

Gun and pickup truck ownership: Very high.

Crime rate: It used to be very low, but the casino, which opened in 2008, attracted an unsavory element, and crimes of all kinds have been on the rise ever since.

Drugs: Readily available in town and throughout the county. Out in the boondocks, meth making remains the most lucrative, if dangerous, profession. Other of our rural entrepreneurs deal in everything from heroin to pot, assuring that no one here with a drug habit goes unserved. Opiates—the bane of rural America—are the biggest problem, and for every one thousand residents of the county nine hundred eighty-eight dopioid prescriptions were written last year. People here seem to be in a lot of pain.

Economy: Struggling, especially after the Northland Consolidated Paper Mill, long the town's biggest employer, closed five years ago. The casino and Peter's resort hotel provide jobs, but few of them pay much, and most of the worker bees live in cheaply built apartments on the outskirts of town. Aside from Peter's family, there isn't much old money around to buy our way out of obsolescence, and it's probably fair to say Pineland is a relic from an economic model that no longer exists.

Indian affairs: Only a few choice bigots will admit it, but the Ojibwe who run the casino are widely disliked in Pineland, despite the money and jobs they've imported. These ill feelings seethe just beneath the surface, so overt displays of bias are rare. But the prejudice is there, and I doubt it will go away anytime soon.

Best place to eat: At home.

Bottom line: Because the casino and hotel are three miles west of town off Interstate 35, Pineland is isolated, a drive-past town in flyover land. In winter particularly, there's a sense here of being unmoored from the rest of the world, like one of those "lost Swede towns" Fitzgerald mentioned in *The Great Gatsby*. But even lost places have their own small virtues and pleasures. As my father, who lived a life untainted by optimism, once said, "There are worse places you could live." For once my father was right.

When I ran for county attorney, I won the unflagging support of our local newspaper, the aptly named *Paradise Tattler*. The paper is a story in itself. For many years it was known as the *Pineland Pioneer*, and it was a hopelessly dull rag, filled with less-than-scintillating accounts of church socials, city council meetings and the occasional tractor rollover or auto accident. Like so many small-town newspapers, the *Pioneer* eventually fell on hard times, and the local owners sold it to a regional chain based in Duluth. The new owners turned it into a shopper devoid of anything like real news, and in that condition it was on the verge of dying of its own irrelevance until Tommy Redmond came to the rescue.

Arriving in town from points unknown, Tommy bought the failing *Pioneer* for a song, renamed it the *Tattler*, and quickly turned it into a quirky mini-tabloid full of gossip, crime news and, of late, frequent editorials extolling the underappreciated excellence of Donald Trump. Here's a sample of recent headlines: "Wildcat Stalking Local Dogs," "Minneapolis Man Found Naked in Casino Parking Lot," "Farmer Says UFO Landed Near His Barn." You get the drift. Naturally, the good people of Paradise County found this sort of news so distasteful they couldn't get enough of it, and Tommy achieved a kind of non-digital miracle, transforming his little publication into an improbable moneymaker.

He also writes a blog called "Paradise Detective Bureau" that's devoted exclusively to crime news, much of it of a decidedly minor variety. Now and then, though, he gets into something more serious and usually pisses off Arne to no end in the process. I'm one of the blog's five hundred or so subscribers, because I often learn more from it than I do from local law enforcement.

Tommy is known around town as "Red," not just because of his last name but because he always wears a bright red sportscoat that makes him as instantly recognizable as an approaching fire truck. All he lacks is a siren. He's a sharp stick of man in his mid-thirties, with a dark complexion, big brown eyes, and a wild swirl of curly black hair. He pursues stories relentlessly, and he's never been afraid to take on the "Swindeller," as he likes to call Peter. I've leaked or steered a number of good stories to Tommy and he considers me a prime source.

So I wasn't surprised to find him at my doorstep Saturday evening, a few hours after the Serenader had delivered his first message. "Hey Paulie, how's it going?" he asked as Camus came up to assess the situation. "I would have called but I thought we should talk in person."

For some reason, Tommy always calls me "Paulie." I guess it makes him think I'm his friend. I'm not, but I do find him very useful at times.

"Come on in," I said. "I figured you'd be in touch."

Tommy bent down and rubbed one of Camus' ears. "I like this guy. Where'd you get him?"

"He got me. He came up to the door one day just after I moved in. He invited himself in, accepted a donation of chopped baloney, and then went to sleep on my couch. He had no tag, no chip and no owner I could ever find. He was a free being in the world, so I named him Camus."

"Funny name for a dog," Tommy said, "but I like it."

Once we sat down Tommy said, "Boy, lots of big news, isn't there? The Swindeller's gone missing and then that crazy stuff on the courthouse door. I'm wondering, why did he send you that text this morning?"

Here we go, I thought. The smaller the town, the harder it is to keep a secret, and if Tommy knew about Peter's message, so did everyone else in Pineland by now. There was no point denying I'd gotten the text. All I could do was try to set the record straight, which I did.

"So you don't really know why he texted you?"

"Right. It's a mystery to me. And I can't tell you anything else because I don't know anything about why or how Peter went missing. Talk to Arne."

Tommy looked at me in disbelief. "You know Arne hates my guts, so he's not saying shit. C'mon, Paulie, you gotta help me out on this. Biggest story ever here, as far as I know. I want to be out front on it. What about this Serenader business and the message on the courthouse door? Very weird, if you ask me."

"I agree, but I have no theories as to who the Serenader is or what he's up to."

"So you have no idea why you were mentioned with the others?"

"Afraid not."

"How about that thumb drive, which is also pretty weird? Any idea what's on it? Arne won't tell me squat."

"Sorry, Tommy, I'm in the dark about that. Arne doesn't confide in me, either."

"I know. But guess what? I've been hearing stuff about Arne and Peter."

"Such as?"

"Let's just say I have good reason to believe some big shit is going to hit the fan before long."

"Care to be more specific?"

"No can do, friend. But you'll be reading all about it, I promise you. Let's get back to Peter's disappearance. Like I said, I want to be all over the story. I wouldn't be surprised if it goes national."

"You'll just have to keep digging, Tommy. I'll keep you in the loop if you do the same for me."

I gave him my new cell number and he said, "Okay, you've got a deal. Oh, one more thing. What about that Black woman in the photo? Know anything about here?"

"Not a thing," I said. Soon, I would know a great deal more.

7

The call came in Sunday afternoon on my land line, just after I'd returned from a long, rambling walk with Camus.

"Hello, my name is Cassandra Ellis. Is this Mr. Zweifel?"

I didn't recognize the name or voice. "It is. Can I help you?"

"I hope so. I'm in town from Chicago and I'd like to talk to you about an important matter. Is it possible we could meet today? I'd really appreciate it."

"What sort of matter?"

"I'd prefer not to talk about it over the phone but it involves Peter Swindell."

"I see. And you have some information about him?"

"Possibly. Is there private place we could meet?"

"Sure. Why don't you just come over to my house?" I gave her the address and directions.

"Thank you. I'll be there shortly."

Cassandra Ellis appeared at my front door twenty minutes later. Camus came up for an inspection, gave her two quick sniffs and went away, evidence he found her satisfactory. She introduced herself again and said, "I hope I'm not interrupting anything."

"Not at all. Please come in."

She was slender and athletic looking, mid-thirties, with café au lait skin, short hair, and sharp brown eyes. She carried an elegant leather handbag that did not come from K-Mart. Her perfectly tailored gray suit was of a kind and quality rarely seen in Pineland, and her clipped voice lacked the slight Scandinavian lilt that forms Minnesota's predominant accent.

It took a moment before I recognized her, and if the Pope had come to bless me, I might have been less surprised. Cassandra Ellis was the woman from the photo found in Peter Swindell's SUV.

"Well, this is certainly unexpected," I said. "You may not know it, but you're something of a mystery woman in these parts."

"Really? I don't understand."

"Let's just say your face has become familiar," I said, inviting her into the living room, which was a litter dump of legal documents, books and magazines. I cleared a space on the couch. "Please, have a seat and I'll do my best to explain what's going on."

Before she sat down, she handed me her business card. It was from a Chicago law firm called Randall, Morton, Muir and Feinstein and identified her as a "senior litigator."

"You must be very good," I said. "I haven't run across many senior litigators of your age."

"I'm a quick study," she said. I didn't doubt that for minute. Some people radiate intelligence, and she did. "I really do appreciate your taking the time to see me," she continued. "I flew up from Chicago this morning and, of course, I don't know anyone here. But I thought I might begin with you."

"May I ask why you selected me?"

"I did some research. This is all foreign territory to me, as I think you can understand, and I didn't want to come up here and have to deal with, well—"

"A bunch of racist yahoos?" I suggested.

"I'm not saying that. I just wanted to talk to somebody who wouldn't be put off by who I am. I ran across your name as the county attorney here and learned you'd once been a public defender in Minneapolis. You handled a big case there representing a group of Black defendants being unfairly targeted by the police. So I figured you were somebody I could deal with."

She was right. I'd won the case, which involved a group of small-time pot dealers who were hardly upstanding citizens. But it was blatantly obvious the cops had been doing a little color selection when it came to their busts, and I'd managed to get the charges dismissed.

"I'm impressed with your research," I said. "But it's not why you're here, so we might as well get to the point. I'd really like to know how you're connected to Peter Swindell. By the way, are you aware he disappeared yesterday?"

"Yes, I just found out. I picked up a newspaper at the airport in Minneapolis. Now I have a question for you: what did you mean when you said I'm a 'familiar face' here?"

I told her about the photo. "Since you're from Chicago, I'm guessing that's where the picture was taken."

"Very strange," she said, a hint of alarm edging into her voice. "Do you have the photo?"

"No, the sheriff here has it. But it looked like it was taken with a long lens. I doubt you knew you were being photographed."

"You think someone was stalking me, is that it?"

"Could be. In any case, I'd really like to know what brought you here. It must be quite a story. And if you don't mind, I think I should record our conversation, since anything you tell me could have evidentiary value."

"I'd rather not do that now. I'll give a full and complete account of what I know at the proper time to the proper authorities."

"Spoken like a true lawyer," I observed.

"Do you have a problem with that?"

I could almost see bristles growing out of her forehead. Cassandra Ellis clearly wasn't much for humor at her own expense.

"No problem," I said. "But we're not in court here."

"I'm aware of that," she said curtly. "Let me show you something."

She dug into her svelte Italian handbag, and I caught a glimpse what looked to be the grip of a pistol tucked inside. She left the gun undisturbed and instead produced a manila envelope. It contained a letter, which she placed on the coffee table in front of us.

"I received this two days ago," she said. "It may be evidence, so you shouldn't touch it. Go ahead and read it. It will explain why I'm here."

The letter read as follows:

My Dearest Cassandra,

I have been meaning now for many years to write to you, but something has always held me back. Now that I find myself very near the end of my life, however, it is time to bring this matter to a close, so that I may leave the world with a peaceful heart.

My name, Cassandra, is Peter Swindell, and I am your father. I know you will find this hard to believe, but I assure you, with all my heart, it is true. Your mother, who I knew only briefly but loved very much, gave birth to you on Sept. 30, 1983, in Chicago, and gave you up for adoption soon thereafter. I learned of this only later, and as you may imagine, I was heartbroken. Your mother is gone from this world now, and so I alone am able to tell our story.

Cassandra, I am a white man and your mother was Black. We truly cared for each other but at that time ours was an illicit love, and I could not do the thing then that I should have done, which was to marry your mother and raise you as our daughter. For this, I am truly sorry.

I have searched for you for many years—adoption records, as you must know, are sealed under court order—and it was only recently that I was able to learn at last of your whereabouts. Since then, I have read everything I could find about you in the Chicago newspapers, and I hope you can at least imagine how proud I am of you and how thrilled I am at your success in life. Your adoptive parents, George and Helen, certainly raised you well and I am grateful for that. I only wish I could have found you sooner.

There is much, much more I would like to tell you, but more than anything else I want to see you, to look into your beautiful face and ask for your forgiveness, before I die. I am too ill to travel—the doctors say I have only a matter of weeks—but if you could come here to my home in Pineland, which is just north of the Twin Cities, we could spend my remaining days together.

I know this is a great deal to ask after so long a time. I will understand if you choose not to come. But there is nothing in life I want now except to see you. I have not called you because it would somehow seem wrong to intrude on you in that way. However, please feel free to call me at any time if you wish. I can only conclude by saying it would mean everything to me if you would respond to this letter and agree to come see me here in Pineland. I would savor every moment with you and perhaps, in what little time there is, you might even come to feel something in your heart for me as well.

With all my love,
Peter Swindell

Beneath the signature was a phone number beginning with a 612 area code, which covers the Minneapolis area but not Pineland, as well as what appeared to be the correct address for Peter's mansion. The signature itself, in blue ink, was written with a shaky hand. I couldn't recall ever seeing a specimen of Peter's handwriting, but I would have expected it to be bold and pretentious, just like the man, and not the reedy scrawl I was looking at now.

Nothing about the letter sounded at all like Peter. I doubted heartache and repentance were part of his genetic make-up. His style was never to look back, and I suspected he'd long ago buried his emotions in a deep pit so he could stomp across the world free from the entanglements of the heart. I simply couldn't imagine him suddenly becoming sentimental about an abandoned child. Nor was he at death's door as far as anyone knew.

"That's quite a letter," I said. "But I have to be honest with you. I don't think—"

"You don't think Mr. Swindell wrote this letter, do you? Why is that?"

I explained my reasoning. I also told her about the Serenader and the message he'd left at the courthouse. "You must be 'the woman.' And since the Serenader seems to have predicted your arrival, it's possible he wrote the letter. Or, at the least, he knows who did."

"So you're saying I was lured here. I suspected as much."

"Then why did you come? If this is all bullshit—"

She cut me off. "It may not be entirely bullshit. It's possible, even likely, Peter Swindell really is my father."

54

"Why do think so?"

"Because I called him, whoever he is. It was an interesting conversation."

I wanted to hear what Cassandra and the letter writer had talked about. But I had to temper my curiosity. She clearly possessed significant evidence relating to Peter and possibly his disappearance. It was time for official business, rather than casual conversation.

"We really need a formal interview at this point," I told her. "I'm sure I could arrange a meeting at the sheriff's office within the hour. Would you be willing to do that?"

"Yes, that would be fine. As I said, I have no problem providing a statement."

I called Arne on his cell and explained the situation. He agreed to meet us at his office in forty-five minutes and said he'd notify the two Jasons to see if they were available as well.

"We're all set," I told Cassandra. "I can drive you to the sheriff's office and back if that will work." She said it would.

Camus, who'd been sprawled on the floor, went over to Cassandra and favored her with one of his patented, soul-searching stares.

She stared back and said, "Your dog seems to finds me very interesting. What's his name?"

I told her, explaining that I'd read a lot of Albert Camus in college. "Then I found myself back in Pineland and it felt kind of absurd, so when this guy arrived at my doorstep one day, I decided to anoint him my Camus in residence."

"And he provides philosophical advice, is that it?"

"Yes. He also keeps burglars away."

"Fascinating," Cassandra said and looked at me as though I just might be crazy.

Before we headed off to Arne's office, I gave Cassandra a brief sketch of Pineland and Paradise County. I assumed she felt uncomfortable, fearing that racists lurked around every corner. It's not like that, I told her, but I did caution that Pineland is not a liberal Valhalla where rainbows of happy diversity sparkle in the sky. I suggested she should be straightforward and nonjudgmental with the locals, and most would respond in kind.

"I'll handle it," she said.

Out of sheer curiosity, I asked about her education and background. She wasn't very forthcoming, but I was able to tease out some information. She'd graduated from Northwestern University with a double major in political science and economics and gone on to Harvard Law School on a scholarship. Then she'd clerked for a federal appeals court judge. It was the kind of resume most lawyers would kill for.

My educational background, I told her, wasn't quite as stellar. I have a bachelor's degree in history from St. Cloud State University, a school of no particular distinction, followed by an L.L.B. degree from William Mitchell College of Law. I didn't mention that it required five years of night classes to get my law degree while I worked an array of odd jobs, all accomplished with student loans totaling close to sixty thousand dollars. I'm still paying them off.

She wasn't familiar with William Mitchell and asked where it was.

"It's an adjunct of Harvard," I said.

"Really? I never heard of it there."

"That's because I'm kidding. It's actually in St. Paul, but it's now the Hamline College of Law."

"Haven't heard of that, either," she said without cracking a smile.

I changed the subject and asked how long she'd worked for her firm in Chicago. She said she'd started at Randall, Morton, Muir and Feinstein right out of law school. The firm specialized in personal injury cases and was known for its aggressive, leave-no-bridges-unburned style of litigation. In Chicago legal circles, she said, the joke was that the firm's initials actually stood for Really Mean Motherfuckers.

"So how do you end up among the sharks?" I asked.

"Simplest reason of all. The firm needed a nice Black face for their affirmative action portfolio, and they dangled plenty of money my way, so I signed on."

"And from there, I gather, it was onward and upward. Now, you're already a senior litigator. I can't tell you how impressed I am."

"It wasn't easy," she said. "I worked really hard. I won some big cases for the firm and when you bring in money you get rewarded. It's that simple."

"Any cases I might have heard of?"

"The biggest was *Richard Washington vs. Chicago Housing Authority*. That was last year. Richard was just fourteen and a shooting left him paralyzed and with a traumatic brain injury. I argued that CHA was negligent in just about every way you can think of, and the jury agreed. He was awarded sixty million, counting punitive damages."

"And your firm will get forty percent of that?"

"Fifty. And that's how I became a senior litigator with a corner office. More importantly, Richard will get the care he needs for the rest of his life."

"You sound like you just might be an idealist underneath all that legal armor we lawyers have to wear."

She smiled for the first time and said, "Oh, I don't know if I'd go that far. So, tell me something. Who's the sheriff I'll be seeing?"

"His name is Arne Sigurdson."

"What's he like?"

"The consensus of one, that being me, regards him as an asshole."

"Wonderful," she said. "Assholes are who I deal with every day."

As we drove to Arne's office, I decided to take a gamble. I knew Arne and the Jasons wouldn't want me in on their interview with Cassandra. But I felt I'd established some rapport with her and I remained deeply curious about the phone conversation she'd had with whoever wrote her the letter. So I told her how I'd become a suspect in Peter's disappearance because of the text message.

"I'm officially considered a suspicious character," I said.

"Well, that's good to know, but I have to say you don't look like a desperado to me."

"Thank you."

"Actually, you have a kind face. That's not true of many lawyers I know."

"It's the one defect in my otherwise sterling character," I said. "Now, if there's anything you want to mention in passing about that phone conversation yesterday, I'd be happy to hear it, in complete confidence of course."

She seemed to be loosening up—maybe she'd decided she could trust me—and she said, "I guess I can give you the quick version. I talked with the guy for about twenty minutes. He knew all about me, where I grew up, what my adoptive father did for a living, where I went to school, you name it. He also talked about my birth mother but wouldn't tell me her name."

"Did he say why?"

"Not in so many words. But he left the impression she might have been a prostitute. He told me he really did love her but marriage was out of the question. Besides, she had a bad drug problem, or so he said."

"Is that how she died?"

"He claimed he didn't know for sure but it might have been a heroin overdose. He told me he'd lost track of her after I was born. Then he moved to the Chicago suburbs and married a woman there. She's dead, too, he said. Cancer."

"How did the guy sound?" I asked, thinking of Peter, who spoke in a silky baritone and always talked very fast.

"He sounded like an old, sick man. His voice was almost a whisper, and he seemed to be struggling to get the words out."

"What time did you call him?"

"About four o'clock yesterday."

Peter had vanished early Saturday morning, well before Cassandra made her call. But if he was still alive, his disappearance a ruse, why would he have gone to the trouble of disguising his voice? And if he was in hiding, why had he urged Cassandra to visit him in Pineland? It didn't make sense.

I shared these thoughts with Cassandra. She said, "That's interesting. Let's assume then that I didn't talk to Peter Swindell yesterday. But whoever it was, he was very convincing. That's why I hopped on a flight this morning."

"I would have stayed in Chicago," I said. "Why risk coming here when you knew you could be walking into a trap of some kind?"

"There are things I need to find out, and I'm willing to take the risk. Besides, I don't scare easily."

"So what exactly are you hoping to find out? That Peter really is your father?"

"Yes, that's the first big thing. The man I talked to on the phone knew way too much to be a simple scammer. He knew the date and location of my birth in Chicago. He also offered up details about the woman he claimed was my birth mother. A lot of what he said was new to me. You have to understand, I was only a few weeks old when I was adopted by a white couple, George and Helen Ellis, from Wheaton, Illinois. They're the only parents I've ever known."

"Did you ever try to track down your biological parents?"

"No. My attitude for a long time was that I really didn't want to know. But I could never quite make the curiosity go away. Last year, I took one of those DNA tests that traces your ancestry. If the test was accurate, I'm half Scottish and Irish."

"Well, for what it's worth, Peter is of Scotch-Irish ancestry. We have an annual parade up here and Peter liked to march in it playing bagpipes and wearing a kilt. I can't say his appearance was fetching."

Cassandra Ellis, on the other hand, was very fetching, and I studied her face closely as we continued to talk. One feature, her eyebrows, stood out. They were long and slightly arched in the usual manner but took a short, steep dive as they neared her nose. It was a striking detail, one I'd also noticed on Peter's face. A genetic marker of sorts or just a coincidence? I didn't know.

As we approached the sheriff's office, which is near the courthouse, Cassandra said, "The only way to tell for sure if Mr. Swindell really is my father would be a DNA paternity test. But now that he's gone missing, that might be a problem."

"Maybe not," I said. "You probably don't know it, but Peter has a son here in town named Dewey. His DNA, if he'd be willing to provide it, would do as well as Peter's for purposes of comparison."

"I'll keep that in mind," she said. "I'm still trying to figure things out."

"Well, for what it's worth, here's the way I see it. Whoever sent you the letter and talked to you on the phone is likely the same person who snapped that photo in Chicago. And now that he's got you here, who knows what his intentions are? You could be in real danger. My lawyerly advice would be for you to leave here as soon as you can until we have a better sense of what's going on."

"I appreciate what you're saying, but what if Peter Swindell really is my father? I need to know what happened to him. Is he dead or alive? Who spirited him away and why? But more than anything else I need to know who I am because I've never been able to answer that question. My adoptive parents are wonderful people but they're not blood, and blood is the one true thing we get when we come into the world. It took me a long time to realize that, but now I do."

I thought of my own tangled bloodlines, a saga of Germans and Irish and Native Americans and God knows who else, and I understood her point. I also saw that there was in her a deep fierceness—how could she, as a prized litigator, not have that quality?—and that she wouldn't back away from danger in pursuit of a worthy goal.

"So I gather you'll be staying here for a while."

"Yes, until I know what I need to know. I'll be at the big resort hotel outside of town."

"Okay. I assume you know who owns the place?"

"I don't."

"Peter Swindell."

"Imagine that," she said. "Small world up here, isn't it?"

Arne and Jason Braddock were waiting for us at the sheriff's department. After introductions were made, I mentioned that Cassandra's car was parked at my house and she'd need a ride back. Jason immediately volunteered.

"You won't have to talk to Mr. Zweifel again," he added. "We'll take everything from here."

Maybe Jason believed that, but I intended to see Cassandra again, and soon.

9

I went home and screwed around with some legal work to pass the time, but I couldn't get Cassandra out of my mind. Her story, especially the part about the letter from her supposed father, had resonated with me. With its plea for reconciliation, the letter was exactly the kind my own father should have written but never did, and I still can't get over it.

My father, the Honorable Phillip Howard Zweifel, was an excellent lawyer, known for his cutting cross-examinations and charming way with a jury. He was also, for ten years in the 1960s and early 1970s, the Paradise County Attorney. It was a part-time job then, more political than anything else, and my father was by all accounts very adept at it.

Once my father stepped out of the courtroom, however, there was less to admire. As with me, alcohol for him was a hard burning thing, not be touched for too long without pain and danger. He was, or so I've been told, an unpredictable drunk known for long weekend benders with his courthouse cronies. Drinking is always an escape, a way out of the world and its endless disarray, and it made my father a risk to others in the way people who try to elude reality always are. He just didn't care, about himself or anyone else, when the booze took hold, and that's how he ended up killing my mother.

Her name was Dorothy Swaboda, and she was by all accounts a lovely woman who'd grown up on a dairy farm near Pineland. I say "by all accounts" because I have no memory of her. All I have are a few photos and some of her old jewelry, including a simple gold bracelet I've worn for years as my way of keeping in touch with her spirit. She was tall, light-haired, with a solid Slavic face. In the photos she always looks stern, or maybe unhappy. She was thirty-five when she married my father and I was born six months later, the baby behind the wedding. I was just shy of two when she died.

It happened one night when I was in the care of my two aunts. My father and mother went out for dinner at Gentry's Supper Club, now long gone. The club was on Fortune Lake, about ten miles west of town, at the end of a twisty county road. After dinner and more than a few cocktails, my father got behind the wheel of his Buick Electra, my mother in the front seat beside him. It was pitch black along the road and my father missed a turn at high speed. The Buick went off the road and overturned, ejecting both occupants. My father survived the wreck. My mother was dead at the scene.

It was a clear-cut case of vehicular homicide but my father never faced charges for his drunken act of destruction because he had friends in all the right places in Paradise County. Still, everyone in the county knew the real story. Two weeks after the accident, my father resigned as county attorney for "personal reasons," according to the local newspaper.

Once my mother was gone, my father didn't relish the thought of raising a child—I think he always saw me as an unfortunate mistake—and he gladly turned me over to Katherine and Anna, my mother's unmarried sisters. They hated him, of course, for killing their sister and did their best to keep me away from him. On the rare occasions we did see each other, he showed little interest in me, and I came to think of him as a ghost barely visible at the edges of my life.

When I was twelve, he moved to Las Vegas and went into practice there with an old friend from law school. We didn't talk or stay in contact, and he was as lost to me as if he'd disappeared in a hurricane on the high seas. Then one day in 2010 he returned to Pineland, a sick old man in search of care and sympathy, and that's how I ended up back in town as well.

Now Cassandra Ellis was looking for her father, and I wished her luck. I really did. But I hoped she wouldn't be too disappointed in who and what she found.

Just after six, Camus began barking at the door and when I looked outside I saw Jason Braddock dropping Cassandra off. He waited for her to leave in her car before driving away. I wondered how her interview with Arne and Jason had gone, but I figured she could take care of herself, and I didn't think she would have said anything to get me into more trouble than I already was.

Not to worry. More trouble would find me before long.

Camus always sleeps with me, but he's a restless soul, and he'll often get up in the middle of the night to wander around and bark at phantoms in the dark. I try to ignore his nocturnal yapping, but when it becomes especially loud and persistent I know something is going on. The day before, Arne had set him off by approaching the front door. Now, at four a.m., Camus was going crazy again, and I dragged myself out of bed to investigate. I found him at the front door, making tight counterclockwise circles and sounding as though Armageddon might be at hand. But it wasn't the end of the world. It was a wooden cross burning in my front yard.

I turned on my yard light and went outside, just in time to see a vehicle racing away from my cul-de-sac. The driver was running without lights and I couldn't make out a license or identify the make of the vehicle. The cross, about four feet tall, was burning fiercely, sending out angry sparks, and I was worried my house might catch fire. As I turned to go back inside and call 911, I saw something else—the letters "KKK" chalked on my driveway.

Cassandra Ellis had appeared at my door just twelve hours earlier and now she was clearly the target of a hate crime. It made me sick. But the burning cross and the reference to the Ku Klux Klan also had a deep personal meaning for me. There was an old, awful sin in the Zweifel family history and whoever had staged the ugly scene in my yard appeared to know all about it.

I called 911, then went looking for my kitchen fire extinguisher. But it was dead, so all I could do was wait and watch until help arrived. The fire had all but burned itself out, the cross vanished into a pile of ashes, by the time a deputy sheriff pulled up. Two fire crews appeared a few minutes later with pumper trunks but there was little for them to do except hose down the last of the embers.

"What the fuck?" Arne said when he stopped by my office at the courthouse later in the morning and took a seat across from my desk. "You're just in the middle of everything, aren't you? You sure that was a cross in your yard?"

I hadn't managed to get any photos of the cross, and that seemed to make Arne suspicious. "Of course it was a cross," I said. "Besides, you know about the message."

"Yeah, my deputy got pictures," Arne said as he dug out a Marlboro and lit it.

"There's no smoking in Paradise County public buildings," I reminded him.

"I'll let the BCA know. I have no doubt they'll get right on it, assuming they're not busy trying to find any remains of that cross. It's a weird deal, if you ask me."

"Listen, it's more than weird. It's scary. You know who that message was directed at."

"Do I?"

"Yeah, you do. It has to be Cassandra Ellis."

"Okay, if she was the target, why was a cross burned on your lawn? Who even knew she'd been to your house?"

"That's a fair question, Arne. Let's see now. There's me, there's you, the Jasons, some of your deputies—"

"Oh, I get it. The KKK has a secret cell in my office and they're out burning crosses on your fucking lawn. That's a genuinely pathetic idea."

"Let's hear a better one then."

"I don't know. You're the only person who saw the cross. You tell me."

"So I did it all myself? Is that what you're thinking? That idea doesn't even rise to the level of pathetic. But how about we get back to Cassandra Ellis? She's still in town from what I understand. Has anybody told her about the cross burning and the message?"

"Not that I know of. The fact is, there's no real evidence to say it was directed at her. Could just be some stupid kids."

"Who happened to select my lawn to do their dirty work? Not a chance, Arne. It was a carefully premediated act. There's something else you should know." I told him about my family connection to the KKK.

"No shit," Arne said. "So you've got some white hoods in the family closet. But it was a hundred years ago. Who the hell would know that besides you? Makes a person wonder, doesn't it?"

"Wonder away, Arne. Just make sure you tell Cassandra what happened. And while you're at, suggest to her in the strongest possible terms that she return to Chicago. She's in jeopardy here."

"Sure, we'll do that. But you met the woman. She'll do what we she wants to do and that's it."

"Sounds like you had a tough interview with her. How'd it go, by the way? Any big revelations?"

Arne dumped his cigarette into any empty cup on my desk and stood up. "None of your business," he said as he went out the door.

I wasn't convinced Arne would tell Cassandra the full story so I called her at the hotel as soon as Arne left. There was no answer in her room. I left a message for her to call me just as my nosy assistant, Doug Wifferding, came into my office. He was holding a newspaper and looked very concerned, which is how he looks almost all the time.

"Saw Arne walking out," Doug said. "What did he want?"

"He just wanted to say how much he admires me," I said. "So what's up?"

"Have you seen the *StarTribune* this morning?"

"Not yet."

"I just got it. Have a look at this."

Doug laid the newspaper's regional page in front of me. A headline jumped out: "MYSTERY MESSAGE FOLLOWS DISAPPEARANCE." The story below included the Serenader's message word for word and reported, more or less accurately, how I had found it. This news was attributed to "a knowledgeable source in Pineland."

"I wonder who the source is?" Doug said. "Arne's going to be really pissed."

"Arne's always pissed," I said.

As to who'd the leaked the message to the Minneapolis newspaper, I had no idea. But I fully expected Arne would lay the blame on me.

10

My favorite watering hole in Pineland is the Dead Lumberjack Saloon and Eatery. Its original owner was Ron Berglund, who'd actually been a logger. Ron lost an eye and a
small piece of his face when a chainsaw went berserk on him
one afternoon in the woods, and in the early 1970s he won
a multimillion dollar settlement from the manufacturer. His
attorney, by the way, was my father. Ron used his new-found
fortune to open the saloon.

Ron is long gone and his granddaughter, the magnificent
Kaitlyn Berglund, now runs the place. Kat, as everyone calls
her, has long brown hair that cascades past her shoulders,
inviting hazel eyes and a dewy freshness that belies her age,
which is somewhere in the vicinity of forty. She's Pineland's
resident sex goddess, and when men come into the bar you
can almost see their fantasies swirl around them, like steam
coming out of their pores.

I've known Kat since I came back to Pineland and we're an intermittent couple. She's not the sort of woman who feels the need to be in a steady relationship, much as I'd like that, and so we go out now and then and enjoy an occasional romp between the sheets. I'd marry her tomorrow if I could—she's smart, funny, good-hearted, and flat-out gorgeous—but I know that will never happen. She's she just too independent to be bound by matrimony. Kat also functions as rumor central in Pineland because men always like to tell a beautiful woman secrets, especially if she's plying them with alcohol.

"Well, here comes another lost soul," she said when I wandered in for a drink Monday night. "The usual?"

"Why not?" I said, bellying up to the saloon's long bar. Hanging behind it is one of the Dead Lumberjack's chief accoutrements—a gigantic old painting of General George Custer, golden locks flowing in the wind as he bravely meets his end amid a scrum of Indians at Little Big Horn. The painting, a piece of hack work from the 1890s, depicts the Indians as raving savages in a predictably offensive way, and I once asked Kat why she kept the damn thing, which her grandfather installed when he built the place.

"It's a testament to human stupidity," she told me. "What could be more appropriate for a bar?"

Although Jack Daniel's is my usual drink, I always order a margarita at the Dead Lumberjack. It brings to mind tropical sands, warm ocean waves and Kat lulling about in a bikini. A man just has to dream.

When Kat delivered my margarita, she said, "I hear you had a little excitement last night."

"Yeah, the KKK rides again, or so it seems."

73

"Any idea who might be behind it?"

"Nope. So much shit has happened the past couple of days my brain can't keep up with it."

"Maybe a margarita will help."

"Won't hurt. So, Kat, since you're the closest thing to an omniscient sage here in glorious Pineland, what do you think happened to Peter?"

"Somebody took him," she said. "He's probably dead by now."

"What makes you think that?"

"I know Peter, and, no, it's not because I ever slept with him. But he did come in now and then to have a drink and stare at my boobs."

"Can't blame him for that."

"Thank you, mister chauvinist pig. When Peter wasn't busy ogling, he always talked about how happy he was to be back in Pineland with his mansion and his fancy cars. You know what he actually told me once? He said, 'I'm the king of Paradise County and it's good to be king.'"

"What a dickhead."

"True. But the point is that he was clearly enjoying himself here. I also know for fact he wasn't in any financial trouble. So there'd be no reason for him to take off and disappear."

"How did you find out about his finances?"

"That qualifies as a bartender's secret. I'll tell you something else. From what I hear, Peter doesn't have a will. So if he is no longer among us, darling Dewey will get the money. The estate's supposedly worth ten million or more, not counting the mansion."

"What about Peter's ex-wife?"

"I'm told she's dead."

"That's interesting," I said. "Somebody else just told me the same thing."

"And who would that be?"

I gave Kat a brief account of my visit from Cassandra Ellis. "There are so many leaks in Arne's office I'm sure half of Paradise County already knows about her," I said.

"That half includes me," Kat admitted. "Heard the news from a party who shall go unnamed less than an hour ago. Any chance this Ellis woman might really be Peter's daughter?"

"Yes, there's a chance. A DNA test will tell the tale if she can get Dewey to cooperate."

"Dewey's a turnip. I doubt he has any blood. Maybe they can get some of his saliva. But you can bet he won't jump at the chance to see his inheritance cut in half."

"I'm sure he won't. Speaking of the Swindell family, who do you think snatched Peter?"

"Not a clue as to that, I'm afraid. Maybe our new friend, the Serenader, knows."

"Sounds like he's already the talk of the town."

"He is. You know what the strangest thing about it is? The name. Why does the guy call himself the Serenader?"

"Maybe he'll start singing to us before long," I offered, "and then we'll know. But you're right. It's a very odd name. It has to have some special significance."

"My regulars are already speculating on who the guy might be, but it's just the usual barroom bullshit. How about you? Any ideas? Think of me as your voice to the community."

"No, I'm in enough trouble already, so I think I'll keep my stupid mouth shut." I swigged the last of my margarita and swung off the bar stool. "One and done for me tonight. But if you hear any interesting talk about the Serenader, let me know, will you?"

"Your wish is my command," Kat said.

"In that case, I wish you'd come over to my place later tonight."

"Not tonight, my lonely man. But soon. We'll have some drinks and play. How's that?"

"I can hardly wait," I said.

On my way out I ran into Ed Boudreau, one of the Dead Lumberjack's regulars. Ed is a full-blooded Ojibwe and the chief financial officer for the Grand Lac Band, who own and operate the Paradise Pines Casino. He's about fifty, tall and craggy, with a wide, friendly face and long black hair tied into a ponytail. I found him in his usual costume of faded blue jeans and a buckskin jacket. Ed speaks fluent Ojibwe, passable French, has an MBA from Wharton, can work magic with a spreadsheet, and is of the general opinion that white people are crazy. He is also profanely funny.

"You already done staring at those marvelous tits?" he asked. "The evening is still young."

"Your turn, Ed. But remember, George will be watching you."

"Well, we all know the only good Custer is a dead Custer," Ed said with a grin. "That's an old Indian saying, if I'm not mistaken. Speaking of assholes, what the hell happened to Peter?"

"Nobody knows," I said. "Any thoughts?"

"Maybe. But I prefer to stay out of white mischief."

Ed was well acquainted with Peter and his activities. The Grand Lac Band helped finance the Paradise Resort Hotel, and there were rumors Peter had cemented the deal with some suspicious payments to certain Indian "charities." But if Ed was involved in some dirty business with Peter, I'd never find out about it. The band was its own little world, one in which I had no jurisdiction.

"You're not fooling me, Ed. You love white mischief. It gives you something to make fun of. If you do know something that might relate to Peter's disappearance, I'd love to hear it."

"All right, here's a 'maybe' for you, but you didn't hear it from me. Agreed?"

"My lips are sealed."

"Then you might want to look at something called the 'cloud fund' in Peter's accounts."

"And why should I do that?"

"I'll leave that for you to figure out. Let's just say I think Peter had a secret and it was costing him a lot of money."

"And you know this for sure?"

Ed put a hand on my shoulder, which surprised me, and said in a solemn voice, "Wise old Indian never lie. He see much. He know much. Be wary, white man."

Then he let out a great roar of a laugh and headed into the Dead Lumberjack. "Titty time. Bye, Paul."

Ed's cryptic reference to the "cloud fund" piqued my interest. He liked to screw with people, especially those of the white variety, and maybe that's all he was doing now. Even so,

I decided to make some inquiries, just to see if such a fund existed.

As I drove home, I found myself thinking about the hateful message left on my driveway and about a famous photograph taken in Pineland in 1924. Called "Night Rally at the Courthouse," the photo is the work of an unlikely genius named Wilford Shay. The photo features my grandfather, Paul William Zweifel, who died before I was born, and it exposes my shameful family history.

The fact that the photo is perhaps Shay's masterpiece doesn't help matters. A lifelong resident of Paradise County, Shay between 1910 and his death in 1937 recorded in large-format, black-and-white images everything he could about our little slice of the world. He was a classic rural eccentric, a farmer's son who became a full-time tractor mechanic and part-time antiques dealer when he wasn't busy behind the camera. He lived his entire adult life in a tiny cottage along the Paradise River. When he died, his "estate" was valued at less than five hundred dollars.

Yet Shay had one invaluable possession, a fabulous eye, and it was God's own gift. His photos—found carefully titled, numbered, dated, annotated and stored away after his death—are the closest thing to high art ever produced in Paradise County. There are nearly six hundred in all, most of them still owned by the county historical society, to which I proudly belong.

Shay took photos of threshing bees, farm families, political rallies, old barns, small-town businesses and anything else that appealed to his dazzling eye. He was no Grandpa

Moses, however, and his images aren't the usual sentimental stuff celebrating the glories of pastoral existence. His portraits show faces hard-edged and broken, and the buildings and places he memorialized always look on the brink of ruin. Hardship and loss were his themes, but he also found strange beauty in the midst of both.

"Night Rally at the Courthouse," now in the collections of the Chicago Art Institute, was taken in Pineland on July 19, 1924. It shows a rally of the Ku Klux Klan, then nearing the apogee of its power, in the courthouse square. From my office window I can see the exact spot where the local Klan chapter's ridiculously titled Grand Giant, my grandfather, addressed the crowd. Dear old granddad was the first Zweifel to practice law in Pineland and was known to be a forceful speaker. According to newspaper accounts, he spewed out a witch's brew of hatred for Blacks, Jews, swarthy immigrants and anyone else lacking good Aryan bloodlines.

Shay was right there, his camera mounted behind my grandfather. The image Shay took has a Satanic sheen, torches flaring in the darkness amid a small cluster of men in white robes and peaked hats, their sweaty faces emerging out of the light as my namesake delivers his toxic oration. The photo, widely reprinted, has appeared in several books tracing the history of the Klan, thereby immortalizing Pineland for all the wrong reasons.

The Klan is long gone from Pineland, but the idea of white supremacy isn't. A few skinheads slunk out of the woods a while back and staged a small rally by the courthouse. It wasn't a success. A crowd consisting largely of protesters showed up, and the skinheads were shouted down before slithering away. I'd been among those who spoke out against them, and I wondered if they'd burned the cross on my lawn. But it didn't seem likely because I doubted they knew anything about Cassandra. Nor did I think they had the collective cranial capacity to think up or manage the elaborate scheme by which she was lured to Pineland.

The Serenader, on the other hand, clearly knew about her and very probably wrote the purported letter from Peter. But why did he want her in Pineland? And who'd come to my lawn in the dead of night to threaten Cassandra, if not the skinheads? And what about Peter? Was he dead or gone into hiding for reasons yet to be discovered?

It was a puzzle with more pieces than I could manage, at least for the moment. When I got home, I put some Mozart on my turntable and sat down for a long talk with Camus. He was very understanding but offered no immediate morsels of wisdom.

11

When I reached my office Tuesday morning, my secretary, Jane Niskanen, told me Vern had called.

"Okay. Any other messages?"

I was hoping Cassandra had gotten back to me, but Jane said Vern's message was the only one. "He said it's very urgent," she added.

"Of course he did. Anytime Vern wants to tell me I'm screwing up, it's always urgent."

I knew my favorite county board chairman wanted to talk about Cassandra Ellis and the Serenader and whatever crap Arne was peddling at the moment. He'd also want to remind me how I could serve the greater cause of humanity by recusing myself from the case of Peter's disappearance. But I was in no rush to speak with Vern. Let him stew for a while.

The usual paperwork awaited on my desk and after an hour of heavy legal lifting that included such scintillating items as vetting a new contract for the county's dog catchers,

I called Vern. The conversation went exactly as I expected, Vern probing me for more information about Cassandra and telling me once again to step away from the case or else. I refused, unpleasant words were exchanged, and I hung up.

Even so, I assumed my removal from the case, forced if necessary, was merely a matter of time. How long did I have? For an answer, I went to the adjoining office for a chat with Doug. As usual, he was hunched over at his desk, staring at the giant, home-theater-sized computer monitor he'd somehow finagled the county into buying for him. I'd caught him once watching porn—no great offense, but not a wise thing to do in a government office—and after that he'd always been more discreet.

"Hi, Paul," he said, his bright little face a study in poorly disguised duplicity. "Quite a deal at your house this morning, wasn't it?"

"Excitement is my middle name," I said. "I suppose the news is all over town already."

"Could be. I heard it at breakfast from a deputy I know. I'm betting we'll have a bunch of news people up here by the end of the day. A burning cross! Wow! That's something. The reporters will want to talk to you, that's for sure."

His words came tinged with regret, and I knew why. Doug wanted desperately to be the county attorney, and he'd been laying the groundwork to run before I blitzed him with my out-of-nowhere campaign. When I took office, the county board all but forced me to keep Doug on— he'd been an assistant for a number of years—and I reluctantly agreed.

Tall, thin and swarthy, Doug wears seersucker suits and white shoes year round, likes to talk in a low conspiratorial whisper, and favors antique terminology, once informing me that a Black woman he'd seen working at the casino was "probably an octoroon." I told him he was probably an idiot for trotting out that word, which left him deeply offended. He's not a native Pinelander—he grew up in Iowa, or maybe it was Indiana—and somehow landed here, for reasons he's never explained. My guess is that he loves the weather.

Despite Doug's manifest eccentricities, he's a decent lawyer. He's also an able and practiced maneuverer who functions as king of the courthouse gossip circuit. Vern and his cronies seem to love him, and I've often wondered whether he has some sort of hold over the board, knowledge perhaps of an indiscretion here or a little payoff there that ensures his continued employment. I have no doubt he regularly reports on my activities, so I'm always cautious around him.

"I'll be avoiding reporters today and in the days ahead," I said. "If they call while I'm out, just say I've gone fishing."

Doug, whose sense of humor suffers from being nonexistent, immediately noted that the county's lakes were still iced in and that fishing season had yet to begin.

"You can share that insight with the reporters, too," I said. "By the way, what's the betting on how long I'm going to be on Peter's case? I'm sure the rumor mill is working full time as we speak."

Doug at first feigned ignorance. "Oh, I really couldn't tell you, Paul. But people are talking. You know how it is."

"No, I don't, Doug. Enlighten me."

"Well, there are a lot of questions what with that text from Peter and all and you being mentioned in the Serenader's message. Vern and the board just think you're a little too close to things and that bringing in an outsider may be the way to go. You know, just to be on the safe side."

"Well said, Doug, but how about we trying being honest with each other? Do I have a week before the board tosses me off the boat?"

A coy smile appeared on Doug's lying face. He very much liked that I was in trouble with the board. "Gosh, Paul, all I can say is I wouldn't bet on it."

Knowing what a high rank Doug holds in the ranks of weaseldom, I saw no reason to doubt his forecast.

Back in my private office, I logged on to my computer to check the day's e-mail. It was all the usual stuff except for a message from Dale Shiffley, who runs the only funeral home in town. Dale is married to one of my cousins, Merrilee Swaboda. Merrilee, a vacuous woman I try to avoid, inherited the mortuary but found little inspiration in sucking the innards out of corpses, so Dale does the embalming and runs the business.

The funeral home itself is a landmark in Pineland. It was designed in the 1950s by Frank Lloyd Wright, and it's a weird circular building unlike anything else in town. Dale, on the other hand, doesn't have an unconventional bone in his body, and I don't see him very often because he's sort of a bore.

His e-mail, however, grabbed my attention. It read: "Paul, I was out at Memorial Cemetery for a funeral this a.m. and happened to go by your dad's grave. Looks like some jerk knocked over the headstone. You might want to have a look and talk to the caretaker about having the stone reset. Dale."

I'd buried my father only a month after returning to Pineland. Cancer drained the life out of him, and it was a hard, sad time. I don't make a habit of visiting his grave, but the news that someone had vandalized it upset me more than I thought it would. So after lunch I took Dale's advice and drove out to the cemetery to see what had happened.

Memorial Cemetery is just west of town along the county road that leads from Interstate 35 to the casino and resort hotel. The cemetery has one outstanding feature. At its center, atop a slight rise, lies the largest mass grave in Minnesota, home to about three hundred victims of the great Pineland Fire of 1892.

The fire is Paradise County's original sin, a ghastly storm of flames that one hot September day roared through the combustible remains of a vanished forest before heading straight for Pineland. It was a man-made disaster. The loggers who had cut down all the pines cared nothing for the vast heaps of dead limbs and branches left behind. The violated land was a catastrophe waiting for a spark, and when Armageddon came, it must have seemed like God's fiery vengeance.

Nearly four hundred people in all died in the incinerator. Temperatures reached two thousand degrees Fahrenheit as the firestorm swept through, consuming a half-dozen communities, Pineland among them. The collapsed walls of two brick buildings—a railroad depot and a school—formed all that was left of Pineland, which had been home to nearly a thousand people. When the time came to sift through the debris, survivors found charred bodies scattered through town like grotesque lumps of charcoal. No one could identify most of these unlikely remains, and so in the end three hundred or so lumps believed to be bodies or parts of bodies were buried in the mass grave. Six years later, a forty-foot obelisk was erected near the grave to commemorate the fire and its victims.

The obelisk, which still towers over the grave, holds a particular significance for me. It's made of a beautiful, fine-grained sandstone with the trade name of Paradise Pink. It was quarried by a firm whose owners included my great-grandfather, Johannes Zweifel. He'd come to the United States from Bavaria as a boy in 1870 and eventually found his way to Pineland, where he opened a general store and became involved in the quarry business in the late 1880s. By the time of the fire, he was married and had a year-old son.

Johannes was behind the counter of his store when the fire appeared at the edge of town like a "red demon," as the newspapers of the day described it. According to an account left by his clerk, Johannes took off his apron, put down the pipe he smoked constantly, and told his wife to take their son and "run like the wind" toward the Paradise River. Then he went out to warn others of the impending inferno. He was last seen heading for the river, but he never made it, and he presumably lies now in the mass grave, a quiet hero lost to time.

My great-grandmother and her son, my grandfather, survived in the cooling waters of the river. With nothing left for them in Pineland, they moved to St. Paul, where my grandfather eventually studied law. Around 1910 he returned to Pineland, by then fully rebuilt and beginning to revive as a small trade and manufacturing center. He put out his shingle and built a successful practice before involving himself in the Klan. He didn't marry until he was forty and had only one child, my father, born in 1934. All of Pineland's Zweifels are buried at Memorial, and it's where I—likely the last of the line—will go into the ground as well.

By the time I reached the cemetery the day had turned to classic April crud, with sharp little particles of sleet cutting through the air beneath a cold pewter sky. I drove up to the family burial plot, which isn't far from the memorial obelisk, and searched for the overturned headstone, but I saw no evidence a vandal had been at work. I got out of my car and went for a closer look, hunched over against the pelting sleet. I found that my father's black granite headstone was perfectly upright. I also found the Serenader's second message.

Protected by a clear plastic envelope, it was taped to the headstone. A thumb drive was visible inside the envelope. I got down on one knee to read the message, typed like its predecessor on a standard sheet of copy paper. It said:

> *Peter will not return. The conspirators cannot hide their terrible deeds for long. Ask how Jill Lorrimer really died. THE WOMAN has arrived. Let the truth shine forth.*
>
> *The Serenader*

My discovery of the message was no accident. The e-mail from Dale, I soon learned, was a fake. Someone had hacked into his account and sent the e-mail to lure me out to the cemetery. It had worked beautifully, and now I was once again left with all manner of explaining to do.

The explaining took two hours once Arne, several deputies and the two Jasons arrived at the cemetery. The Jasons began documenting the scene while Arne took my statement. He listened impatiently, then suggested I'd planted the message, even after I showed him the phony e-mail from Dale.

"It's funny how you just seem to turn up where these messages are," he said as we huddled in his car.

"Somebody is playing us, Arne. Can't you see that?"

"Or maybe you're the one who's doing the playing. I just don't get why."

"Come on, why would I go around posting messages and then make sure to find them myself so everybody will suspect me? Or setting a cross on fire on my lawn, for that matter?"

"Could be that's going to be your defense. How could a smart guy do so many dumb things, etcetera, etcetera. Lawyers love that kind of shit."

"Believe me, I'm not that subtle. But you know what, you might have some problems of your own, Arne. Our friend the Serenader seems to think we need to take another look at Jill Lorrimer's death. Why do you suppose he dredged that up?"

"How the hell would I know?" Arne said. "It was a clean investigation."

Jill Lorrimer been found dead in her car, parked outside her apartment building not far from the Big Pine Casino, just after dawn on New Year's Day. Toxicology tests revealed she'd died from a lethal mix of heroin, crack cocaine and alcohol. It looked like an accidental overdose, and a regional coroner in Duluth ultimately issued a finding to that effect.

But there were lingering questions because of documents found in her apartment. One was a list of clients, including several prominent Twin Cities businessmen, from whom she'd received up to five hundred dollars for "special massages" at the Paradise Resort Hotel. Two county deputy sheriffs were also on her list, but their "massages" cost a mere fifty dollars. And finally there was notebook showing payments to Dewey Swindell averaging close to one thousand dollars a month.

It was all highly suspicious, and Arne called in the BCA to investigate. He also suspended the two deputies, but only after Tommy Redmond at the *Tattler* got wind of the story. I recused myself from the case, and the assistant state attorney general who took over—a haughty jerk by the name of Chad Barrington—kept me in the dark. As far as I knew, the investigation remained active. Dewey had been worried enough about it to bring up Jill's name to me, and now the Serenader was also interested.

Before the BCA assumed control of the case, I'd read the coroner's report on Jill's death, but nothing jumped out at me. Her death had all the hallmarks of a classic misadventure with drugs. Now I wasn't so sure.

"So you don't have any doubts about what happened to her?" I asked Arne. "Not even with the prostitution and the fact Dewey and maybe even Peter were involved with her?"

"Like the coroner said, she accidentally overdosed. Case closed. There's no reason to go fucking around with it now."

"You're one hundred percent sure?"

"I'm not one hundred percent sure the sun will rise tomorrow, but I have my hopes."

"Well, I think we'll have to take another look at the case."

"What, you don't have enough to do now?"

And so it went, another round of the Arne and Paul show. The Jasons finally came over to declare a truce. They also wanted to take their own statement from me. I told them exactly what I'd told Arne, but they didn't appear to believe me. I couldn't say I blamed them. I was looking more suspicious by the minute.

It was nearly dark by the time I escaped the land of the dead and headed home. Cassandra was on my mind. I wondered why she still hadn't bothered to call me back. I also wondered if Arne had told her about the cross burning. Now there was another message from the Serenader referring to her as "THE WOMAN." It was an ominous development, and she needed to know about it.

I called her at the hotel and was relieved when she answered the phone. I told her about the message at the cemetery, but she didn't have much of a reaction, which I thought was odd.

I switched the subject. "How did your interview with Arne and the Jasons go?"

"It wasn't difficult. I gave them the letter from the man claiming to be my father and the taped phone conversation. They in turn showed me the photo left in Mr. Swindell's SUV."

"Were you able to figure out when it might have been taken?"

The question seemed to offend her. "Of course I did. It was taken last October, about a block from the federal courthouse in Chicago. I had a motion to argue there and I remember the suit I was wearing."

I suspected Cassandra could tell me what she'd worn every day of her life. My ex-wife was like that. I, on the other hand, can't remember which of my five blue suits I had on yesterday.

"That's not encouraging news," I said. "Whoever lured you here spent a lot of time on his plans. Six months at least. It's pretty creepy."

"Well, I'm here now, so we'll see what happens." She didn't sound as concerned as I thought she should be. I asked if she'd learned anything else of interest during her interview.

"Yes, I learned some very interesting things. We can discuss them later. I'm going over to the casino now. Why don't you me meet around nine at the bar there? There are some matters we need to clear up."

"That would be fine," I said,

After I disconnected, I fed Camus and took him for a walk while I communed with his animal spirits. He seemed anxious, stopping now and then to go into one of his dervish-like spins.

"Be calm," I told him, but he just kept spinning, going nowhere fast. Maybe he was trying to tell me something.

The Paradise Pines Casino, like all of its kind, is a noisy, neon-lit machine for extracting money, and I rarely go there on the theory that life is enough of a gamble without doubling down on it. The casino's signature design feature is a curved, cascading roof that the architect—some well tanned fellow from Los Angeles—compared to the notched wings of a raptor. Officially, the idea was to "celebrate" the free spirit of the Indian Nation or some such noble ideal. A less inspiring view is that the casino was designed to resemble a giant bird of prey hovering over all the unsuspecting gulls within.

A bus from Duluth was unloading an eager scrum of old women and the occasional geezer just as I came up to the front door. I waited for the crowd to pass before going inside. The old folks went straight to the cashier cages, where I spotted Ed Boudreau chatting with one of the employees. I went over to say hello.

"Don't see you here very often," Ed said after we shook hands. "Looking to make a killing on the nickel slots?"

"No, I'll pass on that golden opportunity. I'm just here for a drink."

"Let me guess. You're meeting that lawyer from Chicago. I saw her come in earlier. Are the two of you getting cozy?"

"No, we're just getting drinks, but I know what you're thinking and you can forget it. It's all business with her."

Ed has a long and storied reputation as a skirt chaser, and he likes to hang out at the casino, buy drinks for women and then try to convince them to atone for Custer's sins by having sex with him. Like all casino players, he sometimes gets lucky. Maybe he was hoping Cassandra would be his latest conquest, the odds of which I put at zero.

"Well, enjoy your 'business,'" Ed said in a way that suggested he didn't believe anything I'd told him.

The casino's main bar is called the Pineries Lounge. It features a stand of dwarf pines, a small pool and a mural depicting woodland Indians on the hunt, presumably for more suckers to fleece at the gaming tables. I found Cassandra seated in a leather-upholstered banquette across from the bar. She was impeccable as always in a navy blue business suit. A waiter was just coming by, so I ordered my daily dose of Jack, straight-up, then slid into the banquette across from Cassandra.

"So what's this about your family and the Ku Klux Klan?" she demanded in way that strongly suggested I was about to be cross-examined.

"And good evening to you," I said. "You sound unhappy."

"Shouldn't I be? Your pal the sheriff called yesterday to tell me about the cross. He also mentioned your grandfather was quite the Klansman. Funny you never spoke about that to me."

"I tried to. I called you at the hotel and left a message to call me back, but you never did."

"I received no message from you," she said.

"Well then, the hotel screwed up. But I'll lay out the whole unsavory story of my grandfather's Klan activities if you're interested."

"It's a little late for that. I must say I find it very concerning when important information is being withheld."

Her tone was harsh and accusatory, and I didn't like it.

"I wasn't withholding anything," I said. "Besides, what the hell does it matter what my grandfather did a century ago? Fuck him. Are you implying I'm some sort of Klan sympathizer?"

"I'm not implying anything. I'm just trying to get some honest answers about what's going on here. But honest answers seem hard to come by. The sheriff, for example, claims he isn't sure why that cross was burned in your yard. He thinks maybe it was just a teenage prank."

"That's bullshit."

"Yes it is. That cross was a message aimed directly at me. It's clear I'm not welcome in your lovely little town. I guess I shouldn't be surprised. Didn't you tell me Pineland went seventy percent for Trump?"

"I did, but that doesn't mean the town is teeming with racists. People here voted for Trump mostly because they couldn't stand Clinton."

"Oh, so that's it. I feel much better now."

She was really starting to irritate me. "Let's can the sarcasm, okay?"

"Sure. By the way, how did you vote? Don't tell me you're a Trump guy." She was spoiling for a fight—the default position of every hot-shot litigator.

I tried not to take the bait. "I didn't vote. I wasn't a fan of either one of them."

"Or maybe you just didn't want to vote for a woman."

"What's with you? I'm trying to help here. And, if you want to know, I couldn't vote for Clinton because she spent her whole goddamn campaign shaking money out of Silicon Valley millionaires. She had nothing to offer people here and neither did Trump. But at least he bothered to lie about it."

Cassandra, who was sipping on what looked like a Scotch and water, shook her head slowly as though I'd just said something completely nonsensical. Then she pounced.

"So what about your father? I hear he was Klan sympathizer, too."

"Who told you that?"

"It doesn't matter. Is it true?"

"I really doubt it, but then again I really don't know what the hell my father did in his spare time other than drink. We weren't exactly close."

"Well, I'm told he was a big-time white supremacist. I imagine that made him a very popular fellow here in town."

Something was wildly off. My father was an asshole, for sure, and no lover of humanity in general, but I'd never heard even a hint that he was a "big-time" racist. Someone was feeding lies about my father to Cassandra and she seemed eager to accept them as the truth.

"Cassandra, I don't know where you're headed with all of this, but you're starting to sound a little paranoid. Yes, my grandfather was a Klansman, but as far as I know my father had nothing to do with that sort of stuff. Who's telling you that and, besides, what's the point? I'm not my father or my grandfather."

She sipped at her Scotch and said, "The point is that I have real doubts I can trust you after what's happened. I don't like being lied to."

"I haven't lied to you," I said. "But what about you? Since you prize honesty so much, maybe you should start being truthful with me. Who's been whispering in your ear? Arne, maybe? Or have you found another source of misinformation?"

"No, but I have found someone who's actually willing to tell the truth. Imagine that."

A waiter came up to check on our drinks. Before he could say a word Cassandra stood up and said, "Nothing more for me, but Mr. Zweifel will probably want another round. Maybe it'll make an honest man of him."

The waiter and I watched as Cassandra walked off. "Another Jack Daniel's for you, sir?" he said, coolly ignoring the little drama he'd just witnessed.

"Why not?" I said. "The night is still young."

As I nursed my second and last Jack, an unnerving idea popped into my head. If I was right, Cassandra was doing a very foolish thing and possibly putting herself in grave danger.

The next morning I went to the office, told Jane and Doug I'd need an undisturbed hour to contemplate the mysteries of existence, and then retreated to my inner sanctum to examine the Jill Lorrimer file. Arne's investigation had not been particularly thorough. Perhaps he, and I, had missed something. I also wondered why the Serenader had brought up the case. Did he have inside knowledge about what had happened? I hoped the case file might provide some answers.

The file turned out to be thinner than I remembered. There were just thirteen documents, all from the sheriff's office or the coroner, along with autopsy photos and a few others showing Jill's car and her apartment. The official cause of death was acute alcohol poisoning aggravated by a hefty intake of cocaine. Investigators theorized that after becoming deathly ill in her apartment, Jill had gone out to her car, perhaps to drive herself to the emergency room, before collapsing and dying in the front seat.

The conclusion Jill had died of an accidental overdose appeared to make sense, until I found something in the coroner's report I'd missed during my initial review. One of the photos showed her in her car, dead. She was wearing a long winter coat, a fur hat, and tall leather boots. But the boots were angled outward in a way that suggested they were on the wrong feet. This seemed strange. She'd apparently been able to put on her coat and hat with no trouble before she went out to her car, but not her boots. It led me to wonder if someone else had hurriedly dressed her, possibly after she was dead, and gotten the boots mixed up.

Something else struck me as odd. If the investigative file was to be believed, Jill had spent the late hours of New Year's Eve alone. She'd worked a full shift at the casino from noon to eight and then supposedly returned to her apartment to binge on a lethal combination of alcohol and cocaine. But was it really likely a high-priced call girl like Jill would have been alone that night and not helping one of her customers celebrate? I also discovered from the file that no cocaine or other illicit drugs were found in her apartment. Nor was any mention made of discarded liquor bottles.

All of which raised the possibility she'd actually been out partying on New Year's Eve, perhaps with her "pimp" Dewey or, better yet, with his father. I had no evidence of this, but the idea didn't seem farfetched. Peter was known to revel with attractive women, the younger the better. Perhaps Jill had gone out to Peter's mansion for a night of carnal recreation, only to collapse and die in his presence. After that Peter or one his minions could have put her in her car and driven her back to her apartment so she'd be found dead in the parking lot there.

I wondered if the BCA, as part of its investigation into Jill's activities with Dewey, had already uncovered evidence that her death was no accident. Another possibility was that Arne and his deputies had covered up her death at Peter's direction. That might explain why Arne's investigation had been so cursory.

Then again, maybe I was just building castles in the air ready to vanish with the first fresh breeze of new evidence. I needed solid proof and so far I had very little of it.

Around noon Doug stopped in. Naturally, he'd already learned the contents of the Serenader's second message and he took the opportunity to pump me for more information.

"Boy, that Jill Lorrimer thing came out of nowhere, didn't it?" he said. "Wonder why he brought it up."

"I'll ask the Serenader when we meet. How about you? Any bright ideas?"

"Not really. It was pretty much an open-and-shut case as far as I remember. Do you think it needs to be reopened?"

"Probably not," I lied. In fact, I'd already decided to take a second look at the case, but I didn't want to tell Doug because he'd spread the news around the courthouse as fast as he could. I preferred to act discreetly so as not to tip off anyone who may have been involved in a coverup.

Doug nodded and said, "It's always hard to reopen an old case. I mean, why create trouble if you don't have to?"

"Words to live by," I agreed and headed out to lunch.

Koffeeken's, which sounds like a Finnish name but isn't, qualifies as one of Pineland's unlikely success stories. It opened a few years ago in an old storefront on Paradise

Avenue with the idea that Pinelanders raised on anemic Lutheran church basement coffee might actually enjoy a better brew. The place is owned by Ken Michaels, who relocated to Pineland after supposedly encountering some drug-related "hassles" with the police in Minneapolis, where he'd also run a coffee shop.

It was widely assumed that a place selling four-dollar lattes could never make a go of it in Pineland, but Ken proved the skeptics wrong. He installed a fancy Italian espresso machine, brought in the usual collection of stuffed chairs and other second-hand furniture for that rumpled-but-inviting coffee shop look, and hung bad paintings by local artists on the walls. Then he started making friends by dispensing really good coffee along with wraps, sandwiches and salads. Koffeeken's is now a favorite for locals but also draws a few casino-goers tired of the lousy restaurants along the interstate.

Ken's a wiry, ex-army guy in his thirties, with shaggy black hair, a Van Dyke beard and puppy-dog brown eyes. He usually wears fatigues adorned with combat medals, talks in the jumpy manner of a man who's fully caffeinated, and has a bottomless store of Kuwait-Iraq-Afghanistan-Wherever war stories, some of which may even be true. He's also Pineland's chief purveyor of conspiracy theories, the more outrageous the better. Aliens, the military industrial complex and Ivanka Trump—an unholy trifecta if there ever was one—seem to obsess him above all else. Still, I like him, and I like his coffee and food even better.

"Yo there, Mr. Zweifel," Ken said when I took a seat at the counter, ready for my usual luncheon repast of a chicken salad sandwich and soup. "What's new on the crime front? Any more messages from that Serenader fellow?"

"Yeah, he told me I should always eat lunch here if I know what's good for me."

Ken let out a big rolling laugh and said, "A wise man, that Serenader. Except, maybe he's not as smart as he thinks he is."

"What do you mean?"

"Haven't you heard?"

"Apparently not. But I'm sure you're about to tell me."

"The sheriff knows who he is. That's what I've been told. There'll be an arrest shortly."

"Well, that's certainly big news. And what do you suppose the Serenader will be charged with? Littering?"

"Ha, that's a funny one."

"I'm serious. The Serenader has left two messages. Neither was in the form of a terroristic threat. As I said, maybe we can get him for littering but that's about it, unless there's some proof he was behind Peter's disappearance. So who's telling you an arrest is imminent?"

"It's just something I heard," Ken said. "You know how it is. I talk to a lot of people."

A fine, straightforward evasion if I ever heard one. "I'm sure you do," I said. "Anything else you're hearing that I might enjoy with my lunch?"

"Oh, I don't know. There's a lot of buzz about that Black woman who's in town."

"I can only imagine. So what's the word?"

"From what I hear, she's talking to a lot of people, trying to dig up stuff about Peter. But I guess you've spent enough time with her you'd know more about that than I do."

Ken was speaking in small-town code but I knew where he was going.

I said, "Okay, before I enjoy my lunch, I will state to you for the record, under oath if necessary, that I am not sleeping with her, have never slept with her, and have no intention of sleeping with her. Now, what's the soup today?"

I was just finishing my lunch when Marty Moreland came in and took the stool next to me.

"Paul, good to see you again," he said. "I'm just taking a little coffee break. Don't feel like eating." His voice, usually a baritone that oozed confidence, had an uneasy edge to it, and a nervous pallor had replaced his usual sheen of optimism. "So, how are you doing? You must be a busy man these days with everything that's going on. Did they catch those kids who burned that cross on your lawn?"

"Not sure it was kids, Marty, but we'll see. How about you? I suppose everyone in town wants to know why this Serenader guy decided to pick on people like you and me."

"Boy, I really don't know. It's just the craziest thing. That's what I told Arne. No idea, I said, no idea what this is all about. I wonder where all this stuff about conspirators and whatnot is coming from? I haven't done anything wrong and neither have you, I'm sure."

"Sounds like you know all about the second message. I haven't seen anything about it in the press yet."

"You know how it is. Word gets around. Hard to keep a secret in Pineland. Sometimes I wish it was easier. It's weird that Lorrimer woman was mentioned, isn't it? I thought the ruling was that she died of an accidental overdose."

"That's the official verdict, at least for now."

"So are you looking into it?"

"I can't comment on that, Marty."

"Oh sure, I understand. I wouldn't know anything about it anyway. You know, I was just thinking it's funny how you found both messages."

"Hilarious," I agreed. Marty's hands shook slightly as he cradled his coffee cup, and his face was so ashen I thought he might be ill.

"Are you all right, Marty? You look a little pale today."

"Oh, I'm fine," he said, but the salesman wasn't convincing. Nothing about him suggested he was in a good frame of mind. "Think I might have a touch of the flu or something, that's all."

"Well, I hope you feel better soon. And how's your family? Haven't seen Doris or the kids lately." Marty's wife, Doris, is one of my favorite people in Pineland—a plain, sturdy woman with an earthy sense of humor. She also has a fine voice that earned her roles in the Gilbert and Sullivan productions I staged after returning to Pineland. She and Marty have two teenage sons, both good kids, but it's no secret in town that Marty's philandering has brought their marriage to the brink of divorce.

"Everybody's all right," Marty said in a monotone.

I thought it best to change the subject. "By the way, I saw your name in the newspapers, talking about Peter's disappearance. You're a celebrity, Marty."

He responded with a dismissive snort. "No, it's nothing like that. I just wanted to make sure people understand what Peter did for this community. He was a great guy."

"If you say so. But it almost sounds like you think he's dead."

"That's not true. Not true at all. I mean, who knows? Poof, one morning he's gone and then his house blows up. What are we supposed to think? Believe me, I hope he's alive, but what are the odds? There hasn't been a ransom note or anything like that, has there?"

"Not that I'm aware of. But as you said, who knows? There are people who think maybe Peter had enough of his glorious life here and decided to head for the Caribbean."

"Oh, he'd never do that. He liked it here. He really did."

"He liked you, too, from what I understand. I've heard stories about all those parties at his mansion."

These stories, as Marty surely knew, were mostly of the X-rated variety. Lap dances, hookers, cocaine, all the pointless thrills of high living, Hollywood style, right there on a lonely hilltop in Paradise County. Word in town was that Marty was often among the satyrs at these bacchanalia. Then again, the stories could be greatly exaggerated, since gossip usually comes down to thinking the worst of people.

"Those stories are a bunch of crap," Marty said with considerable vehemence. "People make shit up. Besides, just because I was Peter's friend doesn't mean I did everything he did. It's guilt by association, that's all."

There was a pause before Marty said, "I'm a good person, you know. I really am."

"I'm sure you are."

"Thanks for saying that. You know, I wish, I really wish —." His voice trailed off, as though whatever he wished for could never come true, and then he said, "Well, no matter.

I've got to be going. Maybe I'll see you again sometime. Let's hope, right?"

And with that odd farewell, Marty swung off his stool and left.

Religion in Pineland isn't what it used to be. When I was growing up, churches seemed to be everywhere. The Lutherans, Catholics, Methodists, Baptists and Presbyterians all had substantial houses of worship, while a motley group of smaller denominations made do with simple wooden buildings, always white and always with a big cross pasted over the front door. The mainline churches are still around, but their congregations are dwindling, and if you attend Sunday services at Redeemer Lutheran or First Methodist or Grace Baptist, you'll find yourself in an oversized, echoing space with more pews vacant than filled.

The real religious action these days is in the Pentecostal churches, of the kind that once occupied those little white buildings. Pineland's largest congregation is the Call of God Church, which is out near the interstate in what used to be a big-box discount store. A thirty-foot-high fiberglass cross, complete with programmable LED lighting, rises above the old store building, where the congregation's five hundred members come on Wednesday nights and Sunday mornings to hear the divine word as delivered by the Reverend Ronald Peterson, better known around town as Reverend Ronnie.

He arrived in Pineland a few years ago, took over a small, struggling church and turned it into a powerhouse. Although he's a charismatic fire-and-brimstone preacher of the old school, he also blogs, tweets, maintains a sophisticated website, and views Facebook as God's own playground. I'm not much for religion myself—I had all of it I ever needed as a Catholic schoolboy—but I don't mind the Reverend Ronnie. He's not entirely God crazy and he has a sense of humor, unlike some of the diehard believers I know.

"Is that a sinner I see before me?" he called out in his booming basso as I was leaving Koffeeken's.

I turned around and saw him coming up behind me. As always, the Reverend Ronnie cut a striking figure, dressed in his usual head-to-toe white outfit—jacket, shirt, slacks, and even snow-white sneakers. He's a big-shouldered man in his early thirties, with a long smooth bloom of a beard, jet black hair so shiny it look likes it was buffed with a floor polisher, and small dark eyes. Do away with the beard and black hair and attach some wings and he might pass for an angel come down from heaven to save our miserable souls.

"I haven't managed any sinning yet," I told him as we shook hands. "I usually wait until after dark. How's the God business doing these days?"

"Better than ever. The Good Lord is working wonders for our church, but I also have to deal with some earthly real estate matters. I'm just going over to see Marty Moreland."

"Well, I just talked to him and he's sounding pretty down. Maybe the word of God can cheer him up."

"Sorry to hear that about Marty. He's been a member of our church since the beginning. I'll have a talk with him. Maybe I can be of help. What about you? How are you dealing with your troubles?"

"Which ones? I'm starting a list just to keep track of them all."

"I understand. That cross burning was terrible. Who would do such a thing? And then there's Peter's disappearance and this business with the Serenader. My congregation talks of little else."

"Well, whoever he is, he's certainly been on my case, and Marty's, too."

"May I offer some advice? There'll be no charge."

"Be my guest."

"I believe this man who calls himself the Serenader was sent by God for a purpose we have yet to discover. I know you think that's nonsense, but you don't know the world as I do, my friend. There are hidden currents everywhere, moving around us, and sometimes they push at us, if we are open to their power. God is pushing at us now, to open our eyes and hearts, and the Serenader is the instrument he has chosen."

What could I say? Much of life comes down to whether or not you believe in hidden things—God, Fate, Voodoo, the Trilateral Commission, or anything else that might explain the great, heaving mess of the world.

"Well, let's hope God's instrument isn't also a kidnapper or even a murderer, because that's what he just might be."

"Oh, ye of little faith," said the Reverend Ronnie, but with a smile emerging out of his beard. "We shall see, won't we? Well, I'm off to see Marty. In the meantime, I'll pray for you."

"Can't hurt," I said.

It was my day for unexpected encounters. At the courthouse square I ran into Dewey Swindell. He'd just parked his car in a handicapped spot, displaying his usual class.

I braced for a confrontation, and not just because of our unpleasant phone conversation a few days earlier. Dewey's held a grudge against me for years. It all centers, weirdly enough, on a production of *H. M. S. Pinafore*.

I love Gilbert and Sullivan, and I'm a passable singer and actor, just good enough for community theater. So when I returned to Pineland seven years ago, I rounded up a few like-minded souls and proudly established the Lost Pines Gilbert and Sullivan Society. Thus far our little company has put on *Trial by Jury*, *Patience* and *H. M. S. Pinafore*, all staged with minimal splendor in the Paradise Consolidated High School auditorium.

We were running out of money after putting on *Patience* and that's when Dewey, newly arrived in town, stepped in with a surprising offer. In exchange for a $5,000 donation and the prospect of a major role, he'd help us stage *Pinafore*. As director of the company, I reluctantly agreed. Big mistake.

Once rehearsals began, I discovered Dewey couldn't sing in the vicinity of any known key. I tried to persuade him to take on a role in the chorus or to become a backstage presence, but he wouldn't hear of it. I finally refused to cast him on the grounds he was wholly incompetent. Things then got nasty and Dewey ended up suing me for breach of promise. He lost, primarily because I'd inserted some legally potent qualifying language into his contract with our company. Tommy Redmond covered the whole flapdoodle in the *Tattler*, depicting Dewey as a vain popinjay, and he's never forgiven me.

Now he was itching for a fight. "I've got you," he said, stepping out of his big gray Mercedes. "We're going to talk." There was a whiff of alcohol on his breath.

"No, we're not."

"Yes we are," Dewey said, blocking my path with his wide body as I tried to go around. His meaty face, decorated with a chin mole sporting its own hairdo, came up uncomfortably close to mine.

"Your new girlfriend came by this morning, looking for money," he said. "Do you think I don't know her game? She won't get a cent and neither will you."

As everyone knows, there are people in this world who could best be served by a punch in the face—say, once a day—as a general service to humanity. Dewey was just such a person. But I decided to leave the punching to someone else for the time being. "Okay, Dewey, you're losing me here. Who's this 'girlfriend' of mine you're talking about?"

"Don't play dumb. Here's the deal. There won't be any DNA test. Not now. Not ever. So you can send your little gold digger friend back to Chicago or wherever the hell she came from."

Now the picture became clear. Cassandra Ellis had approached Dewey about taking a DNA test. The encounter hadn't gone well. No surprise there. What I didn't understand was why Dewey thought Cassandra and I were plotting to steal his inheritance.

"Listen up, Dewey. I'm not Cassandra Ellis's boyfriend. I didn't send her to talk with you. She's not a gold digger. She's a very successful lawyer and has plenty of her own money. She's just trying to find out if your father might also be hers. You know how much he screwed around."

"I don't give a shit about the old man," Dewey said in a touching display of affection. "But I goddamn well will get his money—all of it."

"I'm sure you will and that it will make you very happy. But if Cassandra is just a gold digger, why not take the DNA test and clear things up once and for all?"

"You'd like that, wouldn't you? You and your little colored slut would figure out some way to doctor the results, for all I know."

"All right, that's enough," I said. "You can go away now. But I still think you should have that test. Wouldn't it be nice to know you have such a lovely sister?"

That set him off. I'm not much for fisticuffs in the streets, but what the hell. I thought it just might feel good.

Dewey stepped back and took a swing at me. He missed. I put a shoulder to his chest and pushed him back against his car. A comic groping session ensued—two middle-aged guys trying to stage a presentable altercation—when someone pulled me away.

"Stop it, you two," Robby Lindquist said. My least favorite deputy sheriff had been on his way to the courthouse when he came across our feeble attempt at a street brawl. "What are you doing?"

"Just having a little legal disagreement," I said. "Nothing to worry about."

"The fucker attacked me," Dewey proclaimed. "You saw it."

"All I saw is the two of you fighting," Robby said. "Christ, you guys should know better. Now, what say we forget the whole thing? Go about your business, all right?"

"Oh no, you need to file a report," Dewey said. "I was assaulted. I want this man arrested on criminal charges."

Robby took on the pained look of a man with a headache from hell. I suspected he wished he'd just ignored us. I had the same wish. "I don't think I can do that," he said.

"Good call, Robby," I said. "Dewey here started the whole thing, but I won't press charges. No need to make a big deal of this."

Dewey thought otherwise, and much back and forth followed, none of it edifying. But he finally agreed to leave, on the condition that Robby file a report about our little set-to. Robby promised he would.

As he got into his car, Dewey directed some final words of wisdom at me. "I'm going to get you, you asshole. Don't think I can't."

The next person I ran into was Ed Boudreau. He was standing on the courthouse steps, a grin plastered across his lined, coppery face.

"I didn't know you were such a brawler," he said. "Dewey doesn't seem to like you very much."

"I'm not sure anyone does at the moment. But you know how Dewey is."

"Only too well. Feel free to kick him in the ass on my behalf anytime you feel like it. I'd do it myself, but I'm too old. Besides, he's already in plenty of trouble, or so I hear."

"You mean over the Jill Lorrimer business?"

Ed grinned. "Pussy problems are the least of his worries. Haven't you heard? Rumor has it Tommy Redmond is working on a big expose. Dewey's wading up to his big blue balls in debt and a lot of people are looking for a piece of him. That's why he's not shedding any tears over daddy's disappearance. He'd love to get his fat little fingers around Peter's fortune. Some folks think he might have even done away with the old man. Of course, that's just pure speculation."

"Of course."

"Then again, you can never be sure when it comes to white mischief, can you? There's no end to it. You know why this town even exists? Because white folks stole all the land around here in 1837 so they could cut down the trees."

"The Treaty of St. Peters," I said. "I've read about it. The Ojibwe got screwed."

"The history of America," Ed said. "Screw the Indians every which way you can."

"Well, maybe the casino at least buys you a little revenge."

"There can never be enough revenge. But, hey, good things do sometimes happen in this world. Dewey's going to take a fall one way or another. Well, I've got to be moving along. Got to keep my eye on all you white sinners."

"Me included?"

"Ha," Ed said, putting a hand on my shoulder. "We're all sinners, aren't we? And now a bit of friendly advice. I'd start working on a left hook if I were you. Might need it the next time you see Dewey."

"I'm not worried. I can take care of the fat boy."

Unwise words, as it turned out.

15

Peter Swindell was on my mind when I returned to my office. Even if Dewey didn't care about his missing father, I did. Peter's disappearance had brought out the Serenader and set other events in motion, but I wasn't sure how everything connected. All I knew was that Peter had to be the key.

My encounter with Ed Boudreau reminded me of what he'd told me earlier about a mysterious "cloud fund" draining Peter's bank accounts. Ed had said a "secret" lay behind the fund. I decided to do a little digging in hopes of finding out just what the secret was.

The State Bank of Pineland stands at a prominent corner along Paradise Avenue in a heavy stone building that resembles a jail decorated with Ionic columns. I maintain a personal account at the bank, and I'm well acquainted with its president, Toby Lucker. I like Toby well enough—like me he's a native Pinelander—and he seems to be a decent guy.

But around town he has a reputation as a skinflint who not only has the first penny he ever earned but worships it nightly during dark ceremonies in his basement.

I stopped in at the bank just before three. Toby, as usual, was in in his corner office, ensconced behind a mahogany desk the size of a small SUV. My plan was to chat Toby up and maybe, just maybe, find out something about the "cloud fund." In traditional Pineland fashion, Toby and I talked first about the weather and agreed it had been a miserable April so far but that May was bound to be better and then there'd be summer and wouldn't that be lovely. Once we'd shared these brilliant observations, I casually broached the topic of Peter's disappearance.

"I suppose those fellows from the BCA have been going through all of Peter's accounts. It must be quite a job trying to sort out his finances."

"You've got that right," Toby agreed. "An agent came by this morning to examine the accounts. There's a lot to deal with."

I then went directly to that old standby, the bald-faced lie: "You didn't hear it from me, but our office has also been digging up some stuff about Peter. That cloud fund of his has raised a lot of eyebrows. It's very mysterious."

"It is strange, the way he sent those payments to that post office box in St. Cloud, but I'm sure he had a good reason."

"You're probably right, but just between you and me, I was surprised by how much he sent."

"Well, three thousand a month wasn't all that much for a man like Peter. There must have been a charity over in St. Cloud he was supporting. That's about all I can figure."

"Maybe. I've got someone looking into that. It must be quite a charity. What did he spend on that fund in all?"

"I can't say off hand, but it was a substantial amount of money."

"Well, I hope the money went to a good use," I said, although I doubted it had. Instead, I suspected Peter was being blackmailed. What I didn't know was why or by whom.

I couldn't pry much else from Toby, so I thanked him for his time and then walked over to the courthouse. The day had turned dreary under a deck of slate-colored clouds newly arrived from Canada, and snow flurries danced in the air. I was hoping to spend what remained of the day in profound cogitation, but since I'm not good at that, I opted instead for several games of solitaire on my computer. I lost them all, a sign of things to come.

I didn't mention the "cloud fund" right away to Arne or the BCA investigators. They weren't sharing much information with me so I was in no mood to help them. And there was no doubt they needed help because the investigation into Peter's disappearance, only a few days old, already felt as though it had gone cold. His telephone and credit cards remained black holes of inactivity. The same was true of all his bank and investment accounts. No one reported seeing anyone who remotely resembled him, in Paradise County or anywhere else. There was still no ransom note. He remained in the wind.

My own father had also been lost in the wind, at least to me, for many years. That afternoon, as I ruminated over

Peter's disappearance, the Honorable Phillip Zweifel, lawyer at large, kept creeping into my thoughts. For better or worse, I was in Pineland because of him. I'd come back seven years ago to usher him out of the world, not knowing how much his death would change my life.

I was living then in the Twin Cities, serving as a public defender. Helping poor defendants get a fair day in court sounds like a noble occupation, but mostly it was an endless slog of paperwork and plea deals, and a grateful client was as rare as an innocent one. I was burned out, sick of my job and afraid to look in the mirror because I knew I wouldn't like what I saw. Taking stock, I came up with this: I was thirty-seven years old and had absolutely nothing of any consequence to show for myself. I was divorced, childless, barely solvent, drinking every day and all too well aware that my life had turned to utter shit.

And then the invisible man, a.k.a. my father, called on my cell phone one winter night when I was knocking back Manhattans at Mancini's, an old-style steakhouse in St. Paul with a bar straight out of a Staten Island mafia hangout. It had become my watering hole of choice, and maybe I was secretly hoping to get whacked so I'd be put out of my misery. Instead, my long absent father made an offer I couldn't refuse. In a weak and raspy voice, he announced he'd returned to Pineland to die, and would I care to join him there while he did it?

The details came out later. He had advanced lung cancer, the product of years of smoking, and the doctors had given him two months at most. At the time he was still living in Las Vegas, alone. Once he received the grim diagnosis, he put his condominium up for sale at a below-market price, sold it within a week, and then had himself transported to the Riverview Care Center in Pineland. Phillip Zweifel had decided to die at home, or as close to it as he could get.

"It'd be nice to see you," he told me on the phone that night. "Besides, I don't have anyone else."

Well, yes, I wanted to tell him, of course you don't. You killed my mother in a car accident, abandoned me to her sisters, and eventually alienated everyone else in your life. You deserve to die alone, you fucker. Yet I also knew he hadn't been entirely deficient as a parent. I learned from my aunts after the fact that he'd quietly footed most of the bill for my undergraduate education. He probably would have helped with law school, too, but when I found out about the college financing, I refused to accept any more help from him. To me, it was dirty money and I wanted no part of it.

And now he was a sick old man on the phone, begging to see me. I swallowed my stupid pride and said, "All right, I'll come up for a visit."

I imagine this is the part where you expect me to tell you about the wonderful reconciliation that occurred, father and son reunited at last, confessions made, truths revealed, apologies given, grievances vanquished and love finally triumphing before the old man went off peacefully into the sunset. It didn't happen that way. For one thing, my father was heavily sedated and close to comatose by the time I got to his bedside, and he looked so small and damaged, his once robust body turned into a thin bony shell, that I hardly recognized him. But when he was awake, I found he hadn't changed a bit.

He was still as selfish, cynical and mean-spirited as he'd ever been, and he had no interest in reconciliation.

What did interest him was his "legacy," and that was all he wanted to talk about. It seemed ridiculous to me—what the hell was the legacy of a life so badly lived?—but he insisted he'd done "very important legal work" in Pineland that would no doubt fascinate future generations. I told him, honestly, that no one would ever give a shit about his legal career. That made him so angry I'm sure he would have punched me in the nose if he could have.

Later, I regretted saying it, in more ways than one, because someone actually did care very deeply about one of my father's cases, for all the wrong reasons.

After my father died and was duly lodged in the good old earth of Paradise County, I decided, to my own surprise, to stay in Pineland. My friends in the Twin Cities were stunned when I told them of my plans. Even Meredith, married by then to her bald neurologist dreamboat, called to say she thought I was crazy. I think she believed I'd be exiling myself to a Siberian gulag. And maybe I was, a prisoner of my own memories.

Truth is, I can't really explain why I did it, except to say that once I returned to Pineland I felt as though gravity was pressing on me with some extra force. Maybe it was just the weight of my ancestry, of all the Zweifels who'd come and gone in Pineland. Whatever it was, I couldn't resist it. I had to stay and start sorting out my own life, just as I'd tried to sort out my father's.

There was also the fact my father left his entire estate to me. It included investments, annuities, a cache of gold coins and the old family home in town, which he'd rented out for years. All told, the estate didn't come to a princely sum, but there was enough to pay off much of my law school debt and also provide seed money to set up a law office in town. I found a fine old terra-cotta storefront on Paradise Avenue that had once been a Woolworth's store, hired a couple of handymen to remodel it, and in 2011 opened my one-man law firm.

I fared pretty well, initially doing meat-and-potatoes stuff—wills, contacts, real estate—and later taking on some criminal cases as well. It took a while, but I gradually blended into the fabric of life in Pineland. Then, as county attorney, I became, for the first time in my life, part of the establishment, sort of. But unlike my father, who was connected to all the right people in Pineland, I'm still viewed as something of an outsider, the guy who doesn't play small-town ball the way it should be played. Maybe that's a good thing.

That night, I stayed up late, as I usually do, reading and then watching some bad television in hopes it would put me asleep. Instead, I came across a channel showing *Captain Blood*, the old Errol Flynn pirate epic, and it touched off a cascade of memories and regrets.

When I was ten or so, my aunts, who were great readers, gave me a copy of *Treasure Island*, and once I'd devoured it I desperately wanted to be a pirate, despite the inconvenient fact that I lived a thousand miles from the nearest salt water. But when you're ten, dreams are golden and reality not yet a cage, so I built a model pirate ship and sailed it whenever I could in a slack pool of the Paradise River, imagining mighty battles with roaring cannons and cutlasses flashing in the sunlight. What I was really imagining, although I didn't fully understand it then, was an escape from Pineland's narrow world into the great wide ocean of possibility. Being a pirate meant adventure and freedom and the swagger do as I pleased.

I often think now that I should have been a pirate—not in any literal sense, of course—but by living a life closer to the edge. Instead, I settled into a career in law and then married, and if I'd been a good husband I might have had kids, a four-bedroom house in the suburbs, and a Volvo with all the latest safety features. And maybe that would have been the right life for me after all.

Now, I wasn't sure what my life had become. I was neither pirate nor suburban husband, and I hadn't managed to escape Pineland. I was just another middle-aged guy stuck in a small place, blowing through the calendar on my way to nowhere in particular.

Happy thoughts indeed. And yet, as I pursued insomnia, I realized that the last few days had been insanely invigorating, courtesy of the Serenader. Maybe he was the pirate of my dreams, I thought, come to either save or kill me.

16

The next day, a rainy Thursday, began with no great drama on the crime front. I went into town early to drop off Camus with a dog groomer. He was looking ragged and dirty, but he hates baths. He growled unhappily when we reached the groomer's house because he knew what was in store and didn't like it.

"Be nice," I said as I handed Camus to the woman who'd take on the terrible task of making him presentable. "You'll thank me in the end." Then I headed to the office to catch up on routine work.

Doug was already there, and I asked him for the latest update on Peter's disappearance, since Arne and the Jasons had continued to shut me out of their investigation. Doug reported that detectives were hacking away at the case but it remained a stone wall without any signs of a breakthrough. One small mystery had been solved, however. Specialists at the BCA determined the Serenader had typed his messages on a 1960s-vintage Smith-Corona Sterling. It was a commonly used office typewriter in its day but now a museum piece. In time inquiries were made around town as to who might own such a typewriter, but they went nowhere.

By afternoon a handful of newspaper reporters and TV types from the Twin Cities drifted into town, looking for leads. A correspondent from the *Chicago Tribune* also showed up but spent most of his time in the Dead Lumberjack ogling Kat and angling for information from the local barflies, who gladly spread whatever misinformation they could. I had nothing to say—a first for me. All of this outside media attention didn't produce any revealing stories, just the usual microwaved rehashes.

Then Tommy Redmond scooped everybody. That afternoon, his blog popped up with some sensational news. "The Paradise Detective Bureau," he wrote, "has learned exclusively that Cassandra Ellis, the Chicago lawyer who arrived in Pineland earlier this week, is trying to determine if she's the long-lost daughter of Peter Swindell. According to reliable sources, a letter written by Mr. Swindell just before his disappearance stated he is in fact her father, by a relationship he had long ago. Ms. Ellis could not immediately be reached for comment, but it is known she has been making inquiries with County Attorney Paul Zweifel and others regarding the matter. Further details to follow."

I wasn't surprised Tommy had found out about Cassandra's mission in Pineland. Still, I wasn't happy he'd mentioned me in his brief post, which would quickly produce gossip spreading like fine dust all across Pineland. Cassandra and

I were bound to be covered head to toe in it, complicating everything.

I soon had bigger worries. Egged on by Vern, the Paradise County Board of Commissioners decided to defenestrate me from any further involvement in the matter of Peter's disappearance, voting unanimously to fling my sorry ass out the window and replace me with a special prosecutor to be brought in from the Minnesota Attorney General's office. This was accomplished at an "executive session" to which I was not invited.

I found out what the board had done, not from Vern, but from Tommy Redmond. He knows everyone in the courthouse and has the place wired with sources, so it was literally only a matter of minutes before he learned of the board's supposedly secret action. Then he called me. Once he'd passed on the big news, he asked what I intended to do.

"Is this for attribution, Tommy?"

"Only if you want it to be."

"Let's just say I'm considering my options."

"What would those be?"

"Well, I could accept the board's judgment and bow to their superior wisdom."

"Yeah, and I could have sex with Scarlett Johansson."

"Doubt it, but keep dreaming."

"I'm serious, Paulie. What are you going to do? Take the board to court?"

"As I said, I'm thinking about it. But I'll tell you what. How about we do a little information sharing and go from there? What are you hearing about the investigation into

Peter's disappearance? From what I've been told, it's already going cold."

"Maybe it's a little warmer than you think," Tommy said.

"In what way?"

"Let's just say those BCA fellows are beginning to suspect Dewey might have some involvement in it."

"You're kidding. Why would they suspect him?"

"Two words: Jill Lorrimer. The story I'm told is that daddy was getting ready to throw Dewey under the bus over that prostitution stuff at the hotel. In exchange for his testimony, he'd face no charges."

Tommy had covered the Lorrimer story extensively and knew about Dewey's supposed role as pimp in residence at the hotel. But he was waiting for Dewey to be charged—if in fact that happened—before writing a story. Otherwise, Tommy would be fair game for a career-ending libel action. I didn't doubt Tommy had good sources of information. Still, I wasn't quite ready to believe a plea deal with Peter was in the works, if only because I knew he had really good lawyers capable of papering over anything he might have done with Jill Lorrimer.

"It sounds to me like a tall tale," I said. "Where'd you hear it?"

"Come on, Paulie, you know I can't tell you that. Anyway, it's time for some quid pro quo. Tell me all about this lawyer lady who says Peter's her father. Do you think it's true?"

"I have no idea. But she isn't saying she's his daughter. She doesn't know for sure. It's just a possibility."

"Well, it's hot stuff, she being Black and all. Then there's also the KKK thing. Had no idea your grandfather was mixed up in that shit."

"Not something to be proud of," I agreed.

"I guess you never know about people, do you? Anyhow, like I was saying, this business with that Ellis woman has got everybody buzzing. You wouldn't believe how many comments are on my blog post already. Some of them are kind of nasty."

"No doubt the trolls are having an ugly field day," I said. "In any case, there's nothing more I can tell you about Cassandra Ellis. But I do have a tip for you. Stop by the offices of the district court clerk later on. You'll find a newsworthy motion there."

Tommy was on hand when I filed the motion just before the clerk's office closed for the day. I claimed the county board's action to bring on a special state prosecutor was illegal under Minnesota law, which for all I knew it could have been, not that I really cared. I just wanted to buy some time. The longer I stayed officially connected to the case swirling around Peter's disappearance the better the chances I'd be able to figure out what was really going on.

It had been an interesting day. The evening would prove downright fascinating.

I rescued Camus from the dog groomer just after five and headed home. As I pulled into the driveway, I saw a sheet of paper posted on my front door. A small black object was attached to it with a piece of tape. I knew at once I was looking at a message from the Serenader, and I felt a sharp shudder, as though the point of a knife was poking at my spine. Maybe for the first time in my life, I wished I had a gun in my pocket. I wanted to get out and read the message, but I thought better of it. What if the Serenader was inside the house, waiting to ambush me or whisk me away?

I rolled down my window as Camus started barking. If he was suspicious, so was I. Best not to take a chance. I backed out of the driveway and swung into the street, stopping at point where I had a sweeping view of the house. Then I dialed Arne's office.

Robby Lindquist was the first deputy to arrive. He pulled up next to my car and asked, "What's going on?"

I explained the situation, but Robby didn't seem all that alarmed. "Maybe the UPS guy left a message or something."

"Trust me, it's not a message from UPS."

"Okay, if you say so. Arne is coming so we'll wait for him."

Arne was on the scene within fifteen minutes, and as usual he wasn't happy to see me. He invited me into the front seat of his cruiser and said, "So, are you writing more mysterious messages?"

"Right, and now I'm putting them on my own front door, just so no one will suspect me. I'm a regular criminal genius."

"Maybe you are. Well, let's go have a look."

"You need to clear the house first. He still could be in there."

"I doubt that, but we'll take the usual precautions."

We drove up the house, Robby right behind us. The front door was locked—maybe no one had gone in after all—and I opened it. Camus started barking again as Arne and Robby, Glocks drawn, went inside. I stayed by the door with Camus and read the message. The thumb drive attached to it presumably contained another audio file.

"Nobody in there," Arne said when he and Robby emerged from the house, "and it doesn't look like anything was disturbed. So I guess there's no need for you to tremble in fear, counselor."

"Christ, Arne, don't be such a dick. I was just being careful. In case you've forgotten, Peter has disappeared and he was probably kidnapped. I didn't want to be the second victim."

"Well, we'd certainly miss you. Tears and lamentations would engulf Paradise County, I'm sure."

I wanted to punch Arne, but he had a big gun and I didn't. "All right, be a shithead, but the message is pretty disturbing, if you ask me." Like the Serenader's earlier communications, the message—affixed to the door with four thumbtacks—was brief but evocative. It read:

Who will be next? Old sins are the worst sins and evil is casting its shadow. Only THE WOMAN can see through the lies. Do not forget Lorrimer. Let the truth shine forth.
The Serenader

The Jasons, who seemed to have become permanent residents of Pineland, arrived at my house less than an hour later and seized the message and thumb drive as evidence. Arne was apparently under orders to defer to the two wizards from the BCA, so he was content to stand around and smirk when the Jasons turned their attention to me. As the man who appeared to be doing public relations for the Serenader by conveniently finding his messages, I was naturally a subject of great interest.

Jason Braddock, who was taller and smarter than the namesake who tagged along with him, immediately hinted, as had Arne, that I'd posted the message and thumb drive myself.

"And why would I do that?" I asked. "To get attention? To be irritating just for the hell of it? Because I have an old typewriter that's growing rusty and needs some use? Or because, as Arne seems to believe, I'm simply a moron?"

"I like that last one you mentioned," Jason said with a smirk.

"You know, I'm really tired of the accusation that I'm the world's stupidest human being. It offends me, Jason. For the life of me, I don't know why you and Arne are so convinced I've concocted some stupid scheme to write and then find my own messages. It doesn't make any sense."

"Maybe you're just being doubly clever. You're a smart guy who's pretending to be dumb. I've seen it before."

Arne had once made the same argument and I was tired of it. "So by your logic, if I were pretending to be smart, you'd never suspect me. Did you ever read *Catch-22*, Jason? You might find it enlightening."

"I'll put it on my reading list. But here's the deal: this is becoming a very suspicious pattern with you. Do you really expect us to believe somebody is going to such elaborate efforts just to make you look bad?"

"Yes, I do," I said, "with all my heart."

What more could I say? Jason wouldn't believe the truth, which was that I was being targeted by the Serenader as part of his game, so I finally dummied up. "We've been through all this before. I've told you what I know, and that's all I can do. But here's a friendly suggestion: Maybe you should be looking into the Jill Lorrimer case. The Serenader thinks something untoward occurred. Why don't you see what Arne has to say about it? You might even discover a big cover-up. That would look good on your resume."

Jason, who made an art of condescension, emitted something from his tight little mouth that resembled laughter and said, "You'd like to send me off on a wild-goose chase, wouldn't you? Won't work. Nobody gives a shit about some hooker who ODed."

The BCA's resident genius would live to regret those words sooner than he could imagine, but in the meantime he kept after me until I finally told him he should get the hell out of my house. He was sitting in a big stuffed chair Camus had always viewed as his own, and when he stood up to go, Camus made a beeline for the chair, growling at Jason along the way.

"Sorry, but my dog is something of a rebel," I said. "He's suspicious of authority figures."

"Seems to be a trait in this household," Jason said. "By the way, before I leave, I'd like to search your house for additional evidence. Just a routine thing."

"I'm sure it is and you're perfectly welcome to do so as long as you have a warrant."

"Have it your way," he said, heading toward the door. "We're not through."

"Good to hear. I'm always delighted to see you."

17

The message on my front door was the beginning of a frantic spell of days. Pineland, where time usually beats with a slow, steady pulse, unhurried by circumstance, lost all sense of rhythm and order. There were new crimes and revelations, and a sense that our little town was unraveling. The news media, attracted to mystery and mayhem, arrived in force to broadcast our miseries to the world. All the while the Serenader moved among us, our ghost in residence, and we couldn't be sure if he was our nightmare or our savior.

I was preparing for my nightly battle with insomnia just after eleven when Arne called.

"Hope I didn't wake you up," he said, not very convincingly. "You're not with that Ellis woman, are you?"

The question irritated me. Did everyone in town, Arne included, think Cassandra and I were an item?

"No, Arne, she's not here, so you can dismiss whatever prurient thoughts you're having."

"I'll leave that sort of thing to you, counselor. Any idea where she might be?"

"Why are you asking?"

"Well, we went over to the hotel to ask her a few questions but were told she'd checked out. We found her cell number and called it but it went straight to voice mail. So we're just wondering if you've seen her today or talked with her."

"I haven't, but that's not surprising. I'm sure somebody told her about Tommy Redmond's blog post. I doubt she wants that kind of attention. She doesn't seem to have much confidence in me of late, either. I have no idea where she went or what she's up to. She's never shared her cell phone number with me, so I wouldn't even know how to reach her. Maybe she went back to Chicago."

"If she did, her office doesn't know about it."

"Well then, I guess it's a mystery. But you know the woman. Cassandra isn't the trusting sort. I get the impression she thinks she can figure out what's going on here all by herself."

"Yeah, well, let her think what she wants. All I know is that we need to talk to her right away."

There was urgency in Arne's voice, and it worried me. Had something happened to Cassandra? "What's going on, Arne? Are you suggesting she may have met with foul play?"

"How the fuck would I know? All we're sure of is that she left the hotel in a hurry early this evening even though she'd been booked for the full week."

"Did she say why she was leaving early?"

"Well, that would have been mighty nice of her but, no, she didn't."

"Why are you so eager to talk to her? Rumor around town is that you've identified the Serenader. Does it have something to do with that?"

"No comment," Arne said. "But if you do see her, you let me know pronto."

"Sure. There's one other thing you should be aware of." I told him about my run-in with Dewey and Cassandra's request for his DNA. "Maybe Dewey knows something."

"Okay, I'll check with the fat boy," Arne said and then disconnected.

I stared at my phone for a minute as though it was the Rosetta Stone, holding the key to a great mystery. But the phone offered no immediate answers. Where had Cassandra gone? Dark thoughts rose up from the depths and the night suddenly seemed alive with danger. There wouldn't be much sleep for me.

The only work of art on my living room walls is an expensive print of an Edward Hopper painting called *Gas*. It shows a man tending a rural gas station's pumps at twilight. Across the road from the station and its bright lights a dark green forest fades to black, suggesting mystery and menace. Like many of Hopper's paintings, *Gas* turns light into melancholy and darkness into a threat, and maybe that's the reason I like it so much.

Drive out of Pineland along a rural road as night falls and before long you'll feel the woods closing in and the darkness becoming as deep and final as darkness can be. It's Hopper's night, and there's a kind of lonely exhilaration in it, a sense of leaving one world for another. And yet if you know Paradise County you know that bad things lurk out on the woods, and darkness can be your enemy.

When I somehow fell asleep on the couch, beneath that lonely gas station, I dreamt of being in the woods and seeing Cassandra there in a white gown and bright red scarf. She seemed to be floating through the trees, as though carried by the wind. I called out to her but before she could answer a sharp pinging sound startled me awake. I looked at my phone and saw that a text message had just come in, at twelve forty-five a.m. As far as I knew, no one except Arne, Doug and Cassandra had the number of my new cell phone. I assumed the message was from one of them. I was wrong. The text was from Dewey Swindell and all it said was, "Are we set?"

I'd never had a text message from Dewey before and I certainly had nothing "set" with him. Had the message been intended for someone else? Or, for that matter, had Dewey actually sent it? Was I being played by someone? And how did Dewey or whoever sent the message know my new number?

The message left me uneasy. Peter had sent me a puzzling message in the middle of the night and now his son was doing the same. I decided to respond because if I didn't, it might look like I was actually plotting something with Dewey.

"I don't understand," I replied. "Set for what?"

"You know. The mansion. See you there."

"No, I don't know. Who is this?"

I waited for Dewey to text back but it didn't happen. Now what? Call the authorities to report Dewey, or someone pretending to be him, had sent me message I didn't understand? Not exactly the stuff of an urgent 911 call. About all I could do was contact Dewey in the morning and see what he had to say.

I somehow fell asleep again but my dream state was short-lived. Around two thirty Camus started barking and, just to make sure I'd heard him, ran his tongue across my face. Unlike the night a week earlier when I'd slept through the explosion at Peter's mansion, I woke up immediately and heard distant sirens. Normally, I would have bribed Camus into silence with a strip of beef jerky and then gone back to sleep. But I kept on hearing more sirens, a regular parade of them, and that was unusual.

I got up and went to the kitchen, where I have an occasionally operable police-fire scanner. I fiddled with it until I found the Pineland Fire Department's frequency, and I quickly discovered what all the excitement was about. The old Darwin Swindell mansion was on fire.

Long before Peter built his sprawling estate outside of Pineland, another member of the family—his grandfather, Darwin—did the same thing, only in town. Darwin's gleaming white mansion, built in 1922 to resemble a Southern plantation home, stands on Adam Street a few blocks from the courthouse square. Like all rich men in love with their own importance, Darwin decided his mansion required an impressive-sounding name, so he dubbed the place Pinehurst. With its columned portico and grounds occupying an entire block, the mansion in its brief prime must have seemed like a shimmering antebellum mirage, Pineland's very own Tara.

No one seems to know how Darwin made his initial pile of money, but he had already amassed a small fortune by the time he became a major investor in, and then president of, the Paradise Paper Company, which opened its mill in Pineland in 1922. By then Darwin was married and had a young son, Harold, who would go on to become Peter's father. Once Darwin assumed command of the paper mill, which employed three hundred workers, he became Pineland's undisputed nabob. Like his grandson, Darwin loved the role of big man in town and played it to the hilt.

Wilford Shay, our resident photographic genius, took a wonderful picture of the mansion and its grounds in 1928, when Darwin was still on top of the world. The photo, titled "At Play on Pinehurst's Lawn," presents a sweeping, deep-focus view of a croquet game in progress. Men in white linen suits and women in light summer dresses occupy much of the scene. But the picture, like so much of Old Willy's work, offers a subversive surprise in the foreground, where an elderly Black servant, tray with icy drinks in hand, stands at the ready, his weathered face offering a subtle study in contempt.

Every time I look at the photo, I wonder who the Black man was and how he ended up that long ago afternoon on Darwin's perfectly manicured lawn. According to the 1920 census, Paradise County had just four African-American residents, none older than thirty-five, so Darwin must have recruited the servant from elsewhere. I suspect he wanted a Black servant to complete his Southern plantation fantasy, and so he got one, much in the way he might have chosen a piece of furniture to create the proper décor.

The servant didn't stay for long because Darwin enjoyed only a brief ascendancy at his magnificent estate. He was a plunger, deeply leveraged with optimism and debt, and his paper fortune went down with the stock market in 1929. A few years later, after declaring bankruptcy, he was forced to move out of his heavily mortgaged dream. Pinehurst remained vacant during the Great Depression, but a new owner finally acquired the property around 1940 and turned into a boarding house. Later, it became a nursing home, then cheap apartments as it gradually took on the air of a genteel ruin. Even so, a dozen tenants called the place home.

But when Peter came back to Pineland, he announced plans to purchase the mansion and restore it to a state of luminous grandeur. It was matter of family pride, he said, and he promised to spare no expense to make Pinehurst once again the jewel of our town. In due time, he tossed out all the tenants, who were too poor to object, and hired a contractor to begin work.

Reality soon intruded. Pinehurst turned out to be a mammoth money pit, full of rotten wood and bad plumbing, and it was too daunting even for Peter's deep pockets. After a few months he abandoned the project. In the process, Peter stiffed the contractor for a hundred thousand dollars, claiming he'd done shoddy work.

I sued Peter on the contractor's behalf. It was my first big case in town, and I went after it with all I had. After eighteen months of thorny litigation, I won a settlement, though not for the full amount. Smarting from his loss, Peter decided to give a giant finger to his perceived tormentors by tearing the mansion down and replacing it with a big apartment complex intended to attract casino workers. So much for family pride. The neighbors objected, however, as did the handful of people in town interested in historic preservation.

Another legal battle ensued, but I wasn't involved. Peter finally prevailed in court early this year, dooming the old mansion. After all the legal dust had cleared, he called me one afternoon—just as he had in the case of the sweetheart hotel road project I'd blocked—to reiterate what a pain in the ass I was. "I should have burned the fucking place down," he said, "and saved myself a lot of trouble."

Now, it seemed, his dream had come true.

18

Lawyers aren't supposed to chase ambulances, but there's no rule against following fire trucks, so I drove into town. I had to park three blocks away from the mansion because a huge crowd had already gathered to watch the conflagration. A dozen fire trucks were at the scene, their crews shooting arcs of water into the roaring flames. The old mansion was a giant bonfire, flames leaping from every window and bursting through the roof. Crews from neighboring communities had joined Pineland's volunteer fire department to fight the blaze, but their efforts looked futile. There would be no need to tear the mansion down. It was gone.

I roamed around a bit and spotted many familiar faces. Tommy Redmond was there, no doubt working on some inflammatory prose for the next edition of the *Tattler* or his blog. I spotted Marty Moreland chatting with Ken Michaels, perhaps getting in an early coffee order. Our local Lutheran pastor showed up and so did Reverend Ronnie. Mayor Mary

Jane Bakken, looking suitably appalled, was talking to Kat Berglund and Vern Blankenberger. Even Dale Shiffley, keeper of our local dead, had been roused out of his slumbers to take in the pageant of destruction. I didn't spot Arne, but a couple of sheriff's deputies were milling around, trying to look as though they actually had something to do.

The one person notably absent from the crowd was Dewey Swindell. His message to me had indicated he'd see me at "the mansion." Now, the only mansion of any consequence in Pineland was burning down before my eyes but there was no sign of Dewey. It was all very strange.

"Holy cow, isn't this something!" Doug Wifferding said, interrupting my thoughts. I hadn't noticed him until he suddenly appeared beside me. His ferret face glowed from the fire's reflection. Or maybe he was just excited. He had a tablet with him and was shooting video. "I've never seen anything like it."

"Think of it as desperately needed entertainment for the masses," I said. "Looks like everybody in town is here."

"It's kind of funny, isn't it?" Doug said.

"What do you mean?"

"Well, you know, first Peter's mansion explodes and burns and now this. Two mansions owned by the same family gone within a week of each other in the same way. I guess it could be a coincidence, but—"

"I really doubt it," I said. "Any word on how the fire started?"

"Not that I've heard."

I left Doug to his video endeavors and went over to talk with Mary Jane Bakken. She's one of Pineland's good souls.

Her lesbianism produced its share of foul talk around town when she ran for mayor. But she ended up winning by more than three hundred votes, and now the talk has subsided to a few lonely whispers. Attitudes change, even in Pineland.

"Looks like a lost cause," I said. "I'm hoping no one was in there."

"Me, too," she said, "but you never know. Kids like hanging out in there at night and we've had to shoo them out more than once. The funny thing is, Peter had a demolition permit and the place was supposed to come down next week. Makes a person wonder."

"That somebody set the fire? Seems kind of pointless at this stage."

"I agree. Still, I don't know how the fire could have started on its own. Jim's over there" —she pointed off to her right, where Pineland's police chief was standing next to a squad car— "and he might be able to tell you more."

Like Arne, Jim Meyers isn't one of my favorite people. He can be arrogant and pushy, and he uses his bulk—he must weigh close to three hundred pounds—as a means of intimidation. He was talking on his cell, and I came up behind him and listened in, just because it seemed like a good idea.

"Has to be arson," Jim was saying. "There's nothing in the place that would cause a fire. Yeah, heat and electricity were off. An old biddy across the street claims she saw a guy running from the scene. Couldn't describe him, of course. Young, old, tall, short, she didn't have a clue. Could be kids. They fuck around here all the time. But I don't know. Seems like too much of a coincidence. Yeah. Yeah. Right. Okay. Thanks, Jason. Bye."

"Hi, Jim," I said, slipping around in front of him. "Quite the fire, isn't it?"

He didn't look overjoyed to see me. "I guess so."

"It must be arson, don't you think?"

"Too early to say. The fire guys will have to deal with that."

Liar, I thought, but didn't say anything. Trying to keep me out of the loop had now become standard operating practice among the local doyens of law enforcement.

Jim's cell jingled and he answered. "Gotta take this," he said, moving away. "See you around."

"Sure," I said, "and, hey, say 'hi' to Jason for me. Look forward to learning more about the big arson investigation."

I got out my phone and read Dewey's message again. Was it possible he'd set the fire and invited me to watch his handiwork? If so, what was his motive? I didn't know, but I believed the fire had to be intentional and a continuation of everything that had happened over the past week. All of it was directed, in one way or another, at Peter and his family, and there was a pungent smell of retribution in the air, as the Serenader's messages demonstrated.

But retribution over what? Peter hadn't led a blameless life—who has?—and his career was a litany of dodgy business deals and reckless behavior. Maybe he'd even bribed some public officials along the way. It was also well known he'd cavorted with more than his share of hookers, Jill Lorrimer possibly among them. Yet none of these offenses struck me as sufficiently awful to fuel someone's white-hot urge for vengeance. There had to be something deeper—an old and terrible violation—behind what was going on. All I had to do was figure out what it was.

I finally spotted Arne talking to Pineland's fire chief, Erik Shulstad. I joined them. The mansion was still burning fiercely, its wooden studs resembling prison bars as the clapboard siding peeled away. It was only a matter of time before the roof collapsed and mansion fell in on itself, ready for its final consummation. I debated whether to mention Dewey's message to Arne but decided against it. I wanted to talk to Dewey first. Maybe he could clear everything up.

"Well, I see you're awake," Arne said. "I thought you specialized in sleeping through explosions and fires."

"I've learned the errors of my ways. So what do you think, chief? Is there a crime here?"

"Don't know," Erik said. "Arson is certainly a good possibility. We've got the state fire marshal coming up to take a look."

"I take it you don't think anyone was in there."

"No one we know of. But it's going to be a big mess come daylight and it'll take us awhile to get through the ruins."

"Don't worry," Arne said with all the insincerity he could muster, "You'll be the first to know if we find anything."

"Lovely of you to be thinking of me, Arne."

"You're welcome," he said. "Keeping you happy is what I was put on Earth to do."

I finally dragged myself away from the fire and got home at four-thirty with a marvelous plan for sleeping in. But once I'd sprawled out on the bed with Camus, my mind went into its racetrack mode, thoughts spinning around in an endless oval. So I got up and went out to the couch, thinking a change of position might improve my prospects. No such luck. I still couldn't sleep and neither could Camus. We stared at each other for a while before he went back to the bedroom and dragged out his favorite toy, a plush squirrel I'd named Treerat. Time for a game of hide-and-seek.

"Jesus, Camus, I'm running out of places to put the damn thing," I said. No matter. Camus was up for a game and he'd nag me until we played. So I sent him back into the bedroom, closed the door, and started looking for a hiding spot. Under the kitchen sink? No, it would be the first he'd look because he liked the smells there. Behind the brooms in the hallway closet? Too easy. Out in the garage? Bad idea. He'd try to squeeze under the car and probably hurt himself.

After a few minutes of wandering around the house, I gave up and went for the obvious. I stuffed Treerat under the cushions of the couch. Then I fetched Camus, who raced to the kitchen while I sat down atop his toy. To my surprise, Camus rummaged through every room in the house before he finally nosed out Treerat and earned his beef jerky reward. I theorized my smell must have disguised the toy's or at least made it more difficult for Camus to hone in on the right scent.

While Camus chewed away, I stretched out on the couch and tried yet again to get some rest. But my mind wouldn't let up. The richest man in town had vanished, his mansion torn to shreds by an explosion. Now his ancestral family home lay in ruins, destroyed by an arsonist who'd also undoubtedly set fire to a cross on my lawn. And then there was Cassandra Ellis, suddenly gone missing.

It didn't take a genius to sense that an elaborate plan was at work, unwinding on its own terms and at its own pace. Was the Serenader the man behind it or was he someone who knew just enough to warn us about what might be coming? Hard to say. But whoever he was, he had to be, like Camus's toy, so close at hand he was almost too obvious to see.

19

I managed a little sleep before ejecting myself from bed in time to reach the courthouse for a routine hearing at nine o'clock. On my way, I drove past the remains of the Swindell mansion. Two fire trucks, a fire marshal's car and a bevy of squads were at the scene, along with a BCA mobile crime lab. A cluster of uniformed men and two technicians in white jumpsuits were sorting through the ruins. I wanted to stop and take a look for myself but I didn't have time. Court was calling.

First, though, I tried calling Dewey from my office, which is just down the hall from the county's main courtroom. His secretary said he wasn't in but promised she'd have him call me back. That would be fine, I said, and rushed off to court.

The hearing, over a small-fry meth case sure to end in a plea bargain, lasted all of ten minutes. Afterward, the presiding judge, the Honorable Alan Arthur Anderson, invited me into his chambers for a talk. "A. A.," as he likes to be called, is perfectly cast for his role. He has a leonine mane of white hair, craggy features, and an imperious manner. He's been a judge for twenty years and he enjoys, far too much, the magical power of the black robe. His other defect is that he's a weasel who politicks behind the scenes and sucks up to the rich and powerful. Also, he thinks I'm a big jerk who lacks proper respect for authority. Imagine that.

I'd won quite a few cases in Paradise County District Court as a private attorney, but most of them had been in front of another judge. A. A. wasn't much for lawsuits challenging anyone in power, and I'd tried to avoid his courtroom whenever possible. He knew this, and it must have pained him when I was elected county attorney. But he liked sending people to prison and so hadn't given me much trouble as a prosecutor. I had a feeling that was about to change.

His chambers, little changed since the day the courthouse was built, are large and impressive. Trophy photos decorate the mahogany-paneled walls—A. A. travels to Africa every few years to kill whatever he can—and there are also pictures of his wife and children. The rumored mistress, said to reside in Minneapolis, is nowhere to be seen, however.

I took the usual hot seat, a rickety, uncomfortable chair strategically positioned in front of A. A.'s desk, a mammoth antique affair that, with the addition of a few heavy guns, could pass as a battleship. I'd been in the chair many times before. The arrangement was carefully designed to make you feel like a small child summoned to the principal's office for discipline.

"So, how are things, Paul?" A. A. asked, leaning back in his leather chair and spinning a pencil between his fingers. "There's a lot going on for you at the moment."

"So I've noticed. I'm doing all right."

"Well, that's all we can ask, isn't it? Still, I see you've filed a motion claiming the county board can't replace you with a special prosecutor in this business with Peter. I'll be handling the motion. Now, let me ask you this: do you think your motion is a wise thing to do? It doesn't seem to me Vern and the board are being unreasonable given the circumstances."

Vern, I knew, had A. A.'s ear. The two of them are long-time golfing buddies who spend their summer afternoons at the Paradise Pines championship course. There's nothing like golf to weld old white guys together. I don't play, which is probably why I'm widely viewed among Pineland's elite as a suspicious character.

"Well, judge, I believe there's a genuine legal issue involved and that's why I filed my motion."

"I don't see it that way. The facts aren't in your favor. This fellow who's writing the messages and causing trouble seems to have you on his mind. Of course, you're the one who's been finding the messages, which is also a peculiar thing. And with Peter missing and now his old family mansion burned down, well, it's just a very messy situation. It puts you in a bit of bind, don't you think?"

"How so?"

I was being deliberately dense. A. A., no doubt at Vern's bidding, was ready to rule against my motion and thus clear the way for removing me from the investigation. But he really wanted me to step up like a good boy, recuse myself and thereby save him the trouble of kicking me off the case.

"It should be obvious," he said, irritation edging into his voice. "You've become entangled in the investigation. I'm not saying it's your doing, but it's happened and you have to deal with it. You're simply not in a good place for a prosecutor to be, wouldn't you agree?"

Even bad judges can be right sometimes and A. A. had a valid point. But I wasn't in a mood to please. Too many people in power were eager to push me out the door. There was a stink in the air, and it was in my town and my father's town and the town of all the Zweifels before them. I just didn't like what was happening.

"Maybe you're right, judge, but I don't think we'll be in a better place if I'm off the case. I'm not afraid of finding out the truth."

"Oh, so you're a shining light who's going to do that for us, is that it?"

"More like a flickering candle," I said. "But I want to see this thing through. If you and Vern want me off the case, then you can sign an order to that effect and I'll fight it at the Court of Appeals. Could be interesting and there'd probably be lots of publicity, don't you think?"

"Vern has nothing to do with this," A. A. said, rising from his chair, and I knew the lion was about to roar. "You're being an insolent son-of-a-bitch. I'm denying your motion and the appeals court, I guarantee you, will do the same. Now get out of my office."

As I was leaving A. A.'s chambers I ran into Ken Michaels.

"Suing somebody?" I asked, "or just here to take in the wonders of the courthouse?"

"Naw, I just delivered coffee and donuts to the soil and water conservation board. They're having a big meeting of some kind."

I figured the town's caffeine provider-in-chief might have some good, lively dirt, so I asked him about the latest gossip at his coffee shop. Cops and sheriff's deputies are among Ken's clientele, and I consider his place and the Dead Lumberjack to be Pineland's most reliable sources of useful, if not necessarily accurate, gossip.

"Everybody's talking about that Black lady," he said.

"I imagine they are, especially after Tommy Redmond spilled the news about her possibly being Peter's daughter."

"Yeah, but here's the funny thing. Nobody's like crazy surprised about that. Peter was an old horndog. He probably slept with the entire United Nations. But some of my regulars are convinced the woman is up to something."

"And that would be?"

Ken's gravelly voice dropped to a conspiratorial whisper even though nobody else was around.

"They think she's an undercover cop. Maybe for those state guys or even the FBI. Word is Peter was into all sorts of dirty stuff—money laundering and things like that—and they're trying to track where all the money went."

"By sending in a Black lawyer from Chicago? How's that supposed to work? It's pretty hard for her to keep a low profile here, don't you think?"

Ken shrugged. "Hey, don't ask me. But something's going on that ain't quite kosher, if you know what I mean. She was in my place yesterday afternoon. Have to say she isn't hard on the eyes."

"Glad to hear you admire her pulchritude, Ken. So did the two of you have a little chat?"

"As a matter of fact we did. She wanted to know all about Peter and Dewey. Family background stuff, mostly. I'm kind of a history buff so I tried to help her out."

"I didn't know you're an expert on the Swindell family."

"Hey man, I'm no expert, but I know a few things. Anyway, I filled her in on what I could, and she seemed to eat it up. You know what else? She told me something very interesting before she left. She said a lot of people here have the wrong idea about the Serenader."

"How so?"

"She said the Serenader is actually trying to help solve Peter's disappearance. She said he may even know where Peter is but can't say for some reason."

"Well, that's an interesting theory."

"I said the same thing. I think she's a nice lady. Left me a ten-dollar tip."

"How sweet of her," I said. "Glad she's found at least one person in town she can trust."

The rumor that Cassandra was an undercover agent didn't surprise me, especially coming from Ken, who suspects almost everyone is plotting something. Still, I was intrigued by his claim that Cassandra seemed to view the Serenader in a positive light. Did she know something I didn't? I'd have to ask her when I got the chance.

An hour later, I was about to step out for lunch when Doug rushed into my office. He had the eager look of a retriever carrying a freshly dead duck.

"They found a body in the old mansion," he announced. "It was down in the basement, all covered up by debris. That's why they didn't find it last night. They haven't made an ID yet because the body is so badly burned. A regular crispy critter, I guess. But they're sure it's a man."

I thought I knew the answer but asked the question anyway: "Any clues as to who he might be?"

"Maybe."

"What do you mean?"

Doug smiled, and it was the smug, knowing smile of someone in possession of a tantalizing secret.

"Out with it," I said. "What do you know?"

"Well, maybe it's just a coincidence, but Dewey Swindell was reported missing this morning."

20

It wasn't a coincidence. Dewey went missing because someone put a bullet through his head and then set the mansion on
fire with him in it. Using dental records, the regional coroner
in Duluth made the official identification the next morning.
A .38-caliber slug was recovered from Dewey's skull, and the
autopsy showed he was dead before the fire turned him to
char. The coroner calculated Dewey had been killed around
midnight, two hours before the fire broke out.

Arne and the BCA investigators were able to trace Dewey's movements in the hours before his death. A security
camera at the Paradise Pines Hotel, where he maintained
his offices and a large apartment, showed him walking out
the front door at two minutes before eleven Thursday night.
He was dressed informally in chinos and a light jacket and
walked quickly as though he might be late for an appoint-
ment. Moments later, a parking-lot camera caught him get-

ting into his gray Mercedes and driving off in the direction of the interstate and Pineland.

Investigators then asked the obvious question: Where was the Mercedes? It wasn't parked anywhere near the mansion, suggesting Dewey had either walked there or been driven by someone. A search began for the car, and early Saturday afternoon a patrolmen spotted it parked behind a building Dewey knew well, the historic Glenning Apartments, the crumbing old heart of what's left of downtown Pineland.

If you're looking for the Disneyesque version of small-town America—the one with quaint brick buildings, jolly Victorian houses sporting gingerbread porches, and tidy little shops overseen by kindly grandfathers in aprons—you won't find it in Pineland. Rebuilt quickly and none too well after the Great Fire, "downtown" Pineland even in its most auspicious days wasn't much to look it. Even so, there was a solid commercial corridor along Paradise Avenue. When I was a kid the avenue's lineup included a Woolworth's, a sporting goods store, two hardware stores, men's and women's clothing stores, a drug store, a liquor store, two banks, three bars, a Ford dealership, a couple of restaurants, an old movie theater, a Super Valu grocery and a seedy motel named, predictably, the Starlight, where my aunts believed people did terrible things such as having sex.

The avenue in those days was part of the fabled Highway 61, so there was plenty of traffic, especially in summer when people from the Twin Cities headed north to Duluth and lake country. I'd like to think Bob Dylan came through town more than once, on his way down from Duluth to find fame and fortune. Maybe he even stopped for lunch or dinner at one of the restaurants—Burger Bobby's, long since closed, was everybody's favorite—before Paradise Avenue turned into Desolation Row.

The interstate highway, which opened in the 1960s, and later the casino sucked the life out of downtown, and it's hard to think it will every come back. A few stores are hanging on—the Our Own Hardware owned by Vern and his family may be the most successful—but much of Paradise Avenue has become a bleak repository of decaying buildings and shuttered storefronts. It's sad to see, and whenever I go there I feel as though I've wandered onto a stage set left over from some dimly remembered performance of civic life.

A few years back, however, it looked as though downtown Pineland might experience a renaissance of sorts, courtesy of Peter and Dewey Swindell. The two floated a scheme to transform the moribund area along Paradise Avenue into a sort "ye olde towne" outfitted with boutique shops, cute little restaurants and even a fitness center for the two of three people in town who are known to work out. But the key to the scheme was something called the Lone Pine Club, an upscale gambling salon for high rollers that would be operated, like the casino outside town, by the Grand Lac Band of Ojibwe.

The club was to be located in the Glenning Apartments, which had originally been a hotel. Situated a block from the Northern Pacific Depot, the three-story hotel in its day was the pride of Pineland. Its namesake, Daniel Glenning, opened the place in 1905 at a time when twelve passenger trains a day stopped in town. The hotel, which boldly proclaimed itself "the finest in the Northwest," did a booming business and even offered a gambling den behind the lobby where craps, blackjack and high-stakes poker games flourished.

But the number of trains began to decline after the 1920s, and by the 1950s they stopped coming altogether. The depot was abandoned, the Northern Pacific vanished into a merger, and then the interstate arrived with new motels and restaurants at the outskirts of town. That was the end of the Glenning. It closed in 1972, a year before I was born, and the building was converted into low-rent apartments.

Peter bought the place in 2013 and announced Dewey would oversee the project to transform it into a luxurious new venue. A lot of people thought the club idea was ridiculous—would high rollers really be attracted to the minimal glories of downtown Pineland?—but the Swindells forged ahead. Dewey took charge of evicting the building's mostly impoverished tenants, a task he accomplished as gracelessly as possible. Once the building was cleared of its human detritus, renovations began.

A few months later, the work abruptly stopped, for reasons that were never fully explained, although word around town was that a key financial backer had bailed from the project because of certain "irregularities" in the Swindells' bookkeeping. "We're having some minor financial issues," Peter told the *Tattler* at one point, "but we'll be back on track soon." That didn't happen. Peter and Dewey abandoned the project and decided instead to build their resort hotel next to the casino. The Glenning then became a vacant hulk, and as it turned out, a good place to commit murder in the dead of night.

There were no witnesses to Dewey's murder, hardly a surprise, since downtown Pineland after dark usually pulses with all of the excitement of an abandoned graveyard, except for whatever zombies have gathered at the Dead Lumberjack. But two residents of nearby apartments reported that they'd been awakened by a loud noise, likely the shot that killed Dewey, around midnight. Both thought it might be a car backfiring and promptly returned to their slumbers.

The most useful evidence came from Dewey's Mercedes. The front passenger side window was shattered, and a heavy spray of blood—later determined to be Dewey's—decorated the driver's side window and the area around it. Clearly, he'd been shot by someone standing outside the car. More blood was found on the ground next to the Mercedes, leading investigators to believe the killer had pulled Dewey's body from the front seat and then presumably placed it in another vehicle for transportation to the Swindell mansion. To say it was a bizarre crime would be an understatement.

Arne called Saturday afternoon to confirm that Dewey was indeed the victim in the mansion. It wasn't a courtesy call.

"You need to come down to my office for a talk right away," he said.

"Be happy to," I said. "I was going to come in anyway. I've got something to show you."

I knew why Arne wanted to see me. It was all about my ridiculous tussle with Dewey in the courthouse square. Dewey had all but forced Robby Lindquist to write a report on the comic encounter, but it looked much more sinister now that Dewey was dead.

Jason Braddock from the BCA joined Arne for the interview. Arne said our friendly little talk would be recorded, adding: "You have the right to have an attorney present if you feel the need for sound legal advice. We wouldn't want you to get tripped up and accidentally blurt out the truth."

"Thoughtful of you to bring that up, Arne, but I think I can manage on my own," I said. "And believe it or not, you will hear the truth. Now, before we begin, let the record show I am handing you an LG cell phone. I am the owner of said phone. On it you will find a text message left at twelve forty-five a.m. yesterday by a person claiming to be Dewey Swindell. You will also find text messages I sent in response."

I scrolled to the message thread and handed the phone to Arne while Jason looked over his shoulder.

"Interesting," Arne said. "I'm guessing you're now about to tell me you have no idea on God's green earth why Dewey sent you that message."

"Correct."

"Did Dewey send you any other messages or did the two of you talk at all yesterday?"

"No."

A few more routine questions followed before Arne brought up my dustup with Dewey. "Sounds like a nasty little fight you two had. Duking it out right there in the square. My, my, very unseemly behavior for a county attorney, if you ask me."

"I'm prostrate with grief over it," I said. "Please do me a favor and get to the point."

"The point is that you were angry enough at Dewey to shove him. What were you so mad about?"

"First of all, he was the one who started it by taking a swing at me. Second, he was pissed off at me and not the other way around."

I explained how Dewey had confronted me because he thought Cassandra and I were plotting to steal his inheritance. "He was being ridiculous. He also smelled like the bottom of a whiskey barrel. That's all there was to it."

"So you say. But maybe a lot more was going on between you two."

"Such as?"

Jason piped up and said, "Why don't you come clean, Mister Zweifel, and tell us what really happened? The lies have to stop. It's time to clear the air once and for all."

"Is that a fact? Well, as far I see it, the air is already crystal clear. I didn't murder Dewey Swindell and I have no clue who did. But here's an idea Arne might appreciate. What about that money Dewey was getting from the late Jill Lorrimer and what about those deputies who were getting reduced-price blow jobs from her? Now that might be something to really look into. Might even be a motive for murder if Dewey knew too much about certain important people."

"Bullshit," Arne said. "Don't you dare—"

Jason intervened. "Let's calm down," he said and then asked if I had an alibi for the night Dewey was murdered.

"I was home, as usual. Camus would gladly testify to that but he's not very talkative."

Jason looked confused. "Who's Camus?"

"It's his goddamn dog," Arne said before I could answer.

"And a fine dog he is," I said. "Now, gentlemen, I have a suggestion. Check that cell phone I just gave you. There's a cell tower two blocks from my house. I have no doubt you'll find the messages I sent to Dewey pinged off that tower, proving I was home when I said I was. And that's all I have to tell you this afternoon on the subject of the late Dewey Swindell. But since we're here, maybe you can tell me if you've tracked down Cassandra Ellis. I'm worried about her."

"In case you haven't noticed, we've got more important things to worry about right now," Arne said. "No one's filed a missing persons report, so there's nothing to investigate. She went someplace. That's her business."

"She's dropped completely out of sight and that doesn't concern you?"

"Not at the moment. But feel free to hunt her down in your spare time."

"I'll do just that," I said. "No thanks to you."

After I left Arne's office I drove out to Walmart to buy yet another cell phone, then went home and took Camus for his daily cavort through the countryside. A lot of border collies like to pluck Frisbees out of the air, fetch sticks or go after bouncing balls, but Camus has never shown the least bit of interest in such plebian activities. Instead, he appears to view them as beneath his dignity. But like his namesake he is a believer in the absurd, so he regularly chases after birds, squirrels and other moving objects he has no chance of ever catching.

I was starting to feel the same way about the Serenader. I wanted to run him down and extract his secrets, but so far he'd proved as elusive as one of Camus's squirrels. Maybe he was just too smart for me, not to mention Arne and the Jasons and everybody else in town. Or maybe he'd just been lucky in avoiding detection. Either way, it was maddening.

When I coaxed Camus, who had been running free, back to the house, I received a pleasant surprise—my first in quite a while. Kat Berglund called on my land line with an enticing proposition.

"You need a break, poor man," she said. "I'm off duty at the bar tonight. I've got a couple of nice Italian reds and some excellent edibles from a friend in Colorado."

No man in his right mind would turn down a night with Kat, and as far as I could tell, I was still in my right mind. "That would be lovely," I said. "See you soon."

There are women in Pineland who regard me as a "catch," perhaps because I have a full head of hair, a belly as yet undistended by beer, and I make enough money that I'm not living in a trailer in the woods. In other words, standards aren't especially high when it comes to Pineland's limited crop of unattached middle-aged men.

Of course, not all of Pineland's eligible females view me as a prime specimen, and I've had a number of dates that ended badly. It's also true there aren't a lot of women in town who interest me beyond the obvious attraction of sex, which I certainly like but which is of itself just a flaring match in the dark, quickly extinguished. I've always been most attracted to smart, capable women, probably because that's who I grew up with.

My aunts Katherine and Anna, who raised me, never married, but not for a lack of suitors. I think they simply felt no need for children of their own once my father turned me over to their care. They doted, as aunts will, but they were rock solid and didn't let me get away with any craziness. They were both well read, very smart, and highly accomplished. Katherine ran a successful floral business and Anna was the head nurse at Mercy Hospital in Pineland. But no matter how busy they were they always had time for me. They saved my life every day, which is what good parents do.

Sometimes out of the blue I'll find myself thinking of them and their no-nonsense approach to raising me. Anna, tall and big-boned, was an especially commanding presence, and I'll never forget the time, when I was twelve or so, that she sat me down to reveal the facts of life. It was, in retrospect, a hilarious occasion—Anna calmly reciting the ABCs of sex and the male and female apparatus while I squirmed with embarrassment—her lecture ending with the memorable observation, "You'll start having wet dreams soon." I did.

Both of my parent-aunts, as I like to think of them, died in their sixties. Anna went quickly from a brain aneurism. Katherine took ten months to die from pancreatic cancer. Their funerals were the saddest days in my life and I hope they always will be.

The aunts prepared me well for how to relate to women, or so I thought. When I met Meredith, an aspiring artist and part-time grade school teacher who came from a wealthy suburban Minneapolis family, I thought for sure I'd found my life partner. We were married six months later. It was one of those over-the-top weddings, awash in flowers and designer dresses and sumptuous food, all paid for by her rich father and presided over by a pale-faced Episcopalian minister at a fancy club on the money-drenched shores of Lake Minnetonka.

The wedding wasn't my style but I really loved Meredith. She was bright and funny and sexy, and for the first couple of years we were happy together. Then everything started coming apart, as though some unseen hand was driving a wedge between us, and my work began to consume me and so did whiskey. The alcohol grabbed me, just as it had my father, and took me out of myself. Of course, I allowed it happen— the bottle comes with warnings, but no blame—and before I knew it Meredith was gone.

Since returning to Pineland, I haven't had a "serious relationship," however that's defined. The pop-psych explanation would be that I was traumatized by my divorce, which in fact I was, and that I now avoid commitment for fear of being grievously wounded again. That explanation could be right. But it also could be that I was born to live alone—I truly believe some people are—and that my three years of marriage were an aberration, a fork in the road I never should have taken in the first place.

As I drove into town, my thoughts turned back to Kat Berglund. She's the one woman in Pineland who could entangle me again in the hopeless intricacies of love, but I know that will never happen. Kat is triumphantly self-sufficient, a living force who owns her life with a totality I could never match, and she views men as interesting but not essential. She invites visitors to her bed as she wishes, but no one stays overnight.

Kat lives in a second-floor apartment on Paradise Avenue, just three blocks from the Dead Lumberjack and across the street from the vacant Glenning Hotel. Her place is above the rather run-down offices of the *Tattler*, where Tommy

Redmond produces his delightfully tasteless rag sheet on an old basement press. There were originally two upstairs apartments in her building but Kat combined them into one big unit, which she decorated in an eccentric style that somehow combines her love of sea shells, wolves, and Navajo pottery.

She was wearing a strapless, black velvet jumpsuit when she greeted me at the door. "It's my cat woman outfit," she said. "I'm hoping you're ready to meow."

I was, and we had a fine time of it, sharing a bottle of Barbera and sampling some of Colorado's finest before falling into bed. It was a romp to remember, and afterwards we talked for hours, about her life and mine, and eventually we became sober enough to puzzle over the mystery of the Serenader and everything else happening in Pineland.

One of those puzzles concerned the thumb drive I'd found along with the Serenader's second and third messages. I'd asked Arne what was on the drives but he refused to tell me, calling it "privileged information," as though he was in possession of a national secret. But secrets have a way of surfacing in Pineland, and Kat told me she knew all about the contents of the latest thumb drives.

"One of my regulars is a deputy sheriff," she said. "He had a few drinks last night and loosened up. One thing led to another and before long he told me what was on the drives. It was 'that music again,' he said. But there was also something new: faint voices in the background."

"On both files?"

"Yes."

"Could anyone make out what the voices were saying?"

"I don't think so. But the deputy said the BCA's lab technicians in St. Paul will probably manage to enhance the voices without too much trouble. It just may take some time."

"What about the music? Any luck identifying the tune?"

"Apparently, the BCA is also working on that. There are all sorts of apps designed to identify a piece of music, but so far they haven't had a hit, or at least that's what the deputy told me."

"Maybe it's an unknown Barry Manilow masterpiece," I suggested.

"Hey, don't make fun of Barry. I saw him once at the casino. He can still sing."

"Good for him. Did you find out anything else?"

"That's about it from rumor central."

In return, I filled Kat in on my precarious situation with the county board and Judge Anderson, not to mention my semi-official status as a suspect. I also shared my worry about the missing Cassandra Ellis.

"I certainly hear a lot of talk about her," Kat said. "Is she or isn't she Peter's daughter? I'd say it's a fifty-fifty split on that question at the moment. I haven't met her, but the word is she's extremely hot. You working on getting into her pants?"

"I must say, Kat, I am absolutely appalled by the crudity of your question."

"No you aren't and you haven't answered it."

"Okay, I will say she's very attractive, and smart as can be, but no, she's not my type. I think she'd require extremely high levels of daily maintenance. Still, I really do wonder where she's gone. I hope she hadn't gotten herself into big trouble."

"Such as?"

"I'm not sure. It's just a sense I have. Cassandra is one of those people who believes she can handle anything or anybody. That kind of absolute self-confidence can be dangerous. Nobody is smart enough to have everything figured out. Let's just hope I'm wrong and she's safe. In the meantime, I can use your help. If you hear something at the bar—"

"Have no fear, I'll keep you informed," Kat said. "As for you, try to stay out of trouble, will you? It sounds like some serious shit might be coming your way."

"Don't I know it," I said, rolling out of bed and putting on my clothes. It was past midnight and Kat's man clock was running out on me. "I'm sure things will straighten out before long. I'll be fine."

Mark those down as remarkably foolish words.

I gave Kat a goodbye kiss and went downstairs and out toward my Prius, which was parked in front of the dark, vacant Glenning. A car went past as I started across the street but otherwise silence prevailed in the barely beating heart of downtown Pineland. That's when I saw a beam of light and found the Serenader's fourth message, posted along with the usual thumb drive, on the Glenning's boarded-up front doors:

Now there are three. Zweifel, Sigurdson, Moreland. They have the answers but cannot be trusted. Buried secrets lie among the stones. THE WOMAN is gone but will return. Let the truth shine forth.

The Serenader

22

"This is getting ridiculous," Arne said after we'd gone through yet another session of questioning. "Either you're pulling everybody's chain or the cleverest fucking asshole in the world is on your case."

I'd already talked to Jim Meyers at the Pineland Police Department, and once he'd pulled all the meat he could off my bones he turned me over to Arne to pick at the leftovers. We were now in Arne's spartan office, it was two in the morning, and neither of us was particularly happy to be there.

"The clever asshole theory works for me," I said.

"Yeah, I bet it does. But I don't think it works for anyone else."

Arne had a point. I could hardly believe myself how expertly I'd been set up to discover yet another message. The beam of light directing me to it had come from a flashlight placed on the sidewalk, all part of a carefully timed arrangement.

When I arrived outside Kat's apartment, I'd seen no flashlight or message. Presumably a few souls had wandered along Paradise Avenue during the hours Kat and I were recreating. If any of these passersby had seen an illuminated message on the Glenning's doors, they almost surely would have reported it to authorities, given the Serenader's notoriety in Pineland. But no one made such a report. That meant the message must have been posted not long before I left Kat's place, which in turn suggested the Serenader had been nearby the whole time, watching and waiting. I told all of this to Arne and said Kat would back me up.

Arne was skeptical. "You two an item?" he asked.

"Come on, you know no one is an 'item' with Kat. I was just spending some quality time with her."

"Playing tic-tac-toe, I'm sure. Must be that law degree of yours that attracts woman. It can't be your face. But who's to say she wouldn't lie for you?"

"Well, you go right ahead and ask her if she'd do that. I think you know what the answer will be."

"Oh, I'll ask," Arne said. "You can count on that."

While I entertained Arne in his office, evidence technicians swarmed the Glenning, looking for fingerprints, DNA, a fugitive strand of hair or anything else that might lead them to the Serenader, or to me. The forensics wizards found nothing. The Serenader was the antiseptic man. No surveillance camera footage turned up, either. Few businesses in downtown Pineland bother with cameras because there's so little worth stealing.

After my slow waltz with Arne, I went home and tried to catch some sleep. But the Serenader's new message kept banging around in my head, concussing me with questions. I wondered most of all what he meant by "buried secrets lie among the stones." An idea eventually occurred to me, but I didn't like it because, if I was right, a new storm of suspicion could blow my way.

Once daylight arrived, I took a long shower, ate a stale bagel, drank stale coffee, sent Camus outside to hunt for small sentient creatures, lured him back into the house with a piece of stale chicken, and then drove into town to enjoy coffee and donuts with the Jasons, who wanted another interview with me. They were their usual charming selves as I explained my discovery at the Glenning to them. Many questions followed, many answers were duly provided, and then I bid them a fond and hearty farewell. I knew the two BCA stalwarts were even less inclined than Arne to believe me, but I was past caring. If they wanted to waste their time trying to prove I was playing some kind of weird game, so be it.

When I reached my office, I found Doug manning the phones because Jane, who does not exhaust herself as my secretary, was already on one of her famously long coffee breaks. Doug greeted me with his usual duplicitous enthusiasm and said, "Sounds like you had another wild night. Isn't it something how you keep on finding those messages? Why do you suppose that is?"

"It's a mystery for the ages. By the way, has Vern called?"

"No more than ten minutes ago. How'd you know?"

"ESP, Doug. Runs in the Zweifel family. I'll get back to him."

I went into my private office and closed the door. I knew why Vern had called and I knew what I had to do. My discovery of the Serenader's latest message was a final coating of radioactive dust that made it inevitable I couldn't go on as part of the investigation into Peter's disappearance and Dewey's murder. The county board had already voted to remove me from the case. Judge Anderson, Vern's old pal, had denied my motion for a temporary injunction. I had little or no chance at the state Court of Appeals. I had to go, and Vern was undoubtedly pants-wettingly eager to tell me just that.

When I reached him on the phone, I delivered the joyous news he'd been waiting for. "I'm recusing myself from the case as of today. You and the board can rest easy. You'll have the paperwork on your desk within the hour."

"Well now, that's a start," Vern said. "That fellow from the AG's office in St. Paul, Chad Barrington, is all set to take over. I'm sure he'll do a fine job."

Unlike me, in other words. I had a hunch what was coming next. "I'll also need your resignation," Vern said, as though it was a settled matter. "I don't see how you can continue as county attorney with so many questions being raised."

"Won't happen, Vern. The voters can decide at the next election if they want me out of office. It's not your call."

"We'll see about that," Vern said, and abruptly disconnected.

"Fucker," I said to the dead phone. I didn't see how Vern could force me from office, but he was devious and ruthless enough to give it a try. I'd have to be very careful in the days ahead.

Doug Wifferding, who's something of a computer whiz, handles all of our office's online business, sending out news of indictments, jury verdicts and other developments via social media. I, on the other hand, try to steer clear of Facebook, Twitter, Snapchat and the like for the simple reason that I have no particular opinions, wonders or achievements to share with the world. Nor do I wish to know whose grandchild has just completed potty training. But I pay close attention to the news on a dozen or so websites and I also consult local blogs to sample the latest gossip.

Tommy Redmond's "Paradise Detective Bureau" is usually the first blog I turn to, and when I went to it that afternoon I learned he already had the news of my recusal. The only surprise was that he hadn't called me already for comment. His blog report was accurate, except for a sentence that read: "With Zweifel now removed from the investigation, the local knowledge he brought with him will be lost and will be hard to replace."

I didn't quite see it that way. Although I was officially off the case, I wasn't out of the game, and I intended to use my "local knowledge" to discreetly investigate on my own. After all, the Serenader had made a point of calling me out in his messages. He'd also called out Dewey, who was now dead. Was I next? Or would it be Arne or Marty Moreland?

As I went out that evening for my usual exercise with Camus, I tried to figure out how the Serenader had selected his targets. Clearly, we hadn't been named at random. We all belonged to well known Paradise County families. In the message posted on my door, the Serenader had written that "old sins are the worst sins," suggesting he was preoccupied with something that happened years earlier. He followed with a message referring to "buried secrets." But how were all of us—or our families—supposedly involved? What was the common thread?

The law was one possibility. Marty Moreland's late father, Theodore, was a Paradise County District judge for many years, and his father before him had been on the bench as well. Arne's father, also dead, was the redoubtable Magnus Sigurdson, who served three terms as sheriff. And of course various Zweifels have practiced law in Pineland since the early 1900s. The Swindells, however, didn't have lawyers, judges or members of law enforcement in their family as far as I knew. What they had was money, lots of it, going back to the days when Darwin Swindell helped found the paper mill and built his now destroyed mansion.

Still, there might be a connection to the law. Perhaps one of the Swindells—Peter?—had been involved in a court case that touched off the grievance suggested by the Serenader's messages. A lawsuit that left the loser with a festering sense he'd been wronged? A property eviction? A costly divorce settlement? An unjust criminal conviction? It could be anything. And then there was the Jill Lorrimer case. How and why did she fit into the picture?

I knew that whatever ignited the events now taking place likely centered on something Peter had done, since he was the first target for revenge. Was it something that happened in Pineland, perhaps in the courts, or was it before that, when Peter lived in Chicago? There was no way to know for sure. But if it was linked to an old court case, I faced a big problem.

Paradise County court records didn't go digital until the early 2000s, which means most older files are still on paper, without any kind of useful search function. Sifting through them—in search of exactly what?—would be a vast and probably fruitless undertaking. And I couldn't interview any of the old family members—Theodore Moreland, Magnus Sigurdson or, for that matter, my father. They were all dead, as were Dewey and probably Peter Swindell. That left Cassandra as possibly the last of the Swindells, but she knew very little about the family's history.

The next generation didn't seem to hold much promise, either. Arne would have no interest in helping me, and I doubted Marty would know much about his father's judicial career. That left me. I still had my father's office records, stored in a half dozen filing cabinets in the old Zweifel family home, which I own, on Eden Street. It seemed like a fool's errand, but I decided to go through them, if I could find the time, in search of hidden treasure.

23

The opening wave of a news tsunami rolled into Pineland Tuesday morning. The first truck came from a television station in Duluth and soon three more arrived from the Twin Cities, all equipped with antennas, satellite dishes and well-coiffed news people. The trucks parked around the courthouse square and expelled their reporters, who immediately spread out in search of sacrificial victims willing to go on air. Dewey's murder, the discovery of his body in the fiery ruins of the old Swindell family mansion and the Serenader's latest message had combined to form an irresistible story.

"Quite a scene out there," Doug said when he came into my office, where I was doing my best to escape detection.

"Must be our lucky day," I said.

"Have you seen the story in the *StarTribune*?"

"Not yet."

I wasn't looking forward to reading it. A reporter from the Minneapolis newspaper had already left two phone messages, which I'd ignored, asking for comment, among other things, on why I'd recused myself from the investigation.

Doug handed me the front section of the paper, which offered a page-one story under the heading "Deepening Mystery Grips Pineland." The story trotted out all the usual clichés. Pineland "is a close-knit community." People "are locking their doors for the first time." At the local coffee shop—Koffeeken's, of course—"regulars talk of little except the Serenader and a crime spree no one can understand." There was also much speculation about Cassandra and how she might be linked to investigation. But the story didn't exaggerate when it said people in town had become "genuinely frightened" about what was happening.

"You're mentioned on the jump page," Doug said, helpfully.

Sure enough, a paragraph placed like a land mine reported that "all four messages from the Serenader were discovered by Pineland County Attorney Paul Zweifel, who on Monday recused himself from the case. Investigators have questioned him at length on several occasions, according to law enforcement sources. Zweifel, who did not return calls asking for comment, apparently stepped down from the case because of suspicion he may be linked in some way to the Serenader."

Arne was quoted extensively elsewhere in the story, and he offered the helpful observation that I had not been "entirely cooperative" with investigators. How nice of him to say so. Before long, Arne would have much more to say to the media and none of it would put me in a good light.

After lunch, I dodged a couple of reporters loitering by the front doors of the courthouse and went up to my office. Marty Moreland was waiting for me, chatting with Jane Niskanen as he sat in the anteroom. He was in his standard businessman's costume—dark blue suit, patterned red tie, crisp white shirt, well-shined black oxfords—but somehow nothing about him looked right.

"Hey, Paul," he said, standing up to shake my hand, "do you have a minute to talk?"

"Sure, come into my office." As had been the case during our talk a few days earlier at Koffeeken's, Marty looked profoundly out of sorts, churning with some inner turmoil. His face had gone to chalk, and he seemed on the verge of breakdown.

"Hold any calls for a while," I told Jane, who smiled at Marty and said, "I forgot to ask: how's that lovely wife of yours? Haven't seen her at church in a while."

"I guess she's been really busy," Marty said, "but she's fine."

We went into my office and I closed both doors—the one leading to the anteroom and the other that connected to Doug's little den, where I hoped he was busy watching porn and wouldn't disturb us.

I didn't see any point in small talk. "Marty, you don't look good. Is there some way I can be of help?"

"This has to be confidential," he said, glancing around as though in fear of hidden cameras and microphones. "Will you give me your word on that?"

"I will, and you know my word is good. So what's going on?"

Marty gulped down a deep breath and said, "It's about Jill Lorrimer. Maybe it wasn't an accident. "

I should have guessed. The Serenader had suggested Jill's death was suspicious, and I'd come to the same conclusion after reexamining her case file. Something had happened at Peter's mansion the night she died and maybe it wasn't an accidental overdose. Had Marty witnessed Jill's murder?

"Were you at the mansion with Peter the night she died?"

"I didn't say that. But believe me, I didn't have anything to do with that poor woman's death."

"All right, I believe you. But if you saw something you need to come forward as a witness."

"It's not that easy."

"Because?"

Marty let out a forlorn little laugh. "Because that could be dangerous."

"Do you mean someone is threatening you? Who?"

Marty leaned forward, his elbows propped on my desk and said, "Maybe I shouldn't be talking about any of this. I probably have enough trouble as it is."

He was being ridiculously elusive. He might know something about Jill Lorrimer's death. Somebody might be threatening him. He might be in some kind of trouble.

"I truly cannot help you, Marty, unless you stop being so vague," I said. "Either some things have happened or they haven't. Just tell what you know."

It took a while but Marty finally spilled out his story, and it came as a surprise because Arne was at the center of it.

Marty told me he'd received an ominous phone call the day before from Arne. "It was about Jill Lorrimer and Arne basically told me to keep my mouth shut or else."

"How was Arne involved with Jill?"

"He used to go to some of the parties at Peter's mansion. I did, too. I'm not proud of that. It was stupid, really, really stupid. Jill was one of Peter's party girls and, you know, would entertain us."

"As in having sex."

"Yes."

"And she had sex with you and Arne?"

"I don't know about Arne. I only saw him once at a party and Jill wasn't there. But I think she must had sex with him another time because, well, that's why Arne called me, don't you see? He was worried word might get out about how he'd been at a party with Jill. I guess those messages from the Serenader spooked him."

I doubted it was just sex with Jill that had Arne so worried. "You think Arne was somehow involved in Jill's death, don't you?"

"I don't know that for sure. But here's the thing: Peter always had a lot of drugs at his parties and you know, maybe he gave too many to Jill and she died and then he had to figure out what to do with her body."

"And Arne helped him out?"

"Could be. Really, I don't know."

"Because you weren't there that night, or so you've said. Yet you seem to know a lot about what happened and now Arne is calling you and telling you to keep quiet. I'm having a little trouble believing you weren't there."

"I don't want to go to prison for something I didn't do," Marty blurted out, and I saw he was beginning to tear up. "So I'm not going to put myself in jeopardy. Okay? There are other witnesses. I'm not the only one. "

"You mean other people at Peter's parties?"

"Right. I don't know their names but I'm sure you could find out. They were mostly high-roller types from Twin Cities. The parties were a perk for people who stayed at Peter's hotel and gambled at the casino."

"How nice for them. Let's get back to Arne. What exactly did he say when he called you yesterday?"

"He said that if I talked to anybody about him and Jill I'd be 'done for.' That's how he put it, 'done for.'"

"And you interpreted that to mean what? That he might hurt you or even kill you?"

"You know Arne. He's a scary guy. He's shot people. So, yes, I'm worried what he might do. Maybe I need one of those protective orders to keep him away."

"That might be a stretch, Marty. Did he actually say he would harm you?"

"Well, not in so many words, but I knew what he meant."

"I'm afraid that's not enough for a protective order. There has to be a more specific threat."

Marty got out a handkerchief and daubed his eyes. "I don't know what else to do. I'm in a corner here, Paul. Do you understand that?"

"I do, but there's a way out if you want to take it."

"What's that?"

"First get a lawyer. I can recommend some good ones. Then go to the state prosecutor who's coming up here to take charge of the investigation into Peter's disappearance and Dewey's murder. His name is Chad Barrington. Tell him your story, but only after you've received immunity from any possible criminal charges."

"I don't know. I'd have to testify, wouldn't I?"

"You would if the case goes to trial."

"Okay, let me think about this some more. Can I call you if I need to?"

I jotted down my cell number and gave it to Marty. "Any time."

He stood up and reached cross the desk to shake my hand. "Thanks a lot, Paul. I knew I could count on you. It'll all work out, won't it?"

"I'm sure it will," I promised. "Just do the right thing Marty, and you'll be fine."

I spent the rest of the afternoon hip deep in the usual dreary paperwork, doing my level best to keep Paradise County on the right side of the law. There were minor criminal and civil matters to be dealt with, motions to be filed, letters to be written, paving contracts to be approved. I also had to prepare for an upcoming court hearing centering on a tricked out, eighty-thousand-dollar Yukon Denali seized by one of Arne's deputies in a drug case. The owner wanted his big toy back and I could sympathize. The seizure laws were ridiculous. Then again, who but a drug dealer in Paradise County could afford an SUV worth eighty grand?

Still, no matter what flotsam floated across my desk, I couldn't help but think about Marty, glum-faced and anxious, caught up in something that threatened to destroy his life. I was all but certain he'd been at Peter's mansion the night Jill Lorrimer died. Had Arne been there, too, and was that why he'd made the ominous call to Marty? If so, Arne might have done more than merely cover up Jill's death as a favor to Peter. Maybe he'd killed her, for reasons unknown, and Marty had witnessed the crime. And then maybe Arne had made Peter disappear and murdered Dewey, because . . . .

Slow down, I told myself. There's nothing like a conspiratorial frame of mind to stimulate wild thinking, and it's easy to leap right off the cliff and nosedive into all manner of craziness. I was just making guesses. I really didn't know what Marty had seen at Peter's mansion, and I wouldn't know until he decided to tell me. I made a mental note to call him by the end of the week to see if he was ready to speak out. In the meantime, I'd keep what Marty had revealed about Arne's sexcapades with Jill as an ace in the hole, ready to play when the right time arrived.

24

The next day, amid a trickle of rain and fat whirling snow-flakes, the national media swooped down on Pineland like big dark birds hunting for prey. A CNN crew led the way in search of bad news in the heartland, and their report, full of drama and angst, was merely the beginning. FOX, CBS, and NBC quickly followed. The *New York Times*, not to be outdone, sent a reporter to suss out the situation. He spent two days in Pineland, looking painfully out of place amid the rustics, and then produced a long story—"A Town on Fire"—filled with piquant details about the hockey-playing, God-fearing, Budweiser-drinking, Trump-loving hosers who inhabit our remote backwater. It was quite a read, and wrong in a hundred ways about Pineland, which like all small towns is not nearly as simple a place as outsiders like to assume.

The glare of the media always attracts moths eager to fly into the light, and plenty of Pinelanders stepped forward for a once-in-a-lifetime chance at self-immolation. Arne, to my amazement, was chief among them. I thought he'd try to duck the press, but instead he embraced the cameras and microphones, quickly morphing into Pineland's very own media celebrity. His rumpled, grumpy presence and tart manner made him a natural for television, the classic Podunk sheriff, and before long his ornery face was showing up on screens across the country.

He presented himself as a folksy-but-sly lawman, full of old-time country wisdom, and even talked in fake drawl like a good old boy from south of the Mason-Dixon line. "We got a skunk here we need to smoke out and you can bet we'll do just that," he told one interviewer. He assured another that while "we're just simple people up here in Paradise County, don't think for a minute we're stupid. We got some whip-smart folks investigating this thing and they'll get to the bottom of it pretty quick."

Big city media types are easily snookered when they venture into the exotic realm of small-town America, so they fell for Arne's aw-shucks routine and depicted him as a man of shrewd, if not downright dazzling intelligence. But as the Einstein of Pineland exhaled his mighty gusts of wind, he made sure to throw me under the media eighteen-wheeler, suggesting I was "a person of interest" in the investigation. He didn't specify what made me so interesting, not that it mattered. Calls started coming into my office, producers for some of the on-air correspondents began nosing around and before long my mug appeared on CNN. "Questions raised about county attorney," read the Chyron beneath the image.

I wanted to blast back at Arne—Marty had provided me with plenty of ammunition—but decided against it. A big public war of words with Arne would just draw more attention to me and I didn't want that. I also figured the national media would decamp after a day or two, looking for chewy mayhem elsewhere, and we'd all catch our breath.

It didn't quite work out that way.

The media weren't the only irritant I had to deal with. Just before noon, Chad Barrington from the Minnesota Attorney General's office in St. Paul showed up to formally dismiss me from the case and demand that I turn over any and all investigative files. I'd first met him when he took over the corruption investigation involving Dewey and two sheriff's deputies after Jill Lorrimer's death. I didn't like him then and I liked him even less now. He's tall and thin, in his late thirties, a frequent marathoner who loves recounting his running achievements mile by dreary mile. He wears more expensive suits than I've ever owned, possesses a law degree from Yale and speaks with an affected East Coast accent. What's there not to dislike about him?

"Of course I'll cooperate in any way I can," I said in my politest manner. "You can count on me, Chad. Incidentally, how's that corruption investigation going? Now that Dewey Swindell has been murdered, I imagine it's heating up."

"I can't comment on that," he said.

"I suppose not. Well, have fun with Arne. I'm sure he's eager to work with you to clear up everything here. Should be a piece of cake, don't you think?"

"I wouldn't know," he said, and I couldn't have agreed more. He didn't know—about Pineland, about Arne, about all the cross-currents at work—but he was in for an education.

While the news media were busy carving up Pineland for the amusement of America, the investigation of which I was no longer a part gave scant evidence of progress. Peter remained lost, and even though I had an idea where he might be buried I wasn't ready yet to present my theory to Arne or anyone else in law enforcement. It was too risky for me, and I saw no harm in waiting awhile to speak up.

Dewey's murder wasn't proving any easier to crack. No trace evidence of the killer was found at the Glenning, in the ruins of the old Swindell mansion or on what was left of Dewey's body. Dewey's phone records revealed no suspicious calls or messages. His e-mail was equally unremarkable. No useful footage was found from the few surveillance cameras in the vicinity of the Glenning or the mansion, nor did any eyewitnesses come forward. Whoever shot Dewey and hauled his body to the mansion to be incinerated had managed to move unseen through the night.

Investigators were able to determine, to no one's surprise, that arson was the cause of the fire that destroyed the mansion. The arsonist had gone about his work skillfully, setting at least two fires simultaneously to insure a rapid burn. He used accelerants—paint thinner and lamp oil—found on site and constructed timers from simple household items all but impossible to trace.

Dewey himself went from the fire to a refrigerated drawer at the coroner's office in Duluth, and he stayed there for weeks because no one claimed his charred corpse. When I learned of the situation, I filed legal work to arrange a county-sponsored burial. Even jerks deserve a decent farewell.

Kat Berglund called as I was leaving the office just before five.

"Heard something you might be interested in," she said. "Got a minute?"

"For you, always. What's up?"

"Do you know Jimmy Shields, over at the Paradise Pines Hotel? He's one of the desk clerks."

"The name's vaguely familiar," I said.

"Well, he comes into the bar every afternoon after his shift at the hotel is over. He has a couple of bumps and then plays euchre with his buddies."

"Euchre?"

"I know, who plays that? But he does. Anyway, while he was enjoying his afternoon shots of Jim Beam he mentioned he'd seen 'that fancy Black lady from Chicago,' as he calls her. Apparently, she checked back into the hotel today."

This was good news, if only because I knew Cassandra was all right. At the same time, I wished she hadn't taken the risk of returning to Pineland. She'd decided to investigate on her own—leaving me and everyone else in the dark—and I had no doubt she was convinced she could ferret out the truth. Maybe she could. Or maybe she was unknowingly setting herself up to become the killer's final victim. In either case, the sooner I could speak to her and try to regain her trust, the better.

"Well, I'm glad she's safe and sound," I told Kat. "I'll have to go out to the hotel and have a long talk with the wondrous

Cassandra. Maybe she'll open up a bit and share what she knows. She hasn't exactly been candid with me."

"Or maybe she just doesn't like you," Kat offered. "She wouldn't be the first woman with that problem."

"Sad but true, despite my inherently lovable nature. So did your barfly pal Jimmy have anything else to say about Cassandra?"

"Actually, he did. He said she asked him a bunch of questions about Pembroke Woods Park."

"What sort of questions?"

"How big the park is, if it's really isolated, whether other people would likely be there this time of year. Questions like that. I guess she gave Jimmy quite a grilling. Sounds as if she's planning to go out to the park."

"Why would she do that?"

"I serve drinks, Paul. I don't read minds."

"Damn, I was sure you did. Thanks for the info. I owe you one."

"No problem. Talk to you soon."

Pembroke Woods County Park is two miles northeast of town along a quiet stretch of the Paradise River. Although the park encompasses only forty acres, it holds a great prize in the form of a virgin stand of red and white pine that eluded both loggers and the Great Fire, in large measure due to a crusty character named Thomas Pembroke. He homesteaded the land in the 1870s and refused to sell his patch of woods to Jonathan Paradise's all-consuming lumberjacks. No one knows why he kept the loggers at bay. Maybe he just liked trees or maybe he saw beauty where no one else did and believed, against all odds, that it was important. He was also lucky. The Great fire somehow swooped around his woods, as though giving him credit for his preservation efforts.

Pembroke's descendants kept the woods in their pristine state for almost a hundred years before donating the property to Paradise County in 1970. The park's big trees, some three hundred years old and over a hundred feet high, are the last of their kind in Paradise County, giants from a lost age. The park draws hikers in summer and cross-country skiers in winter, but there are few visitors during the damp, chill days of April.

I used to roam the park as a kid, lost to the everyday world and dreaming of great things. The dreams are mostly gone now but the park remains one of my favorite places, and I often go there in summer to enjoy its fragrant air and deep, soothing quiet. It's even better in winter, insulated in deep snow and immune to the world's noisy nonsense.

After talking with Kat, however, I wasn't feeling at all peaceful. What would possess Cassandra to go out to the park, if in fact she had? I put in a call to the hotel and asked to speak to her, but there was no answer. Maybe she'd gone out to dinner. Or maybe she'd gone somewhere else. There was only one way to find out. Instead of heading home, I drove north out of town, toward Pembroke Woods.

25

When I reached woods around five-thirty, I saw a red BMW in the parking lot. Cassandra presumably had a rental car and she'd be just the type to go first-class with a Beamer. There are times when your gut is way ahead of your brain, and I could feel my stomach tightening as I parked next to the car. I checked the driver's side door and was surprised to find it open. The interior was clean and tidy, nothing in disarray. I looked in the glove compartment and found a Hertz rental agreement with Cassandra's name. Not good. What was she doing out here in the woods by herself? It didn't feel right.

I wondered why Cassandra hadn't locked the car. Was she just in a rush or had someone grabbed her, or worse? I popped open the trunk latch. My stomach was double knotted by the time I went around to look into the trunk. It was empty.

I closed the trunk and looked out toward the old forest, a dark green wall at the edge of the parking lot. The mix of snow and rain had stopped, patches of blue poking through the clouds as angled shafts of sunlight sliced through the big trees. But night wasn't far away and once it clamped down Cassandra would be lost to the woods. A stiff wind had come up from the northwest, crashing through the crowns of the pines with a whooshing, jet-engine roar. I suddenly thought of my Hopper print, with its ancient American darkness closing in on the lonely gas station. Paradise County is like that, the woods and their hidden mysteries never far away, mocking the thin claims of civilization.

Although I had no proof anything was wrong—for all I knew Cassandra had a deep interest in forestry and was simply out for a hike—I felt a roiling sense unease. I got out my cell phone and called 911. I identified myself to the operator and asked that a sheriff's deputy be dispatched at once to the park.

"What is the nature of the emergency?" the operator asked.

"I believe a woman named Cassandra Ellis may be in danger."

Everybody in Pineland knew about Cassandra, and the mention of her name had an immediate effect.

"All right," the operator said, "we'll send out a unit. Will you meet the deputy there?"

"Yes, I—"

The crack of a gunshot tore through the wind, close enough to startle me.

"I'm hearing gunfire," I said. "Send more deputies. I'll be in the woods."

A well-maintained trail circles through the park, and I ran toward it. The wind was still blasting through the trees, and if Cassandra was somewhere in the woods I doubted she could hear my voice above the roar, but I tried anyway.

I called out her name and said, "It's Paul Zweifel. Where are you?"

No response. I called out her name again. Nothing.

The park's pines stand in dense, huddled groves, and once I started along the trail the parking lot quickly faded from view. Nothing much blooms in Paradise County until May, and the forest's understory of aster and hazelnut and chokeberry was still struggling to thrust through the thick layer of pine needles covering the ground. I moved quickly down the trail, the wind pushing at my chest like some bruiser trying to knock me off my feet. The branches of the pines swayed overhead, blotting out much of the sky, and I had the eerie sensation that I'd left the familiar world and passed into another far older and more dangerous, home to Little Red Riding Hood and the big bad wolf.

I called out Cassandra's name every few steps, to no avail. Maybe she wasn't in the woods after all or I'd somehow missed her and she was back at her car. Or maybe she'd been taken away or even murdered by the same the man who appeared to be waging war against the Swindell family.

About a quarter of a mile in from the parking lot I reached a sign along the trail pointing to Old Tom, the largest and tallest white pine in the park, named after its savior, Thomas Pembroke. A narrow path leads to the three-hundred-year-old skyscraper, long a popular rendezvous for late-night teenage beer fests. I glanced over toward the stately old giant, in the shadow of which I'd committed my share of youthful follies, and that's when my heart almost stopped.

Next to Old Tom a man stood stock still, staring at me. I stared back. The man was all in black—leather jacket, gloves, cargo pants, high-topped boots—and he could have been a lost hiker except for that fact that he was also wearing a black ski mask. I thought of the old Colt Python revolver—a hand-me-down from my father—that I kept at my house, and I wished I had it with me as the proverbial chill ran down my spine. Now what? It didn't take long to find out. The man in black gave a kind of waving salute with his right hand, as though we were friends who'd just spotted each other at a party, and then turned and ran.

"Hey, you, stop!" I shouted.

I was in my usual suit-and-tie uniform, with loafers as footwear, which meant I was hardly prepared for bush-whacking through the woods. Still, I was ready to give it a try until I heard footsteps coming up behind me. I turned around and there was Cassandra, in designer jeans and pow-der blue sneakers and a gray cashmere sweater worth half a week of my salary. A small leather bag was tucked under her shoulder. She was her very own fashion show in the woods. Her ensemble also included a snub-nosed, silver-barreled re-volver, presumably the same one I'd seen earlier in her purse. She was pointing it straight at me.

"You with him?" she asked, glancing over at the man in black, who was rapidly disappearing into the woods. Her hand was shaking. The gun shook with it. She was scared. So was I. I was also angry.

"What the hell are about talking about? Why would I be with whoever that is? I'm out here looking for you because I thought you might be in trouble. Didn't you hear me shouting? And would you please lower that gun. I'd really prefer not to get shot today."

"Sorry," she said, putting the revolver in her bag. "Just a precaution. I heard you calling my name but I wasn't sure it was you."

"Really? I thought you'd be familiar with my voice by now. What about the gunshot? Did that guy threaten you?"

"I'm not sure. I saw him and he started coming toward me in way I didn't like. So I shot in the air just to let him know he'd better not fuck with me. And now here you are and the guy's waving at you like he knows you. What am I supposed to think?"

"He was just being an asshole. I have no idea who he is, but I doubt we could catch him now and find out. Jesus, Cassandra, I'm just glad you're all right. This could have ended very badly. I've already called nine-one-one and deputies are on the way. I'd really like to know what you were doing out here by yourself."

"I was looking for something."

"What?"

"Let's just say I received information that I might find something of interest here."

Could she be any less revealing, or more exasperating? "Come on, cut the crap," I said. "You came out here with a gun in your pocket and you won't tell me why. You know you're still shaking, don't you? What's going on?"

Cassandra took a deep breath, drawing in the air as fiercely as though it was an intoxicating chemical about to send her off on a wonderful trip. She said, "Let's talk later, okay? I've got to sort everything out."

Cassandra's phone sounded from one of her jeans pockets. She got it out and looked at the screen.

"A message from a friend?" I asked.

"Shit," she said. "This is getting really weird. Like I said, just give me some time and we'll talk."

I began to hear faint sirens. Deputies were on their way.

"Have it your way," I said. "Maybe it doesn't matter to you, but I'm truly relieved you're safe. And please don't do anything this stupid again. I think that guy was stalking you."

"Yeah, you may be right. I'm just not sure. But I appreciate that you came looking for me."

It was an apology, sort of, but I still didn't think Cassandra was being totally honest with me. As we started walking back to the parking lot, I glanced over at Big Tom, where a flash of white caught my eye. I moved a few steps down the trail for a better view. The white appeared to be a sheet of paper attached to the tree's massive trunk. I knew what it had to be.

"I think we just missed the Serenader," I said.

I didn't want to be the one who found the message posted on Big Tom, and Cassandra didn't either, so we went straight back to the lot. The sirens grew much louder. Then a white Ford pickup with flashers sped into the lot, closely followed by two squads. The pickup stopped next to us and Arne stepped out, dressed in a corduroy jacket and slacks and a white Stetson hat. I guess it was his Texas Ranger look.

"Well, it seems you're safe after all, Miss Ellis," he said. "Now what's all this about? The counselor here seems to think you were in some sort of trouble. Is that right?"

"There was no trouble," Cassandra said to my surprise. "Mr. Zweifel was mistaken."

Cassandra, it seemed, was still playing games. I was about to chime in but Arne cut me off. He only wanted to talk to my less-than-truthful companion.

"I gather you went out here for a stroll through the pines," he said. "Not the best day for it, I have to say. The thing is, you don't look like the woodsy type. What were you doing here?"

Cassandra said, "And just what does the 'woodsy type' look like, sheriff? Not Black, I imagine."

"Woodsy types come in all colors, and they wear hiking clothes and boots and warm jackets, none of which you seem to have. There's also the matter of a gunshot Mr. Zweifel here claims to have heard. Can you tell me anything about that?"

I thought Cassandra would deny she had a weapon but she didn't. "I fired a shot by accident. It was very careless of me. I was just putting the gun in my bag when it happened."

She handed the bag to Arne and said, "See for yourself."

"Well, that's nice to know," Arne said as he dug into the bag and pulled out a short-barreled revolver.

"I have a permit to carry, in case you're interested," Cassandra said.

"I'm sure you do," Arne, said, breaking open the cylinder and inspecting the revolver. "My oh my, a Ladysmith three-fifty-seven magnum. A lot of gun in a small package.

Hope you weren't doing some target practice out here. It's illegal, you know, to discharge a firearm in our county parks."

Cassandra said, "As I told you, it was an accident. Beyond that, all I can tell you is that I went out for a walk today. That is not illegal. I carry a duly-licensed firearm for personal protection. That is not illegal either. I have nothing else to say at the moment, so I'll be leaving. Before I go, I'd like my gun back."

Arne gave her his best blow-torch stare. Cassandra stared right back.

"Well, perhaps you'd be willing to give a statement soon," Arne said, smiling. "You've probably heard we have dead and disappeared people around here and it looks as though you may be related to them. So, yes, we need to talk."

"Fine," Cassandra said. "I'll be Paradise Pines Hotel. Call me tomorrow. Now, my gun please."

Legally, Arne could have kept the weapon under one pretext or another, but he handed it back to Cassandra. "Wouldn't want you to go unprotected," he said. "You have a nice day. Sorry for all the bother. Mr. Zweifel was just a little excited, I guess. He gets that way sometimes."

Cassandra slipped the gun in her jacket pocket without a word, went over to her BMW and drove off. After she left, I said, "There are two things you should know, Arne. The first is that I saw a man out in the woods, disguised with a ski mask. I think it was the Serenader. The second thing is that he left another message, nailed to Big Tom."

I didn't mention that Cassandra had lied about how she came to fire her revolver, assuming, of course, that she'd told me the truth. Clearly, she didn't trust Arne. But did she trust me? I wasn't sure.

Arne sent his deputies to swarm through the woods in search of evidence while I answered more questions. Jason Braddock from the BCA arrived just after six thirty and joined the on-scene interrogation. There wasn't much I could say, other than explaining how I'd come to search for Cassandra before encountering the mysterious man in black.

"Maybe it was Bigfoot," Arne offered at one point.

"Yeah, he's famous for wearing a leather jacket and ski mask," I said. "A great disguise."

Arne was skeptical of my story from the start, suspecting I'd planted yet another message and then lured Cassandra out to the park for nefarious purposes. I said that was absurd, but he and Jason kept pushing at me until someone else demanded their attention. A deputy came rushing out of the woods, a phone screen glowing in his hand like a magical lantern, and said, "We found the message, I took a shot of it. There's also another of those thumb drives with it."

I stood behind Arne, Jason and the deputy as they read the message, which had a decidedly biblical quality:

The end days are near. Sins will be exposed, sinners punished. Fires will rage. THE WOMAN will eat of the tree of knowledge. Let the truth shine forth. The Serenader

"It's just more crazy shit," Arne said.

I knew better but didn't pursue the point. Instead, I told Arne I'd enjoyed his stimulating company but it was time to go. He couldn't stop me—there was no probable cause I'd committed any crime in the woods—but said he'd have more questions later.

"Can't wait," I said, and left.

I headed home, stopping first to grab an exquisite meal at the McDonald's along the interstate. Camus, his bladder swollen to the size of a hot-air balloon, was extremely happy to see me. I let him out to do his business, chewed on my hamburger at the kitchen table and decided that one way or the other, I was going to have a come-to-Jesus moment with Cassandra Ellis because I was all but certain she'd been in secret contact with the Serenader.

26

I called Cassandra at the hotel first thing in the morning but as usual there was no answer on her room phone, so I went into work and tried to pretend I was interested in the many routine tasks that fall to a county attorney. Doug came in to pump me for information but I shooed him away and then went for a break at Koffeeken's. Its loquacious proprietor was on hand, armed with high doses of caffeine and gossip. I soon learned Cassandra's sylvan adventure with me the evening before was already the talk of the town.

"And what is the rumor mill grinding out at the moment?" I asked Ken as he detonated a depth charge and set it in front of me.

"Word has it she was meeting the Serenader at the park but then you came along and spoiled her plans," Ken said. "Or maybe it was the other way around. I even heard one version that you were out there in a black ski mask trying to scare her."

"No, that was Bigfoot," I said. "A word of advice, Ken. Spread all the gossip you want, but be very careful what you believe."

Ken had other news to offer, none of it scintillating, and after loading up on caffeine I returned to the office, well buzzed. I logged on to my computer, scanned several official county emails imploring me to do one profoundly important thing or another, then called up the latest edition of Tommy Redmond's "Paradise Detective Bureau."

There, to my surprise, I found the Serenader's message word for word. The deputy's cell phone snapshot had somehow found its way into Tommy's possession. His blog went on to report that a thumb drive had also been found, but I only learned later that it held yet another snippet of unrecognizable music and muffled background voices.

I expected a call from Tommy, but the afternoon went by without a word from him. Ditto Cassandra. She still wasn't answering her phone at the hotel. My come-to-Jesus moment with her appeared to be on hold.

I was crossing the courthouse square on the way to my car when Tommy Redmond finally caught up to me. He hailed me with a desperate arm wave as though I was the last taxi in a rainstorm and came rushing up, notebook in hand. He was wearing his usual flamboyant red sportscoat, a stoplight you didn't dare go through.

"Nice blog today," I said. "How did you manage to get your sweaty little paws on that photo?"

"I have friends in high places," Tommy said with a grin.

"Last time I checked, there were no high places in Paradise County."

"Ha, good one, Paulie. Maybe I should have said low places, you know, where all the dirt settles. Anyway, how about we have a chat?"

"There's not really much I can tell you, Tommy. As you so ably reported the other day, I'm off the case."

"Sure, and yesterday you were out in the woods with that Ellis woman looking for the Serenader. Doesn't sound like you're off the case to me. I even hear you saw him."

"I can't comment on that. Maybe Arne will let you read his report of the incident, assuming you haven't seen it already."

"Right. Arne and I have a regular love affair."

"I can't wait to read all about that in the *Tattler*. But really, I don't have much I can share with you. I'm like everybody else in town. I'm trying to figure this whole thing out."

Tommy's saucer eyes registered disappointment and I thought he'd start pressing me for more information. Instead, he said, "Okay, I'm really busy anyway so I'll let you go. But let's stay in touch, Paulie. You help me, I help you. If you find out anything, you know who to call."

"You're on my speed dial," I lied and watched Tommy head back across the courthouse square. He walked quickly and purposefully, his red coat saturated in the late afternoon light, and he looked like a man afire. Maybe he was. A new edition of the *Tattler* was due out Friday and I expected it would offer plenty of incendiary news.

I was at home, tending to Camus's need for constant attention, when my land line rang just after seven. Caller ID said it came from a cell phone with a 312 area code. That would be Chicago.

"This is Cassandra," the familiar voice said. "Can you meet me at the hotel bar tonight? I've done some unfortunate things and I need to set matters right. Would nine o'clock work?"

I said it would.

I pulled into the parking lot of the Paradise Pines Hotel just before nine. The twelve-story hotel is the county's tallest building by far. Peter had always been inordinately proud of his creation, claiming it brought "a touch of real class" to our benighted corner of the world. Curved in the form of a broad arc, the hotel sports a tropical color scheme in pink and aqua green, a bit of Miami Beach magically transported to the frozen hinterlands. The hotel is promoted as "your private paradise," but I've always thought of it as a bawdy architectural hooker, designed to seduce. At two hundred dollars a night it's too expensive for locals, who instead perform all the minimum-wage grunt work needed to keep the place running.

The hotel's glitzy bar, called Tropics, offers the usual assortment of overpriced alcohol in a faux atmosphere decked out with murals of tanned beachgoers cavorting in the sun. The place wasn't crowded on a Thursday night, and I found Cassandra—the only Black person in evidence —sitting in a small booth beneath one of the murals. She was wearing a no-nonsense dark blue suit and gave me a courteous handshake before I took the seat across from her.

"You've got the floor," I said. "I really would like to hear what you and the Serenader have been up to."

Cassandra was drinking something with water—bourbon or maybe Scotch. She took a very demure sip and said, "How'd you know I've been in touch with him?"

"Detective work. You told me you'd called the man who sent you the letter, presumably the Serenader, before you came up here. Then before long you went undercover—I guess that's how I'd describe it—and I thought, maybe it was because of something you'd learned from another chat with the Serenader. My caffeine-dispensing pal Ken Michaels also mentioned you'd told him you thought people had the wrong idea about our mysterious message man. I took that to be further evidence you'd been in contact with him. So why don't you tell me all about it?"

"All right, I owe you explanation. You're right. We talked four times, over the phone. He used a device to disguise his voice so I wouldn't be able to identify him. He said he was in local law enforcement—he didn't specify which agency he worked for—and couldn't come forward because he feared for his life. He described a huge conspiracy involving the sheriff, Dewey Swindell, a guy name Marty Moreland, and you."

"Wow. A vast conspiracy right here in Pineland. And you believed him?"

"I did."

"That was foolish."

"Yes," Cassandra said softly. "It was. But he was very convincing and he had lots of information. The conspiracy, he said, centered around me, and Dewey Swindell was at the heart of it."

"Come on, Cassandra, that's just pure bullshit. Dewey—may he rest in peace—couldn't have conspired his way out of a paper bag."

"Okay, but I didn't know that."

Cassandra unspooled the conspiracy story as revealed to her by the Serenader. It was nothing if not baroque. Dewey had found out she was his step sister, and he feared she'd try to get her hands on a big chunk of daddy's money. So Dewey lured her up to Pineland with a phony letter even as he kidnapped and presumably murdered his father to keep him from ever revealing the truth about his Black daughter. Dewey then planned to kill Cassandra, with help from Arne, Marty Moreland and myself, all alleged co-conspirators in a magnificently intricate scheme. But something went wrong and the conspirators had to take out Dewey. Meanwhile, there was also the business with Jill Lorrimer. The Serenader claimed Arne, Marty and I had been at Peter's house when Jill received a lethal overdose of drugs. We then conspired to cover up the true manner of her death.

When Cassandra was done, I said, "The story he told you has, oh I don't know, maybe a thousand holes in it. It doesn't make an ounce of sense if you think about it. But I have a pretty good idea why you fell for it."

"Do you? If you're going to tell me I'm stupid—"

"No, I'd never say that. But I think you believed the whole crazy story because you wanted to. You came up here expecting to find a bunch of Trump-loving racists. Pretty soon a cross gets burned on my lawn. Then maybe you actually encounter a Trump-loving racist—yes, we have a number of them here—who says something that confirms your worst suspicions. So when the Serenader starts whispering conspiracy theories in your ear, you're very receptive. They must be true because we're all no-good people here anyway who hate Blacks and liberals and immigrants and well, you name it."

"Spare me the chamber of commerce bullshit," Cassandra said as a waiter arrived and took my order for a Jack straight up. "Maybe everybody here isn't a racist, but you'd have a hard time convincing me of that. It's not like I've been welcomed with open arms. A lot of people here look at me like I'm from outer space."

"Well, you are from Chicago. That's outer space as far as most people here are concerned. Anyway, how about we get back to yesterday's events? I assume the Serenader, or whoever you talked to, convinced you to go out to Pembroke Woods."

Cassandra nodded and gave her drink another swirl. "Yes. He said I could find evidence there that would prove who was behind Peter Swindell's disappearance."

"Did he say what kind of evidence?"

"No, but he gave me exact directions about how to find it. The plan was to turn it over to the BCA so they could arrest the conspirators. Once that happened, the Serenader said he'd reveal himself."

"You shouldn't have gone into those woods by yourself," I said. "Not in a million years."

"Well, I did," Cassandra said. "I had to know the truth."

"Okay. What happened next?"

"I drove out there. The parking lot was empty and there was no sign of anyone. I started walking along the trail, following the directions I'd gotten. But give me at least a little credit. I was suspicious and I had my gun, which you'd better believe I know how to use. I was in the middle of the woods when I saw the guy in black. He was trying to sneak up behind me but I heard him. I turned around and saw him coming right at me, maybe twenty yards away. That's when I fired a shot, not at him, but to scare him off. He got the message and he started backing away fast. You know the rest. I ran into you and then mister ski mask gave us a wave and vanished."

"Well, you were lucky. He might have killed you."

"I wasn't lucky. I had a gun and I was ready to defend myself."

"Okay, Annie Oakley, whatever you say. But then I came along, one of the supposed co-conspirators. I'm surprised you didn't shoot me."

Cassandra's dark brown eyes, usually hard and unreadable, seemed to soften. She shook her head slowly and said, "I guess I had one of those 'aha' moments. I can't really explain it, but I could sense you were there to help me. That you were my friend."

"Sounds like religious experience," I said.

"Maybe it was. There's also the fact that ninja guy scared the shit out of me. Remember that text message I got as we were leaving the woods? All it said was, 'Sorry I missed you. See you again soon.' It really creeped me out."

"I can see why. It's pretty obvious he's watching you. So let me ask you this: if you suddenly realized the Serenader was a big fat liar and maybe was even threatening you, why didn't you tell Arne the truth? You told him nothing happened in the woods."

"Look, I'm willing to put my trust in you right now but no one else. I still think the sheriff may be involved in some bad things here. Maybe that Moreland guy is, too. So here's the deal. How about the two of us find out what's really going on? Screw the authorities. We don't know if they can be trusted."

She had a point, although I reminded her that I was, technically at least one of the dreaded "authorities."

"But I heard you've recused yourself from the case," Cassandra said.

"'Kicked off' would be a better way of putting it," I said. I studied Cassandra's face for a moment. I saw strength, resolve, courage and a hint of obsession. She would make a formidable if possibly unpredictable partner.

"You've got a deal," I said. "Where do we start?"

27

"We can start with some things I've already found out," Cassandra said. "I know who my birth mother is. Her name is Patricia Gordon."

"Well, that's big news. How did you manage that?"

"I hired a private detective in Chicago last week. He's done work for our firm over the years. He's a big Albanian guy, a cousin of John Belushi or so he claims. Everybody calls him Jocko, although that's not his real name. He used to be a process server and he really knows his way around the Cook County Courthouse. He got a look at my adoption records."

"They weren't sealed?"

"Tight as can be, or so Jocko informed me. But it's Chicago, if you know what I mean."

"I take it money changed hands."

"Large amounts. Jocko has a source in the clerk of court's office and after a couple of days of digging around he was able to locate the file through my birth date and the names of my adoptive parents."

"It must be wonderful to know who your birth mother is."

"I guess so, but I don't know. It's strange because I doubt I'll ever be able to see her or talk to her. But I do have an old mug shot of her Jocko found. She was really beautiful."

"A mug shot? So she had a criminal record?"

"Yes, mostly for prostitution. Anyway, my Albanian stalwart tracked down quite a bit of information about her. She was born in nineteen-fifty-four in Chicago, mother seventeen years old, no known father. Arrested three times for prostitution and once on a simple assault charge after some sort of altercation in a bar. Her last arrest was in nineteen eighty-two, the year before I was born, at the Blackstone Hotel, which is a very posh place. That tells you she had a high-class clientele."

"Sounds that way. Any idea what happened to her?"

"Well, I know she didn't die in Chicago because there's no death certificate on file for her in Cook County."

"Is it possible she's still alive? We have only the word of whoever wrote you that fake letter that she's dead."

"I suppose it's possible. She'd be sixty-three now, but prostitutes lead dangerous lives and they don't tend to live to a ripe old age. Besides, Jocko says she went off the radar in the mid-nineteen-eighties. I'm pretty sure she's dead."

"How about your father? What did the adoption papers say?"

"Father unknown, according to the records. But I'm certain now Peter Swindell was in fact my father."

"How so?"

"Just like you, I did some detective work. I asked Jocko if Peter could have been one of Patricia's customers. A little jungle fever and all of that. But he said the cops didn't bother arresting johns back in the eighties, especially if they were rich. A payoff usually took care of the problem. But when Jocko sent me the arrest records, I noticed something interesting. Patricia's case in nineteen eighty-two, the one at the Blackstone, was ultimately dismissed for lack of probable cause. The lawyer who represented her was named Richard Seymour. On the court documents he was listed as having a phone number with a Minneapolis area code. That struck me as peculiar."

"Because why would a lawyer from Minneapolis be representing a hooker from Chicago on a run-of-the-mill prostitution charge?"

"Exactly. I wasn't sure if Seymour was dead or alive, but it didn't take long to get an answer. Jocko traced him through his old law firm in Minneapolis. We found out Seymour is retired and living with his daughter in Evanston, just outside Chicago. He said he'd be happy to visit with me, so I flew down to see him. He's in his eighties but very sharp. We had a nice talk,   during which he casually mentioned he'd also represented Peter Swindell in an adoption proceeding in Chicago."

It took a second—I'm getting old and slow—before I realized what Cassandra had just told me. "Your adoption," I said.

"Right. In nineteen eighty-three. Seymour was pretty stunned when I told him who I was. He said Peter never actually admitted he'd fathered me by Patricia Gordon, but it was obvious what had happened. As Seymour put it, why would Peter have hired him otherwise?"

"Okay, so there can't be any doubt Peter's your father, just as that letter you received claims. But where does that leave us? We still don't know who wrote the letter. I really doubt it was Dewey. Maybe it was the Serenader but we don't even know who he is or what he's up to besides sowing chaos. And how does the fact you're Peter's daughter connect to his disappearance or Dewey's murder for that matter?"

"I have an idea about that. Seymour told me something else that really caught me by surprise. He said he'd heard Peter became involved in another adoption case a year or two after mine."

"In Chicago?"

"No. Seymour said the case was somewhere in Minnesota. A small town, he said. He couldn't remember the name of the town so I threw out a suggestion to see if it might jog his memory."

"Pineland," I said.

Cassandra flashed a big smile. "However did you guess? There's more. Seymour said he'd had a few brief contacts with the lawyer in Pineland handling the adoption. He remembered that the lawyer had a funny name. It started with a zee."

"Holy shit. It had to be my father."

"That's what I'm thinking. What was his first name again?"

"Phillip. He knew Peter, of course, so it would have made sense that he represented him. Do we know who the mother of the child here was?"

"No, but we have to find out."

Cassandra was usually all business with me, so I was stunned by what happened next. Without warning, she began to cry. Something old and deep had welled up inside her and poured out in tears before she could contain it.

"Fuck," she said, grabbing some tissues from her purse.

"Are you all right?"

"Yeah, yeah. I'm fine," she said, daubing at her cheeks. "I apologize. Just a little episode. Nothing to worry about."

"No need to apologize. Who doesn't want to cry now and then?"

She said, "I had a sudden intuition. I have a feeling about Peter's adoption case here. It could be very significant. We need to look at it, the sooner the better."

"Okay, but this isn't Chicago. Bribery's not a way of life here, so getting access to a sealed court file won't be easy, if it can be done at all, as you've already discovered. Let's see. Your adoption proceedings were in nineteen eighty-three, right?

"Yes. So we'd be looking for an adoption that occurred in eighty-four or maybe eighty-five. I assume the records would be at the courthouse here. I'll see what I can find tomorrow morning."

I could imagine Cassandra rummaging through files in the county clerk of court's office, probably pissing off any number of people in the process. "I think that would be a bad idea," I said.

"Why?"

"Because once you show up at the clerk's office, the news will be all over town in five minutes, and everybody will start wondering what the uppity Black lawyer from Chicago is looking for. Let me see if I can locate the file. Even just getting a file number might help. There's also another place I can hunt for information. My father's legal files are still stored in his old office here and maybe they'll reveal something."

"All right, but promise me you'll start looking right away."

I said I would. I knew why Cassandra was so interested in Peter's second adoption case, but I didn't think it would lead anywhere. If Peter did have another child by Patricia Gordon, it seemed highly unlikely Cassandra's lost sibling would have been born in Pineland, where a pregnant Black mistress would definitely have caused a stir.

Cassandra said, "By the way, that asshole sheriff of yours gave me a hard time today and I finally had to tell him to back off."

"You had a formal interview with him, I take it. What did you tell him?"

"As little as possible. In fact, I pretty much stonewalled him as to why I was out in the woods. All I admitted was that my gun had discharged accidentally. Anyway, he was very unhappy with me. But as you know, I don't trust him."

"That may be wise," I said, and recounted my conversation with Marty Moreland and how he believed Arne had threatened him over the Jill Lorrimer case.

"So it sounds like I'm right. The sheriff's dirty."

"Maybe. All I can say for sure is that you need to be cautious around him, at least for now."

"I will be. What about the BCA? Won't they investigate him?"

"Don't hold your breath. I'm not sure the BCA agents here know what they're doing. Pineland's a mystery to them. They might as well be in Outer Mongolia."

"I know the feeling," Cassandra said.

We talked for a while longer and I ordered another Jack. Cassandra was drinking Glen Moray Scotch, which is far out of my price range, and had a second drink as well. The extra alcohol seemed to loosen her up a bit. She leaned back and looked me over, as though inspecting some exotic specimen of homo sapiens, and said, "So what did you do before losing yourself in Pineland?"

"I'm not lost," I protested. "Just confused, as usual."

"But you were a hot-shot lawyer in the Twin Cities for quite a while, weren't you?"

"'Hot shot' wouldn't be the right term. But yeah, before I became a public defender I was a partner in a small firm with a guy named Geoff Armbruster. Care to guess what our advertising slogan was?"

"No, tell me."

"Armbruster and Zweifel: We meet your legal needs from A to Z."

"Wow. Did you come up with that yourself?"

"Pure genius, if you ask me."

"What kind of law did you practice?"

"Well, despite our silly slogan, we knew we needed a niche. The high road wasn't available so we went low. We started representing clients accused of DWIs and other serious driving offenses. The two of us were pretty creative and managed to get a lot of our clients off, so word began to spread we were the guys to see if you were caught drinking and driving. We handled some bigger felony cases as well. Armed robbery, assault, that sort of thing. We also did some civil stuff. In other words, we did whatever we could to pay the bills."

"So the firm was a success?"

"For a while. I made close to two hundred thousand in our best year, but it didn't feel good. One guy we'd got off on a DWI went out three months later and plowed his SUV head-on into a minivan. Killed a woman and her six-year-old daughter. He was drunk of course. It still makes me sick to think about it."

"But it wasn't your fault. You were just doing your job."

"Sure, but if you start to feel bad about what you're doing, you need to stop doing it. So I left the firm and decided I should try something else. I got a job as an assistant Ramsey County attorney in St. Paul. I didn't like that either. Too much bureaucracy and I hardly ever got to try a case. Everything was a plea deal."

"And then you switched sides again to become a public defender?"

"Right, in Minneapolis. I liked the work but it was exhausting. I had a ridiculous number of cases and most of my clients were real lowlifes. But every once in a while I'd get some poor guy who really was innocent, and that gave me a chance to fight the good fight on his behalf. I always liked that feeling."

"But you quit that job and came up here to Pineland. Why?"

"It's a long story, but the short version is that my father was dying and I came back to shepherd him off to the great beyond."

"I'm sorry," Cassandra said. "I didn't know. It must have been very difficult for you. Were you close to your father?"

"No."

"And your mother?"

"Dead, a long time ago."

"You're not really interested in getting into all of this, are you?"

"Correct," I said. "And to save time, I'll tell you I'm divorced and don't have any children."

"So, you're a man on the loose here in beautiful Pineland. Do you have a girlfriend in town?"

"I don't know if I'd call her that, but there's a wonderful woman I hang out with on occasion. How about you? Is there a man in your life?"

Cassandra stared a moment at her expensive Scotch and said, "No, but there is a woman."

That got my attention, but I didn't know what to say other than, "That's nice. Are the two of you married?"

"No. Maybe one day. I must say you look a little surprised."

"A little, but I'll survive."

"I'm sure you will," Cassandra said with a bemused smile. "Well, maybe we should call it a night. We've got a lot of work ahead of us."

She jotted down her cell phone number on a napkin and handed it to me. I gave her my cell number as well. "We should stay in touch every day from now on. Agreed?"

"Agreed," I said and downed the last of my Jack. Another one would have been lovely, but I resisted the urge. Too much liquor always sends me to the devil's workshop, and I preferred to be on the side of the angels, assuming I could find any in Pineland.

28

The next morning I went to the clerk of court's office. The clerk is a bilious little man named Carl Stock, who is best avoided. Fortunately, he's known to take a long coffee break every morning at half past ten, and it was five minutes after that time when I wandered into his office. Wanda Swanson, the deputy clerk, is always far more helpful than Carl, not to mention more ripe with gossip, and I was pleased to see her alone behind the counter. Wanda's in her early fifties, heavy-set, a bit of a flirt, but very capable.

"Morning, Wanda," I said in my friendliest voice. "Looks like you're holding down the fort by yourself. Is Carl getting his coffee fix?"

"No, he's out of the office today. Some sort of virus."

"That's too bad. I trust he'll have a speedy recovery."

"Right," Wanda said with no evident enthusiasm. She wasn't fond of her boss. "So how are you, handsome?"

"My life certainly isn't dull these days. There's a lot going on."

"No kidding. It's scary what's happening, isn't it? You wonder who'll be murdered next or have their house burned down. Do the police have any idea who's behind all of this?"

"I don't think so, but they'll find out. It's just a matter of time."

"Well, I hope so. I want my quiet little town back."

"Me, too," I said, then got down to business. "So, Wanda, I have an odd little request. An issue has come up regarding an old adoption case, and I'd like to see if I could find the file number. All I know is that the case went through the courts in nineteen eighty-four or eighty-five. Is there any easy way to look it up?"

"Not really. Everything was paper then. But if you want to go through the register for that year, be my guest. We still have it in the back. You know, of course, that adoption records are usually sealed, so—"

"I'd need a court order to see them. No, I just want to get a case number and any other paperwork that might be public."

"No problem. Just give me a minute."

Wanda went into the back bowels of the office and returned with a pair of outsized, leather-bound volumes, one for 1984 and the other for 1985. Each book contained a listing of all the criminal and civil cases filed in the Paradise County courts for that year. Cases were recorded by name and number, in the kind of elegant handwriting that used to be required of every court clerk. I slogged all the way through the books and found just one adoption case, filed in

July of 1985, that looked promising. Its title, "In re the Matter of Baby Doe," told me the child was a boy.

I jotted down the case number and asked Wanda to see if the file contained any documents not under seal. She returned with a slim folder. "This is all I can give you," she said.

The folder contained a single sheet of paper in the form of a court order, dated July 26, 1985, stating that a hearing would be held on August 5 regarding Baby Doe. The order was signed by Judge Marshall Moreland, Marty's father. One other name appeared on the order—that of the attorney of record in the case, the Honorable Phillip Zweifel.

"So how do we get a look that file?" Cassandra asked after I called her with the news.

"What did you have in mind? A break-in?"

"No, but there must be a way. Money's no object, if it comes to that."

"As I recall, bribery is still against the law in Minnesota, and I'm not going to be part of any Chicago-style skullduggery, if that's what you're thinking."

"At least we can get things done in Chicago," Cassandra said, sounding displeased that a certain level of honesty appeared to prevail in Pineland. "So what about a court order? It might be worth a try."

"We'd need some good grounds to convince a judge, and I don't know what they'd be."

"I could figure out something. I'm good at making shit up."

"Every good lawyer's most important skill," I agreed. "But I really doubt it would work in this case. Besides, I'm not very popular with the local judiciary at the moment. Our best bet now might be to have a look at my father's office records. I'm not sure what kind of shape they're in so it might take a while to get through them."

"I could help," Cassandra offered.

"Let's wait and see. I'll start digging into the records tomorrow and then let you know if I need help."

Doug came into my office that afternoon bearing the latest edition of the *Tattler*.

"Tommy's really on top of things," he reported with something close to glee. "Looks like he's got all the dirt that's fit to print."

"Wonderful," I said. "More dirt is always helpful."

I dismissed Doug and sat down to read Tommy's lead story, which didn't wallow in as much gossip and speculation as I expected it would. Instead, the story offered plenty of solid information, although most of it wasn't news to me. Near the end of the story, however, I found an eye-opening paragraph.

"The *Tattler* has learned that the flash drives accompanying all of the Serenader's messages contain in addition to an unknown piece of music the voices of a man and a child. The BCA reportedly has been able to determine what the voices are saying but is not revealing that information to the media at this time."

It was a tantalizing detail. I believed an old grievance lay behind all that had happened over the past two weeks. Was it a grievance that went all the back to childhood? If so, the child's voice on those mysterious audio files could be the voice of someone who grew up to be a murderer.

When my father died, he left me the old Zweifel family home on Eden Street. My grandfather the Klansman built it in 1910. It's a very late Victorian sporting towers and turrets and a wraparound porch decked out with every manner of turned, twisted and sawn woodwork its builders could devise. The house is also one giant pain in the ass to maintain, which is why my father encased it years ago in vinyl siding to avoid the onerous chore of painting every few years. The vinyl turned out to be a mistake—it faded and warped—and the house, shorn of most of its Victorian garb, now has the woeful look of an old starlet done in by bad cosmetic surgery.

My grandfather, who more or less designed the house himself, incorporated a spacious office on the first floor where he conducted his law practice. Presumably, he kept his white robe and peaked hat elsewhere. After my father inherited the practice, he kept the rent-free office but moved out of the drafty old house, which he subdivided into three rental apartments. I'm now the landlord. My tenants—two older women and a retired couple—enjoy the benefit of very reasonable rents, since I'm content to break even on the house rather than try to milk a big profit.

Even though my father moved to Las Vegas in the 1980s, he liked the idea of collecting rent so he didn't sell the house. But in his hurry to depart he never bothered to clear out the old office. Instead, he just locked it up and left it as a kind of Zweifel Legal Museum complete with cabinets full of old files, a desk and chairs, and an assortment of antiquated office equipment including typewriters, dictating machines, dial telephones and even a vintage TRS-80 computer from Radio Shack.

I was thirteen when my father moved away, and before he left he invited me to the office for a brief farewell address. He was wearing his usual three-piece suit, a fat gold watch chain dangling from one of the pockets, and as always he was formal and distant, Father talking to Son. He promised he'd see me whenever he came back to town, although he didn't know when that would be. He said my aunts were doing a wonderful job of raising me and so had no worries about my future. Maybe, he added, I'd even come out to Las Vegas for a visit when I was older. That didn't happen—he'd been gone from my life so much I hardly knew him—and in any case he'd killed my mother, so screw him, I thought. It would be twenty years before I saw him again.

I suppose because of that rotten leave-taking I never had much interest afterwards in seeing the office, although I rummaged through it one day after the house came into my possession, just to see if I could find any family photos. There were none. I didn't bother to look at any of the old files, which I assumed had little to offer except the dry dust of forgotten litigation. Yet even dust can sometimes have a voice, and so on Saturday afternoon I went to the office in search of Baby Doe.

One of my tenants, Agnes Miller, was just leaving as I came up to the front door and we chatted a bit before she went on her way. I went inside and unlocked the only door to the office, which smelled of old books and lost lives. A massive oak desk first used by my grandfather occupies the center of the office like a giant family totem, and I set my coat there before going to work.

I had hoped the files would be a model of clarity and order. Not so. The Zweifel office filing system, if it could be called that, had been the work of many secretaries, each of whom was apparently a law unto herself. There were files sorted alphabetically by client name, files sorted by year, files sorted by judicial case number, and even files sorted by nothing other than what looked to be secretarial whim. The good news was that the files appeared remarkably complete, documenting minor legal matters going all the way back to my grandfather's day.

I waded into the morass and eventually located all the files from the 1980s. They were sorted by year but I found no adoption cases listed in the 1984 or 1985 files. I checked 1986 and 1987 just to be certain and again came up empty. Then, in the bottom drawer of the filing cabinet, I came across a fat folder labeled "Miscellaneous Cases (Unpaid)." Baby Doe was there.

The file didn't have a great deal to offer. Nothing pointed to the baby's identity, but I did find two letters from Peter Swindell disputing my father's bill, which apparently had come to just over two thousand dollars. Peter thought that amount was excessive. A letter from my father begged to differ, but Peter apparently never paid the bill in full. The only other document in the file was a copy of the court order setting a hearing date for the Baby Doe matter. It was the same order I'd found in the file at the courthouse, except that it also contained a brief note scrawled in pencil, possibly by my father. The note said, "Earl Bradley, Freedom Beach," followed by a phone number with Pineland's area code.

Both Earl Bradley and Freedom Beach were familiar names to me, and to many others in Paradise County. It was all very curious. I took the file with me, drove home and called Cassandra. She'd be very interested, I knew, in the story of Freedom Beach.

29

We met again that night at the Tropics Bar. Cassandra, who must have traveled with trunks full of clothes, was in purple—an elegantly cut jacket over a tight, knee-length skirt. When the waiter came by, I ordered a margarita. She settled for a glass of Sauvignon blanc.

"I thought you were a Jack Daniel's man," she said.

"Not always. We're in the Tropics Bar, so I might as well go with the theme tonight."

"Didn't you mention once you had problems with alcohol?"

"Big problems. It's under control. Or I should say I think it is. But I know for sure that if I have more than two drinks, I'm gone for the night. It's like a magic line I can't cross or the demons appear. I suppose you could say I'm a part-time alcoholic."

"I've never heard of such a thing."

"Me neither. Maybe I'm just kidding myself and one of these days I'll go off the deep end again and stay there. But as of this evening, I remain a model of sobriety."

"Well, stay that way. I need you to be sober. Now, tell me about this Earl Bradley fellow and Freedom Beach," she said, so I did.

The story of Freedom Beach began in 1962, when Bradley, who owned a plumbing and heating business in Minneapolis, made a deal to buy ten acres of land on Fortune Lake, a clear, deep body of water at the southwest corner of Paradise County. As it so happens, the supper club where my father and mother went drinking the night she died was near the same lake. Small world, as they say.

The lake was already well developed by the 1960s, with cabins and houses along much of its shore. No one thought much of the deal Earl Bradley had struck until a story in the old *Pineland Pioneer* revealed he was Black and that he intended to build several cabins on the property, to be used as summer rentals by families of color from the Twin Cities. Minnesota in 1962 had laws that made public accommodations such as resorts open to all. But Blacks rarely felt welcome at lake resorts, which catered to an almost exclusively white clientele. Bradley, a striver of the old school who had overcome all manner of bias on the way to building his successful business, believed Black families needed a summer retreat of their own where they could relax free of any racist hassles.

He looked for lakeside property for months before he learned of the land on Fortune Lake. The acreage was part of a farm owned by a crusty old Norwegian bachelor named Einar Gimmestad. Approaching seventy, Gimmestad was preparing to retire and wanted to sell off the lakeside portion of his farm to raise some cash.

Bradley went up to visit Gimmestad and the two men, perhaps to the surprise of both, immediately hit it off. Unlike most of his neighbors on the lake, Gimmestad had no particular attitudes about Black people, and he agreed to sell the property to Bradley. "I see no reason why I shouldn't sell to him," Gimmestad later told the *Pioneer*. "He's a good, hard-working man and there's nothing wrong with his money."

Pretty much everyone else on lake, however, objected to the proposed sale and tried to block it through their property association. The group ginned up a lawsuit in district court that was clearly motivated by nothing more than naked prejudice. The sale, it was claimed, would violate various county land use regulations relating to lot size, drainage, septic systems and anything else the association's clever lawyer could think of.

That lawyer was my father, then just beginning his practice in Pineland. But not even the fine legal mind of Philip Zweifel could make sausage out of shit, and a judge threw out the case. Bradley eventually built ten cabins on the property, which he named Freedom Beach.

"It's still going strong," I told Cassandra after I'd spun out the tale. "Families from as far away as Chicago own the cabins now."

"So it sounds like your father was a racist, too," Cassandra said. "Interesting."

"I don't know that. He certainly wasn't a KKKer like dear old granddad. He didn't argue the case on racial grounds, from what I know."

"Okaaaay," Cassandra said, drawing out the word in a way that left little doubt what she thought my father must have been. "I'll take your word for it. So, what do you make of Earl Bradley's apparent connection to Baby Doe? Is it possible he may actually have been the baby's father, rather than Peter Swindell?"

"I doubt it. I'm guessing that by nineteen eighty-five Bradley would have been in his late sixties or early seventies. A little old for siring kids, don't you think?"

"Probably. Besides, that lawyer I talked to, Seymour, was definitely under the impression Peter had fathered another child here in Pineland." Cassandra leaned back and thought for a minute, then said, "Am I safe in assuming there weren't many Black folks around here in nineteen eighty-five?"

"You are. I'd bet there were even fewer then than now."

"You know what I'm thinking?"

"I have a pretty good idea, but tell me."

"Well, I'm thinking maybe the reason Earl Bradley became involved with Baby Doe is that the baby was Black. Or at least had a Black mother."

"And that could well be Patricia Gordon if Peter was the father."

Cassandra nodded and said, "It looks like I might have a brother. Jesus, it's strange. I'm not sure I can believe it."

"Well, we don't know for sure. But if you do have a brother, he could be in Pineland right now, name unknown, and he has to be the person who sent you that letter pretending to be Peter. That would also mean he's very probably the Serenader and maybe a murderer as well. This isn't good, Cassandra. I don't think he has a happy family reunion in mind."

"Doesn't seem that way, does it?" She was shaking her head, still trying to make sense of the situation. She took a sip of wine and said, "He must look white. Otherwise he'd stand out here."

"He definitely would."

"Shit. This is all too goddamn crazy." She paused, then said, "I suppose Earl Bradley must be dead by now."

"Seems likely."

"Do you know if he had a family?"

"No idea, but I'm sure we could find out. He must have been a well-known figure in Minneapolis's Black community, and I'm guessing the fight over Freedom Beach drew some attention in the Minneapolis newspapers."

"Makes sense. I'll call Jocko and have him do some digging. He's a genius at tracking down people, dead or alive. If Earl Bradley has surviving family members, they shouldn't be too hard to locate."

"I wish you luck," I said, "and please, please, be vigilant."

"I will. How about you. What's next?"

"I don't know. The way things are going, I feel like Wile E. Coyote down at the bottom of the canyon, waiting for the next anvil to drop."

"You'll be all right. I think you're quick enough to dodge an anvil or two."

"Let's hope so," I said.

After I finished my margarita, Cassandra left to return to her room—she had some work to do for her law firm—and I headed out to the parking lot. I wasn't in a mood to go home so I drove into town to the Dead Lumberjack. The place was packed. A less-than-stellar country western band was at work on a small stage at the rear, grinding through a song about bad whiskey and worse women, or something to that effect. I looked around for Kat but didn't see her behind the bar. The band was just finishing their song when I spotted Kat in a booth, talking to Ed Boudreau. I went over to join them.

Kat saw me coming and directed me to her side of the booth.

"You're just in time," she said. "Ed's been telling me a secret. It's about Peter."

Ed didn't look drunk—I'd never seen him that way—but he was enjoying a nice buzz, not to mention his favorite pastime of staring at Kat's bosom. He said, "As you know, I consider Miss Berglund a fine person who can be trusted to keep whatever I tell her in the strictest confidence until she passes it on to everybody at the bar. Care to share in our little secret, Paul?"

"What good are secrets if you can't share them?" I said.

"Exactly. So here's what I was telling the lovely Miss Berglund. It's about that 'cloud fund' Peter was pouring money into. Well, guess what? It was blackmail money. Somebody had their hooks into him."

I'd entertained the same idea, but with no proof, and I wasn't sure Ed could be believed. He likes to tell stories about white mischief in all of its varieties, but sometimes he greatly embellishes the details. "How do you know this?" I asked.

"Let's just say I have a very reliable source in the banking community."

"As in Toby Lucker at the State Bank of Pineland," I said, recalling my earlier conversation with Peter's main finance guy in town. "He told me he thought the money was going to charity."

"I have no comment in regards to that," Ed said. "But believe me, Peter admitted to a certain person that he was being blackmailed."

"Over what?"

Ed shrugged. "Who can say? Peter was a man with many vices. My guess is that it was some sort of sex thing. Peter never could keep his dick in his pants."

"Definitely a problem with Peter," Kat agreed. "Restless dick syndrome, I think the doctors call it."

"Many must have it," I said, then asked Ed how much money the blackmailer had supposedly extracted from Peter.

"Close to a hundred grand from what I've been told. Not a fortune for a man like Peter but enough to worry about."

"And you think the blackmailer may be the same person who caused Peter to disappear?"

"That's for you to figure out," Ed said as he slid out of the booth. "Me, I'm just an old Indian trying to keep white people honest. It's a never-ending job."

"Don't complain," I said. "At least you've found a way to take white people's money. Didn't the casino have a record profit last year?"

"It did and this year is looking even better. The Great Spirit works in mysterious ways."

"He really wants to sleep with you," I said to Kat after Ed left.

"Do you think? Talk about restless dick syndrome. He has a perfectly lovely wife at home, so I'll pass. Now, are you drinking tonight, Mr. Zweifel?"

"One more margarita," I said and then told her about my meeting with Cassandra at the Tropics.

"Sounds like you two are on a mission," Kat said.

"You're right, and Cassandra's a really good partner to have. She's a tough customer."

"So are you planning to sleep with her?"

"You're acting like you're jealous, Kat. We've been through this before. I like Cassandra but, no, she's not my type. I'm not hers either. "

I didn't mention that Cassandra had told me she preferred women to men. That was her business, not mine, and I saw no point in bringing it up.

"I am not jealous," Kat protested. "Just curious, that's all."

My margarita arrived, and I hoisted the glass. "Well, here's to us, Kat, and also to my mission, which is trying to find out what the hell is going on here. I've developed a permanent headache just from thinking about it."

"I can tell you something that won't make your head feel better," Kat said. "One of Arne's deputies was in earlier tonight and he said the BCA has prepared a profile of the Serenader. Care to hear what it says?"

"Sure. I need the aggravation."

"The Serenader is a white man in his thirties or forties, a resident of Paradise County, a white-collar worker or professional, possibly divorced, a loner, and someone who, believe it or not, probably drives a high-mileage car like a Prius. Sound like anybody you know?" Kat asked with a grin.

"Can't think of a soul who'd fit that profile," I said, feeling the noose tightening around my neck. "The BCA must be mistaken."

30

On Sunday Pineland went to church, I did some reading at home, and Camus enjoyed an intoxicating ramble through fields and forests while warm sunshine buttered the countryside, hinting that spring might finally be near. But as darkness fell, a hard wind came in from the east and sirens began piercing the air.

After Paradise County's old pines were cut down and their remains incinerated in the Great Fire, a new growth of far less impressive trees—mainly aspen and birch—filled the void. These scrub species, worthless as lumber, did have value, however, as a potential source of pulp for papermaking. Darwin Swindell, Peter's grandfather, saw a moneymaking opportunity at hand and in 1920 he and other investors, among them William Zweifel, founded the Paradise Paper Company. They secured financing from a big Eastern bank and built a massive brick-and-concrete mill beside the Paradise River at the east edge of town, along with a dam to provide hydroelectric power.

All hailed the new mill when it opened in 1922. It provided hundreds of jobs and proved Pineland was an up-and-coming place, not just another forgotten hamlet in the woods. But progress is never perfect, and from day one the mill excreted from its tall smokestacks a sharp, sulfurous stink that on many days made much of Pineland smell like a huge pile of rotting garbage. Some people left town because the odor was so bad, but everybody else just got used to it as the olfactory price of prosperity.

The plant's signature product was Soft Swirl toilet tissue, which for many years could be found on every grocery store shelf next to the Charmin and Scott's. A YouTube video posted by some enterprising Pinelander shows a Soft Swirl television ad from the 1960s. In it a Betty Crocker-style housewife stands proudly in her immaculate bathroom, a toddler at her knee, and proclaims Soft Swirl "as smooth as a baby's bottom."

Naturally, Pineland's most famous product was the source of much earthy humor. As a teenager I certainly found it amusing, and when the town sponsored a contest one year for a new municipal motto, I offered an anonymous suggestion: "Pineland, we wipe America's ass." To my profound disappointment, it didn't win.

For a long time, Soft Swirl was money in the bank, at least for the Swindell family, but not even nice toilet paper can be eternally profitable. Peter's father sold the mill in the 1970s, and after that it went through several owners before a big Canadian paper company acquired it in the early 2000s.

But the old mill rapidly faded into obsolescence, and it closed for good in 2012. About one-hundred-fifty jobs went with it, but at least the big stink was gone. The Canadians were in no hurry to spend millions to demolish the mill and remediate the polluted ground beneath it, so the old industrial hulk still stands as Pineland's largest ruin.

Around ten o'clock Sunday night, as banks of low clouds slid beneath a waxing crescent moon, a homeowner a mile or so from the mill heard a loud boom and went out to investigate. Before long he saw an orange glow off to the east and knew at once the old mill must be burning. Pineland's volunteer fire department arrived at the mill twelve minutes later and encountered a towering conflagration well beyond their means to contain.

Firefighters also found a dead man and they all knew who he was. His body was slumped up against a chain-link fence in a dog walk area the mill's owners leased to the county. A single bullet hole pierced the man's forehead. There was also an interesting piece of paper folded in the breast pocket of his flannel shirt.

Marty Moreland's troubles were over. Mine were about to become much worse.

The fire, later determined to be the work of an arsonist, raged all night and left behind another ruin to go with the two Swindell mansions. More importantly from my point of view, the location of the fire—the mill is just outside Pineland's municipal limits—meant Arne's office had jurisdiction over Marty's murder. The wolf, it seemed, would be in charge of looking into the unfortunate demise of the sheep.

I didn't hear the sirens because my house is on the opposite side of town from the mill, but I did hear my phone just after midnight. Arne was calling. He instructed me to come to his office at once for an interview.

"What about?" I asked.

"Just get your ass down here."

"No, I think I'll stay in bed with Camus. He likes to cuddle this time of night. Of course, if you'll tell me why you're so desperate to see me—"

Arne finally shared the bad news. He added, "Marty left behind a note and your name's on it. So we need to talk. Understand?"

I probably should have known my name would come up front and center in Marty's death. I'd become the magnet attached to every bad thing that had happened over the last week. Now I'd have to tussle yet again with Arne, and I wasn't looking forward to it.

The dreary concrete-block building occupied by the Paradise County Sheriff's Department is a stone's throw from the courthouse. Arne's office is just off the main entrance, and I found him there working on a Marlboro as he scrolled through his iPhone. His office is as spare as a monk's cell, as though any sort of memorabilia or even family photos might be a sign of weakness. I was surprised to find Arne alone.

"Where are the BCA boys?" I asked. "Don't they want a piece of me?"

"They're on their way. Apparently they don't like it here so they go home on weekends. I really miss them."

"Me too."

Arne handed me his phone. "Here's a picture of the note we found in Marty's shirt pocket. Why don't you tell me what it's all about?"

The printed note read: "If anything happens to me, ask Zweifel what I told him."

I ignored the note and said, "I assume you've notified Doris."

"Yeah, I went over to the house and talked with her a little."

"How's she doing?"

Arne shrugged. "Poorly. What would you expect? Her husband's on the way to the morgue. But let's talk about you and that note."

"First I need to know more about Marty's death."

"There's not much to say. He left his house around nine, supposedly to go out for a few drinks. That's the last Doris saw of him. We found his car in the lot at the dog park. Somebody met him there and put a bullet through his brain."

I had no faith that any investigation conducted under Arne's direction would be fair and impartial, given the fact he appeared to have a good motive for killing Marty. But I wanted to see if Arne was at least going through the motions.

"So you don't have any suspects at this point?"

"Maybe I'm looking at one. Didn't you and Marty used to walk your mutts at the dog park?"

"Camus is not a mutt and, yes, I was out there with Marty and his dog a few times. So were many other people."

"Okay, so the two of you were dog-walking pals. That's nice. Now, how about you fill me on what Marty told you?

Must have been something important or he wouldn't have bothered to mention it in his note."

Arne's face is usually as impassive as granite, but I sensed he was anxious, probably because he suspected what Marty had told me.

"Yeah, Arne, you could say it was something important," I said before delivering a full account of my last conversation with Marty. When I was done, Arne slowly shook his head and said, "Well, that's too bad. I don't blame Marty, though. He's been a sick man for quite a while now."

Arne clearly had his defense all lined up and ready to go. "And just what kind of illness was Marty suffering from?" I asked.

"From what I understand, he's been depressed. That's what Doris said. Maybe he was a little paranoid, too. He thought people were after him. And I guess he believed I was one of them. Let me show you something."

Arne opened his desk drawer, dug out a pair of traffic citations and passed them over to me. "In the last month alone Marty was cited twice by my deputies for speeding—one time he was doing seventy in a forty zone—and I'm sure it made him suspicious I was somehow out to harm him. I became the enemy in his mind and so he struck back at me."

Did Arne really expect me to believe such nonsense? "Ah, I see. He was so unhappy about two speeding tickets he decided to implicate you in Jill Lorrimer's death. Quite a leap on his part, wouldn't you say?"

"Strange but true, I'm afraid," Arne said, his hard blue eyes as dead as last spring's flowers.

"So let's be clear. Are you saying you never called Marty and told him to 'shut up or else' about Jill Lorrimer? That sounds like a threat to me."

"I called him and told him he shouldn't be spreading malicious rumors. There was no threat."

"And you didn't have anything to do with Jill's death?"

"Of course not. I hardly knew the woman."

There was no point in going further. Marty's statements to me didn't amount to real proof of anything, as Arne was well aware. He'd just deny everything and there wasn't much I could do about it.

"Now, back to you, counselor," Arne said. "Where were you tonight?"

"Home, sleeping, until you woke me up."

"Alone?"

"Camus was with me."

"Yeah, and he's a great alibi witness. So I'll ask: Did you kill Marty?"

"No, and besides, what would my motive be?"

"Who the fuck knows? Who knows anything about all this shit that's going on. It's driving me crazy. None of it makes much sense."

"I agree, but maybe it will before long."

"What do you mean?"

"I'll say no more. Nobody's sharing anything with me these days so I'll return the favor."

"So you're playing boy detective, is that it?"

"Something like that," I said, but I didn't tell Arne that the real detective, looking into her own family history, was Cassandra Ellis.

Camus was barking at the front door when I pulled into my driveway. Dawn was still hours away, but I knew I wouldn't be able to get back to sleep. Camus and I had a long discussion while he chewed on a bone. By the time daylight arrived, I'd made up my mind what to do.

First, I called Cassandra to update her on the latest news, including Marty Moreland's murder and my interview with Arne.

"Was Mr. Moreland a friend of yours?" she asked.

"An acquaintance. He was a decent guy."

"Well, I'm sorry to hear about it. Do you really think the sheriff was involved with his murder? That's a scary idea."

"Yes it is, but I think it's possible. All I lack is anything that resembles concrete proof. What about you? Making any progress on the Earl Bradley front?"

"Not sure. Jocko is working on it. "

"All right, keep me posted."

"Will do," she said and disconnected.

My next call went to Jason Braddock at the BCA. "I have some interesting information for you," I told him. "Where can we meet?"

Jason had been staying at a motel out by the interstate, with a Perkins restaurant next door. We met there and found a booth well away from other diners. Jason was in a well-tailored blue suit that showed off his muscular frame. His shaved head—standard cop issue—gave him the menacing, tough-guy look law enforcement types seem to prize. He'd been an asshole in his dealings with me, but I was hoping he would at least listen to what I had to say.

"This better be good," he said, and he wasn't talking about the omelets we'd ordered.

"I promise you, it will be, if you're willing to keep an open mind." I then shared all the details of my talk with Marty and Arne's reaction to it. I finished by lining up the pieces as I saw them. "I think you should look into the possibility that Arne killed Marty to shut him up about what happened to Jill Lorrimer. And if there was a coverup, and things started going south, who's to say Arne didn't have something to do with Peter's disappearance and maybe even Dewey's murder?"

"Well, that's quite a tale," Jason said. "I don't suppose you have any proof?"

"All I know is what Marty told me, and I think it was pretty close to a dying declaration. What reason would he have to lie?"

"Maybe he was paranoid, just like Arne said. Or maybe you just like to lie."

"Do you really believe that?"

"Doesn't matter what I believe. You of all people know that. So you've told me this wonderful story. Now, what the hell am I am supposed to do about it?"

"Start looking at Arne, and in the meantime don't trust him for a second. It's the only way you'll ever get at the truth."

"You know what, the one thing I've learned since coming to this snake pit of a town is that I can't trust anybody here, least of all you. So, thanks for the information. I'll take it all under advisement. How's that?"

"You're making a big mistake, Jason," I said, and for once I was right.

31

Marty was sliced open for an autopsy in Duluth that afternoon. The coroner's report, followed by ballistics tests at the BCA, revealed that the .38-caliber slug recovered from Marty's brain had come from the same gun that killed Dewey Swindell. Since no cartridges were found at either murder scene, the assumption was that both men had been shot with a revolver.

Toxicology tests showed Marty had no alcohol in his system, indicating he'd lied to his wife about going out for a drink. No drugs of any consequence showed up, either. If Marty was depressed, as Arne claimed, he wasn't taking anything for his condition. A careful examination of Marty's body and clothes uncovered no trace evidence that might help identify his killer. Whoever was on a crime spree in Pineland remained a ghost, invisible as the wind.

The e-mail, sent to my official Paradise County address, arrived just after three p.m. It read, "Go to the quarry. You know why."

The message came from an AOL account identified as "rmhiller." I had no idea who that was but I was pretty sure who'd actually sent the message and what it meant.

I briefly considered my options, then made another phone call to Jason Braddock.

Ten miles northwest of Pineland the Paradise River races through a foaming stretch of rapids at the bottom of a narrow sandstone gorge. Known as Paradise Dalles, it's the county's beauty spot and it forms the centerpiece of a popular state park. The mile-long run of whitewater attracts canoeists and kayakers from miles around, and in late spring when the river is high the gorge can get downright crowded with thrill seekers. A thick second-growth forest laced with trails overlooks the gorge, which has the look of a wild, untouched place.

It isn't. Long before the whitewater enthusiasts arrived, the southern end of the gorge, where cliffs rise forty feet, was the site of a quarry operated by the Paradise Stone Company. My great grandfather Johannes Zweifel was a founder of the company, which opened in 1889 amid the usual high hopes. A spur railroad line was built to serve the quarry, and a small village called Rockledge sprang up nearby, complete with two saloons and a general store.

Neither Rockledge nor the quarry lasted for long. Like Johannes, twenty of Rockledge's inhabitants perished in the Great Fire of 1892, and the town was never rebuilt. The quarry survived the fire and did well for a few years, shipping stone to as far away as Chicago and St. Louis. But its signature product—the smooth, radiantly colored sandstone known as Paradise Pink—fell out of favor after 1900 and the quarry closed for good in 1907.

An unmarked dirt road known only to locals leads to the old quarry. Jason and I, joined by two state troopers familiar with the area, drove down the deeply rutted road late that afternoon. Jason had been skeptical when I showed him the e-mail message, but he was just curious enough to go out to the quarry, which is mostly used these days as a late-night rendezvous for teenagers interested in the ever popular trifecta of alcohol, drugs and sex. A thickly overgrown jumble of waste rocks littered with bottles, cans and used condoms forms the base of the main quarry face.

"You stay put," Jason said when he parked his state-issued SUV. "I'll look around with the troopers."

The three men fanned out as I stood by the SUV. They stumbled around the ragged piles of rocks for fifteen minutes before Jason returned, cell phone in hand, and told me to get back into the SUV. It wasn't a request.

"Did you find something?" I asked.

"Maybe," he said but wouldn't elaborate.

Arne showed up a half-hour later with a retinue of deputies. Looking royally pissed, he had an animated conversation with Jason out of my hearing range. Then he came over to Jason's SUV, where I was still ensconced in the back seat.

"Why didn't you call me, you fucker?" he said when I rolled down the window.

"Why would I? I don't trust you, Arne."

249

"And you trust that shithead from the BCA? Well, go ahead and see where that gets you. Now that they've found Peter's body, he'll be looking to nail your ass."

Other pleasantries were exchanged before Arne stomped off, but at least I knew what Jason and the troopers had discovered.

Just before sunset a BCA mobile crime and evidence team rolled in from St. Paul. I learned all the details later. Under banks of bright lights, the crime technicians dug into the stony ground and found Peter Swindell's partially decomposed body, wrapped in black plastic lawn bags. Curiously, he was naked and no clothes were found nearby. It didn't require the expertise of a forensic scientist to determine the cause of death. Peter had been executed with a shot to the back of the head, and by the look of his body, he'd been dead for at least two weeks.

All police interview rooms tend to look alike, and I suspect there's a malicious designer somewhere who specializes in making them as claustrophobic and discomforting as possible. The interview room at Arne's department is a fine representative of its kind—windowless, walled with gray acoustic tiles and just big enough for a table and four chairs. It also offers the usual two-way glass mirror so that the proceedings can be observed by parties unknown.

"So, let's go over this again," Jason Braddock said as he stared at me from across the table. "How'd you know which quarry to go to? I understand there are several of them up along the river."

We'd been at it since eleven o'clock and by my watch it was now half-past midnight. Arne was sitting next to Jason, forming the usual interrogatory tag-team. As teams go, however, they weren't very cohesive. Jason wanted to take the lead but Arne kept horning in, and occasional bouts of bickering broke out. I wondered if Jason had taken my warnings about Arne to heart. Or maybe he just didn't like him. Even so, the two lawmen were in complete agreement that the evening's events cast me in a dubious light.

As for how I'd led Jason to the right quarry, I said, "It was the logical choice because it was established by my great grandfather. The Serenader has been targeting me from the start and that's why he sent me that e-mail. He knew which quarry I'd go to."

Arne said, "This Serenader fellow must be quite a Zweifel family historian. The quarry's been closed forever and yet he knows all about it. How do you suppose that is?"

"Maybe he reads, Arne. Some people do. As I recall, there was a story in the *Tattler* a few years back about the quarry and its history. It's not a big secret."

Jason ignored the history lesson and said, "And you're telling us you had no idea Peter's body was buried out there, correct?"

"No idea whatsoever, until I got the e-mail. That's when the possibility occurred to me."

In truth, I'd begun to suspect Peter's body might be at the quarry after the Serenader referred to "buried secrets" lying "among the stones." I'd even been tempted to go out to the quarry to look around to see if I was right. But I decided against it because I didn't want more suspicion coming

251

my way. That's why I'd called Jason after receiving the e-mail. Better to have authorities find the body than me.

"And you think the e-mail was from the Serenader?"

"That's my guess. I'm sure your tech people can track down where it came from."

They did. The AOL account belonged to Roy and Mildred Hiller, an elderly couple who live in Pineland. Someone had hacked into their account by the simple expedient of breaking into their house while they were gone. The burglar then logged on to the couple's computer, the passwords to which were conveniently written down in a desk drawer. It was a hack that couldn't be traced.

I was about to call it a night when Chad Barrington joined the interrogation. He'd apparently been watching and listening and now he had a few questions of his own. He was wearing a banker's three-piece suit—no casual late-night garb for him— and he took the last available chair in the interview room, next to me. I smiled at him. He didn't smile back.

After adjusting his perfectly knotted red silk tie, he swung around to face me, his blue eyes as cold and sharp as icicles, and said, "I'm struck, Mr. Zweifel, by how much everything that's happened here seems to involve you in one way or another. The text messages from the Swindells, both now deceased. All those postings from the Serenader you have an uncanny way of finding. The note in the late Mr. Moreland's pocket. And now an e-mail that leads you to direct the authorities to Peter Swindell's grave. It's really quite extraordinary. How do you manage it?"

A dozen smart-ass responses came to mind but I opted for a straightforward answer. "It's obvious someone is very deliberately putting me in the center of things for reasons I don't understand. But I'm sure now that you've joined the investigation, Chad, the mystery will be solved in no time."

"Oh, we'll figure this out, Mr. Zweifel," Barrington said, "I assure you of that."

I did not take those to be comforting words.

I got home around one o'clock in the morning and called Cassandra despite the hour. She picked up immediately.

"Sorry to disturb you," I said, "but I've got some bad news."

I told her about the discovery of Peter's body and filled in what details I could. "He was shot, probably not long after he was kidnapped. Beyond that, I don't know very much."

There was a long pause before Cassandra said, "I suppose I shouldn't be surprised. It wasn't likely he'd still be alive. But damn, I would like to have met him, just once, you know, and talked."

"I understand. You wouldn't have cared much for him—Peter really was an asshole—but maybe at least you could have gotten some answers."

"Like why he abandoned me and never even tried to get in touch? Yeah, that would have been nice."

We talked for a good half-hour. I could tell Cassandra was shaken even if she'd never known her father, and about all I could offer were the standard consolations. As always, they seemed grossly inadequate.

"What will happen to the body?" Cassandra finally asked.

"The medical examiner will have to perform an autopsy, of course, and then I guess it'll be up to somebody to bury Peter. You may be the only family he has left."

"Unless I have a brother," Cassandra said. "But I doubt he'd be interested in attending the funeral. So what about you? I imagine you're under suspicion again."

"When haven't I been? I feel like the Serenader's pawn-in-residence. Whenever he needs to make something happen, he moves me into place. I'm getting sick of it. In any case, the BCA guys are particularly eager to pin something on me."

"Well, if you need a good lawyer, you know who to call."

"I don't know that I could afford you."

"Don't worry," Cassandra said. "I'd give you a special deal."

"Thanks, I may need it."

After I got off the phone, my old buddy Jack began to beckon, but I didn't give in. Sometimes painful sobriety is the suffering a person requires, and I was in that situation. I couldn't afford to let the world get away from me. I went straight to bed, Camus plopping down beside me, and slept until nine a.m.

By the time I reached my office, Doug was well into his usual dissection of the day's press coverage. "The *StarTribune* and the *Pioneer Press* have the story online. It's a big deal now that they've found Peter's body and of course there's also that new message from the Serenader."

Well, shit. During their hours of questioning me, Jason and Arne hadn't mentioned any new message.

"Where did you read about the message?" I asked Doug. "Does Tommy have it already?"

"He sure does. Right in his blog. Word for word. I don't know how he does it. Arne and those BCA guys must really be pissed."

Too bad for them but good for me. I opened Tommy's blog and there it was:

Now there are two, Zweifel and Sigurdson. What do they know and how do they know it? THE WOMAN is searching for an answer, but will she find it? Let the truth shine forth.

The Serenader

Tommy's blog included a photo of the message, which had been affixed to a smooth slab of stone near Peter's body. The usual thumb drive was taped to the bottom of the message.

Like Doug, I wondered how Tommy had insinuated himself so thoroughly into the investigation that he had access to crime scene photos. More importantly, I wondered what was coming next. The Serenader had alluded to five men in his first message. Now, in just over a fortnight, three of them were dead. The odds weren't comforting. Was I the next target? Or Cassandra? I had no idea.

Maybe it was time to dig out my father's old revolver.

32

I called Cassandra right away to report on the Serenader's latest communication, which we agreed wasn't especially revealing. She also had some news for me.

"I just heard from Jocko. He's located a daughter of Earl Bradley. She lives in Minneapolis and works there. I'm going to drive down today and try to make contact with her. I'm hoping she'll be willing to talk to me."

"Sounds promising," I said. "Let me know what you find out."

I tried to keep a low profile for the rest of the day but it wasn't easy. The discovery of Peter's body touched off a new media frenzy. I received a dozen phone messages and e-mails from TV news people, all eager to tell my side of the story in a thirty-second sound bite. *Good Morning America* thought I'd be an interesting guest, and a writer from *Vanity Fair* wanted to insert me into his impending saga of trouble in flyover land. I stiffed the lot of them and spent most of the day holed up in the courthouse law library, away from the news-hungry hordes.

Services for Marty Moreland were scheduled for ten o'clock Wednesday morning at Swaboda's Funeral Home, which is known around town as the "pregnant spaceship." The building, perhaps not one of Frank Lloyd Wright's masterpieces, is round, bows out slightly in the middle and has small circular windows. Wright came down from space and landed in Pineland because of my uncle, Jack Swaboda, who built the funeral home.

Crazy Jack, as everyone in the family called him, was my mother's only brother and a famous character around town. He might still be alive if he hadn't, at age seventy-five, tried to run his snowmobile across a lake coated in ice about as thick as his fingernails. He and his sled were found a day later under thirty feet of water and everyone agreed it was a suitably outlandish way for him to die. Long before his final snowmobile adventure, Jack had become smitten with Wright's work after seeing a gas station the legendary architect designed in a nearby town. So Jack ordered up a Wright of his very own, at great expense.

Although the building proved to be trouble from the start—Jack had to patch the leaky roof every year—he loved his big architectural toy and in the end his faith was rewarded. A small but steady stream of tourists, some from as far away as Japan, began arriving in Pineland to gaze upon the wonders of what was billed as "Frank Lloyd Wright's Only Mortuary." Jack happily accommodated them by offering "special guided tours" for a mere twenty dollars a head, turning his house of death into a nice little money machine.

My cousin-in-law Dale Shiffley still provides tours, for thirty dollars, but he doesn't share Jack's passion for the building. Dale would like to sell it if he could, but a buyer has yet to appear out of the Wrightian woodwork. I don't usually communicate much with Dale, since mortuary science isn't among my fervent interests, so I was surprised when he called Wednesday morning shortly after seven.

"Are you coming to the service for Marty?" he asked.

An odd question, I thought. What did it matter to Dale whether I showed up or not? And why the hell was he calling me at such a ridiculous hour? "A little early to be asking that question, isn't it? Don't worry, I'll be there. But the service is at ten. What's going on?"

"It's hard to explain, but could you come to the funeral home right now? There's something you need to see."

"And what would that be?"

"Just come over, okay? I don't know what to do here. I need your advice."

I couldn't get any more out of Dale, so I told him I'd be there as soon as I could. When I drove up to the funeral home a half-hour later, Dale was waiting for me outside the front door.

"Thanks so much for coming," he said. His face, normally caked in mourning makeup, was alive with agitation. "This is all very weird, Paul. Very weird. I'll show you. He's in the basement."

"Who are you talking about?"

"Marty. That's what I called you about. You'll see."

I followed Dale down the basement into a large, tile-lined embalming room equipped with all the handy tools morticians use to make the dead look even deader. The odor of formaldehyde wafted into my nostrils. A dark steel casket, its lid open, was propped on a cart in the center of the room. Marty was in it, dressed in a black suit with a red tie.

"Have a look for yourself," Dale said.

I did, and it was certainly an unexpected sight. Carefully placed atop Marty's crotch was an eight-by-ten-inch color photo that showed Arne with a topless young woman sitting on his lap. She was well endowed, and there was a striking tattoo of a nude, winged female figure beneath her breasts. Arne, who had a drunken grin on his face, was playing with one of her nipples. The photo included a message, neatly typed on a half-sheet of paper. It read:

Sigurdson at Peter Swindell's mansion. Reward for services rendered. Bring the sheriff to justice and let the truth shine forth. The Serenader.

Although the woman's face was turned away from the camera, I knew who she had to be. Marty had been right about Arne and a dalliance with the late Jill Lorrimer. Arne's supposed investigation into her death suddenly looked like a sham, and he was about to be in the deepest of deep shit. I couldn't say I felt bad for him.

"Any idea how the photo got here?" I asked Dale.

"Somebody broke in last night and must have left it. I found the back door jimmied open when I came in this morning. I thought we'd been burglarized, but I didn't find anything missing."

"Are there any surveillance cameras by that door?"

"No. I mean, why would there be? Who'd want to break into a funeral home?"

"Okay, so what happened after you discovered the break-in?"

"I looked around to see if anything had been disturbed but everything seemed to be okay. Then I opened Marty's casket for a final check and that's when I saw the photo. It was a real shock, I'll tell you that. Have you ever heard of such a bizarre thing? Anyway, I thought I should call you before anyone else. What should we do?"

Good question, Dale. The picture, assuming it wasn't a Photoshopped fake, was a bomb designed to blow up the investigation into everything that had happened over the past two weeks. Arne would come under intense scrutiny, not just over the photo but also in connection with Marty's death, not to mention Peter's and Dewey's. At the least, Arne would be fatally compromised, and he and possibly his entire department would be forced out of the investigation.

I'd be in for more trouble as well. Dale's decision to contact me before anyone else meant that I was once again linked to the Serenader's handiwork. The usual suspicions were sure to follow.

"Just leave everything where it is," I told Dale. "I'll call Jim Meyers and let him deal with it."

Before I tapped in the Pineland Police Department's number on my cell, I took a few shots of the photo showing Arne and Jill and sent everything up to the cloud. I figured it wouldn't hurt to have my own copies of the photo, just in case. Arne was quite possibly a criminal in uniform, Jim

Meyers had his own agenda and I didn't trust the two Jasons. Better safe than sorry.

Dale went over to a small desk in the corner of the room and sat down. I was surprised to see him pull out a pack of Marlboro Lights. He fired one up and took in a long draw of smoke.

"I didn't know you smoked, Dale."

"I don't," he said. "But sometimes—"

Dale offered me a cigarette and I took it.

"I don't smoke, either," I said, and enjoyed my first hit of tobacco in twenty years.

Jim Meyers and two of his finest arrived at the funeral home just after eight. When Jim saw the photo in Marty's casket, he could barely contain his glee. He despised Arne, who had once called him "Dumbo Jim" to his face, and now sweet revenge perfumed the air.

"Oh my, look who got caught with his hand on the titties," Jim said. "So, do we know who the bimbo is?"

"I'm not sure," I said, "but the tattoo should make her easy to identify."

"Yeah, right. Probably one of the party girls from the casino."

"Could be," I acknowledged. Like Arne, I'd never been dazzled by Jim's intellect, and he didn't seem to be making the connection that had occurred to me when it came to identifying the woman. I saw no reason to give him a hint.

Dale, who'd been working himself into a panic, now piped up: "Chief, we've got a funeral scheduled here in two hours and people will expect to see, you know, the casket and Marty."

"Sorry, but you'll have to postpone the funeral. Tomorrow should be fine. "

"Well, it's very late for that and I'm not sure—"

"Doesn't matter. We'll have to spend some time here, go over everything with a fine tooth comb and, you know, all of that."

"Shit," Dale said—the first time I'd ever heard him utter that word—before he went upstairs to work on rescheduling the services.

Meanwhile, Jim managed to locate the police department's only evidence technician, who was no doubt enjoying a peaceful breakfast, and dragged the poor guy in to look for fingerprints or other evidence on the photo. Jim also called Jason Braddock at the BCA, but I didn't catch their conversation. Then Jim interviewed Dale and me, separately, but there wasn't much we could tell him.

"Jesus, I'm a nervous wreck," Dale said after we were finally cut loose. He grabbed his Marlboros and headed out for a smoke.

"You'll be all right," I said. "They don't suspect you of anything. I'm the one who's in the muck."

Once we got outside, Dale offered me a smoke but I turned it down. "One was enough," I said, knowing that what I really wanted was a drink. Maybe several.

I went straight to the courthouse after leaving Dale and got out the Lorrimer file, just to be certain. I took a good look at the autopsy photos and saw that Jill Lorrimer had tattoos on her ankles, her upper arms and beneath her chest, where a winged woman cast her eyes toward heaven. Arne, on the other hand, appeared to be heading in the opposite direction.

I called Cassandra from my office and told her about the incriminating photo in Marty's casket. She thought it was hilarious.

"Nice to see the sheriff has some shit of his own to deal with," she said. "Who knew there could be a sex scandal in Pineland?"

"You'd be surprised what goes on here," I said, "but sex may be the least of Arne's problems at the moment. What about Earl Bradley's daughter? Have you talked to her yet?"

"No, but I've got her work number. She's a drug counselor. Her office told me she's on some of kind of retreat and isn't taking any messages. She'll be back late Friday. I'll try to catch her then."

"Okay, but stay down in the cities for the time being, all right? There's nothing you can do here."

"Doesn't sound like you're accomplishing a whole lot either."

"Not true. I'm keeping the Serenader busy. Too bad I don't know who he is. I'd love to have a chat with him."

"Maybe you already have," Cassandra said before she disconnected, "and you just don't know it."

That night, I poured a shot of Jack, downed it, and was reaching for another round of solace when Camus came up and gave me a disapproving look. Camus is the moral arbiter of our household, and I sometimes think he was put on Earth for no other purpose than to keep me from doing really stupid things. With a few exceptions, among them my pointless binge on the night Peter disappeared, I've carefully rationed my drinking under my loyal companion's watchful blue eyes.

Now, he was staring at me, and I knew what he'd be saying if he could talk. Don't be a fool, Zweifel. Don't be a fool. As always, Camus was right. I put Jack back on the shelf and went into the bedroom. I felt very tired. I took off my shoes and lay down on the bed. Camus came up beside me. I stroked his head and then he rolled over for the inevitable belly rub. After a while, we both fell asleep.

33

Most funerals in Pineland are still of the traditional dust-to-dust religious variety, tolling the gloomy bell of life's brevity while offering the distant prospect of resurrection. But "celebrations of life" are becoming more common, the idea being that no matter how measly or misguided your existence, you deserve a cheery sendoff at a hope-filled gathering designed to dispel the grim likelihood of oblivion. Marty managed to get both treatments. Reverend Ronnie and his flock prayed over Marty at a Wednesday night service at the Call of God Church. I skipped that prayer fest, but I was on hand at Swaboda's Thursday morning for Marty's delayed final good-bye.

Dale greeted me at the door. "How you doing? Have those two guys from the BCA talked to you yet about the photo?"

They had, the day before at my office, and the Jasons were intrigued when I identified the woman in the photo as Jill

Lorrimer. They were now seriously entertaining the possibility Arne had murdered Marty to cover his own crimes

"Yes, we had a lovely time," I told Dale. "I hear they had a much longer talk with Arne last night."

"Geez, I bet he had some explaining to do."

"Knowing Arne, I'm sure he had a wonderful fable all ready to go. We'll see. How about you? Did the Jasons pay you a visit?"

"They interviewed me yesterday morning. It wasn't too bad. I think they understand I was just an innocent bystander."

In my experience bystanding doesn't always equate with innocence, but no matter, because Dale quickly morphed into his official bereavement mode. "So sad about Marty, isn't it? He was such a sparkplug. Who would want to kill him like that?"

"Don't know," I said, truthfully, then offered up a cliché of my own, "Time will tell."

"Well, I'll be glad to get this business behind me," Dale said. "I'm heading to Las Vegas for a convention next week. I can't wait. Four days of sun and showgirls. Just hope nobody else dies before I leave."

"Won't you have to handle Peter's funeral pretty soon?"

"Not that I know of. I'm not even sure who'll take charge of the body when the time comes."

"Maybe all of his bankers," I said. "They like to stay close to their money."

A couple of hundred people showed up for the service, jamming into the large circular room that forms the heart of the funeral home. Family and friends clustered near the casket. Every business owner in town, Ken Michaels among them, was on hand, as were all five members of the Pineland City Council. I spotted Ed Boudreau, who was chatting with Kat Berglund and Tommy Redmond. The *Tattler* would no doubt have much to report about Marty's demise in the next edition. Reverend Ronnie was in the crowd as well, appearing to be in a much less celebratory mood than everyone else. Vern arrived on the late side and made a point of ignoring me. My beloved assistant, Doug, also made a last-minute appearance.

Arne, of course, was a no-show. Although the photo deposited in Marty's coffin was in theory a closely held piece of evidence, word of it had quickly spread. My guess was that one of Arne's disgruntled deputies, and there were several, had leaked the titillating information. People in Pineland are as interested in sex as everyone else, but they're still religious enough to think it's a dirty business, and the news that Arne had been caught cavorting with a half-naked woman at Peter's mansion was a thoroughly delicious morsel of gossip.

Law enforcement was not absent from the scene, however. Jim Meyers, in one of his used-car salesman suits, roamed the room with his usual officiousness. The Jasons were also on hand, presumably looking for clues. I could only wish them luck.

As I sat in the back row, scanning the crowd, I wondered if the Serenader was in the room. I strongly suspected he was. Whatever else he might be, the Serenader was one of ours. He moved so easily and confidently through town that he simply couldn't be a stranger. He was someone we'd say hello to the street, someone we thought we knew but who was in fact hidden behind the mask of his life. And if he really was Cassandra's brother, moving to the sounds of his own disturbing music, I feared our troubles were far from over.

There was a makeshift dais up front, and next to it Marty lay in his coffin, minus the fetching photo of Arne. Marty was nicely embalmed but still looked convincingly dead. Mayor Mary Jane Bakken served as master of ceremonies. The service lasted ninety minutes, about eighty-five more than mine will require. Amid bursts of inspirational music, friends and colleagues rose one after another to extoll Marty's virtues, many of which I had somehow failed to detect during his lifetime. As the tributes droned on, I was struck by the fact that Marty's wife, Doris, chose not to speak. Instead, she sat quietly in the first row next to her two teenage sons.

I suspected the boys had been closer to Marty than Doris was, and the younger one's shoulders heaved in grief as a recorded version of Warren Zevon's "Keep Me in Your Heart" injected a genuine note of sadness into the proceedings. Doris did her best to comfort him, but if she shed any tears, I didn't see them. Marty's infidelities, I assumed, had driven a giant wedge between them, and maybe she was all out of tears for him by the time he died.

I joined the line of well-wishers after the services, and when I reached Doris to offer condolences, she smiled and said, "It's so good to see you, Paul. It's been awhile."

"It has," I agreed. "I think the last time we talked was when we were doing *Pinafore*."

"Wasn't that great fun?"

"It was." Doris had played Mrs. Cripps in the production, and her lovely contralto was the best voice in the cast.

"Do you suppose you could come by the house tomorrow?" she asked. "I have something I want to talk about with you."

"Sure, but if it has to do with Marty's death, keep in mind I'm no longer involved in the investigation."

"I heard that. But I'd still like to talk tomorrow."

"I'd be happy to do that. How about around ten?"

"That would be great," Doris said. "See you then."

As the mourners began to disperse, the Reverend Ronnie came up for a talk. As usual, he was a vision in white, which I thought was odd. Everyone else had opted for the standard mourning attire.

He must have read my mind because he said, "I suppose you're wondering why I don't wear black at funerals. The answer is simple. Marty is now among the angels and while I mourn his passing I also know he has ascended to a better place. Marty was very much a man of God in his own way."

"I didn't know that," I said, "but I'll take your word for it."

"It's true. Of course, you wouldn't know it by what just went on. I didn't feel God's presence here today."

"Well, if it's any consolation, neither did I."

"Ha, the atheist speaks! One day, you'll see the light, I promise you. But that can wait. I have something to tell you. I had a long talk with Marty the day he died. We met at the church office late in the afternoon. Marty was carrying a terrible burden, as you're well aware. He told me about his conversation with you."

"Did he say what this burden was?"

"He told me he'd witnessed a serious crime at Peter's mansion but was afraid to report it because the sheriff had threatened him."

"And he actually used the word 'witnessed'?" Marty hadn't admitted as much in his talk with me.

"Yes."

"Did he go into any detail as to who committed the crime and what it was?"

"No, Marty was vague about that. I'm not sure why. But he did want to know if failing to report what he'd seen was a sin in the eyes of God."

"What did you tell him?"

"I told him it was. We are all our brothers' keepers, are we not? God expects us—indeed, demands of us—that we do what is right. So I told Marty in no uncertain terms he should go to the authorities—someone other than the sheriff, obviously—and make a report. He was wrestling with it, trying to find the right path, and after we talked for an hour or so, he finally told me he'd do it."

"You mean, report what he'd seen at Peter's mansion?"

"Yes. I told him he'd made the right choice and that God would reward him. And then, a few hours later, he was murdered. I have to admit I'm a little concerned with my own safety now. If someone killed Marty because of what he knew, then—"

"You're thinking you might be next. Have you told the authorities about your talk with Marty?"

"No, but I suppose I should."

I gave him Jason Braddock's phone number. "Call him right away," I said. "He—"

"So, you doing a little conversion work, reverend?" Tommy Redmond said, inviting himself into the conversation. He'd come up behind me, looking as always for a scoop. "I know for a fact Mr. Zweifel here is a godless fellow. Isn't that right, Paulie?"

"The godless, let it be known, sometimes do God's work," Reverend Ronnie said. "It is one of the wonders of the world. I must be going. Have a good day, Mr. Redmond. You, too, Mr. Zweifel, and thanks for your help."

"There's a hypocrite if I ever saw one," Tommy said once Reverend Ronnie was out of earshot. "I hear he's getting quite a bit of action from some of the ladies in his congregation, if you know what I mean."

"Well, good for him. Action of any kind is always welcome in Pineland. Is there something I can do for you, Tommy?"

"Yeah, why don't you tell me what the hell is going on here? I'm hearing some very interesting things about our beloved sheriff. Too bad about Marty, by the way. Any idea who shot him?"

"Tommy, you should direct your questions to the BCA, not me."

"Do you really think those BCA assholes will tell me anything? Not a chance. Come on, Paulie, help me out here."

"My lips are sealed," I said, "especially when it comes to that old case involving Jill Lorrimer and what Marty might have seen at Peter's mansion. I really couldn't tell you a thing about it."

A cold rain was falling when I got outside. I took refuge in my Prius, started the engine, turned the heat up at full blast, and suddenly felt very tired. There was work to do at the office but I wasn't up for it. I drove home, entertained Camus for a while, then took a nap. I had a dream that took me back to Paradise Consolidated High School, where I was about to fail a math test because I'd inconveniently neglected to study for it. Oddly, music played in the background as I stared hopelessly at the test sheet, lost amid differential equations. I heard voices, too. I guess you could say the dream was an omen.

I awoke to a ringing telephone. Arne wanted to chat. He was still sheriff—the compromising photo with Jill Lorrimer wasn't evidence of a crime—but Vern and the county board had "persuaded" him to take an immediate leave of absence.

"You arranged all of this all, didn't you?" he said in a slurred voice. He sounded drunk and angry, not a good combination.

"Little early in the day to be drinking, isn't it? And, no, I didn't arrange anything. You jumped into a pile of shit all on your own."

"Fuck you, Zweifel. Fuck you. You're not going to get away with it. I know where you got that picture."

"Really? Tell me then." I wondered who'd snapped the photo of Arne with Jill Lorrimer on his lap. I had an idea but no proof.

"I'm not telling you shit, Zweifel. But you just watch yourself. Your day is coming."

"What's that supposed to mean. Are you making threats?"

"I don't make threats, you fucker. I am the threat."

He hung up before I could say anything else. Arne is the most dangerous man I know, and now he'd put a target on my back. It was not a good feeling.

The Moreland family home, near the northern edge of town, is one of those foursquares from the early 1900s you'll find everywhere in Minnesota. It's sturdy and unpretentious, like all of its kind, with white clapboard siding and an open front porch. Marty and Doris had lived there ever since their marriage.

Doris met me at the door. She was wearing jeans, a checkered blouse and a bright red bandanna around her neck. Her salt-and-pepper hair looked a bit unkempt and there were bags around her eyes suggesting she hadn't had a good night's sleep in a long while. Tall and well-built, Doris is German to the core—she came from a well-known family of Schultzes in Pineland —and she always seemed stronger to me than Marty. She'd been a teacher for years before becoming the principal of Pineland's only elementary school.

"Come on in," she said. "The boys are back in school—I didn't want them to sit around and mope—so we've got the place to ourselves."

She ushered me into a cozy living room furnished with what looked like mostly hand-me-down items. In one corner a gas fireplace flickered with welcoming warmth. A long row of family photos decorated the mantel. I didn't see Marty in any of them.

"Coffee?" Doris asked as I sank into a big leather chair with rolled armrests.

"No thanks, I'm fine. How are you doing?"

"I don't really know, but I guess I'm all right," she said, sitting down across from me on a well-used couch. "At least, that's what I tell myself. But the boys are taking it hard."

I hadn't really known Doris well until she won the role in *Pinafore*. She was delightful to work with—she had no big ego but plenty of self-confidence—and we'd been casual friends ever since. I'd talked with her enough to sense that her marriage wasn't flourishing, but she never went into details, even though Marty's unsavory adventures at Peter's mansion were much discussed round town.

"That was a nice service yesterday," I said by way of making conversation. "I imagine you had to plan the whole thing."

"Actually, I let Dale do most of it. But I did insist on the Warren Zevon song. I wanted to make sure the boys understand how important it is to keep their father's memory alive."

"Important for you, too."

"Sure," Doris said, but the assurance wasn't delivered with much conviction. "Truth is, Marty and I lived separate lives for years. But neither of us wanted a divorce until the boys were out of high school and on their own. I give Marty credit for that. He cared about his sons."

"I know he did."

Doris nodded and said, "Maybe that made up for his sins. I'd like to think so. There's something else you should know. Marty was in a really bad way before he was killed. He was hiding a secret, and it was something a lot worse than the fact he was fucking all those hookers up at Peter's place. I knew about that."

I thought back to my last conversation with Marty in my office and decided to share with Doris what he'd told me about Arne and Jill Lorrimer.

"Oh God," Doris said, her head sagging. "Marty always trusted people too much. Everybody except me, that is. Maybe I wasn't a good wife to him. He just wouldn't share anything. Why didn't he tell me what was happening?"

"I think you were a fine wife," I said. "Marty was one of those guys—there are a lot of them—who have to have secrets, especially from the people closest to them. So instead of talking to you he took his problems to me. He also talked to the Reverend Ronnie."

"I hope you know the reverend is a fucking snake," Doris said with surprising vehemence. "I can't tell you how much money Marty threw into that stupid church. Ronnie the fake—that's what I always called him. I mean, who really believes in God anymore?"

"Lots of people," I said.

"Well, more power to them, I guess." She paused, heaven lost with her husband, and started to sob.

I waited quietly for a few moments before offering that universal bromide, "It will be okay." As if I knew.

"Sorry," Doris said. "It just happens sometimes."

"There's nothing to apologize about," I said. "I'm here to listen if there's more you want to tell me."

She daubed her eyes with a tissue and said, "Yes, there's more. I talked to those two agents from the BCA last night. From what they said and what you've told me, Arne is a suspect in Marty's murder. Honestly, do think he did it?"

"I truly don't know. Arne's capable of killing—we know that—but executing Marty point blank? I'm just not convinced that's something Arne would do."

"Me either," Doris said. "Maybe it was someone else who knew what happened to Jill Lorrimer and wanted to silence Marty."

"Could be. Did Marty ever say who the regulars were at Peter's parties?"

"Oh, I don't know, from what I've heard half the men in town showed up there at one time or another. Did you ever go?"

The question caught me off guard. "Actually, no. Peter didn't much care for me."

"But would you have gone if you'd been invited?"

"That probably would have depended on how drunk I was at the moment. Sober, I'd like to think I would have passed, but—"

"If your dick was calling, you couldn't resist."

The conversation was veering off into weird territory. Was Doris flirting with me or just expressing her general disgust with the male of the species? I wasn't sure. Maybe both.

"Doris, let's forget my libidinous instincts for the moment and get back to those parties at Pater's mansion."

"Well, I can't answer your question because Marty never talked about who was at the parties. It's not as if he came home afterwards and said, 'Honey, let me tell you all about the wonderful time I had at Peter's place with his friends and his hookers.'"

"Okay, it was stupid of me to ask. I'm sorry."

"No, it's not your fault. I sound angry, don't I?"

"You do, but you have a right to be. Marty could have been a better husband."

Doris slowly shook her head, her eyes closed. She opened them and said, "Do you ever wonder what happened to your life, and how it could have been much different?"

"All the time."

"Yeah, I guess everybody does. And so here I am, age forty-three, two teenage boys still to raise, precious little money in the bank, looking out my window at the glories of Pineland, Minnesota, where the odds are strong I'm going to die."

"Well, as my no-good father used to day, you could do worse. And, of course, you've got the boys, which is more than I have."

"God, aren't we a pair! Well, screw it. Life goes on and all of that. So, there's actually a reason why I invited you over. I want to show you something."

She went to a desk behind the couch and brought back a copy of Paradise Consolidated High School's 1988 yearbook. "It's Marty's senior yearbook. I found it down in the basement rec room last night. It was left open to page sixty-six. Marty wrote something there. It's kind of strange."

I turned to the page and found an article about the high school's band director, a man named James Biersdorf. The article, which included a photo of Biersdorf leading the band, mentioned he had written a "special composition" for the school's annual ice cream social and fundraiser that year. The composition was called "Evening Song," but it was the subtitle—"A Serenade to Pineland"—that caught my eye. Marty had circled the subtitle in pencil and written next to it, "Serenade. Serenader? Strange what happened to Mr. and Mrs. Biersdorf. Any connection?"

"You're sure Marty wrote this?" I asked Doris.

"Yes. It's definitely his handwriting."

"Did he ever show you this or talk about it?"

"No, but he was always circling things he found in books and newspapers or whatever. It was a habit he had. Maybe it was just the word 'serenade' that got his attention, you know, because of everything that's been happening here."

"I take it Marty would have known Biersdorf."

"Sure. Marty played trombone in the school band. You must have known him, too."

"Not really, I was a few years behind Marty. I think Biersdorf was gone by the time I got to dear old Paradise Consolidated."

"Same here. I could try googling his name if that that would help."

"No, I can do that. But I would like to borrow this yearbook if I could. I'll get it back to you."

"Sure. Keep it as long as you like."

"All right. I really should be going. Thanks for all of your help."

"You're welcome," Doris said with a smile. Before I left, she went into the kitchen and returned with a bag of her legendary chocolate-chip cookies, which I'd first sampled during our Gilbert and Sullivan rehearsals.

"You'll need some sustenance," she said. "And please let me know if you find out more about Marty's death. You're the smartest person I know. If anyone can get to the bottom of it, you're the one."

"If I'm the smartest person you know, Doris, you need to meet more people. But I'll do what I can."

"I know you will," she said, and kissed me on the cheek. There was yearning in it, and I knew that if kissed her back we could have made love right there in the living room with no one the wiser. But it didn't seem right, for me or her, and I said, "Let's talk again when everything calms down here."

"I'd like that," she said. "But you need to be careful. There's a lot of crazy stuff going on."

"So I've heard," I said. "Maybe your cookies will help me figure everything out."

When I got into my car, I wolfed down two cookies and decided it was the best thing I'd done in a quite a while, so I had a third. The sugar rush worked and by the time I reached my office thoughts of "A Serenade to Pineland" were making music in my head.

I googled "James Biersdorf" on my office computer. His name generated a surprising number of hits because of how he and his wife, Janice, had died. The couple had been murdered in 2001 in a foster home they operated in St. Cloud, about seventy-five miles from Pineland. Both had been shot to death. As far as I could tell, no one had ever been arrested for the murders. There was something else of interest. Two months after their deaths, the Biersdorfs' vacant house, described in one account as "St. Cloud's finest Victorian-era residence," burned to the ground. Investigators determined the fire was arson, but as with the murders, the crime went unsolved.

So where was I? Maybe on the edge of a breakthrough, or maybe nowhere. It all hinged on Marty's scribbled words in the yearbook. They seemed to suggest that an obscure school song, and the murder of its composer and his wife sixteen years ago, were linked to the Serenader. But was there any proof of such a connection? Or had Marty simply made a wild guess based on the title of an old song he remembered? I didn't know, but I intended to find out.

35

Cassandra was in touch first thing Saturday morning. "What are you doing tomorrow?" she asked over the phone.

"Nothing much. It's a Sunday. Maybe I'll spend the day doing penance and praying for divine intervention."

"I've got a better idea. Let's go out to Freedom Beach."

"Why? Are you just curious?"

"It's more than that. I talked to Earl Bradley's daughter and she had some very interesting things to say. It's quite a story."

"So what's the gist?"

"I don't have time to get into it today. I'm really jammed up with work. The partners are getting antsy in Chicago. They think I'm spending way too much time up here."

"They're probably right. As I've said—how many times now?—you'd be better off—"

"Yeah, yeah, yeah. I'm not changing my mind. I'm driving up from the cities tomorrow and I'm going to Freedom Beach. Period. Now, do you want to come along or not?"

"All right. I guess two fools are always better than one."

We arranged to meet at a Cenex truck stop along the interstate ten miles south of Pineland. From there, we could take a county road directly to Freedom Beach.

I pulled into the Cenex lot Sunday morning and found Cassandra standing by her rental car, the same BMW Series 7 sedan I'd seen in the parking lot at Pembroke Woods. She was looking very sharp in dark gray slacks and a sleek, peplum-style leather jacket that had a thousand dollars written all over it.

I parked next to her in my Prius, and when I got out she said, "I don't think I can handle another ride in that sporty beast of yours. Let's take my car."

The Beamer was a beauty and I quickly discovered why Cassandra had rented it. She liked to drive fast, and once we got onto the lightly traveled county road leading to Fortune Lake and Freedom Beach, she rarely let the speedometer dip below eighty.

"Any late news from Pineland?" Cassandra asked before I could jump in with questions of my own.

I filled in her in on my talk with Doris Moreland, including the odd item she'd found circled in Marty's high school yearbook. I also told her how James and Janice Biersdorf had died.

"Shit, that's really weird. And you think this Biersdorf guy may somehow be connected to the Serenader because of that song he wrote? Sounds like a stretch to me."

"I agree. Still, I'd like to find a recording of his 'Serenade to Pineland' to see how it compares with the melody on those thumb drives."

We took a sharp turn at high speed and I grabbed the handle above my door.

"Before you kill us both, tell me why we're taking this little trip," I said. "Nobody will be at Freedom Beach this time of year."

"I know," Cassandra said, "but there's a guy who lives not far away we can talk to. His name is Arlen Sandquist and he's expecting us."

"How did you happen to run across him?"

"I learned about him from Earl Bradley's daughter. Her name is Dorothea. I was finally able to reach her Friday night. Once I told her what I was looking for, she invited me over to her condo in Minneapolis and we had a long talk."

"I take it her father is dead?"

"Yes. He passed in 1995 and his wife, whose name was Clementine, followed two years later. I asked Dorothea about the family cabin at Freedom Beach and what happened in nineteen eighty-five when her father's name came up in connection with the adoption of Baby Doe. Long story short, she was working in Louisville in the 1980s and didn't spend much time at the cabin. But she did have an album of family photos. I went through them with her and I found one photo that explains a lot."

Cassandra tapped the brakes and pulled over to the shoulder. She scrolled through her iPhone. "Here's the shot I took. The development date on the actual photo is June nineteen eighty-five."

The image showed a matronly, white-haired Black woman. Posing next to her was a much younger, light-skinned Black woman, who was cradling an infant in her arms. Behind them was a wall paneled with knotty pine. Part of a curtained window was also in the view.

"The older woman is Clementine Bradley, Earl's wife," Cassandra said. "The younger woman must be Patricia Gordon. The photo was taken in the Bradleys' cabin."

Patricia was beautiful and I was struck by how closely she resembled Cassandra. "Can't be any doubt she's your mother," I said. "I assume you think the baby is your brother, the second child Patricia had with Peter."

"Has to be."

"Is that what Dorothea told you?"

"No. She didn't know the baby's identity. She said her parents—and this was surprise to me—never talked about Patricia or the baby. She didn't find out about them until she ran across the photo when she putting together the album of family pictures just before her mother's death. According to Dorothea, her mother's memory was failing by then and she couldn't remember the name of the woman with the baby or how she'd ended up at the cabin or even if the baby was a girl or a boy. But everything adds up. That's why your father wrote Earl Bradley's name on that court file. I think the Bradleys cared for the baby before he was adopted."

"And where was Patricia in all of this?"

"Excellent question. She just disappeared. Jocko hasn't been able to find a thing about her after June of eighty-five. And if he can't track her down, nobody can."

Cassandra nudged the Beamer back into gear and quickly got up to speed. "Are we close to Freedom Beach?"

"Yes, and you need to slow down. The turnoff to the lake isn't far now."

Where the county road makes a sharp right to follow the shore of Fortune Lake, a weed-filled clearing marks the site of Gentry's Supper Club, which burned down years ago.

"This is where my mother died," I said. "Supposedly it was an accident."

"What? You never told me about that," Cassandra said, braking to stop.

"There was no need to. It's ancient family history."

"What happened?"

I gave her the three-minute version of the car crash and my dead mother and my lost father and the aunts who raised me.

"Do you remember your mother at all?"

"No. She's just a name and some old photos."

"What happened to your father?"

"Nothing. No charges were ever filed. He knew all the right people."

"And then he more or less abandoned you?"

"I'd emphasize the 'more' part," I said.

"Jesus," Cassandra said, "no wonder you seem fucked-up sometimes."

"Sometimes?"

"Okay. Most of the time." Then she broke out in the widest smile I'd ever seen from her. "But I like you anyway."

"The feeling is mutual," I said. "Drive on. We're almost there."

Fortune Lake, like thousands of others in Minnesota, is a big puddle of greenish-blue water fringed by birches and evergreens. Cabins and a few year-round houses peek out amid the trees, and in summer docks shoot out like long fingers into the lake. But April is closer to winter than summer in Minnesota, and a crust of ice still covered the lake by the time we got our first view of it.

"Freedom Beach and Fortune Lake. Kind of cool the way those names come together," Cassandra said.

"The lake is actually named after Richard Fortune," I said. "He was an early settler. The name didn't bring him much luck, though. I read somewhere he drowned while he was out fishing."

I directed Cassandra down a narrow gravel road that parallels the lake's eastern shore. It was twisty enough that she had to drive slowly. We rounded one last curve and saw a weathered wooden sign supported by a pair of log posts: "Freedom Beach, est. 1963."

A series of driveways led off on the right and Cassandra crept along until we found one with the address Dorothea had provided.

"So does Dorothea own the cabin now?" I asked.

"No, she sold it about five years ago to another Black family. But I'm sure they won't mind if we take a quick look at the property."

There wasn't much to see because the cabin was gone, its remains outlined by the concrete blocks that had formed its foundation. Ash and pieces of charred wood littered the area. Clearly, the cabin had burned down.

"Damn," Cassandra said. "I wonder when this happened?"

"Recently, by the looks of it, and I'd be willing to bet it was an arson fire."

"We're on the right track then, aren't we? This can't be a coincidence."

Arlen Sandquist lived in a year-round lakeside home a quarter mile north of Freedom Beach. It was a ramshackle place that had begun life as cabin before a series of what looked to be handbuilt additions transformed it into a house. Sandquist met us at the front door. He was in his eighties, stooped and bony in the way old men often are, but he moved quickly and his mind, we discovered, hadn't slowed a bit.

After the usual introductions, he invited us into his knotty-pine living room, where a picture window looked out over the lake. The room was tchotchke heaven, a museum of bad taste that had taken years to assemble. I liked it right away, if only because it reminded me of my aunts and their love of Catholic kitsch in all its varieties. Sandquist brought in a pot of coffee and a pile of glazed donuts and told us all about Earl Bradley and Freedom Beach and the events of 1985.

"Most people around here didn't want to have nothing to do with the coloreds down at the beach, but I didn't see a problem. People are people, right? Anyway, me and the wife went over there one day and introduced ourselves and that's how we met Earl. Salt of the earth, Earl was, and boy, did he know plumbing. Helped me put in a new bathroom and wouldn't take a cent for his work."

"I've heard he was a fine man," Cassandra said, letting Sandquist's reference to "coloreds" pass without comment. "We stopped by his cabin but it was burned to the ground. Do you know when that happened?"

"About three weeks ago. Somebody torched the place. Sheriff thinks it was kids screwing around. We've got some real delinquents around here."

"I'm sorry to hear that," Cassandra said. "May I ask how long you've lived here?"

"Well now, that's a story. Me and Jeanie—that was my wife, she's dead now—bought this place from Peter Swindell in nineteen eighty-five. It was just a cabin then. Mr. Swindell was anxious as all get out to sell the place so we got a good price. And now somebody's murdered him and his son and that other fellow. Isn't that something?"

"It surely is," I said. "A big mystery if there ever was one. It's interesting to learn your place once belonged to Peter. I didn't know he had a cabin out here."

"Oh yeah, it was in his family for years. It was real nice as cabins go. Full bathroom, big kitchen, even a nice concrete patio Peter put in just before we bought the place. Then Earl came along and helped us add on."

Sandquist was a roundabout narrator, and we went with him along several long loops before finally reaching the story of Patricia Gordon and her baby.

The essence of Sandquist's account was that a "colored" woman—he never learned her name —had appeared at Freedom Beach in the summer of 1985 with an infant she claimed was Peter's son. Sandquist said he'd learned this juicy tidbit from Earl Bradley, who with his wife had temporarily taken in Patricia and her child.

"I guess you could say it was regular scandal, but everything got fixed up in the end," Sandquist said. "Earl told me Peter made arrangements to have the baby adopted and sent off to be raised somewhere else. St. Cloud, I think it was."

Cassandra and I exchanged glances. She said, "Do you know the name of his adoptive parents there?"

"Let's see, Earl told me once. It was a German name, I think."

"Biersdorf?" I suggested.

"Yes, that could be right, but I really don't remember. It was a long time ago."

"It was," Cassandra agreed. "I'm curious about one other thing, Mr. Sandquist. Do you know what might have happened to the mother of the baby?"

"No. I never met her, and she was gone by the time I bought this property from Mr. Swindell. Say, do you think they'll ever figure out who murdered him?"

"I'm sure they will," I said. "It's just a matter of time."

"I hope so. Now, if you need to talk to me again anytime soon, I'll give you a phone number where you can reach me. I'm going down to Maple Grove for a couple of weeks to visit my daughter."

He jotted down the number on a scrap paper Then he went over to one of the room's many tchotchke-choked shelves and returned with a small plastic statue, which he handed to me.

"Saint Jude," he said, "Patron saint of lost objects. Maybe he'll help you find what you're looking for."

"Can't hurt," I said and put the little saint in my coat pocket. Down the road, he'd prove more valuable than I could ever have thought.

On our way back to the Cenex lot, Cassandra was so jazzed I thought she'd drive us into a ditch.

"I've got to get a shitload of work done today and tomorrow, but how about we go to St. Cloud Tuesday morning?" she said. "There might be records from the Biersdorf home, if that's where the baby went. Maybe even some photos of the kids who were raised there."

"Okay, we can do that. I take it you plan to stay in town for a while."

"Oh yeah. We're close now. I can feel it."

36

At home late that afternoon, I took Camus for his usual walk and had just settled in to plow through the Sunday *New York Times* when my front doorbell rang. I looked out the side-light and was surprised to see Alice Sigurdson, Arne's wife. She was wearing a long trench coat of the kind favored by secret agents in spy movies. I had no idea what she was doing at my doorstep.

"I'm really sorry to bother you," she said when I opened the door. "May I come in?"

"Of course," I said. I looked down the driveway toward her parked car. "Is Arne here, too?"

"No, I came alone. I know I should have called first, but I didn't want to leave a trail, if you know what I mean, so I thought I'd take a chance on catching you at home."

"I'm not sure I understand," I said, ushering her inside. "Is this supposed to be some sort of secret meeting?"

"It has to be," she said, "or I'm in big trouble. Doris said I should talk to you."

"Doris Moreland?"

"Yes. We've been friends for a long time, but now, well, I just don't know what to do. She said you might be able to help. "

I didn't know Alice all that well. I'd met her only a few times, usually at courthouse Christmas parties, where Arne made a conspicuous point of ignoring her. She's a short, stoutish woman in her fifties, with long black hair fading to gray and a plain country face adorned with the kind of big plastic eyeglasses that went out of style years ago. We'd talked a bit at some of those courthouse festivities, and I'd always enjoyed our conversations. She worked part-time for the county parks department and knew plenty of gossip, which she dispensed with a bone-dry wit. Alice and Arne had two grown children, both living in the Twin Cities, and she liked to talk about them. But she never had anything to say about Arne, and she'd struck me as lonely and unhappy, trapped in the classic dead marriage.

Camus came up to examine Alice, and she seemed pleased by his attention.

"What an interesting dog," she said. "What's his name?"

When I told her, she said, "Isn't that funny. When I was in college, I read a lot of Camus, and then I wanted to go to France and smoke cigarettes and talk about important things all night long."

"A worthwhile goal," I agreed. "I had the same thoughts in college, but I guess neither one of us ever made it to France."

"Not even close."

We moved into the living room, and once we sat down I figured we might as well get to the point. "You said you wanted to talk. I'm listening."

"It's about Arne, what else?" she said. "The fucker." She pronounced the obscenity with real conviction.

"I suppose this is all about that photo," I said. "I'm really sorry—"

She cut me off. "That's old news. Arne's been screwing around for years. But you know what? He's got more to worry about than the fact the bimbo in his lap turned up dead. You know, don't you, that he's a suspect in Marty's murder?"

"Yes."

"Well, I didn't know until two agents from the Bureau of Criminal Apprehension came to my office Friday and started to ask a lot of questions. "

"I assume it was the two agents named Jason."

"Those were the ones. Not very friendly types."

"What did they want?"

"Mostly they wanted to know where Arne was on the night Marty was killed."

"What did you tell them?"

Alice cupped her hands under her chin and slowly shook her head. She looked ill at ease, maybe not with me but with herself. She said, "I told them he was home, snug in bed with his dear wife."

"Was he?"

"No. I lied. We haven't slept together in years."

We were entering dangerous legal territory. I was officially off the case, and I had no business talking to Alice about her husband's alibi or anything else involving the criminal investigation. My lawyer brain said I should halt the conversation at once and direct Alice back to the two Jasons at the BCA. I ignored my lawyer brain.

"Where was he that night?"

"Who knows? Maybe out on an investigation. Maybe screwing some bimbo. Maybe murdering people. All I can tell you is that a lot of nights he doesn't come home from the office until very late, and I don't see him until I get up in the morning, if at all."

"And he never calls to say where he is?"

"Are you kidding? Arne doesn't bother with excuses anymore. He just does what he does. What I think doesn't matter to him."

I tried to compose some consoling words but nothing came to mind. A dead marriage is a toxic swamp and outsiders wade in at their peril.

"Did Arne tell you to say he was home all night?"

"No. But if I'd said he was gone, I knew I'd be in big trouble."

"You're afraid of Arne?"

"Wouldn't you be?"

No argument there. Arne could definitely be a scary guy.

"Are you worried he'll harm you?"

"I'm not sure. There's never been any physical abuse, and he was actually a pretty good father to our kids. But the truth is I don't know Arne after all these years. He's just a stranger I live with."

We talked a while longer, Alice unburdening herself as though speaking to a marriage counselor. Much as I sympathized with her situation, I wasn't sure how to proceed.

"I'm afraid there isn't a lot I can do," I said. "A special prosecutor has taken over all of the investigating, and I don't have any real say in what happens. I'm just an interested party now. But if you really think Arne was involved in Marty's murder, you don't owe him an alibi. You should go to the BCA agents and tell them the truth."

"And what if Arne finds out ?"

"I hate to tell you, but he will. The BCA guys will be discreet. You don't have to worry about that. But at some point they'll have to bring Arne in for more questioning and then they'll start pressing him as to his whereabouts on the night Marty was murdered. If he says he was home they'll challenge him and he'll figure out pretty quick that his alibi has gone up in smoke."

"And then Arne will come after me."

"I hope not. But you can request protection if need be. I guess it all comes down to what you think is the right thing to do."

"I know. Sometimes I feel like I'm watching a movie and I'm seeing my life disappear right before my eyes. Maybe that's what will happen. But if Arne really did kill Marty, I couldn't live with myself thinking I'd covered up for him."

"I understand. The thing is, your life doesn't have to be over. Have you thought about leaving Arne?"

"Sure, but, well, I don't know, it's just hard. I don't want to be alone."

"It sounds like you already are," I said.

"So it seems." She stood up. "Well, I should go. I'll figure this out."

"You will," I said and hoped I was right.

"I have a question," I said to Kat Berglund that night at the Dead Lumberjack, where I'd gone for a margarita infusion. "Why do so many women want to confide in me?" I'd told her in a general way about my conversations with Doris and Alice.

Kat said, "You're just that kind of guy."

"What do you mean?"

"It's hard to explain, but women understand. A lot of guys, they've got a nice shiny surface, and they might be good for sex or money or even some semblance of love, but good luck trying to ever really know them. They're dense objects designed to repel any exploration of their core. You're strong, Paul, maybe stronger than you know, but you're not dense."

"I think that's a compliment, though I'm not sure."

Kat leaned over the bar and gave my margarita a quick stir. "It is. Women can tell you're not a closed book and that you'll actually listen to them. A lot of men, they don't listen at all."

"Did you just say something?"

"Very funny. Now, here's a chance for you to listen to this woman. Watch out for Arne. A source who shall go nameless says Arne's convinced you're the one who planted that photo in Marty's casket."

"I know. Arne already called me to tell me he thinks I'm the culprit. We had a delightful talk full of sharply worded observations."

"I'll bet you did, but don't make light of this. My source says Arne is drinking hard and looking for revenge. You know him, Paul. You know the kind of man he is. I wouldn't put anything past him. If he killed Marty—"

"He'd kill me. I get it. Don't worry. I'll watch my back."

"Do you have a gun?" The question surprised me, but I could tell Kat wasn't joking. "Because if you don't, I can lend you one."

"Well, that's quite an offer. I didn't know you're an NRA type."

"I'm not. But my father was and he left me a dozen rifles and handguns. I sold most of them but kept a couple of pistols just in case. You're welcome to take one for personal protection."

I polished off my margarita and said, "Thanks, but I'll pass. The truth is, if Arne comes gunning for me, I won't win the showdown at OK Corral. He's a lot better at shooting people than I am. Besides, I'm not convinced Arne would kill me in cold blood."

"I hope those aren't famous last words," Kat said.

"Me too," I said and gave Kat a kiss on the cheek before I went out into the night.

Around the time of Marty's funeral, Pineland began experiencing a wave of residential break-ins. Doors were jimmied open, windows shattered, jars of change taken from kitchen cabinets and the occasional cell phone stolen. It was petty stuff, and the police believed teenagers were to blame.

In the early morning hours of Monday, April 24, the old Zweifel family home at 310 North Eden Street became the latest target. The burglar made enough noise to awaken my first-floor tenant, Agnes Miller. She promptly called the police.

A Pineland police officer was duly dispatched to the scene at four in the morning. There were no signs of a break-in but

Agnes was waiting at the front door and let the officer in. Thinking the burglar might still be hiding inside, the officer called for backup. Only two patrolmen work the night shift in Pineland, and the second officer arrived within minutes. Guns drawn, the lawmen checked on the other tenants, none of whom had seen or heard an intruder. The officers then noted that the door to my father's old law office was open and went in for a look. They found no one; the burglar was gone.

Although the long dormant office is hardly a repository of treasures, the burglar had ransacked it, going through desk drawers and file cabinets. Nothing of value was taken because there wasn't anything worth taking. But it wasn't long before the patrolmen made a startling discovery. Sitting atop my father's desk was a vintage Smith-Corona Sterling typewriter. A sheet of plain white paper curled around the typewriter's platen, and a thumb drive rested on the keys. The paper contained a message:

Moreland knew too much and paid the price. Where was Sigurdson when it happened? Where was Sigurdson the night Jill Lorrimer died? Ask him. Let the truth shine forth.

The Serenader

37

The phone call from Jim Meyers came at six in the morning. "I'm at that house of yours on Eden Street," he said. "There's been a break-in and you need to get over here right away."

Jim wouldn't provide any more details, but when I arrived twenty minutes later most of Pineland's police force was there to greet me, along with two sheriff's deputies and Jason Braddock in the pinstripe suit he presumably sleeps in.

"Looks like you've been doing some more writing," Jason said after showing me the message. "I'm told you use this office now and then. Belonged to your father, apparently. So, let's finally end all the bullshit. It's time for you to tell us the truth."

"Sure. The truth is that our friend the Serenader broke in here and typed out this message to implicate me."

"Is that a fact? Well, you know what? I've been looking at the typewriter. It's a Smith-Corona-Sterling. Quite an antique. Just the kind of thing your father might have had in this office. And I'm thinking the odds are about one hundred percent that all the other messages were typed on this machine."

The machine looked vaguely familiar. Had I spotted it somewhere in the old office? I couldn't be sure. Naturally, I didn't reveal my doubts to Jason.

"I've never seen this typewriter before," I said. "It's a plant."

"Oh, I see, a guy carrying a big old typewriter broke in here. That might be a new wrinkle in the annals of crime. And how did he get in? There's no sign of forced entry. Or do you usually leave the office door open?"

"No, I always keep it locked. And why don't you can the sarcasm? Do you really think this was a random burglary? Not a chance. I'm being targeted and have been from the start."

"All a big mystery to you, is that right?" Jason said.

"Look, do you have more questions for me are you just going to continue with your running commentary? Because if that's the case, I'll be leaving now."

"All right, why don't you tell me when you were last in this office?"

I suspected Jason already knew the answer, since he'd probably talked to the tenants. Agnes Miller in particular was a busybody and for all I knew maintained a meticulous record of my comings and goings.

"It would have been a week ago Saturday. I'm sure Mrs. Miller mentioned seeing me."

"What were you doing here?"

"Just looking over some old family memorabilia," I lied. "I come by every so often to go through things. And, again for the record, when I was here last this typewriter wasn't on the desk or anywhere else I could see."

"So you've said. Was there anything in particular you were looking for while you were here?"

"No."

"What time did you leave?"

"I think it was around noon."

"And you haven't been back since then?"

"That's correct."

Jim Meyers, who looked like a lost elephant stumbling around the office, joined Jason to continue the interrogation. Both clearly believed I was the Serenader. But that didn't mean I was about to be hauled off to jail. Writing messages and posting them in various places isn't illegal, and the discovery of the typewriter, however suspicious it looked, wasn't probable cause for my arrest. What the two stalwarts of law and order needed was evidence linking me to the three murders and the arson fires, and they didn't have it.

The jousting continued for a while, Jason in particular setting little traps in hopes of luring me into trouble, but I refused the bait. "You know it's just a matter of time before we put all of this together," he finally said. "I'm really going to enjoy seeing you behind bars."

"You must live a very dull life if that's your idea of enjoyment," I said. "Speaking of time, the bewitching hour has arrived. I have nothing more to say. You know where to find me if you need me."

"I've got some bad news," Cassandra announced. She called around nine just after I'd gone to my office. She sounded tired and irritated.

"Not what I needed to hear," I said. "I've got some bad news, too. You first."

"I can't go to St. Cloud tomorrow. A hearing got scheduled out of the blue in a big civil suit and I have to handle it or the partners will have a collective heart attack. I have to fly back to Chicago and start prepping. The hearing will be tomorrow afternoon. With luck, I'll be back here on Wednesday or Thursday and we can go to St. Cloud then, unless you want to go on your own first."

"No, I'll wait for you. I've got plenty to keep me occupied at the moment." I told her about the staged burglary at my father's office and the discovery of the message in the typewriter.

"That's not good. Do you think the typewriter belonged to your father?"

"A firm 'maybe' is the best answer I can give. But I'm pretty sure it will turn out to be the machine the BCA is looking for."

There was pause before Cassandra said, "So what's the next big find going to be?"

"I wish I knew."

"If I were you, I'd be worried."

"I am worried," I protested.

"You need to be even more worried. This Serenader character has plans for you and he's not done. He's very clever."

"Too clever for me, apparently. I keep trying to figure out what he's going to do next but he always seems way ahead of me."

"Well, it's pretty clear he's setting you up for something."

"And he's doing a mighty fine job of it so far."

"You know what, maybe you should go to St. Cloud tomorrow. If my unknown brother is actually connected to all of this, and if you can find a photo or some other way of identifying him as someone who's in Pineland right now, you'd have the answers we need."

"Too many 'ifs,'" I said. "Besides, I've got to stick around town. If I take off for a day, suspicions will only mount."

"Okay. I'll be back a soon as I can. In the meantime, try to stay out of more trouble,"

"I'll do my best," I said. Too bad that wasn't good enough.

Cassandra's call led me to think more about Baby Doe, her lost brother. If he was living incognito in or near Pineland, he'd be thirty-two years old. How many men about that age did I know around town? A few possibilities came immediately to mind. Then again, adult Baby Doe could be someone I didn't know, a stranger who'd made it his business, for devious reasons of his own, to cast me as the Serenader. In that case, uncovering his identity could be extremely difficult unless St. Cloud offered some answers, and now that would have to wait.

The giant manure spreader that rains down gossip on Pineland didn't take long to broadcast news of the incriminating discovery in my father's old office. Doug had already heard the whole story by the time I ventured into his office to fetch some legal documents. Naturally, he tried to pry out additional details while faking sincere concern for my well-being.

"I bet you were really upset when you found out about that typewriter," he said. "It must have been a shock. Any idea how it got there?"

"Teleportation," I said.

"No, seriously, do you think somebody actually brought it into that office and left it there? I mean, how weird is that?"

"Doug, I will stipulate it was weird."

"Well, I'm just saying it was a bizarre thing for somebody to do. Why do you suppose this Serenader guy is on your case?"

"I'll ask him when I see him. So tell me, Doug, what's Vern been whispering into your fevered little ears these days?"

Doug did his best to sound offended. "Why would you say that? I hardly ever talk to Vern. I don't know what he's thinking."

"Okay. Maybe I was mistaken. Say, Doug, how old are you? Somebody asked me the other day and I didn't know."

"Thirty-five."

"You look younger," I said and went back to my office.

Arne called in the afternoon to share his thoughts. I could practically hear the sound of his gloating over the phone.

"How does it feel to be shithead king for a day?" he inquired with his usual delicacy.

I told him it didn't feel nearly as good as getting a lap dance from a hooker and hung up.

The next morning Vern marched into my office with the look of a man about to shoot an injured horse. He seemed to think I'd be happy to be put out of my misery for the good of all concerned.

"You've got to go," he said. "My phone is ringing off the hook. First Arne, then you. That typewriter is the last straw. Why the fuck are you writing those messages? Have you gone nuts?"

"Crazy as a loon," I said. "Except I'm not the Serenader. Never have been, never will be. It's all a big set-up. Meanwhile, our wonderful county sheriff is being accused of murder. Seems to me you should be asking him to resign."

"Leave Arne out of this. There's no proof he's done anything. You're the one who's making all these crazy accusations."

"No, I'm not."

"Deny it all you want. I don't care. People have lost confidence in their government. It's time to clean house."

"As I recall, that's what the last election here was about."

"And the voters elected you of all people. Big mistake. Well, right now you look bad and people don't like it. Put in your resignation. If you didn't do anything wrong, that will all come out in the end and if you want a goddamn apology then, I'll give you one. How's that?"

I told Vern once again that I wouldn't resign, and there wasn't much he and the county board could do about it. In Minnesota, removing an elected county official for malfeasance requires a cumbersome petition process, and it would take months to force me out that way, if it could be done at all.

"Sorry, but you're stuck with me," I said

"Asshole," Vern replied with his usual devastating wit, then stomped out.

I went to the Dead Lumberjack after work to share my woes with Kat Berglund. I slammed down two margaritas and was contemplating a third when she intervened.

"I wouldn't do that," she said. "You know your limit."

Kat knew my alcohol ceiling because when I first returned to Pineland to deal with my dying father, I'd spent a lot of time getting drunk in the Dead Lumberjack. I'm not the world's worst drunk—I don't start fistfights or harass the nearest female—but as my former wife could attest, I tend to become blushingly candid and a sardonic pain in the ass. Kat wasn't interested in listening to any of that old Zweifel nonsense.

"You're right," I said, "sobriety wins. Make mine a ginger ale on the rocks. And since I'm keeping my wits about me, maybe you can tell me what you're hearing. Do the good citizens of Pineland think I'm the Serenader?"

"Too early to say. But you and that typewriter are certainly the talk of the town."

"And what do people speculate my motive might be? Because I certainly don't know why I'd be the Serenader."

"I've heard various theories. That you and Peter and Dewey were part of some sort of kickback scheme with the hotel and you didn't get your money. Or that you're involved in what happened to Jill Lorrimer and you're covering your tracks. Or that you've simply gone crazy. The list goes on. It's all bullshit, of course."

"Wonderful. Do I have any defenders?"

"Tommy Redmond seems to be on your side, believe it or not. He's planning a special edition, by the way. He'll probably be in touch with you soon."

"Well, he's got plenty to write about."

"That he does. One other thing, Paul. Be cautious around the office. Word has it that the Little Sneak"—Kat's less than endearing term for Doug—"has been whispering sweet nothings into Vern's ear. He'd love to have your job if the time comes."

"Not exactly a big reveal," I said. "The wonderful Mr. Wifferding has a made career of backstabbing and maneuvering."

"Sure, but did you know he's also been talking to those BCA agents in town?"

That I didn't know, but I probably should have. The little fucker.

"So what's he been saying?"

"He's apparently convinced you're the Serenader."

"And what do you think?"

"I think you're in for some interesting times," Kat said, pouring my ginger ale. "Want any peanuts with that?"

As I headed home to talk over my troubles with Camus, Jason Braddock delivered some more bad news.

"So we've looked at that typewriter," he said over the phone. "It's a positive match. All the messages were typed on it. You're looking dirtier by the minute."

"I'll take a shower when I get home. Maybe that will help."

"You do that. But it won't do any good. We're not done. You're going down, smart ass. Have a nice day."

38

As the newly presumed Serenader, I became a hot news item once again. Media from the Twin Cities started calling incessantly, asking for comment. I ignored the calls but I knew what was coming. Another media swarm would arrive in town, and I'd be their prime target.

Even by Pineland's standards, word of the discovery in my father's office had spread with extraordinary speed. Arne, I suspected, had been the leaker-in-chief. Even though he was on leave, he had plenty of loyal deputies to keep him well informed, and he wouldn't have missed the opportunity to make me look bad.

Tommy Redmond, who'd broken news of the typewriter and message in his blog, wandered into my office Wednesday afternoon, and I decided I'd talk to him. I'd helped him out in the past, and I knew him well enough to believe he'd give me a fair shake in the *Tattler*. He was as excitable as ever when I ushered him into my inner sanctum.

"Geez, Paulie, isn't this business something?" he said.

"It's something all right," I admitted. "But it must be good business for you."

"For sure. I'm coming out with a special edition Friday. Lots of juicy stuff. Gonna do a print run of six thousand. That's twice the usual."

"Wonderful. Are you going to have any big scoops?"

"Maybe. Just between the two of us, I've found out more about what's on those thumb drives."

"You mean more about the music?"

"No. Nobody knows what the hell the song is. I'm talking about the voices in the background."

"You have my complete attention, Tommy. Tell me more."

"Only if you'll talk to me about that typewriter. I need to have an exclusive on your explanation. I mean, I'm sure you have one."

"I do, and you've got a deal."

"Okay, here's what I know. On one of the thumb drives there's a man's voice saying, 'Come down right now. It's dinner time.' And then you can hear what sounds like a boy saying, 'I won't, I won't.' According to my source, that's all there is to it."

"What does your source make of it?"

Tommy shrugged and spread out his arms. "Nobody knows. It's another big mystery. Okay, Paulie, your turn. I'm dying to hear about that typewriter."

He took a digital voice recorder from his coat pocket and set it on my desk. "I'm ready any time you are."

I had a recorder of my own and placed it next to Tommy's. "Two recorders are always better than one," I said. "I think that's an old adage." Tommy seemed a little put out but didn't say anything.

"Okay, here we go," I said and launched into the same arguments I'd used with Jason and Jim in my father's office. It was all a big setup, I assured Tommy, and I hoped he would believe me.

"I am not the Serenader," I stated as forcefully as I could, "and I don't know who is."

"Okay, you're made yourself clear about that. So you're not going to resign, I guess."

Tommy obviously had talked with Vern.

"You can state that for the record. I'm not walking away from a job the people of Paradise County elected me to do." God, I thought, I sound just like a politician. So be it.

Tommy asked a few more perfunctory questions before turning off his recorder. "You make a good case for yourself," he said. "Of course, I never really believed you're the Serenader. Maybe some people do, but I don't."

"'Some people' being?"

"Well, Arne for one, but he's got his own troubles to worry about."

"He does. What's he been doing on his leave of absence besides making trouble for me?"

"I hear he's holed up at his farm house and still trying to run the office even though his chief deputy, Jack Brown, is supposed to be in charge. I also hear those BCA guys are seriously looking at Arne for Marty's murder, not to mention that stuff with the hooker. Arne's in a lot of shit right now. He'll be in even deeper come Friday."

"Sounds like you have some revelations in the works," I said.

"Oh yeah, let's just say my special edition will be well illustrated."

"I look forward to reading it. So what else are you hearing these days?"

Tommy looked at me with his eager eyes and said, "Well, there's some interesting dope about that girlfriend of yours."

I wasn't aware I had a 'girlfriend,' at least not at the moment. "And who would that be?" I asked.

"You know, that Black lawyer from Chicago. I hear she's been spending a lot of time with you."

"Listen, Tommy, Cassandra Ellis is not my girlfriend. Where did you get that idea?"

"Nowhere in particular. But the word around town is that you two are really close."

"As in we're having sex? That's bullshit, Tommy, so don't go there."

"Okay, okay. It's just something I heard, that's all. Well, I should be going. I have lots of work to do. Thanks for talking to me, and make sure you read the *Tattler* on Friday. There'll be some surprises."

"I can hardly wait. One more thing. I've done you plenty of favors, Tommy, and you owe me a few of your own. If you find out any big news about what's going on here you give me a head's up, all right? I need to be the first to know."

"Fair enough," Tommy said.

Cassandra was stuck in Chicago. She'd called on Monday to say the hearing had been delayed. By Wednesday the news was even worse.

"It's just one fucking thing after another," she said over the phone. "I won't be able to get up to Pineland until Saturday at the earliest. Sorry, but there's nothing I can do about it."

"I understand," I said, then told her about my conversation with Tommy and the voices on the thumb drive.

"That's really strange, but the voices must be of real importance to the Serenader."

"Agreed, but we're in the dark unless we can figure out who the voices belong to."

"Well, let me know if you learn anything more. By the way, you were in the *Sun-Times* yesterday."

"Really? Was I named lawyer of the year?"

"No. But there was a big feature story about Pineland and the Serenader. The story mentioned that you're suspected of writing the messages. Thankfully, it didn't include the latest news about the typewriter."

"My lucky day, I guess. I hate to tell you, but you may be in for some publicity as well. Tommy passed on a widely-circulating rumor here that we're bed mates."

"So, if I'm a Black woman I must be sleeping around, is that it?"

"I'm pretty sure the same rumor would be floating around if you were white. Apparently, people think I'm so charming women find me irresistible."

"You're not all that charming," Cassandra said. "So what about this Redmond guy? How much do you think he knows?"

"Hard to say. Tommy's the town magnet. He attracts all sorts of junk and he doesn't always bother to sort it out. There are also times I think he just makes up things to stir the pot."

"Fake news, Pineland style?"

"Something like that. Tommy's big story is coming out Friday. I'll save a copy for you."

"Okay. I'll give you a call when I get in Saturday. Are you still up for going to St. Cloud?"

"Sure," I said. "It'll be nice to get out of town."

I spent the next day dodging reporters and ignoring phone calls, except for one, from Alice Sigurdson. She said she'd talked to the two Jasons and recanted her alibi for Arne.

"I'm moving out," she added. "I told Arne yesterday."

"How did he take it?"

"He actually seemed surprised. Can you believe it?"

I could. Husbands can be incredibly stupid when it comes to reading their wives, a behavior with which I was personally familiar.

"Where are you going to go?" I asked Alice.

"I've found an apartment in town. It'll work for the time being."

"Okay. Good luck, and let me know if you have any problems with Arne. I can be of help if need be."

"Thanks so much," she said and disconnected.

With his alibi gone, Arne became the prime suspect in Marty's murder. He wouldn't be for long.

The special edition of the *Tattler* arrived at my office Friday while I was at lunch. Doug always bags it at his desk, so he'd read every word by the time I returned.

"Wow, some interesting stuff," he said, tossing the newspaper on my desk. "You and that Black girl are big news. Is she, you know, pretty hot, or shouldn't I be asking?"

"Go away, Doug," I said and started reading.

Tommy's special edition, all six pages of it, offered up a journalistic jambalaya filled with several well-spiced stories written in his usual delirious style. There was also a full-page ad from the Word of God Church suggesting repentance would be a good idea for everybody. The Reverend Ronnie clearly knew a good advertising vehicle when he saw one because the special edition was sure to be read by just about everyone in Paradise County.

The longest and least interesting story was a rehash of the latest news about the murders, fires, and the doings of the Serenader. But two other front-page stories were real eye catchers. One of them unspooled next to a three-column reproduction of the photo showing Jill Lorrimer on Arne's lap, her nipples blurred so as not to offend the delicate sensibilities of the reading public. The story below recounted Arne's various troubles and did not shy away from speculating about his possible involvement in the deaths of Jill and Marty.

It was a riveting read, but Tommy also had plenty to say about Cassandra Ellis in a separate story. The headline said it all: "Evidence Mounts Chicago Lawyer is Peter Swindell's Daughter." Tommy had no shortage of details, including a more or less accurate description of the letter that had lured Cassandra to Pineland. The story went on to say Cassandra "worked very closely with County Attorney Paul Zweifel before he recused himself from the case." Readers were left to judge what "very closely" might mean.

Although Tommy had already linked Cassandra to Peter in his blog posts, the story in the *Tattler*, with its details about the letter, promised to ratchet up the pressure on her. The national media, I feared, would take renewed interest in the story and come chasing after Cassandra. She wouldn't like that, and neither would her fancy law firm.

The only other story of interest was tucked away on the back page under the headline, "Zweifel Says He's Not the Serenader." I plowed through it and discovered I'd come off reasonably well. Tommy being Tommy, however, there were wildly overwrought details—did I really have "bags like dark, angry bruises" under my eyes?—and he managed to garble a few facts. But on the whole I had no cause to complain.

That evening I called Cassandra and told her about Tommy's story.

"Well, that's just wonderful," she said. "I'm becoming a regular media sensation in the middle of a triple-murder case. The partners will be very unhappy."

"I imagine they will be. My advice when the media horde comes for you is to issue a brief statement of some kind. You know, you were simply trying to trace your roots, you're not sure Peter is in fact your father but you're saddened by his death, etcetera, etcetera, and you'll have nothing more to say at present."

"Fuck," Cassandra said. "I don't need this shit right now."

"I agree. Maybe you should forget about coming back here for a while. Let things simmer down."

"No, I have to see this through. I'll be back Sunday. Pineland's such a beautiful goddamn place I just can't stay away."

39

Saturday was a day of rest and evasion. I slept late, then took Camus out to Pembroke Woods for a long traipse. I started thinking of the man in black and Cassandra and all that had happened, but after a while the old trees spoke to me. They counseled calm and patience, and by the time I coaxed Camus back to the Prius I was feeling better than I had in days.

The good feelings didn't last. My land line at home began to ring incessantly. Reporters from across the continent wanted to talk to me. Even someone from the *Wall Street Journal* called, no doubt in search of insightful financial advice. I've never been interested in being front-page news, but that hardly mattered. The Serenader was now manipulating my life, and I was merely along for the ride at his amusement park of chaos.

I wanted to pursue a night of oblivion with Jack but the part of me that isn't a complete fool counseled sobriety. I listened to that part. When night finally arrived, I went out on my back patio with Camus and looked at the stars. The air was calm, the sky clear, the stars a spangled salute to the flight of time. I don't believe in omens or dream visions or anything that might foretell the future. But I do believe that lodged in our old animal brains, well beyond the boundaries of conscious thought, there are intimations of things to come, swirling around like ghosts in a haunted house. And as I gazed up at the lonely stars, the ghosts were telling me something very bad was about to happen.

I woke up Sunday morning at nine o'clock to the sound of my cell phone ringing. The call was from Tommy Redmond, one of the few people I'd entrusted with the number. What he had to say roused me from my sleep like the crack of a gunshot.

"You didn't hear this from me, but those BCA guys are looking to get a search warrant for your house. They got a tip about some crucial evidence you're supposedly hiding. Apparently they consider the information very credible."

"What kind of evidence?"

"Don't know, but the BCA guys think it could blow the whole case wide open."

"How'd you find out so quickly about the tip?"

"That's my business. But you said I owed you a favor, and now you've got it. So what are you going to do?"

"Await the posse," I said. In fact, I wasn't at all sure what I'd do, but I didn't want to share any plans with Tommy. He was a conduit and the current flowed both ways.

"Well, good luck," he said. "I think you're going to need it."

I had no idea what the supposedly "crucial evidence" was or who had tipped off the BCA. Maybe the Serenader had shifted course and wanted to implicate me as well as Arne in Marty's murder or other crimes. If that was the case, the Serenader wouldn't have alerted the authorities about my house unless he knew it contained highly incriminating evidence. But how would he know?

Camus interrupted my thoughts by dragging out his leash. He wanted to go for a walk and he'd start barking until I complied.

"All right," I said, snapping on the leash. "But we won't be gone for long."

At that instant, I had a disturbing thought that produced a big, ugly knot in my stomach. It concerned Camus and the message the Serenader had posted on my front door days earlier. I'd assumed his motive was simply to cast suspicion on me as the possible author of the message. But now it dawned on me that the Serenader had selected a most fortuitous day to do his work. Camus, guardian of the household and no friend to questionable strangers, was away all that day being groomed—a rare event. In fact, it was the only time in weeks he hadn't been stationed at my house.

If the Serenader knew Camus would be absent, he would have had a perfect opportunity to rummage through my house before leaving his message. Which meant he could have taken things from the house, or, better yet, left a prize clue behind to be found later by Jason Braddock and his crew.

I'm not a tidy housekeeper. My modest estate is a dense-
ly packed repository of items that should have been thrown
out long ago, much of it stored in two back bedrooms piled
high with boxes, old pieces of furniture and the accumulat-
ed detritus of a life not particularly well lived. I also have a
basement and garage filled with junk. All of which meant I'd
be hard pressed to find a carefully hidden piece of evidence
without a lengthy search. Trouble was, I didn't think I had
much time.

I took Camus for a very short walk, my mind a race-
horse, and by the time we returned a couple of bright ideas
had found their way into my brain. I went into the kitchen,
where I keep my everyday keys, all neatly labeled, on little
hooks. Duplicate keys and others I rarely use are scattered in
a drawer below. My regular keys were all in place, including
the one to my father's office. That key has a duplicate, however, which is supposed to be in the drawer. It wasn't there. So
now I knew the Serenader had been in my house at least once
and had found the duplicate key to the office, thereby allow-
ing him to plant the incriminating typewriter. But what, if
anything, had he left behind while he rummaged through my
home?

My land line, an elderly Panasonic handset, is in the
kitchen, with a second phone in the bedroom. The kitchen
line looked okay. Not so the bedroom. There I found a tiny
black transmitter with two wires attached to the phone line
near its plug-in behind my bed. No wonder the Serenader
seemed to know my every move. I left the transmitter in
place, since its presence could be used to argue I'd been a
victim of the Serenader's scheming. If he'd bugged my land

line, I could only assume he might also be listening in on my cell phone calls.

I was certain now the impending search of my house would turn up some damning piece of evidence. But what would "blow the case wide open," as Tommy Redmond had put it? I soon had an "oh shit" moment. I went down to the basement, where I keep most of my father's old belongings, including his Colt revolver. I'd hung on to the gun on the off chance I might need it someday for personal protection but had never fired it. It was supposed to be in a cardboard banker's box marked "father's stuff #1." The box seemed to be in order—the top was still on—but when I looked inside the gun was gone.

I stared at the box for a moment and knew I was in really big trouble. The revolver, I feared, had been used to kill Peter and Dewey Swindell and Marty Moreland. I suspected it had now been returned to my house and squirreled away in some obscure corner. I'd been at Pembroke Woods with Camus for hours the day before. Had the Serenader taken that opportunity to return the gun and then tip off authorities where to find it? Of course he had. Once again, he'd made me his pawn.

A cheery disregard for reality is not among my limited inventory of virtues, so I knew what would happen if searchers found the murder weapon on my property. I'd be arrested on the spot and taken to the jail on suspicion of first-degree murder. That is, if I was around to be arrested.

To obtain a search warrant, Jason would have to prepare suitable documentation, locate a judge—undoubtedly my old buddy A. A. Anderson—to approve it, assemble a team of law officers, and then head to my house, probably around noon at the earliest. Another possibility was that Jason might wait to serve a late-night, no-knock warrant. Such warrants are typically approved in cases where there's reason to think evidence might be quickly disposed of if officers politely announce their presence before conducting the search.

I didn't think Jason would go the late-night route, simply because the longer he waited to serve the warrant, the more time I'd have to find out about it via the local gossip network. I glanced at my watch. It was nine thirty. I devoted half an hour to a search of the house, but I didn't find the gun or any other damning evidence. The clock was ticking down. Jason would be at my door before long. It was time for some seriously creative thinking.

When I left the house an hour later, I didn't have my cell phone with me. But I did have Camus, who was in the back seat, whining. He's never liked car rides.

"Don't worry," I told him, "we don't have far to go."

I drove into town, parked in front of Kat Berglund's apartment, and went up the steps with Camus to see if she was home.

"Jesus," she said when she opened the door, "do you know what time it is?"

"Early for you, but getting late for me," I said as Camus wandered inside to putter around. "I need to a big favor."

Kat, bless her, was willing. "How long will you be gone?" she asked after I'd returned to my Prius to fetch a bag of dog food, a package of Camus's favorite chew toys, and a bed he used when I wasn't around to sleep with.

"A couple of days, no more. Camus will be fine. I think he likes you already."

I'd told Kat an old college friend of mine was dying of leukemia in Minneapolis and had called at the last minute for help with his tangled estate. I lied because I didn't want Kat to get in trouble. The less she knew, the better. I wasn't at all sure she bought my story, but it didn't matter. She was willing to trust me.

I lied again when I asked her to take Camus for a walk while I called my supposedly dying friend. Camus wasn't eager to go without me, but Kat got some venison sausage out of her refrigerator and led Camus nose-first down the stairs.

Using Kat's landline, I called Cassandra. I couldn't lie to her, not with what I wanted her to do, so I laid out my situation.

"You can say 'no,'" I said. "In fact, you probably should."

She didn't hesitate. "Not a chance. I'm coming along. I've already got a three o'clock flight scheduled to the Twin Cities. You're going to need a good lawyer. By the way, where are you calling from?"

I told her. "Do you still have your cell?" she asked.

"No, I tossed it because it could be used to track me."

"Okay, I'll get a couple of burner phones so we can communicate. See you later."

Once Camus settled in with Kat, I gave her a kiss and left. Not much goes on in Pineland on Sunday mornings, and Paradise Avenue was deserted as I slipped into my Prius and headed toward Swaboda's Funeral Home a few blocks away.

Cousin-in-law Dale, I knew, was busy partying in Las Vegas, and I was certain no one alive would be in the funeral home. I parked in the rear lot, which was screened by a row of trees, and got out a heavy crowbar I'd taken from my tool collection. I forced open the back door, which gave way with surprising ease, and slipped inside.

A two-stall garage occupies much of the mortuary's lower level, along with the embalming room where the little surprise had been left on Marty Moreland's corpse. I went into the garage. A shiny black hearse took up one of the stalls. I opened the garage doors, moved my Prius inside next to the hearse and then closed everything up. The Prius, I figured, would be safely hidden from view until Dale returned.

I'd scavenged food from my house – a bag of potato chips, a box of Cheerios and a half-loaf of bread, along with sliced Provolone cheese, milk and orange juice in an ice chest. Not exactly a feast, but it would keep me going until morning. I'd also taken along a duffel bag with spare clothes.

So equipped, I settled in. There was a television set in Dale's office and I watched talking heads on CNN, a Twins game and other fine programming until the local news finally came on at five. I was not mentioned, which was good.

I debated whether to call Tommy to see if a search warrant had indeed been served at my house, but decided against it. Tommy liked nothing better than sharing other people's secrets. He might report to Jason that I'd called, and then it would be easy to track me down via a phone trace.

So I waited around for the ten o'clock news. I tried the ABC affiliate from Duluth first and there I was, the lead story, my less than gorgeous visage plastered across the screen.

A warrant had been issued for my arrest on three counts of murder following a search of my house. The report didn't say what the searchers had found, but it had to be the murder weapon.

Later, I learned that the two Jasons along with a bevy of other law officers had come to my house just after one o'clock. I'd conveniently left the door open, figuring they would have battered it down otherwise, and so the lawmen waltzed in and proceeded to tear the place apart with all the enthusiasm of monkeys at a banana plantation.

I turned off the television and tried to sleep on Dale's leather couch, but it was no use. I was still wide awake by the time Cassandra arrived the next morning.

40

Cassandra pulled into the funeral home's parking just before eight. She was driving a nondescript Hyundai Elantra instead of her usual high-profile Beamer. I'd asked her to rent an inconspicuous car. The Hyundai, I figured, wouldn't attract much attention in the lot.

"What the hell is this place?" she asked when I came out to greet her. I gave her a sort of semi-hug—Cassandra isn't the touchy-feely type—and said, "It's a famous building designed by Frank Lloyd Wright."

"Looks more like some crazy-ass spaceship," she said.

"Too bad we can't fly away in it. Look, before we go any further, I want to be clear about one thing. You can get back in your car and drive away from all this ridiculous shit right now if you want to. Come with me and you'll be harboring a fugitive, and then all sorts of unpleasant things could happen to you and your career."

"I think you're worth harboring," she said. "Just don't get caught. We need time to figure this out. Besides, I'm sure the press would be all over me if I was in Chicago. That story your buddy wrote must have hit the national wires by now, so you could say I'm a fugitive, too."

She had arrived, as always, in a state of elegant attire, wearing dark slacks and a high-necked cashmere sweater that looked expensively Italian. He buckled shoes, from Gucci, weren't cheap either. She'd brought along some breakfast sandwiches and coffee from Starbucks and we went into Dale's office to eat and talk. Cassandra dug into her purse and handed me an LG phone.

"Straight from Walmart," she said. "Nineteen ninety-nine, plus tax. I've got one, too. We have ten hours of use. Make sure you memorize your number and mine."

"Will do. Makes me feel like a real criminal."

"You are, until we can prove otherwise."

"That's going to be the trick. If St. Cloud is a dead end, I don't have a plan B except to be arrested and become a criminal celebrity. And even if we do find what we're looking for in St. Cloud, we'll still have to figure out how to get that information into the hands of the right law enforcement people. The delightful Jason Braddock is convinced I'm guilty and he's running the show here."

"What about that assistant attorney general who's handling the case now? Maybe he'd be the guy to go through. What his name again?"

"Chad Barrington. I've had only minimal contact with him. All I know is that he thinks he's the smartest man in the world because he went to Yale Law School."

"Harvard's actually much better," Cassandra said.

"You would know. Me, I'm just a dumb kid who went to Billy Mitchell."

"You're not dumb. You're plenty smart, no matter where you went to law school."

"Well, let's hope I'm smart enough to get out of this mess. As for Chad Barrington, I'm not sure he can be trusted. In fact, I'm not sure of much of anything when it comes right down to it. I have a feeling this is all going to end badly."

"That's what I like about you," Cassandra said. "You're such a fucking optimist."

Dale's hearse is a 1990s-vintage Cadillac Fleetwood with a vinyl top, a huge V-8 and a front seat wide enough to hold my Prius. White lettering on the front doors identifies the vehicle as belonging to "Swaboda's Funeral Home." I'd found a chauffeur's cap and a black suit coat at the mortuary, along with a nice metal coffin, which Cassandra and I mounted on its stand in the back of the hearse. For all the world knew, I'd simply be a hearse driver on the way to a funeral. Probably, I thought, my own.

We pulled out a few minutes before nine and headed toward St. Cloud. I guided the Caddie along at a respectable fifty-five miles an hour, its engine purring like a fat old house cat. Just out of town a state trooper went by in the opposite direction but didn't appear to give me any notice. Cassandra was in the back seat, behind tinted glass, because I thought the sight of her up front might arouse suspicion as we passed through small towns where Black people are generally seen only on television.

Along the way, we worked out a strategy for our visit to St. Cloud. Under normal circumstances, we would have gone to law enforcement there and made inquiries about the murdered Biersdorfs and their foster children, Peter Swindell's illegitimate son possibly among them. But that wasn't an option now, so we decided our first stop would be at the offices of the local newspaper, the *St. Cloud Times.*

Cassandra had already done a variety of deep online searches looking into the fate of the Biersdorfs. She'd found some straightforward news accounts of the crime, along with photos of the couple, but no images showing any of the children who'd lived at their home. Cassandra said the most detailed stories online all came from the *Times.*

"One said the police had identified a person of interest in the murders but didn't name any names," she told me. "Another one said the cops in St. Cloud believe whoever killed the Biersdorfs also burned down their house. But the bottom line is that the cops weren't able to make a case against anybody."

"So if your brother murdered the Biersdorfs, it looks like he got away with it."

"We'll see about that," Cassandra said. "Maybe he fooled the cops but he won't be able to fool me."

St. Cloud is the largest city in central Minnesota and I didn't think most people there would pay much attention to news out of Pineland concerning a certain fugitive county attorney. I wanted to remain on the loose as long as I could and being in a city of St. Cloud's size provided some measure of anonymity. At least, I hoped it would.

"You went to school here, didn't you?" Cassandra said as we rolled into St. Cloud just before ten.

"I did. I can't remember many of my classes but I got to know every bar in town. It was quite an education. How about you? Any wild college days?"

"Not really. I've never been much of a drinker."

"I wish I could say the same. Believe me, you haven't missed a thing."

Our first stop was at a newspaper box, where we bought a copy of the *Times* and found its office address. The newspaper occupied a one-story brick building in an industrial area on the north side of the city. I parked in a lot out front and stayed in the hearse while Cassandra went into the newsroom. She intended to present herself as a producer for Investigation ID, the all-crime, all-the-time cable network. Her cover story was that the network planned to do a story about the Biersdorf murders and she was gathering background information.

Cassandra was gone for nearly an hour. When she returned, she slipped into the back seat and said, "Start driving. I'll give you directions. I think we may have gotten really lucky."

Our good fortune stemmed from the fact that a reporter working in the *Times* newsroom had written extensively about the Biersdorf murders in 2001. Her name was Marjorie Flahave and she and Cassandra had hit it off immediately.

"Before long I was calling her Marge and we were chatting away like sisters," Cassandra said. "She told me a kid named Phillip Gordon, who was sixteen at the time and lived with the Biersdorfs, was the person of interest in the murder investigation."

His last name told the story. "It has to be my brother," "Cassandra said. "I guess he kept, or was given, my mother's name. As for Phillip—"

"My father's name. Maybe not a coincidence either since dear old dad handled the adoption proceedings. I take it the kid was never arrested."

"No. Apparently the cops put all kinds of pressure on him but he never cracked. He and five other foster kids were at the house the night the Biersdorfs were shot. All of them, Phillip included, claimed to be asleep upstairs and said they didn't hear a thing. The Biersdorfs had a downstairs bedroom and that's where they were killed. There was a safe in the bedroom and it was open when the bodies were discovered the next morning by one of the foster kids. Marge told me the Biersdorfs were rumored to keep a lot of cash in the safe but the cops were never able to figure out how much might have been taken."

"Did the cops think it was a robbery and murder by someone who broke into the house?"

"No. Marge said the cops never bought the robbery idea because the gun used to kill the Biersdorfs was their own. It was a revolver they supposedly kept in the safe. The gun was found on the floor next to their bed. It would be a real stretch to think a burglar broke into the house, managed to open the safe, found a gun inside and then used it to shoot the Biersdorfs."

"So the cops assumed it was an inside job."

"Right. They believed that Phillip, who was the oldest and known to be the most rebellious of the foster children, did the deed. The other kids, three boys and two girls, were quite a bit younger. The oldest was only eleven, according to Marge. She said the cops, despite their suspicions, just couldn't pin the crime on Phillip. "

"They must have done a gun residue test on him."

"They did and found nothing. They didn't find the stolen money either, or fingerprints or any other trace evidence that might link him to the murders. And no matter how hard they pressed him, he stuck by his story."

"Pretty cool, calculating behavior for a teenage boy. So what would have been his motive for killing the Biersdorfs?"

"No one knows for sure, but Marge told me something very interesting. It seems there were allegations of abuse, sexual and otherwise, at the home. An anonymous complaint was made to the St. Cloud police and they opened an investigation just before the Biersdorfs were murdered."

"Did the cops find evidence of abuse?"

"From what Marge said, they didn't really have time to make any findings. So it's hard to say what happened. But if Phillip was abused, that would certainly be a motive for murder. He also had a reputation for being very belligerent and hard to control, so it's pretty obvious he didn't get along with his foster parents."

"Was Marge able tell you anything about Phillip's background?"

"A little. She described him as a 'foundling'—there's an old word for you—and she didn't know the circumstances of his birth. But get this: Marge told me young Phillip was a genius. Supposedly had an IQ of one-sixty-five."

"Great. Too bad he also may be bat-shit crazy. What happened to him after the murder investigation?"

"Marge didn't know. Presumably, he went out on his own when he turned eighteen and left St. Cloud."

"I don't suppose your friend Marge had any photos of him?"

"No. The cops never circulated photos of Phillip or the other foster kids to the media because they were all juveniles. Obviously, we can't go to the cops right now and ask to see a picture of him. But Marge told me where we might find a photo. Turn right up ahead."

We were driving along St. Germain Street, St. Cloud's main drag. I took the next right, went north a few blocks and saw sign for "Sunset Ridge Care Community."

"Park as far from the building as you can," Cassie said as we pulled up. The nursing home was brick, oblong, two stories, and charmless, a warehouse for the old and infirm.

"I take it we're visiting someone," I said.

"We are. Her name is Emma Biersdorf. She's James's sister and his only surviving blood relative. Marge interviewed her after the murders, and they've kept in touch. She had a bad fall recently and her health is deteriorating. Mentally she's still in good shape, or at least she was the last time Marge talked with her. So, do you want to go in with me or should I handle this on my own?"

"I'll tag along. What's the routine? We're not family or anyone known to the staff at the home. I'm sure we can't just waltz in and talk to her."

"I think the TV producer thing might work again," Cassandra said. "You can be my assistant."

"Good, because that's how I think of myself. I imagine you'll want to do most of the talking."

"You imagine correctly."

"Lead on," I said and followed Cassandra into the nursing home.

41

To Cassandra's immense surprise, the nursing home's receptionist was a tall young Somali woman in traditional attire.

"May I help you?" the woman asked, with a Minnesota accent as pure as it comes.

"Why, yes, I think you can," Cassandra said.

She quickly established rapport with the receptionist, whose name was Mara. We learned she'd been raised in Minneapolis, which has a large Somali community. She'd moved to St. Cloud a year ago with her husband, who worked in a meat-packing plant. She didn't mind St. Cloud but thought Minneapolis was better.

Cassandra soon spun out her story about being a television producer from New York researching the Biersdorf case. She introduced me as Roger Smith. Mara didn't know about the Biersdorf murders but Cassandra was entirely convincing, and we were soon heading down a long, antiseptic hallway toward Emma Biersdorf's room.

We stopped just outside and Mara said, "Emma's kind of a crabapple. I'm not sure she'll even talk to you."

"Well, we'll give it a try," Cassandra said as we stepped into the room.

"Emma, you have visitors," Mara announced and then left.

Emma Biersdorf was sitting in a wheelchair at her window, swathed in a pink robe, a colorful afghan spread across her lap. I guessed she was in her mid-seventies. She had high, proud cheekbones, the kind supermodels would die for, and well-proportioned features, but age had made its usual assault. Her face was blotched and puffy, her skin a maze of wrinkles, her long gray hair an untended tangle. Cataract lenses magnified her hazel eyes.

"Who are you?" she demanded.

Cassandra offered up our phony identifications and said, "We'd like to ask about your brother, James. We want to feature him in a story about what happened back in 2001."

"You want to dig that up, do you?" Emma said, wheeling her chair away from the window and eying us like the dubious customers we were. "Why didn't you call me earlier?"

"To be honest, we just found out about you today when we talked to Marge Flahave over at the *Times*," Cassandra said. "She sends her regards, by the way."

The mention of Marge seemed to give us credence. "Where did you say you're from again? Is it the same channel that Kenda fellow is on? I like him."

Cassandra paused, clearly unaware of the exploits of the retired Colorado Springs police detective who'd become a minor celebrity as the "Homicide Hunter."

"That's right," I said. "Joe Kenda is quite a guy. We've enjoyed working with him."

"So what do you want from me?" Emma said, looking pleased that I supposedly knew Kenda. "If you ask me, that kid did it, but they never caught him."

"Yes, I believe his name was Phillip Gordon," Cassandra said. "Did you know him?"

"Not really. I didn't see their kids very often. Jimmy and his wife never had much time for me."

"So you weren't close to your brother?"

"Half-brother. Truth is, I never liked Jimmy. He was ten years younger than me and his father had a lot of money. Mine didn't. That's how Jimmy got that big house. Money from daddy."

"And then he and his wife began fostering children?"

"Yes. I guess Janice couldn't have kids so they started a group home. A whole bunch of kids went through the place. Too many, if you ask me. Who'd want to deal with all that trouble?"

"Did you ever visit them there?"

"Over the Christmas holidays was usually the only time. They decorated the house like there was no tomorrow. Christmas crap everywhere. Just before dinner, the kids would come marching down the steps, all dressed up, with some stupid song Jimmy wrote playing over the speakers."

Our ears perked up. "Did the song have a title?" Cassandra asked.

"It was some kind of serenade thing."

"'Pineland Serenade?'" I suggested.

"Yes, that might be it. How did you know?"

"It turned up in our research," Cassandra said. "We understand your half-brother taught music at the high school in Pineland."

"That's right. But then he got a job teaching here and married Janice. Pretty soon his father died. Our mother was already dead by then, so Jimmy made out like a bandit in the will. Got a big house and a lot of money. After that, Jimmy quit teaching and started the group home. You know what I got in the will? A thousand dollars and 'nice knowing you.' Life isn't fair, is it?"

"No, it most definitely is not," Cassandra said. "Do you know when Phillip Gordon began living at the home?"

"No, but as I recall he was just a baby when they took him in. Grew up to be one of those rebellious types. They probably thought they could save his soul and look what it got them."

Cassandra nodded in sympathy. "Yes, it's very sad. Was your brother a religious man?"

"He claimed to be."

There was a hint of contempt in Emma's response, and Cassandra picked up on it. "I don't want to pry into your personal business, but it sounds like you have some doubts about your brother. We've heard some things as well, concerning possibly improper behavior at the home."

"You mean diddling the kids?"

I had to give Emma credit. She didn't put any sugar on her cereal.

"Yes, that's what we've heard," Cassandra said. "Do you think it could be true?"

"I don't know. What I can tell you is that Jimmy maybe liked children more than a man should."

Cassandra began maneuvering toward our ultimate destination. "It's been very kind of you to talk to us, Miss Biersdorf. There's just one other thing. We'd love to have any family photos of your brother, his wife and their foster kids for our show. It would be especially nice if you have one with Phillip Gordon."

"I don't keep much of that stuff," Emma said. "When you're as old and sick as I am, all you have is your memories and sometimes you wish you didn't because they don't really amount to anything. Your life is going down the drain and who cares? Anyway, Janice's family—they're in Florida now—got most of the things."

Cassandra persisted. "Anything at all you have in the way of family memorabilia would be very helpful."

"Well, I might have something. There's a photo album on the top shelf in the closet over there. Could you get it down for me?"

I fetched the album and gave it to her. She started going through it as we looked over her shoulder.

"Here's one of Jimmy and two of the kids," she said. "Nineteen eighty-seven."

The photo showed a florid, balding man in his late thirties, flanked by a boy and a girl who both looked about ten. I saw nothing familiar in the boy's face and in any case, Phillip would have been only two years old at the time. Emma continued leafing through the album, but most of the photos were of her and various friends. James, Janice and their foster children were ignored.

Then she stopped and said, "Wait a minute. I just remembered something. It'd be at the back."

Her wrinkled hands found the last page of the album. "Here it is. It was the last Christmas card I got from Jimmy and Janice in two thousand. All the kids are there with them."

I stared at the photo. James and the woman who I assumed to be his wife posed in front of a Christmas tree. Next to them, arranged by height, were six children, four boys and two girls. Standing beside James was the oldest child, a boy in his teens. He was tall and slender, with long dark hair and sharp dark eyes that stared at the camera with indifference. I knew his face.

"Yes, that's Phillip," I said, "next to your brother."

Emma was startled. "Have you seen him before?"

"Many times," I said. "He hasn't gone far."

"So now what?" Cassandra said when we returned to the hearse.

"I'm thinking," I said.

Emma hadn't wanted to part with her Christmas card, and our burner phones didn't have cameras. But Mara agreed to take a shot of the card with her phone. She e-mailed the image to Cassandra, who had her laptop with her. We studied the image for a while in the hearse as we tried to figure out what to do next.

I said, "As I see it, we've got a couple of options. We could go to the authorities now and tell them all about Phillip and why we believe he's a murderer. Or, we could do something else."

"'Something else' being?"

"Go back to Pineland and try to make our own case against him before I'm arrested. It'd be a real long shot, though."

Cassandra said, "Well, I don't think going to police would gain you much. The trouble is we don't have any proof at the moment that Phillip is guilty of anything. All we know for sure is that he's in Pineland, using a new name. That's not a crime. He might even admit he's Peter's lost son if the authorities come asking, but so what? He'll probably claim he and daddy dearest were reconciled, and who's to prove otherwise?"

"Does that mean you're ready to try option number two?"

"It does. What other choice do we have? We'll be in jail pretty soon, and once that happens, it'll be much harder for us to make a case against Phillip. He's one clever motherfucker and he's worked everything out. But I don't think he knows we're onto him, and that's the advantage we have right now."

"All right, back to Pineland it is."

We reached Swaboda's by three. I put the hearse in the garage and we went into Dale's office. We'd developed a plan to smoke out Phillip, and it involved playing his own game. There'd be a new message, identifying Phillip as the Serenader and exposing his real identity. We planned to post it at a place sure to get the attention of authorities. Our plan was to post the message after dark and then, to ensure it was found, call in an anonymous tip to the sheriff's office.

We'd stopped for sandwiches at a Subway in St. Cloud but by late afternoon I needed a snack. Cassandra remembered she had a six-pack of granola bars in her car and went out to retrieve it while I continued to work on the exact wording of the message.

I thought she'd be back in literally a minute but she wasn't. Maybe she was digging around for her granola treasure. Another minute went by and I sensed something was wrong. I rushed out to the parking lot. Cassandra's rented Hyundai was there but she wasn't. I opened the driver's side door and peered into the front seat, where a pack of chocolate-chip granola bars lay next to one of Cassandra's pearl earrings. A wave of fear sliced through me, sharp as a sword. I didn't want to believe what I knew in my heart.

Phillip had come for her.

42

In Hollywood movies, when disaster strikes, the hero always knows instantaneously what to do. Orders are issued, forces assembled, everyday people turn magically into gunfighters and stunt drivers, and off they all go to save the day. None of that happened to me.

I stared at the car seat, dumbfounded, a river of questions rushing through my head. What did Phillip intend to do with Cassandra? Where would he take her? How had he found us? Should I call the police immediately to report Cassandra's kidnapping and hope the cops would believe me even as they locked me up?

I took a deep breath and tried to focus. I was pretty sure Phillip wouldn't do immediate harm to Cassandra. He'd want to talk to her, out of sheer spite if nothing else, to contrast his life story with hers, to explain all the injustices that had befallen him after his abandonment and to expound on his brilliant scheme of revenge. It would be a form of malevolent pleasure to have her as his captive audience, and he would take his time. And then? The thought made me sick. I—or the law—had to find Cassandra.

I saw no real choice about what to do next. I went out to the garage and backed out my Prius. Rain was falling, accompanied by blustery winds, and no one was on the streets. I called 911 as I drove east toward Pembroke Woods, where I thought I'd be safe for a while.

An operator answered on the second ring. "Nine-one-one. What is your emergency?"

"I'd like to report a kidnapping."

There was a brief pause—maybe the operator was startled—before she said, "All right, sir, who was kidnapped?"

I provided the details, as succinctly as I could. I stated where and when the abduction had occurred. I gave the operator Cassandra's full name, age, and a physical description, including her clothes. I also described her rented Hyundai and how it had been left in the funeral home's lot. I went on to identify the man who had taken Cassandra, using the name he went by in Pineland. I described him. I said he was almost surely armed and dangerous. I suggested a check of his license information to see what kind of vehicle he might be driving.

The more I unwound the story the crazier it sounded, even to me. I knew the operator would find it equally strange.

The operator finally broke in. "And what's your name, sir?"

"I can't say. But please believe me, there's been a kidnapping and Miss Ellis is in extreme danger."

"Yes, sir. We're sending a unit to the funeral home. Can you tell me why Miss Ellis was there?"

Good question, ma'am. "It's a long story. But if you contact Jason Braddock from the state Bureau of Criminal Apprehension he can fill you in about Miss Ellis." I knew Jason's cell number by heart and gave it to the operator.

"Will you be at the scene when the officers arrive?" the operator asked.

"No. But you have to take this seriously and call Jason. A life is at stake here."

Then I disconnected.

The lot at Pembroke Woods was deserted, as I hoped it would be. A narrow gravel service road used for park maintenance leads off into the pines and I followed it until I was out of view from the parking lot. As a kid, I'd thought the trees, with their long straight trunks, were columns holding up the sky. Maybe they were. Now I felt as though the sky had fallen, collapsed in pieces around me, and I wasn't sure what to do. Stay calm, I told myself, and think.

I assumed Pineland police had gone to the funeral home and found Cassandra's rental car. I also assumed Jim Myers or someone else at the police department had contacted Jason. Then wheels would turn and it wouldn't take long to finger me as the 911 caller.

So now what? I couldn't go to my house because the police would put it under surveillance. Kaitlyn Berglund's apartment might provide a refuge, but I didn't want her to possibly face charges of sheltering a fugitive. I considered turning myself in. But would Jim Meyers or Jason Braddock believe anything I told them? Probably not. Instead, they might conclude I'd done something to Cassandra and that the kidnapping story was just a smokescreen to hide my criminal activity. And if that were the case, precious time would be lost.

Then, from somewhere out in the great blue yonder, an idea wormed its way into my head. There was one man in Pineland who just might have a motive to help me, a man whose chance for redemption might also be my best chance to find Cassandra. It was worth a try.

I picked up my burner phone and punched in a familiar number. A gruff voice answered after the fourth ring: "Who's this?"

"Paul Zweifel. Don't hang up."

Arne said, "What the fuck do you want?"

"I want to find Cassandra Ellis and you can help me. She's been abducted and I know who took her." I identified the kidnapper, as he was known in Pineland, and said, "His real name is Phillip Gordon. He's Peter Swindell's son and he's the man who framed you with that photo."

A long pause followed and I thought Arne was about to disconnect. Then he said, "I'm listening."

I knew when I made the call that Arne was my last hope, despite all that had happened between us. He didn't like me, didn't trust me and blamed me for his recent troubles. He may even have believed I was a murderer. But I also understood how angry he was about the compromising photo with Jill Lorrimer that had put his career in jeopardy and made him the county's laughingstock. I thought if I could show Arne that the photo was part of an elaborate frame-up, by the same person who had also framed me, he just might come around. So I explained, as briefly as possible, everything Cassandra and I had discovered about Phillip Gordon.

"You'd better not be shitting me," Arne said.

"I'm not. I've got an image of Phillip taken when he was at the Biersdorf home." Cassandra had left her laptop in Dale's office when she went out to her car and I had it now. "There's no doubt about his real identify or that Peter was his father."

Arne said, "You know what, counselor, stupid as it sounds, I might just believe you. I knew I was being framed and I thought at first you were the asshole who did it."

"What changed your mind?"

"The gun."

"What gun?"

"The one they found at your house yesterday. They've already done the ballistics. It was the gun used to kill Peter, Dewey and Marty."

"Where did they find it?"

"It was in an old paint can in your garage. A thirty-eight-caliber Colt Python revolver. I used to own one myself. A very nice handgun. There were three live rounds and three expended shells in the cylinder. Once Jason and his crew found it, they put out an arrest warrant for you. You're officially the mad-dog killer county attorney now. You're in shit right up to your nose."

"Well, that's lovely," I said, then told Arne how Phillip had tapped my phone and stolen the key to my father's office. "He also took the revolver—it belonged to my father—and then came back to plant it in that paint can."

"You don't have to convince me. The thing is, when I heard about the gun, I knew something wasn't right. I know you, and you're an asshole as far as I'm concerned, but you're not a stupid asshole."

"How kind of you to say so."

"Yeah, well, the way I look at it, if you shot three people, you wouldn't leave evidence sitting around your house just waiting to be found. The gun would be long gone. Same thing with that typewriter in your dad's old office. The more I thought about it, the more it seemed way too obvious. I couldn't figure out a motive, either. Why the hell would you be writing those messages and maybe even killing people? So I started thinking maybe you were being screwed over, just like me."

"Happy to hear that, Arne. Now, what about it? Will you help me find Cassandra?"

"That's a matter for those fuckers from the BCA and the local cops. I'm officially out of the picture. "

"I know and I've already called nine-one-one. I told them everything I could about what happened to Cassandra. But I don't know how seriously they treated the call. It must be apparent by now I was the caller, and maybe everybody thinks I was trying to send them off on a wild goose chase. I don't know. All I'm sure of is that Cassandra is in terrible danger."

"I get that, genius. But if you don't know where she is, I don't see what you can do."

"Maybe I can figure something out," I said. "If I can't, then just go ahead and arrest me. I'm at Pembroke Woods. How long will it take you to get here?"

"Fifteen minutes. But if you're playing some fucking game with me—"

"There's no game, Arne. See you in fifteen."

Secreted in the pines, I reflected on the doleful fact that Phillip Gordon, a brilliant and twisted soul if there ever was one, had for the last month pulled off an amazing feat. His grand plan, a spectacular creation with many moving parts, had spun out with uncanny precision. He'd taken his revenge on the father who abandoned him to a molester and he'd eliminated Peter's legitimate son and heir, Dewey.

He'd also gone after the sons of Theodore Moreland, Magnus Sigurdson and Phillip Zweifel—three men he saw as facilitators in the terrible fate that befell him. But why had he murdered Marty while settling for a different kind of revenge, in the form of elaborate frame-ups, against Arne and me? I wasn't sure.

Still, the scope of his vengeance was stunning. Besides murdering five people, counting the Biersdorfs, he'd torched and destroyed almost every building associated with the Swindell family. And now he'd kidnapped his own sister. Phillip was a family annihilator, and I had no doubt he intended to kill Cassandra, if only because she'd enjoyed a life of wealth and privilege and he hadn't.

So where were Phillip and his captive now? They wouldn't be at Phillip's house or his place of employment. Too obvious. A hotel or motel room? Not likely. Too public, too many chances for Cassandra to make a scene and call for help. Phillip would want seclusion but also shelter. A cabin in the woods, maybe, but there are lots of cabins and lots of woods in Paradise County.

I felt frustrated, at the end of my rope, and also hungry. I glanced over at the passenger seat, which serves primarily as small dumpster for snacks and the usual miscellaneous junk. The snacks included a four-pack of Oreos, and I reached over to grab what was likely to be my last meal as a free man. And that's when I noticed the little plastic statue of St. Jude Arlen Sandquist had given me.

Of course. It had to be. I knew where Cassandra was.

43

"I'm waiting in the lot," Arne said when I answered my cell. "Where the fuck are you?"

"There in a minute," I said.

I wondered if Arne had come to Pembroke Woods alone or if half the lawmen in Paradise County were with him, ready to slap the cuffs on me. I thought it was a fifty-fifty proposition. Arne was hard to read, and he might still have it in for me.

I drove back to the parking lot and was relieved to find Arne there by himself in his white Ram pickup. I grabbed Cassandra's laptop and joined him in the front seat. A rifle was mounted by the rear window, and Arne had a Glock holstered at his hip. He stared at me with a mixture of expectation and disgust.

"God, but you're a sorry sight," he said. "I should arrest you right now, but what the hell. That's quite a story you told me. Let's see that photo you claim to have."

"Sure, but first things first. I know where he's taken Cassandra," I said and told Arne where we needed to go. "Let's get moving."

"How do you know they'll be there?"

"Believe me, I know. It's the only place that makes sense."

I showed Arne the photo of young Phillip Gordon and sketched in the story of his mother and Peter and the adoption. "Phillip came to Pineland to get his revenge and he's certainly gotten it. Cassandra Ellis is the last piece and he'll kill her."

Arne whistled, grabbed the mic on his police radio and said, "Fucking A. I never would have thought it was him."

"Are you calling it in?"

"Damn right. We're half an hour away. There'll be closer units on patrol in that area."

"I thought you're supposed to be on a leave of absence."

"Yeah, well, that doesn't mean shit right now. I can still make some things happen."

"Okay, but we have to be very careful. If Phillip spots any squads he'll put a bullet in Cassandra's head and then he'll move on to plan B."

"What are you, a mind reader? How do you know what his plan B is?"

"I just know. You have to understand. This whole crazy business is his life. He's stewed over it and planned for it for years. But he's smart enough to know it was always a long shot and there were a million ways it could go wrong. He's probably amazed by how far he's managed to get. But if he figures out we're onto him, he knows he's done unless he can dispose of Cassandra immediately. That means your deputie can't go barging in. Tell them no sirens and to stay out of sight of the house until we get there. And do me a big favor, will you? Don't mention I'm with you."

"Afraid you'll be arrested?"

"No, but I don't want a circus down there when I arrive. The focus has to be on finding Cassandra. You can arrest me anytime."

"All right," Arne said and got on the radio. A deputy was on patrol less than five miles from the house and Arne gave him instructions. "He'll pass all of this on to the acting sheriff and then it'll go to the BCA, the state patrol and everybody else. We'll have a crowd down there in no time."

"That's what I'm afraid of. Let's see if we can get ahead of the pack."

Once we reached the interstate, Arne turned on his siren and flashers and pushed the truck up to ninety. Traffic was light and Arne handled the big pickup expertly.

"Here's a question, counselor. If this guy is Cassandra's brother, why would he kill her? She hasn't done anything to him, has she?"

"No, but she's in the way. Do you know how big Peter's estate is?"

"Millions, I'm sure."

"I've heard it's worth at least twenty million. Plus, he didn't leave a will, or so it's rumored. That means Phillip could announce he's Peter's long lost son, take a DNA test to prove it, and then collect the bulk of the estate because Dewey is dead and Cassandra will be, too."

Arne wasn't buying it. "He'd never get away with it."

"Well, speaking strictly as a prosecuting attorney, I beg to differ. Think about it. There's nothing at the moment to prove he committed any of the crimes. If you asked me to charge him with something, my reply would be: 'With what?' Murder? No evidence. Arson? No evidence. Kidnapping? Only if we can find Cassandra. Otherwise—"

I felt a rising sense of desperation. I'd come to care deeply about Cassandra—as a friend and as a brave and powerful woman—and the thought of something happening to her filled me with dread. Still, I knew she wouldn't go easily. She'd keep Phillip talking as long as she could and she'd never stop fighting.

I glanced at the truck's speedometer. The needle hovered just above ninety.

"How about trying for a hundred?" I suggested.

Arne grinned. "No problem. Good thing we're not in your fucking Prius. That's a pussy car if there ever was one."

I ignored the insult and watched the road ahead. The speed didn't bother Arne, and he became unusually talkative as we roared past one vehicle after another. He didn't have much to say about Cassandra. Instead, Phillip was on his mind.

"That fucker really did a number on me," he said. "I didn't do a goddamn thing to Jill Lorrimer."

"So what did happen?"

"What happened is that, yeah, she sat in my lap once. Okay, so I'm a lousy husband. Alice will tell you that."

I didn't mention she already had.

"But here's the deal: that little scene with Jill took place weeks before she died. I didn't cover up a fucking thing. Al

I know is that she was found dead in her car. We did an investigation. You were part of it. And we concluded it was an accidental overdose. That's all there was to it."

"I think there was more," I said. I told Arne about my suspicions after looking closely at the autopsy report and photos. "Her boots were on the wrong feet and that tells me she didn't put them on herself. I think she was out celebrating that night at Peter's mansion and overdosed on booze and cocaine he provided. After that, somebody dressed her, put her in her car and drove it back to her apartment."

"Well, it wasn't me. And who's to say it went down that way? You don't have any proof."

"Sad but true. By the way, who took that photo of you with Jill?"

"Peter, probably, but it could have been anybody. It was big party and I was wasted. I couldn't even tell you who all was there. I've been thinking about and it's time for me to stop drinking."

"Wise choice," I said. "Maybe I'll have to give it a try myself." Then I said, casually, "What about Marty?"

"What about him?"

"Well, you know Jason is looking into where you were the night Marty was shot. Apparently, you don't have an alibi."

For once, I'd caught Arne by surprise. His eyes burned a hole in my forehead. "That's interesting. Yeah, very interesting. So, how did you know about that?"

"Alice told me."

"Did she, now? Are the two of you friends? She's left me. I suppose you know that."

I could tell where he was going. "Listen, Arne, she came to me out of the blue. She was worried about lying to the BCA to cover for you. She was also worried you might harm her if she told the truth."

"That's crap. I never laid a hand on her in my life. I was out that night. So what? I sure as shit didn't kill Marty. Why would I?"

"I have no reason to believe you did," I said. "Phillip has been sowing chaos. He wants to ruin you, just like he's trying to ruin me."

"What the fuck did I ever do to him?"

"It's the sins of the fathers, Arne, and we're the sons. It's almost Biblical. Phillip got screwed by his father and he thinks we should be screwed, too, because of what our fathers did. I suspect your father helped cover up Peter's activities with Patricia Gordon. She just vanished after supposedly leaving the baby behind, and I don't think anybody from law enforcement ever bothered to look into her disappearance."

"What do you think happened to her?" Arne said, as we roared past a big rig.

"I have an idea about that," I said. "We may know if I'm right soon enough."

By the time we took the turnoff to Fortune Lake, the rain had morphed into a thick, dripping fog. With his siren blaring, Arne roared through the fog until he came up so fast on an old woman in a Buick that he nearly rear-ended her. He swerved at the last second to avoid disaster.

"It would really be nice if we could get where we're going alive," I observed.

"Life is a chance, counselor," Arne said as he gunned the truck back up to eighty. "We'll get there even if I can't see a goddamn thing."

He got back on his radio and learned a sheriff's deputy and a state trooper had already reached the vicinity of the house. More law was on the way. When we reached Fortune Lake Road, I directed Arne toward Arlen Sandquist's house.

"Should we assume he's in the house, too?" Arne asked.

"I don't think so. When Cassandra and I talked to him last week, he said he was planning to spend some time with his daughter down in Maple Grove. Phillip may even have known that. He doesn't leave anything to chance."

We came over a little rise and saw two squads parked near the entrance to Sandquist's driveway. Arne pulled up behind them and we got out to talk. A young state trooper I didn't recognize emerged from one of the squads. Billy Hawkins, a long-time deputy sheriff, was standing by the other unit.

"So you've found the fugitive," Billy said when he saw me step out with Arne. "How come he's not in cuffs?"

"I don't think he's a threat to public safety," Arne said.

Billy was dubious. "Christ, Arne, he's wanted for three murders. You'd better cuff him before Jack comes. He'll be here in ten or so to take command. Until then, he said to hold tight."

Jack Brown was the acting sheriff and no friend of Arne.

"We can't wait," I said.

Billy, a heavyset man who I'd once skewered in court over some mishandled evidence, glared at me and said, "Like I said, you should be in cuffs. In fact my orders—"

"Fuck your orders," Arne said and grabbed me by the arm. "Me and the bright boy fugitive here are going to have a look at that house. If you want to stop us, you'll have to shoot me."

The state trooper, who looked fresh out of the academy and more than a little confused by the situation, said, "Should I go with you?"

Arne said, "No, son, you stay here and babysit Billy. We'll just have a look and let you know what we find."

Billy was obviously pissed but didn't say anything.

"All right, let's go," Arne said, and we started down the drive toward Sandquist's house.

44

The house wasn't immediately visible in the fog and growing darkness.

"How far is it?" Arne asked. He'd unholstered his Glock and held it by his side.

"A hundred yards, maybe."

"Okay. Stop once we can see the place."

A perfect silence prevailed. No birds singing. No animals scurrying through the woods. No wind. Even our footsteps were muted by a layer of decayed leaves. My heart was a metronome beating presto time and my breaths came out fast and hard.

The house, a gray specter, finally came into view. We inched forward, keeping to the side of the driveway, where a row of pine trees provided some cover. It dawned on me we had no real plan, other than to try to find Phillip and Cassandra. After that, it would all be improvisation.

The driveway ended at a detached, two-car garage behind the house. A long white van with rusted wheel wells was parked in front of the garage. Arne whispered, "Looks like you're right. I've seen him driving that van around town."

I'd seen him in it, too, a familiar figure in Pineland, an upstanding community member, or so we believed. Only he wasn't and never had been. Phillip Gordon was a walking epic of deception and guile, revealed only to himself. Our scary, secret man, a poison in our midst. And now, maybe, Arne and I were about to see him as he really was, all the makeup of his phony life removed. It was a daunting prospect, and I was glad to be with Arne and his Glock.

We could see one side and the back of the house, which consisted of a series of additions to the cabin Peter Swindell had once owned. A concrete patio at the rear was furnished with two rusted metal chairs and a charcoal grill protected by a plastic cover. The patio's location was odd. People who live on a lake usually have a porch or deck or patio at the front of their house to take in the view. Why have a large patio at the back, where there wasn't much to see? I also noticed that a bright bouquet of flowers rested on one of the patio chairs. I was pretty sure who'd put it there.

A rear door opened onto the patio, but it looked to be shut tight. Only one window was visible, near the front of the house. Dim light leaked from it, creating a ghostly glow in the fog.

"Somebody's in there all right," Arne said.

I stared at the window, trying to unstrap myself from the burden of fear we all carry around with us. Whatever hap pened next, I had to be ready to act. My old life of doubt was gone for the moment. I was in a new place.

"That's a living-room window," I told Arne. "Let's go have a look inside."

"Hold on, Tarzan. If they're in there and he spots you, he's the kind of guy who might want to go out in a blaze of glory. Then all bets are off."

"What do you suggest? Just standing around and waiting for something to happen? I'm not up for that."

"No, let's get some reinforcements first and we'll go from there."

Reinforcements were already arriving. I heard whispering behind us and saw Jack Brown, Billy Hawkins and two state troopers emerge from the mist.

Jack, a big bear of a man with a touchy disposition, came up to us and said, "I'll take it from here, Arne. You're under arrest, Mister Zweifel. I have a warrant."

He reached for his handcuffs, but Arne grabbed his wrists and said, "Don't be a fucking moron. We've got a hostage situation here. You can arrest him later. Let's figure out first what we're going to do about the hostage and the guy who's in there with her."

"You have no authority here," Jack said, pulling away from Arne's grip. "None. Period, end of story. And how do you even know there's a hostage in there? Is that what Zweifel claims? It could be pure bullshit. Now get out of my way or I'll arrest you, too."

"Just try it," Arne said. "See that goddamn van? It belongs to the guy we're looking for, and he's inside the house with Cassandra Ellis as his hostage."

Well, screw it, I thought. Let the lawmen argue. I started moving, quickly, toward the lighted window. None of the lawmen stopped me, probably because they knew a disturbance of any kind might give away our presence. I reached the window and crouched beside it, listening for voices or any other sounds. Nothing. I peeked inside.

The living room was empty but showed signs of a recent struggle. A table lamp was overturned, magazines and papers littered the floor, and a row of Arlen Sandquist's tchotchkes—ceramic chipmunks, little winged angels, wooden elves and gnomes and sprites—had been knocked from their shelves. A dark stain—blood?—decorated one of the fallen gnomes.

I glanced at the ratty beige couch where Cassandra and I had sat a week or so earlier, drinking coffee with Arlen and learning about a mysterious baby boy. Then my eyes caught something. On the floor between the couch and a coffee table lay a pair of loafers, sleek and black and decorated with brass buckles. Cassandra's Guccis. Across from the couch the front door was halfway open, its window glass shattered.

"See anything?" Arne whispered. He'd come up behind me so soundlessly I was startled.

"I see Cassandra's shoes but there's no sign of her or Phillip. Looks like there's been a fight in there. Maybe they're in the back room. We need to go in right now."

"No, not yet," Arne cautioned. "Jack's got more people coming even if he doesn't know what the hell is going on. We can have this place surrounded in five minutes and—"

An old quotation from Albert Camus suddenly jammed like an arrow into my skull. "Those who lack courage will always find a philosophy to justify it," said the wise man.

Maybe that had been my story, a life of justifications, the easy escape of the bottle, clever talk and small sport. I couldn't remember the last time I'd taken a mortal chance. Now was the moment.

"Not going to happen," I said, and went toward the front door. Arne whispered a curse and followed. I'm a planner, a thinker, a careful man in my own way. Now I was just a guy about to rush through a door and see what happened. Except I didn't get that chance. Arne shoved me aside and went into the living room, his Glock aimed at whatever lay ahead.

That's when I heard a man's voice coming out of the fog behind me. "Cassandra, Cassandra," the man called out. "Where are you, sister dearest?" Then I heard a gunshot. I turned around and started running for the lake.

In Minnesota "ice-out" is a spring ritual, the day when a lake finally gives up its winter mantle. In Paradise County lakes are typically open by mid-April. But winter isn't always eager to leave, even in May, and when I reached the lake I discovered it was still coated with a treacherous sheet of ice and slushy water. I remembered what had happened to my uncle Jack— dead with his snowmobile at the bottom of an icy lake—but I couldn't stop myself. I ran out on the ice, cold slush splashing up against my ankles, and peered into the fog for any sign of Cassandra.

The ice crackled under my feet, a delicate scrim separating me from the frigid waters below. I was dressed for chilly weather—a jacket, a wool shirt, and corduroy pants—and if I went through the ice I'd be about as buoyant as a chunk of lead. I slowed to a walk and then one foot started to break

365

through the scrim. I thought I'd go under, but my other foot held firm. I sensed that another step might be my last, so I got down on all fours, trying to spread out my weight, and started crawling. My shins and knees were soon dripping wet and my hands grew numb from the cold. I lost sight of the shore and then there was nothing but gray ice and gray fog and gray light.

I crawled until I saw a dark shape looming up ahead in the fog. I knew who it was. Phillip was all in black, as he'd been at Pembroke Woods. Like me, he was on all fours, inching along the ice. He was moving away from me at an angle, and I could see a pistol tucked in the small of his back. A frozen river of blood stained the right side of this head. Cassandra had obviously put up a fight.

"You can't hide!" he shouted. "I'll find you, Cassandra. Yes, I will."

Then, I saw another figure farther out on the ice. It had to be Cassandra. She was crawling, too, trying to escape into the sanctuary of the fog. But Phillip had spotted her, and he let out a kind of war whoop.

"There you are!" he said. "Where do you think you're going?"

"Fuck you, you motherfucker," Cassandra said, as only she could say it.

She tried to go faster, but Phillip was gaining on her. I had the weird sensation I was watching a play, a life-and-death drama with a cast of two.

Make that three.

I stood up, ahead of my thoughts for once in my life, and made a run at Phillip, not worrying whether the ice woul

366

hold me. It simply had to. He heard me coming across the snapping ice and was just turning around when I hit him full force. Our combined weight was more than the ice could bear and we broke through into the water as though we'd smashed a giant pane of glass.

Breath rushed from my lungs and my heart seemed to stop for an instant, shocked by the cold. Then I was alive again, and all I could think of was keeping Phillip away from Cassandra, forever. I pushed down on his shoulders and I remember looking into his fierce dark eyes as he disappeared beneath the water. But he kicked away and I couldn't keep him under. He came up, screaming and fighting, and got his hands around my throat, slowly forcing my head down. I tried to grab his gun but I couldn't reach it and I started gulping in water, a dead man in the making.

Then Phillip pulled away and when I popped out of the water, gasping for air, I saw Cassandra at the edge of the ice, lying on her stomach. She was handcuffed but had managed to grab Phillip by the hair and was yanking at him with all her strength. Then she started losing her grip. She slid forward on the ice, screamed out a loud "fuck" and splashed violently into the water.

The cold was inviting me into unconsciousness like a curtain dropping down on my life. The play was about to end. There were sounds—Cassandra crying out, Phillip cursing, water splashing everywhere as though we were just three kids having fun in a backyard pool. Then Phillip had a gun in his hand and I recall thinking, pointlessly, whether it could actually be fired when wet.

"Keep fighting!" Cassandra shouted and I saw her struggling with Phillip, trying to get the gun. But he had a madman's wild strength and bashed the butt of the pistol against her head. She fell away and that's when I heard a muffled sound. The gun dropped from Phillip's hand and I saw blood gushing from a hole in his neck. He looked right at me, with a kind of stony regret, and said, "Almost." Then the man known to everyone in Pineland as the Reverend Ronnie Peterson slipped away into the unforgiving waters of Fortune Lake.

45

I don't remember all of what happened afterwards. Arne told me he tried to reach me after shooting Phillip, but the ice was too thin. I know I struggled to keep Cassandra from going under. She'd received a vicious blow to the head and appeared to be unconscious. I treaded water for as long as I could, holding on to Cassandra by the collar of her blouse, but I began to feel numb, confused and sleepy, a dying man ready to drop out of this world. Then I heard someone yelling at me to "hold on" and that's where my memories end.

Arne saved us with the help of two state troopers who found a ladder and a plastic sled in Arlen Sandquist's garage. One of the troopers, a very brave man, managed to reach us on the ladder. He yanked Cassandra out first and Arne got her into the sled and pushed her back to shore. The trooper held onto me until more help arrived to pull me from the water, a dubious trophy fish if there ever was one.

After that there was movement and light and I was aware my clothes were gone and I was a newborn, swaddled in blankets. I later learned my core temperature registered 88.4 degrees when I arrived at Mercy Hospital in Pineland—cold, but not cold enough to kill me.

Recovering Phillip's body took more time. Rescue crews chopped a channel in the ice and went out with boats and dragging hooks. They found him in fourteen feet of water, his long black beard turned into an icy tangle, as though he was some tentacled, prehistoric fish. Arne's shot, fired from thirty feet away as he lay on his belly, had torn through Phillip's carotid artery, and he was dead by the time he reached the bottom of the lake.

Arne told me later at the hospital that he'd gone out on the ice after hearing Phillip shout Cassandra's name, followed by the gunshot. Like me, he quickly discovered how treacherous the ice was. He was creeping ahead on all fours when another sound caught his attention.

"I heard you go through the ice," he said, "and to be honest, I thought I'd be next. But I kept going and then I saw you and Phillip in the water just as Cassandra was crawling up to help. I have to give it to her: that woman's got genuine brass balls. From what I could tell, it looked like Phillip was pretty well on his way to drowning you, so I had to take the shot."

"I'm very glad you did."

Arne grinned and said, "I suppose I'll be going to hell for saving a lawyer's life."

"Don't worry," I said. "I'll be there to keep you company."

Cassandra's condition was much worse than mine. She was severely hypothermic by the time paramedics got her t the hospital. I found out the next day that she'd also suffered a gunshot wound to the leg. Phillip had shot her as she ran out on the lake and vanished into the fog. It wasn't a critical wound but the doctors said the bullet had missed her femoral artery by less than inch. She'd come that close to bleeding out.

The blow to her head was far more serious, causing a nasty concussion. She was airlifted to Regions Hospital in St. Paul, where she was in intensive care for three days as doctors fought to control swelling of her brain. I went down to see her as soon as I could, but she was in and out of consciousness so we couldn't talk much. Her adoptive parents—the Ellises of Wheaton, Illinois—came up to be with her and I had a chance to meet them. They seemed very nice, but also very quiet and pale, and I knew Cassandra's powerful drive must have come from elsewhere, deep in her genes.

Cassandra finally turned the corner after three days, and the doctors didn't think she'd suffered any permanent damage. By Friday she was well enough to speak to investigators about her terrifying hours with Phillip, and she offered up an immediate revelation, based on what her brother had told her. Hours later a team of Paradise County sheriff's deputies and BCA agents dug out the patio behind Arlen Sandquist's house and found the remains of Patricia Gordon, right where Peter had buried her thirty-two years earlier. An autopsy showed she'd been shot once through the head.

I'd suspected the same thing, especially after seeing the flowers Phillip had placed on the patio. But I had no proof, so was reluctant to call in the diggers until I had solid evidence that Patricia Gordon was buried there. Cassandra provided that.

The exact circumstances of Patricia's death may never be known, but I believe Peter shot her the day after she arrived at his lake cabin with their infant son. Maybe she threatened him with exposure or demanded he marry her or maybe Peter simply decided she was a problem he couldn't afford to deal with any longer. After burying her behind the cabin, he poured the concrete for the patio himself, sealing her away. Then he arranged for Phillip's adoption, claiming Patricia had left for points unknown after abandoning the baby. No one questioned his story—not Arne's father or Marty's father or mine.

How Phillip knew his father had murdered Patricia and buried her behind the lake cabin is a mystery to this day. But Phillip had a genius for finding things out—he spent his whole adult life detecting his own history—and at some point he ferreted out the truth.

Once Cassandra had given her statement, I was able to talk with her. It was a warm Saturday afternoon and she was in a regular room by then, eager to leave her confinement. "Shit food, shit gowns, shit TV and no fucking sleep" was her summation of the hospital experience.

"You forgot to mention how your life was saved," I said. "I think that's a fairly important oversight on your part."

"I know, you're right. The doctors and nurses have been great."

She was propped up in bed, wearing a loose gown and the usual hospital jewelry in the form of tubes and ports and monitors. She looked tired and a little down, her smooth sass chastened by the always informative experience of nearly dying. She was wearing a throwaway hospital cap—a chunk of her hair had been shaved off—and there were bags under her eyes. But she was eager to expel the poison memories of her terrifying hours with Phillip. I think she believed the more she talked about the experience the better she'd feel.

"Well," she began, shaking her head, "I guess it should have been pretty fucking obvious all along. The name was a dead giveaway."

"I suppose, but Peterson is a really common name in these parts. I looked in one of my venerable old phonebooks and found thirty of them in Pineland alone. So I think we can be excused for not making the leap from Peterson to Peter's son."

"Maybe. It didn't seem to occur to anyone else, either. Ronald, by the way, is his real middle name. Phillip Ronald Gordon. It's a name I'll never forgot. "

"Me either. So tell me, what happened when he snatched you from the funeral home?"

Cassandra said Phillip knew we were at the funeral home because he'd attached a tracking device to my Prius—a likelihood I should have accounted for. When Cassandra went out to the parking lot to fetch her granola bars, Phillip suddenly pulled up in a white van and aimed a gun at her head.

"He said he'd kill me in a second if I screamed or made a scene, but I did anyway. I thought I was dead right there so why not at least put up a fight? That's when he whacked me the first time with his pistol. I was stunned. He dragged me into his van and handcuffed me in the back. Incidentally, you're lucky to be alive."

"Tell me about it."

"No, I don't mean what happened at the lake. Phillip wanted to go into the funeral home and shoot you before he left with me. He figured you were the only other person who might know his true identity. But a car pulled into the lot—somebody must have thought the funeral home was open—so he decided to leave."

On the way to Sandquist's house, Phillip delivered what Cassandra described as "a raging madman's monologue. It just went on and on and on. Peter had arranged a wonderful life for me but treated him like shit. I'd gone to Harvard, he'd been abused by a child molester. Nothing was fair. He'd been screwed and now he was exacting the justice all of his tormentors deserved."

"Did he tell you what happened to Peter and Dewey?"

"He confessed to everything. He said he killed them and gloated about it. Your friend Marty was a different story. Phillip didn't plan at first to kill him, but apparently Marty began to suspect who Phillip actually was. After that, Marty had to go."

"And I became the fall guy for his murder."

"You did. Phillip went to a lot of trouble to set you up. The whole Serenader thing was pure genius from his point of view. He was just as proud about what he did to the sheriff. Care to guess where he got that incriminating photo of the hooker in Arne's lap?"

"I'm guessing it came from Peter."

"No, he got it from Marty after that hooker—what's her name again?—died."

"Jill Lorrimer."

"Right. Phillip claimed Marty was actually involved in covering up her death."

"I'm sorry to hear that," I said. "Marty was a decent man but he just fell in with the wrong people. How did Jill really die?"

"She overdosed at Peter's mansion and died right in his living room. The prospect of explaining away a dead hooker didn't appeal to Peter, so he convinced Marty, who'd been partying with him, to put her in her car and drive back to her apartment. You know the rest."

"How did Phillip figure out what happened?"

"Marty was a member of Phillip's church, remember? I guess Phillip became his father confessor of sorts and Marty must have spilled out the whole story. Phillip was really good at insinuating himself into other people's lives and he knew how to make useful friends. He told me he also got a lot of dirt from that scumbag who publishes the *Tattler*."

"Tommy Redmond. That's interesting. I used to wonder why the Call of God Church advertised so much in Tommy's rag. Now we know."

Cassandra shifted in the bed, looking for a more comfortable spot. "God, I want to get out of here. The doctors say maybe tomorrow if everything looks good."

"I hope that happens. What else did your learn from Phillip? It sounds like he wanted to unburden himself."

"He did, and I think I know why. When he kidnapped me and couldn't get at you, he knew the game was over. I was going to be the last piece before he died. I'm pretty sure he planned to kill himself once he killed me."

"The Alexander the Great thing? No more worlds to conquer?"

"Exactly. He'd gone as far as he could with his scheme of revenge and he had nothing else to live for. Even if he somehow managed to claim Peter's estate, I don't think the money would have meant much to him. He would have been a man without a purpose."

"And all that seething anger and hate went back to his time at the Biersdorf home. Did he talk at all about being molested?"

"In graphic detail, believe me. It sounds like it was horrific. That's where that song comes in."

"You mean 'Pineland Serenade.'"

"Right. Biersdorf played a recording of it every afternoon at his group home as a call to dinner. Once they heard it, the foster kids would come marching down the steps and stand at the table. When the music stopped, they'd eat. Phillip told me he played it over the house's speaker system when he shot the Biersdorfs."

"The song must have haunted him. That's why he left snippets of it behind with his messages. In a terrible sense, it was the story of his life."

"I suppose you could say that. In any case, he certainly took his vengeance against the Biersdorfs, but only after they'd revealed Peter was his real father."

"So that's how he found out. What year was that again?"

"The Biersdorfs were murdered in two-thousand-one. Phillip was just sixteen then. He told me the voices heard behind the music on some of the audio files were his and Biersdorf's. He said that on one of them you could hear him say, 'I'll kill you.' The BCA guys confirmed that when I talked to them. It's pretty chilling when you think about it. A kid makes a death threat and then not only carries it out but gets away with the crime."

"Yeah, he was amazing in a terrible sort of way. He commits a double murder at age sixteen, but no one can pin it on him. Presumably, he then goes out on his own when he turns eighteen in two-thousand-three. So what was he doing all those years before he came to Pineland as the Reverend Ronnie?"

"He didn't talk much about that, although he hinted he'd spent some time in prison."

"For what?"

"He was involved in some kind of financial scam, maybe in Texas. The way he put it, he was 'out of commission' for quite a while before he arrived in Pineland. Which was when?"

"Twenty-fourteen," I said. "The same year I was elected county attorney. I remember because he started showing up at court hearings for criminal defendants. He introduced himself and said he was there doing God's work."

"More like the devil's work. Do you know how he took over that church of his? He downloaded child porn on the pastor's computer and then notified the police. The pastor was never convicted because it couldn't be proved he actually downloaded the stuff. But the congregation booted him out anyway and Phillip, who'd gotten one of those phony online divinity degrees, talked his way into becoming the new pastor."

"That's nasty."

"No shit. But you know what? Phillip was bent from the start. Being sexually abused as a child made everything much worse but even before then there was something wrong in his head."

"You think he was a psychopath?"

Cassandra nodded. "Gold-plated. Also nuts, yet incredibly smart and organized. A bad combination."

"I agree. Okay, what happened once you got to Sandquist's house?"

"I knew he was going to kill me and I decided I wouldn't go down without a fight. I tried to keep him talking as long as I could. Everything he said was crazy, wild stuff. It was like the safety valve that allowed him to function as rational human being and make all of his plans suddenly burst open and out came the boiling madness. He went up to me at one point to lecture me eye to eye, and that's when I got hold of a big ceramic gnome and hit him right across the face. I think broke his nose. I ran out the door and onto the lake. He shot at me and I remember it felt like a really bad bee sting. But kept going until he lost me in the fog. And then the Honorable Paul Zweifel came to the rescue."

"I think I'd give more credit to the gnome. And to Arne for sure. All I did was fall into the water."

"Well, I thank you for it," she said. "You are now officially my favorite person in the marvelous town of Pineland."

"I take that as a high honor. So if you do get freed from hospital jail tomorrow, what's your plan?"

"Back to Chicago. The partners have called to offer their deepest sympathies and oh, by the way, will I be able to handle that important case coming up next week? It's nice to know how highly valued my life is."

"Well, I for one appreciate you and all you've done. You just may be the most remarkable person I've ever met." I bent over and kissed her on the cheek. "Take care."

"What about you? Any big plans?"

"I'm too old to have big plans. I'll be going back to Pineland. Camus needs my exquisite company."

"You can't get away, can you?"

"From Pineland? No, I guess not, but I probably should."

Cassandra shook her head. "No, I don't think so. You're a Pinelander through and through. It's where you belong. You know that, don't you?"

"Yes," I said, "I do."

CODA

If you really want justice, an old lawyer once told me, become God. His point was that there are no final settlements in life, only whatever approximations we can devise, and loose ends always dangle in the wind. So it was with the Phillip Ronald Gordon. The BCA dug deep into his past, trying to account for all he'd done, but stubborn mysteries remained.

It was learned Phillip had indeed served time in prison from 2008 to 2013, for his role in a huge Ponzi scheme in Texas. He was supposed to be on probation for another five years but instead disappeared, only to show up a year later as the Reverend Ronnie Peterson in Pineland. He'd managed by then to acquire a wallet-full of fake identifications. He also dyed his naturally reddish hair jet black and added long beard. Although he was a wanted man for violating the terms of his probation, no one in law enforcement had an reason to suspect he might be in Pineland and so he effectively dropped out of sight.

Perhaps the BCA's most intriguing discovery was that Phillip, in his guise as Reverend Ronnie, had traveled to Chicago on the same August weekend in 2015 that Peter Swindell's ex-wife died of sudden cardiac arrest at her home in suburban River Forest. She was alone when it happened and no suspicion was attached to her death. Even so, my old nemesis Jason Braddock at the BCA became convinced Phillip had murdered her, thereby eliminating another potential claimant to Peter's fortune. But no proof of foul play was ever found.

Jason had less success in trying to fill in a full picture of Phillip's crime spree in Pineland. A search of Phillip's house turned up no incriminating evidence but his office at the church did yield some fascinating clues. The office safe contained sixty thousand dollars in cash as well as a two-hundred-page, handwritten manifesto offering Phillip's justification for his crimes, including a hard-to-read account of his abuse at the hands of James Biersdorf. The former school band director had first sodomized Phillip when he was six years old and it had continued for another eight years. Then Phillip had meticulously planned his revenge against Biersdorf and his wife, who apparently knew what was going on but did nothing to stop it.

Most of the manifesto, however, was a long, repetitive exercise in rage and resentment directed at Peter and all of his enablers, my father among them. The wonder was how Phillip could plan and plot with such cool precision even as his insides burned white-hot. What the manifesto didn't offer was an account of Phillip's crimes in Pineland, and as a result Jason and his crew were never able to establish exactly how he lured Peter, Dewey and Marty to their deaths. Nor was it entirely clear whether he'd blackmailed Peter, presumably over Patricia's murder and possibly over Jill Lorrimer's death as well.

But the sixty grand in the safe was certainly suggestive, and I believe it was indeed hush money paid through Peter's mysterious "cloud fund." Still, no paper trail was ever discovered linking the payments to Phillip. Give the devil his due: he was a genius at covering his tracks.

The safe contained one other item of interest—a hand-notated version of "Pineland Serenade," in the key of C major. I had a copy made and Kat Berglund later played it for me on her electronic keyboard. The serenade wasn't a memorable piece of music—it had the air of a trifle dashed off quickly—but it concluded with a strange coda, in A minor, that dropped off into the gloomy depths of the bass clef. I suspect it was the coda that appealed most to Phillip, who must have known his life was destined to end in catastrophe.

When the coroner released Phillip's body, no one knew quite what to do with it. Since Cassandra was his sole surviving blood relative, I called her to ask if she had any ideas.

"I guess we'll have to bury him," she said, "and it might as well be in Pineland."

She sprang for the coffin and a plot at Memorial Cemetery. There was no wake or church service—who would have come to mourn him?—so we rented the local Lutheran minister and had him say a few prayers at the grave. We also hired a violinist to play "Pineland Serenade." Cassandra and I didn't advertise the burial but we let a few people in law enforcement know. Arne was the only one who showed up. The minister went through his prayers as a light rain began to fall and then the violinist serenaded Phillip one last time before he dropped into his grave.

Two days later there was another funeral service, for Patricia Gordon, at Holy Cross Lutheran Church in Pineland. Cassandra once again made all the arrangements. She'd first wanted to bury her mother's remains in Chicago but I suggested Pineland would be a better place.

"Nobody will remember her in Chicago after you're gone," I told Cassandra, "but in Pineland I guarantee that she'll still be a story for years to come."

More than two hundred townspeople showed up for the service, out of sheer curiosity or simply because they thought Patricia deserved the decency of a proper sendoff. Cassandra delivered a moving eulogy for the mother she'd never known, and then we went out again to Memorial Cemetery, where Patricia was buried next to her tortured son.

Peter and Dewey Swindell were also buried in Pineland after suitable services. I went to both. Dewey's funeral attracted few mourners but Peter's sendoff drew a big crowd. Cassandra, however, was notably absent and I couldn't blame her. Peter didn't deserve her final respects.

When summer finally arrived and the old houses along ve and Bliss and Eden streets dozed in their wide green ards, the rhythms and rituals of small-town life returned Pineland. I had a long talk with Camus on one of those drowsy afternoons and we agreed I wouldn't seek a second term as county attorney. I doubted anything like Phillip's wild carnival of crime would ever occur again, and four more years of prosecuting small-time meth makers and trying to placate the county board didn't appeal to me.

Vern Blankenberger was pleased to hear of my decision. "I've always respected you as an honest and able man," he said, lying through his tobacco-stained teeth. "I'll certainly miss your services." No, he wouldn't, but no matter.

Arne, on the other hand, saw his career resurrected by the events at Fortune Lake. His indiscretion with Jill Lorrimer was forgotten, and even Tommy Redmond offered an effusive editorial in the *Tattler* extolling Arne's perspicacity and courage. Come November, Arne is sure to be reelected. Alice Sigurdson, meanwhile, obtained a largely uncontested divorce—Arne wasn't a jerk about it—and she seems to be doing all right. I also see Doris Moreland quite frequently and I know she'd like to have a relationship. But I'm not ready for that just yet.

Meredith even called me a few days after my icy adventure at Fortune Lake to say she was glad I'd survived. We talked for a while but the words were empty and I didn't really know what to say. She's gone and so are whatever dreams we had together. That's all right, and I find I don't need Jack anymore to get me through the occasional bad night. Maybe that's all peace of mind is—the ability to live with doubt and fear in the wee hours of the morning.

It took me a while to figure out what to do with my life, but I finally decided to go back to the defense side of the table. Once I leave office, I plan to establish a first-class legal aid society in Paradise County. The pay won't be much and I'll work long hours, but I think I'll like it.

Kat Berglund also believes it'll be the right job for me, and of late she's allowed me into her magnificent bed more frequently than she used to. She knows I'd like to marry her but I won't propose. Marriage would be a cage for Kat. Best to let her run free.

I regularly fly to Chicago to see Cassandra and she's even come up to Pineland once or twice. She arranged for a DNA test after Phillip's death and the discovery of Patricia Gordon's body. The results were as expected. She and Phillip were indeed the children of Patricia and Peter, only to be taken by chance along two very different paths.

Cassandra is likely to inherit Peter's entire estate once the probate court gets through with it. A few other claimants have oozed out of the ground, not a surprise when twenty million dollars are at stake, but they have little chance of success. Cassandra has already informed me she intends to make a big donation to my legal aid society with some of the proceeds from the estate. I told her that really won't be necessary, but when Cassandra wants to do something, good luck stopping her.

Like soldiers who survived a war, Cassandra and I have become very close, or about as close as two people can be who've never had sex with each other. She's doing very nicely and recently won a police brutality case with a twelve-million-dollar payout. She also has a new girlfriend—a demure young lawyer named, of all things, Patricia—and she seems happy in her own intense, driven way. Once Peter's estate is settled, Cassandra will be a very rich woman, but I doubt it will change her. She's fueled by battle and the courtroom will always be her arena. Still, I can't help but think that one day she'll look out from her beautiful office window and wonder if it was all worthwhile. Then again, who doesn't have those thoughts?

Of late, I've found my own solace in Gilbert and Sullivan. My little company will stage *The Pirates of Penzance* in December in the high-school auditorium. I've cast Doris, the most beautiful singer we have, as Ruth. I found a twenty-something blackjack dealer with a sweet soprano voice to play Mable, and a school janitor will fill the role of Frederic. The biggest surprise is that Jim Meyers, our portly chief of police, turned out to have theatrical aspirations and will do a turn as the Major-General. I will of course be the Pirate King, just as I was so long ago when I dreamed my boyhood dreams and sailed with buccaneers on the still waters of the Paradise River.

So if you happen to be in Pineland around the holidays, make a date to see us perform. Tickets are only ten dollars and a good time is guaranteed for all. Our six-piece orchestra will fire up, the curtain will rise, and our troupe will swing into action. I'll be out on stage in black breeches and a jaunty hat, waving a wooden sword, and I'll sing and dance, momentarily breaking free of this hard old world, for "it is, it is a glorious thing to be the Pirate King. It is! Hurrah for our Pirate King!"

CPSIA information can be obtained
at www.ICGtesting.com
Printed in the USA
BVHW030216301120
594465BV00028B/245

9 781735 727806